George B. Cheever

The Prose Writers of America

a collection of eloquent and interesting extracts from the writings of American

authors

George B. Cheever

The Prose Writers of America
a collection of eloquent and interesting extracts from the writings of American authors

ISBN/EAN: 9783337370756

Printed in Europe, USA, Canada, Australia, Japan

Cover: Foto ©Andreas Hilbeck / pixelio.de

More available books at **www.hansebooks.com**

THE

PROSE WRITERS

OF

AMERICA.

A COLLECTION OF

ELOQUENT AND INTERESTING EXTRACTS

FROM THE WRITINGS OF

AMERICAN AUTHORS.

BY GEO. B. CHEEVER, D. D.

WORLD PUBLISHING HOUSE,
139 EIGHTH STREET,
NEW YORK.
1876.

PREFACE.

Books of common-place are the amusements of
terature. It is pleasant to have at one's side a well-
elected volume. to which he may turn for mental
ecreation, when the fatigue of preceding exertion
as rendered him unequal to intellectual effort. It is
leasant, also, to have before us the eloquent passages
f our favourite authors, so that we may occasionally
waken. and prolong the delightful sensations with
/hich we at first perused them. But the mere power
f conferring amusement is not that, which gives to
ublications of this sort their highest value. To all
hose, whose constant occupation precludes the possi-
ility of spending many leisure hours in the acquisi-
ion of literary taste and knowledge, they may be ren-
ered eminently useful.

The present volume is selected entirely from Ameri-
an authors, and contains specimens of American lit-
rature from its earliest period to the present day. It
s hoped that it may not be found inferior in excellence
r interest to any of those compilations which have
itherto embraced only the *morceaux delicieuse* of Eng-
sh genius.

When we say this, it is without any feeling of na-
ional vanity or rivalry. Our wish is merely to furnish
volume which shall correspond in design and execu-
ion to those which are now so popular abroad, and

INDEX OF AUTHORS.

TABLE OF CONTENTS

.6 .

TABLE OF CONTENTS.

PROSE WRITERS

OF

AMERICA.

Goodness of the Deity displayed in the Beauty of Creation.—DWIGHT

WERE all the interesting diversities of colour and form to disappear, how unsightly, dull, and wearisome, would be the aspect of the world! The pleasures, conveyed to us by the endless varieties, with which these sources of beauty are presented to the eye, are so much things of course, and exist so much without intermission, that we scarcely think either of their nature, their number, or the great proportion which they constitute in the whole mass of our enjoyment. But, were an inhabitant of this country to be removed from its delightful scenery to the midst of an *Arabian* desert, a boundless expanse of sand, a waste, spread with uniform desolation, enlivened by the murmur of no stream, and cheered by the beauty of no verdure; although he might live in a palace, and riot in splendour and luxury, he would, I think, find life a dull, wearisome, melancholy round of existence; and, amid all his gratifications, would sigh for the hills and valleys of his native land, the brooks, and rivers, the living lustre of the Spring, and the rich glories of the Autumn. The ever-varying brilliancy and grandeur of the landscape, and the magnificence of the sky, sun, moon, and stars, enter more extensively into the enjoyment of mankind, than we, perhaps, ever think, or can possibly apprehend, without frequent and extensive investigation. This beauty and splendour of the objects around us, it is ever to be remembered, is not necessary to their existence, nor to what we commonly intend by their usefulness. It is, therefore, to be regarded as a source of pleasure gratuitously superinduced upon the general nature of the objects themselves, and, in this light as a testimony of the divine goodness peculiarly affecting.

Night Season favourable to Contemplation and Study.—DENNIE.

"Watchman, what of the night?"—ISAIAH xxi. 11.

To this query of Isaiah, the watchman replies, that " The morning cometh, and also the night." The brevity of this answer has left it involved in something of the obscurity of the season in which it was given. I think that night, however sooty and ill-favoured it may be pronounced by those who were born under a daystar, merits a more particular description. I feel peculiarly disposed to arrange some ideas in favour of this season. I know that the majority are literally *blind* to its merits; they must be prominent, indeed, to be discerned by the *closed* eyes of the snorer, who thinks that night was made for nothing but sleep. But the student and the sage are willing to believe that it was formed for higher purposes; and that it not only recruits exhausted spirits, but sometimes informs inquisitive and mends wicked ones.

Duty, as well as inclination, urges the Lay Preacher to sermonize while others slumber. To read numerous volumes in the morning, and to observe various characters at noon, will leave but little time, except the night, to digest the one or speculate upon the other. The night, therefore, is often dedicated to composition, and, while the light of the paly planets discovers at his desk the Preacher, more wan than they, he may be heard repeating emphatically with Dr. Young,

"Darkness has much Divinity for me.'

He is then alone; he is then at peace. No companions near, but the silent volumes on his shelf; no noise abroad but the click of the village clock or the bark of the village dog. The deacon has then smoked his sixth, and *last* pipe, and asks not a question more concerning Josephus or the church. Stillness aids study, and the sermon proceeds. Such being the obligations to night, it would be ungrateful not to acknowledge them. As my watchful eyes can discern its dim beauties, my warm heart shall feel, and my prompt pen shall describe, the uses and pleasures of the nocturnal hour.

" Watchman, what of the night ?" I can with propriety imagine this question addressed to myself ; I am a professed lucubrator ; and who so well qualified to delineate the sable hours as

" A meager, muse-rid mope, adust and thin ?"

However injuriously night is treated by the sleepy moderns, the vigilance of the ancients could not overlook its benefits and joys. In as early a record as the book of Genesis, I find that Isaac, though he devoted his assiduous days to action, reserved speculation till night. " He went out to meditate in the field at eventide." He chose that sad, that solemn hour, to reflect upon the virtues of a beloved and departed mother. The tumult and glare of the day suited not with the sorrow of his soul. He had lost his most amiable, most genuine friend, and his unostentatious grief was eager for privacy and shade. Sincere sorrow rarely suffers its tears to be seen. It was natural for Isaac to select a season to weep in, that should resemble " the colour of his fate." The darkness, the solemnity, the stillness of the eve, were favourable to his melancholy purpose. He forsook, therefore, the bustling tents of his father, the pleasant " south country," and " well of Lahairoi ;" he went out and pensively meditated at eventide.

The Grecian and Roman philosophers firmly believed that the " dead of midnight is the noon of thought." One of them is beautifully described by the poet as soliciting knowledge from the skies in private and nightly audience, and that neither his theme, nor his nightly walks, were forsaken till the sun appeared, and dimmed his " nobler intellectual beam." We undoubtedly owe to the studious nights of the ancients most of their elaborate and immortal productions. Among them it was necessary that every man of letters should trim the midnight lamp. The day might be given to the forum or the circus, but the night was the season for tre statesman to project his schemes, and for the poet to pour his verse.

Night has, likewise, with great reason, been considered, in every age, as the astronomer's day. Young observes, with energy, that

"An undevout astronomer is mad."

The privilege of contemplating those brilliant and numerous myriads of planets which bedeck our skies is peculiar to night, and it is our duty, both as lovers of moral and natural beauty, to bless that season, when we are indulged with such a gorgeous display of glittering and useful light. It must be confessed, that the seclusion, calmness, and tranquillity of midnight, are most friendly to serious, and even airy contemplations.

I think it treason to this sable Power, who holds divided empire with Day, constantly to shut our eyes at her approach. To long sleep I am decidedly a foe. As it is, expressed by a quaint writer, we shall all have enough of it in the grave. Those, who cannot break the silence of the night by vocal throat, or eloquent tongue, may be permitted to disturb it by a snore. But he, among my readers, who possesses the power of fancy and strong thought, should be vigilant as a watchman. Let him sleep abundantly for health, but sparingly for sloth. It is better, sometimes, to consult a page of philosophy than the pillow.

Colloquial Powers of Dr. Franklin.—WIRT.

NEVER have I known such a fireside companion as he was!—Great as he was, both as a statesman and a philosopher, he never shone in a light more winning than when he was seen in a domestic circle. It was once my good fortune to pass two or three weeks with him, at the house of a private gentleman, in the back part of Pennsylvania; and we were confined to the house during the whole of that time, by the unintermitting constancy and depth of the snows. But confinement could never be felt where Frank-

.In was an inmate.—His cheerfulness and his colloquial powers spread around him a perpetual spring.—When I speak, however, of his colloquial powers, I do not mean to awaken any notion analogous to that which Boswell has given us, when he so frequently mentions the colloquial powers of Dr. Johnson. The conversation of the latter continually reminds one of "the pomp and circumstance of glorious war." It was, indeed, a perpetual contest for victory, or an arbitrary and despotic exaction of homage to his superior talents. It was strong, acute, prompt, splendid and vociferous; as loud, stormy, and sublime, as those winds which he represents as shaking the Hebrides, and rocking the old castles that frowned upon the dark rolling sea beneath. But one gets tired of storms, however sublime they may be, and longs for the more orderly current of nature.—Of Franklin no one ever became tired. There was no ambition of eloquence, no effort to shine, in any thing which came from him. There was nothing which made any demand either upon your allegiance or your admiration.

His manner was as unaffected as infancy. It was nature's self. He talked like an old patriarch; and his plainness and simplicity put you, at once, at your ease, and gave you the full and free possession and use of all your faculties.

His thoughts were of a character to shine by their own light, without any adventitious aid. They required only a medium of vision like his pure and simple style, to exhibit, to the highest advantage, their native radiance and beauty. His cheerfulness was unremitting. It seemed to be as much the effect of the systematic and salutary exercise of the mind as of its superior organization. His wit was of the first order. It did not show itself merely in occasional coruscations; but, without any effort or force on his part, it shed a constant stream of the purest light over the whole of his discourse. Whether in the company of commons or nobles, he was always the same plain man; always most perfectly at his ease, his faculties in full play, and the full orbit of his genius forever clear and unclouded. And then the stores of his mind were inexhaustible. He had commenced life with an attention so vigilant, that

2

nothing had escaped his observation, and a judgment so
solid, that every incident was turned to advantage. His
youth had not been wasted in idleness, nor overcast by intemperance. He had been all his life a close and deep
reader, as well as thinker; and, by the force of his own
powers, had wrought up the raw materials, which he had
gathered from books, with such exquisite skill and felicity,
that he had added a hundred fold to their original value,
and justly made them his own.

An Apparition.—CLUB-ROOM.

THE sun was hastening to a glorious setting as I gained
the last hill that overlooks the forest; and, late as it was, I
paused to gaze once more on this most brilliant and touching of the wonders of nature. The glories of the western
sky lasted long after the moon was in full splendour in the
east; on one side all was rich and warm with departing
day—on the other how pure and calm was the approach
of night! If I had been born a heathen, I think I could
not have seen the setting sun, without believing myself
immortal : who, that had never seen the morning dawn,
could believe that wonderful orb, which sinks so slowly
and majestically through a sea of light, throwing up beams
of a thousand hues, melting and mingling together, touching the crest of the clouds with fire, and streaming over
the heavens with broad brilliancy, up to the zenith—then
retiring from sight, and gradually drawing his beams after
him, till their last faint blush is extinguished in the cold,
uniform tints of moonlight—who could believe that source
of light had perished ? Who then could believe that the
being, who gazes on that magnificent spectacle with such
emotion, and draws from it such high conclusions of his
own nature and destiny, is even more perishable ?
    I remained absorbed in such reflections till the twilight
was almost gone. I then began rapidly to descend, and,
leaving the moon behind the hill, entered the long dark
shadow it threw over the wood at its foot. It was gloomy
and chill—the faint lingering of day was hidden by the

trees, and the moon seemed to have set again, throwing only a distant light on the rich volumes of clouds that hung over her. As I descended farther, the air became colder, the sky took a deeper blue, and the stars shone with a wintry brightness. The thoughts which came tenderly over me, by the light of the setting sun, now grew dark and solemn; and I felt how fleeting and unsatisfactory are the hopes built on the analogies of nature. The sun sets so beautifully it seems impossible it should not rise again; out in the gloom of midnight, where is the promise of the morrow? In the cold, but still beautiful, features of the dead, we think we see the pledge of a resurrection; but what hope of life is there in the dust to which they crumble?

I arrived late at the inn. It was a large and ruinous structure, which had once been a castle, but the family of its owner had perished in disgrace : their title was extinguished, their lands confiscated and sold, and their name now almost forgotten. It stood on a small bare hill in the midst of the forest, which it overtopped, only to lose its shelter and shade, for from it the eye could not reach the extremity of the wood. I knocked long before I was admitted; at last an old man came to the door with a lantern, and, without a word of welcome, led my horse to the stable, leaving me to find my way into the house. The spirit of the place seemed to have infected its inhabitants. I entered a kitchen, whose extent I could not see by the dim fire-light, and, having stirred the embers, sat down to warm me. The old man soon returned, and showed me up the remains of a spacious staircase, to a long hall, in a corner of which was my bed. I extinguished the light, and lay down without undressing; but the thoughts and scenes of the evening had taken strong hold of my mind, and I could not sleep. I did not feel troubled, but there was an intensity of thought and feeling within me, that seemed waiting for some great object on which to expend itself. I rose, and walked to the window : the moon was shining beautifully bright, but the forest was so thick that her light only glanced on the tops of the trees, and showed nothing distinctly—all was silent and motionless—not a breeze, not a sound, not a cloud—the earth was dim and undistinguish·

able, the heavens were filled with a calm light, and the moon seemed to stand still in the midst. I know not how long I remained leaning against the window and gazing upward, for I was dreaming of things long past, of which I was then, though I knew it not, the only living witness; when my attention was suddenly recalled by the low but distinct sound of some one breathing near me—I turned with a sudden thrill of fear, but saw nothing; and, as the sound had ceased, I readily believed it was fancy. I soon relapsed into my former train of thought, and had forgotten the circumstance, when I was again startled by a sound I could not mistake—there was some one breathing at my very ear—so terribly certain was the fact that I did not move even my eyes; it was not the deep, regular breath of one asleep, nor the quick panting of guilt, but a quiet, gentle respiration; I remained listening till I could doubt no longer, and then turned slowly round, that I might not be overpowered by the suddenness of the sight, which I knew I must meet—again there was nothing to be seen—the moon shone broad into the long desolate chamber, and, though there was a little gathering of shadow in the corners, I am sure nothing visible could have escaped the keenness of my gaze, as I looked again and again along the dark wainscot. My calmness now forsook me, and, as I turned fearfully back to the window, my hand brushed against the curtain, whose deep folds hid the corner near which I was standing—the blood gushed to my heart with a sharp pang, and I involuntarily dashed my hands forward —they passed through against the damp wall, and the tide of life rolled back, leaving me hardly able to support myself. I stood a few moments lost in fear and wonder— when the breathing began again, and there—in the bright moonlight—I felt the air driven against my face by a being I could not see. I sat down on the bed in great agitation, and . was a considerable time before I could at all compose my mind—the fact was certain, but the cause inscrutable. I rose, and walked across the chamber.

I made three or four turns, and gradually recovered my tranquillity, though still impressed with the belief that what I had heard was no natural sound. I was not now in a state to be easily deluded, for my senses were on the alert.

but my mind perfectly calm. The old floor groaned under every tread, but the noise excited in me no alarm; I did not even turn when the planks sprung and cracked behind me long after my foot had left them. But, good God! what were my feelings when I heard distinct footsteps following my own! the light tread of naked feet—I stopped instantly, just as I had made a step—the tread ceased, and a moment after I heard a foot brought up as if to support the walker in this unexpected pause—Could it be echo?— I struck my foot upon the floor—the sound was short and sullen, and was not repeated—I walked on, but the steps did not follow—I turned, and paused again—all was still. I walked back, and as I reached the spot where the sounds had ceased—whether I heard or saw it I cannot tell—but something passed me, and a soft sigh floated along with it, dying away in distance like the moaning of a gentle wind. It was indistinct as it passed, but as I listened to catch its last lingering, I knew the voice of Gertrude!—"Hermann!" it said, in a tone so tender and mournful, that my eyes filled with tears, and I seemed to hear it long after it had ceased. "Gertrude!" I cried aloud—the same sweet sigh answered me, and for an instant I caught the dark beam of her eye—there was no form, but I saw her own look—that deep melancholy gaze—it was but a moment, and it was gone. "Gertrude!" I cried again, "if it be thou, do not fly me—come to me, beloved!" A pause of deeper silence followed; my eyes were fixed on the air where I had lost her, when the shadows at the extremity of the chamber began to move like the waving of a garment; their motion at first was indefinite and hardly perceptible, but gradually increased till they parted and rolled away, leaving a brighter space in the middle. This had at first no determinate form, but soon began to assume the outline of a human figure. I shall never forget the sensation of that moment—my hair rose, my flesh crept, and drops of sweat rolled fast down my cheeks; yet it was not fear—I cannot describe the emotion with which I watched the figure growing more and more distinct; and even when I saw the face of my own Gertrude, all thoughts of earth were swallowed up in those of eternity—I stood in the presence of a spirit, and felt myself immortal! The

2*

triumph was short—it was too like herself—the eyes were
closed, but it was her own graceful form, though attenu-
ated and almost transparent—her own face—pale and languid, but oh, how beautiful!—at last the eyes opened—
they alone were unchanged, and they gazed on me with a
tenderness I could not bear—I sunk on my knees, and hid
my face—I felt her approach—I did not raise my eyes, but
I knew she was near me by a glow of more than human
happiness—a hand was laid upon my head—" Hermann!"
said the same sweet voice, " dear Hermann! but one
year more!"—and the sound floated away. I looked up—
she was already disappearing—she smiled on me, and the
form faded, and the shadows gathered over it.

I had sunk on the floor exhausted; the first feeling I
remember was one of unutterable grief and loneliness;
but the next was joy at the thought that I was not to endure it long—" but one year more, and I shall be with thee
forever"—I could not feel more certain of any fact of my
own experience, than that Gertrude was dead, and I should
soon follow.

I paced the chamber till day-break, and then watched
the sky till the sun rose. I was in no haste to be gone,
for I had but a short day's journey before me, and did not
wish to arrive before night. I remained in my chamber
till the morning mists were dispersed, and then began my
journey. I rode slowly all day, musing and abstracted, and
hardly noticing the objects around me, till I reached the
brow of a hill beneath which lay the village of Underwalden—a few simple buildings gathered close round the
church whose spire just rose above the trees ; beyond was
the gentle slope of green hills parted only by hawthorn
hedges ; and still further on, the home of my Gertrude, can-
opied by tall ancient elms, and gleaming in the yellow light
of the setting sun.

If I had had no other reason, I should have foreboded
evil from the silence of the hour—it is always a quiet time,
but it has a few sounds that harmonize with its solemnity—
the lowing of the cattle, the whistle of the returning labourer, or the distant merriment of the children released
from school, come naturally with the close of day—but
now the cattle were gathered home, and the labourer had

oft the field before the usual hour, the school was shut, and the village green silent and solitary. A few of the better class of villagers, in their decent sabbath dress, were walking over the hill toward the mansion; others, with their wives and children, were standing round the gate of the church-yard, and there was something mournful in the motions and attitudes of all. I knew well what all this meant, but I gazed on it with a vacant mind, and without any new conviction of my desolate lot. I even saw with a sad pleasure the beauty of a landscape, which, like all the world, was nothing now to me. But this did not last long —suddenly there was a hum of voices, and a stir among those who had been waiting at the church—the bell tolled, a faint chant swelled from behind the hill, and the procession came slowly in sight. Then the truth fell on me with an overpowering weight; I threw myself on the ground, and looked on with a bursting heart, till all I had loved was forever hidden from sight.—Farewell, my friend! I am going to Rome for a few months, for it is the seat of my religion, and I would look once more before I die on the mightiest remains of earth. I have watched the fall of the last leaves in Underwalden; I shall return to see them put forth once more, but when they fall again, they will cover the grave of HERMANN

————

Rural Occupations favourable to the Sentiments of Devotion.—BUCKMINSTER.

No situation in life is so favourable to established habits of virtue, and to powerful sentiments of devotion, as a residence in the country, and rural occupations. I am not speaking of a condition of peasantry, (of which, in this country, we know little,) who are mere vassals of an absent lord, or the hired labourers of an intendant, and who are therefore interested in nothing but the regular receipt of their daily wages; but I refer to the honourable character of an owner of the soil, whose comforts, whose weight in the community, and whose very existence, depend upon his personal labours, and the regular returns of the abun-

dance from the soil which he cultivates. No man, one
would think, would feel so sensibly his immediate dependence upon God, as the husbandman. For all his peculiar
blessings he is invited to look immediately to the bounty
of Heaven. No secondary cause stands between him and
his Maker. To him are essential the regular succession
of the seasons, and the timely fall of the rain, the genial
warmth of the sun, the sure productiveness of the soil,
and the certain operations of those laws of nature, which
must appear to him nothing less than the varied exertions
of omnipresent energy. In the country we seem to stand
in the midst of the great theatre of God's power, and we
feel an unusual proximity to our Creator. His blue and
tranquil sky spreads itself over our heads, and we acknowledge the intrusion of no secondary agent in unfolding this
vast expanse. Nothing but Omnipotence can work up the
dark horrors of the tempest, dart the flashes of the lightning, and roll the long-resounding rumour of the thunder.
The breeze wafts to his senses the odours of God's beneficence; the voice of God's power is heard in the rustling
of the forest; and the varied forms of life, activity, and
pleasure, which he observes at every step in the fields,
lead him irresistibly, one would think, to the Source of
being, and beauty, and joy. How auspicious such a life
to the noble sentiments of devotion! Besides, the situation
of the husbandman is peculiarly favourable, it should seem,
to purity and simplicity of moral sentiment. He is brought
acquainted chiefly with the real and native wants of mankind.
Employed solely in bringing food out of the earth, he is
not liable to be fascinated with the fictitious pleasures, the
unnatural wants, the fashionable follies, and tyrannical vices
of more busy and splendid life.

Still more favourable to the religious character of the
husbandman is the circumstance, that, from the nature of
agricultural pursuits, they do not so completely engross
the attention as other occupations. They leave much
time for contemplation, for reading, and intellectual pleasures; and these are peculiarly grateful to the resident in
the country. Especially does the institution of the Sabbath
discover all its value to the tiller of the earth, whose fatigue it solaces, whose hard labours it interrupts, and who

feels, on that day, the worth of his moral nature, which cannot be understood by the busy man, who considers the repose of this day as interfering with his hopes of gain, or professional employments. If, then, this institution is of any moral and religious value, it is to the country we must look for the continuance of that respect and observance, which it merits. My friends, those of you, especially, who retire annually into the country, let these periodical retreats from business or dissipation bring you nearer to your God; let them restore the clearness of your judgment on the objects of human pursuit, invigorate your moral perceptions, exalt your sentiments, and regulate your habits of devotion; and, if there be any virtue or simplicity remaining in rural life, let them never be impaired by the influence of your presence and example.

Reciprocal Influence of Morals and Literature. — Frisbie.

In no productions of modern genius is the reciprocal influence of morals and literature more distinctly seen, than in those of the author of Childe Harold. His character produced the poems, and it cannot be doubted, that his poems are adapted to produce such a character. His heroes speak a language supplied not more by imagination than consciousness. They are not those machines, that, by a contrivance of the artist, send forth a music of their own; but instruments, through which he breathes his very soul, in tones of agonized sensibility, that cannot but give a sympathetic impulse to those who hear. The desolate misanthropy of his mind rises, and throws its dark shade over his poetry, like one of his own ruined castles; we feel it to be sublime, but we forget that it is a sublimity it cannot have til. it is abandoned by every thing that is kind, and peaceful, and happy, and its halls are ready to become the haunts of outlaws and assassins. Nor are his more tender and affectionate passages those to which we can yield ourselves without a feeling of uneasiness. It is not that we can here and there select a proposition formally

false and pernicious; but he leaves an impression unfa-
vourable to a healthful state of thought and feeling, peculiarly dangerous to the finest minds and most susceptible
hearts.   They are the scene of a summer evening, where
all is tender, and beautiful, and grand ; but the damps of
disease descend with the dews of heaven, and the pestilent
vapours of night are breathed in with the fragrance and
balm, and the delicate and fair are the surest victims of the
exposure.

Although I have illustrated the moral influence of literature principally from its mischiefs, yet it is obvious, if
what I have said be just, it may be rendered no less powerful as a means of good.   Is it not true that within the
last century a decided and important improvement in the
moral character of our literature has taken place ? and, had
Pope and Smollett written at the present day, would the
former have published the imitations of Chaucer, or the
latter the adventures of Pickle and Random ?   Genius
cannot now sanctify impurity or want of principle ; and
our critics and reviewers are exercising jurisdiction not
only upon the literary, but moral blemishes of the authors
who come before them.   We notice with peculiar pleasure
the sentence of just indignation which the Edinburgh tribunal has pronounced upon Moore, Swift, Goethe, and, in
general, the German sentimentalists.   Indeed, the fountains of literature, into which an enemy has sometimes infused poison, naturally flow with refreshment and health.
Cowper and Campbell have led the muses to repose in the
bowers of religion and virtue ; and Miss Edgeworth has so
cautiously combined the features of her characters, that
the predominant expression is ever what it should be.   She
has shown us not vices ennobled by virtues, but virtues degraded and perverted by their union with vices.   The success of this lady has been great ; but, had she availed herself more of the motives and sentiments of religion, we
think it would have been greater.   She has stretched
forth a powerful hand to the impotent in virtue ; and had
she added, with the apostle, in the name of Jesus of Naz-
areth, we should almost have expected miracles from its
touch.

Evening Scenes on the St. Lawrence.—SILLIMAN.

FROM the moment the sun is down, every thing becomes silent on the shore, which our windows overlook, and the murmurs of the broad St. Lawrence, more than two miles wide immediately before us, and, a little way to the right, spreading to five or six miles in breadth, are sometimes for an hour the only sounds that arrest our attention. Every evening since we have been here, black clouds and splendid moonlight have hung over, and embellished this tranquil scene; and on two of these evenings we have been attracted to the window, by the plaintive Canadian boat-song. In one instance, it arose from a solitary voyager, floating in his light canoe, which occasionally appeared and disappeared on the sparkling river, and in its distant course seemed no larger than some sportive insect. In another instance, a larger boat, with more numerous and less melodious voices, not indeed in perfect harmony, passed nearer to the shore, and gave additional life to the scene. A few moments after, the moon broke out from a throne of dark clouds, and seemed to convert the whole expanse of water into one vast sheet of glittering silver; and, in the very brightest spot, at the distance of more than a mile, again appeared a solitary boat, but too distant to admit of our hearing the song, with which the boatman was probably solacing his lonely course.

Franklin's first Entrance into Philadelphia.—
FRANKLIN.

I HAVE entered into the particulars of my voyage, and shall, in like manner, describe my first entrance into this city, that you may be able to compare beginnings so little auspicious with the figure I have since made.

On my arrival at Philadelphia, I was in my working dress, my best clothes being to come by sea. I was covered with dirt; my pockets were filled with shirts and stockings; I was unacquainted with a single soul in the place.

and knew not where to seek a lodging. Fatigued with walking, rowing, and having passed the night without sleep, I was extremely hungry, and all my money consisted of a Dutch dollar, and about a shilling's worth of coppers, which I gave to the boatmen for my passage. As I had assisted them in rowing, they refused it at first; but I insisted on their taking it. A man is sometimes more generous when he has little than when he has much money; probably because, in the first case, he is desirous of concealing his poverty.

I walked towards the top of the street, looking eagerly on both sides, till I came to Market Street, where I met with a child with a loaf of bread. Often had I made my dinner on dry bread. I inquired where he had bought it, and went straight to the baker's shop, which he pointed out to me. I asked for some biscuits, expecting to find such as we had at Boston; but they made, it seems, none of that sort at Philadelphia. I then asked for a threepenny loaf. They made no loaves of that price. Finding myself ignorant of the prices, as well as of the different kinds of bread, I desired him to let me have threepenny-worth of bread of some kind or other. He gave me three large rolls. I was surprised at receiving so much: I took them, however, and, having no room in my pockets, I walked on with a roll under each arm, eating a third. In this manner I went through Market Street to Fourth Street, and passed the house of Mr. Read, the father of my future wife. She was standing at the door, observed me, and thought, with reason, that I made a very singular and grotesque appearance.

I then turned the corner, and went through Chestnut Street, eating my roll all the way; and, having made this round, I found myself again on Market Street wharf, near the boat in which I arrived. I stepped into it to take a draught of the river water; and, finding myself satisfied with my first roll, I gave the other two to a woman and her child, who had come down with us in the boat, and was waiting to continue her journey. Thus refreshed, I regained the street, which was now full of well-dressed people, all going the same way. I joined them, and was thus led to a large Quakers' meeting-house near the market place I sat down with the rest, and, after looking

round me for some time, hearing nothing said, and being
drowsy from my last night's labour and want of rest, I fell
into a sound sleep. In this state I continued till the assembly dispersed, when one of the congregation had the
goodness to wake me. This was consequently the first
house I entered, or in which I slept, at Philadelphia.

Passage of the Potomac through the Blue Ridge.—
JEFFERSON.

THE passage of the Potomac, through the Blue Ridge,
is perhaps one of the most stupendous scenes in nature.
You stand on a very high point of land. On your right
comes up the Shenandoah, having ranged along the foot
of the mountain a hundred miles to seek a vent. On your
left approaches the Potomac, seeking a passage also. In
the moment of their junction, they rush together against
the mountain, rend it asunder, and pass off to the sea.
The first glance at this scene hurries our senses into the
opinion, that this earth has been created in time; that the
mountains were formed first; that the rivers began to flow
afterwards; that, in this place particularly, they have been
dammed up by the Blue Ridge of mountains, and have
formed an ocean which filled the whole valley; that, continuing to rise, they have at length broken over at this spot,
and have torn the mountain down from its summit to its
base. The piles of rock on each hand, but particularly on
the Shenandoah, the evident marks of their disrupture and
avulsion from their beds by the most powerful agents of
nature, corroborate the impression. But the distant finishing, which Nature has given to the picture, is of a very different character. It is a true contrast to the foreground.
It is as placid and delightful as that is wild and tremendous.
For, the mountain being cloven asunder, she presents to
your eye, through the cleft, a small catch of smooth blue
horizon, at an infinite distance in the plain country, inviting you, as it were, from the riot and tumult roaring around,
to pass through the breach, and participate of the calm below. Here the eye ultimately composes itself; and that
3

way, too, the road happens actually to lead. You cross the Potomac above its junction, pass along its side through the base of the mountain for three miles, its terrible precipices hanging in fragments over you, and within about twenty miles reach Fredericktown, and the fine country round that. This scene is worth a voyage across the Atlantic. Yet here, as in the neighbourhood of the Natural Bridge, are people who have passed their lives within half a dozen miles, and have never been to survey these monuments of a war between rivers and mountains, which must have shaken the earth itself to its centre.

Moral and intellectual Efficacy of the Sacred Scriptures.—WAYLAND.

As to the powerful, I had almost said miraculous, effect of the Sacred Scriptures, there can no longer be a doubt in the mind of any one on whom fact can make an impression. That the truths of the Bible have the power of awakening an intense moral feeling in man under every variety of character, learned or ignorant, civilized or savage; that they make bad men good, and send a pulse of healthful feeling through all the domestic, civil, and social relations; that they teach men to love right, to hate wrong, and to seek each other's welfare, as the children of one common parent; that they control the baleful passions of the human heart, and thus make men proficients in the science of self-government; and, finally, that they teach him to aspire after a conformity to a Being of infinite holiness, and fill him with hopes infinitely more purifying, more exalting, more suited to his nature, than any other, which this world has ever known,—are facts incontrovertible as the laws of philosophy, or the demonstrations of mathematics. Evidence in support of all this can be brought from every age, in the history of man, since there has been a revelation from God on earth. We see the proof of it every where around us. There is scarcely a neighbourhood in our country, where the Bible is circulated, in which we cannot point you to a very considerable portion of its population, whom its truths

COMMON-PLACE BOOK OF PROSE. 27

nave reclaimed from the practice of vice, and taught the practice of whatsoever things are pure, and honest, and just, and of good report. That this distinctive and peculiar effect is produced upon every man to whom the Gospel is announced, we pretend not to affirm. But we do affirm, that, besides producing this special renovation, to which we have alluded, upon a part, it, in a most remarkable degree, elevates the tone of moral feeling throughout the whole community. Wherever the Bible is freely circulated, and its doctrines carried home to the understandings of men, the aspect of society is altered; the frequency of crime is diminished; men begin to love justice, and to administer it by law ; and a virtuous public opinion, that strongest safeguard of right, spreads over a nation the shield of its invisible protection. Wherever it has faithfully been brought to bear upon the human heart, even under most unpromising circumstances, it has, within a single generation, revolutionized the whole structure of society ; and thus, within a few years, done more for man than all other means have for ages accomplished without it. For proof of all this, I need only refer you to the effects of the Gospel in Greenland, or in South Africa, in the Society Islands, or even among the aborigines of our own country.

But, before we leave this part of the subject, it may be well to pause for a moment, and inquire whether, in addition to its moral efficacy, the Bible may not exert a powerful influence upon the intellectual character of man.

And here it is scarcely necessary that I should remark, that, of all the books with which, since the invention of writing, this world has been deluged, the number of those is very small which have produced any perceptible effect on the mass of human character. By far the greater part have been, even by their cotemporaries, unnoticed and unknown. Not many a one has made its little mark upon the generation that produced it, though it sunk with that generation to utter forgetfulness. But, after the ceaseless toil of six thousand years, how few have been the works, the adamantine basis of whose reputation has stood unhurt amid the fluctuations of time, and whose impression can be traced through successive centuries, on the history of our species

When, however, such a work appears, its effects are ab·
solutely incalculable ; and such a work, you are aware, is
the ILIAD OF HOMER. Who can estimate the results
produced by the incomparable efforts of a single mind ,
Who can tell what Greece owes to this first-born of song ?
Her breathing marbles, her solemn temples, her unrivalled
eloquence, and her matchless verse, all point us to that
transcendent genius, who, by the very splendour of his
own effulgence, woke the human intellect from the slumber of ages. It was Homer who gave laws to the artist ;
it was Homer who inspired the poet ; it was Homer who
thundered in the senate ; and, more than all, it was Homer who was sung by the people ; and hence a nation
was cast into the mould of one mighty mind, and the land
of the Iliad became the region of taste, the birth-place of
the arts.

Nor was this influence confined within the limits of
Greece. Long after the sceptre of empire had passed
westward, Genius still held her court on the banks of the
Ilyssus, and from the country of Homer gave laws to the
world. The light, which the blind old man of Scio had
kindled in Greece, shed its radiance over Italy ; and thus
did he awaken a second nation into intellectual existence.
And we may form some idea of the power which this one
work has to the present day exerted over the mind of man,
by remarking, that " nation after nation, and century after
century, has been able to do little more than transpose
his incidents, new-name his characters, and paraphrase his
sentiments."

But, considered simply as an intellectual production,
who will compare the poems of Homer with the Holy
Scriptures of the Old and New Testament? Where in
the Iliad shall we find simplicity and pathos which shall
vie with the narrative of Moses, or maxims of conduct to
equal in wisdom the Proverbs of Solomon, or sublimity
which does not fade away before the conceptions of Job or
David, of Isaiah or St. John ? But I cannot pursue this
comparison. I feel that it is doing wrong to the mind
which dictated the Iliad, and to those other mighty intellects on whom the light of the holy oracles never shined.
Who that has read his poem has not observed how he strove

In vain to give dignity to the mythology of his time? Who
has not seen how the religion of his country, unable to
support the flight of his imagination, sunk powerless beneath him? It is the unseen world, where the master spirits of our race breathe freely, and are at home; and it is
mournful to behold the intellect of Homer striving to free
itself from the conceptions of materialism, and then sinking down in hopeless despair, to weave idle tales about
Jupiter and Juno, Apollo and Diana. But the difficulties
under which he laboured are abundantly illustrated by the
fact, that the light, which he poured upon the human intellect, taught other ages how unworthy was the religion of
his day of the man who was compelled to use it. "It
seems to me," says Longinus, "that Homer, when he describes dissensions, jealousies, tears, imprisonments, and
other afflictions to his deities, hath, as much as was in his
power, made the men of the Iliad gods, and the gods men.
To man, when afflicted, death is the termination of evils;
but he hath made not only the nature, but the miseries, of
the gods eternal."

If, then, so great results have flowed from this one effort of a single mind, what may we not expect from the combined efforts of several, at least his equals in power over
the human heart? If that one genius, though groping in
the thick darkness of absurd idolatry, wrought so glorious
a transformation in the character of his countrymen, what
may we not look for from the universal dissemination of
those writings, on whose authors was poured the full splendour of eternal truth? If unassisted human nature, spell-
bound by a childish mythology, have done so much, what
may we not hope for from the supernatural efforts of pre-
eminent genius, which spake as it was moved by the Holy
Ghost?

Character of Washington.—Ames.

THERE has scarcely appeared a really great man, whose
character has been more admired in his life time, or less
correctly understood by his admirers. When it is compre-
3 *

hended, it is no easy task to delineate its excellencies in such a manner as to give to the portrait both interest and resemblance ; for it requires thought and study to understand the true ground of the superiority of his character over many others, whom he resembled in the principles of action, and even in the manner of acting   But perhaps he excels all the great men that ever lived in the steadiness of his adherence to his maxims of life, and in the uniformity of all his conduct to the same maxims.   These maxims, though wise, were yet not so remarkable for their wisdom, as for their authority over his life ; for, if there were any errors in his judgment, (and he discovered as few as any man,) we know of no blemishes in his virtue   He was the patriot without reproach ; he loved his country well enough to hold his success in serving it an ample recompense. Thus far self-love and love of country coincided ; but when his country needed sacrifices that no other man could, or perhaps would, be willing to make, he did not even hesitate. This was virtue in its most exalted character.   More than once he put his fame at hazard, when he had reason to think it would be sacrificed, at least in this age.   Two instances cannot be denied ; when the army was disbanded, and again, when he stood, like Leonidas at the pass of Thermopylæ, to defend our independence against France.

It is, indeed, almost as difficult to draw his character, as the portrait of Virtue.   The reasons are similar : our ideas of moral excellence are obscure, because they are complex, and we are obliged to resort to illustrations.   Washington's example is the happiest to show what virtu- is ; and, to delineate his character, we naturally expatiate on the beauty of virtue ; much must be felt, and much imagined.   His pre-eminence is not so much to be seen in the display of any one virtue, as in the possession of them all, and in the practice of the most difficult.   Hereafter, therefore, his character must be studied before it will be striking ; and then it will be admitted as a model, a precious one to a free republic.

It is no less difficult to speak of his talents.   They were adapted to lead, without dazzling mankind ; and to draw forth and employ the talents of others, without being misled by them.   In this he was certainly superior, that he

neither mistook nor misapplied his own. His great modesty
and reserve would have concealed them, if great occasions
had not called them forth; and then, as he never spoke
from the affectation to shine, nor acted from any sinister
motives, it is from their effects only that we are to judge of
their greatness and extent.   In public trusts, where men,
acting conspicuously, are cautious, and in those private
concerns where few conceal or resist their weaknesses,
Washington was uniformly great, pursuing right conduct
from right maxims.   His talents were such as assist a sound
judgment, and ripen with it.   His prudence was consummate, and seemed to take the direction of his powers and
passions; for, as a soldier, he was more solicitous to avoid
mistakes that might be fatal, than to perform exploits that
are brilliant; and, as a statesman, to adhere to just principles, however old, than to pursue novelties; and therefore,
in both characters, his qualities were singularly adapted to
the interest, and were tried in the greatest perils of the
country.   His habits of inquiry were so far remarkable, that
he was never satisfied with investigating, nor desisted from
it, so long as he had less than all the light that he could obtain
upon a subject, and then he made his decision without bias

   This command over the partialities that so generally stop
men short, or turn them aside in their pursuit of truth, is
one of the chief causes of his unvaried course of right
conduct in so many difficult scenes, where every human
actor must be presumed to err.   If he had strong passions,
he had learned to subdue them, and to be moderate and
mild.   If he had weaknesses, he concealed them, which
is rare, and excluded them from the government of his
temper and conduct, which is still more rare.   If he loved
fame, he never made improper compliances for what is
called popularity.   The fame he enjoyed is of the kind
that will last forever; yet it was rather the effect, than the
motive of his conduct.   Some future Plutarch will search
for a parallel to his character. Epaminondas is perhaps the
brightest name of all antiquity   Our Washington resembled him in the purity and ardour of his patriotism; and
like him he first exalted the glory of his country.   There,
it is to be hoped, the parallel ends; for Thebes fell with
Epam'tondas.—But such comparisons cannot be pursued

far without departing from the similitude. For we shall
find it as difficult to compare great men as great rivers.
Some we admire for the length and rapidity of their current, and the grandeur of their cataracts; others for the
majestic silence and fulness of their streams : we cannot
bring them together to measure the difference of their
waters. The unambitious life of Washington, declining
fame, yet courted by it, seemed, like the Ohio, to choose
its long way through solitudes, diffusing fertility ; or, like
his own Potomac, widening and deepening his channel
as he approaches the sea, and displaying most the usefulness and serenity of his greatness towards the end of his
course. Such a citizen would do honour to any country.
The constant affection and veneration of his country will
show, that it was worthy of such a citizen.

However his military fame may excite the wonder of
mankind, it is chiefly by his civil magistracy, that his example will instruct them. Great generals have arisen in
all ages of the world, and perhaps most in those of despotism and darkness. In times of violence and convulsion,
they rise, by the force of the whirlwind, high enough to
ride in it, and direct the storm. Like meteors, they glare
on the black clouds with a splendour, that, while it dazzles
and terrifies, makes nothing visible but the darkness. The
fame of heroes is indeed growing vulgar; they multiply
in every long war ; they stand in history, and thicken in
their ranks, almost as undistinguished as their own soldiers.

But such a chief magistrate as Washington appears, like the
pole star in a clear sky, to direct the skilful statesman. His
presidency will form an epoch, and be distinguished as the
age of Washington. Already it assumes its high place in
the political region. Like the milky way, it whitens along
its allotted portion of the hemisphere. The latest generations of men will survey, through the telescope of history,
the space where so many virtues blend their rays, and delight to separate them into groups and distinct virtues. As
the best illustration of them, the living monument to which
the first of patriots would have chosen to consign his fame
it is my earnest prayer to Heaven that our country may
subsist, even to that late day, in the plenitude of its liberty
and happiness, and mingle its mild glory with Washington's

Labours of periodical Composition.—IDLE MAN.

I KNOW that it is an arduous undertaking, for one whose mind rarely feels the spring of bodily health bearing it up, whose frame is soon worn by mental labour, and who can seldom go to his task with that hopeful sense sustaining him, which a vigorous and clear spirit gives to the soul. To know that our hour for toil is come, and that we are weak and unprepared ; to feel that depression or lassitude is weighing us down, when we must feign lightness and mirth ; or to mock our secret griefs with show of others not akin, must be the fate of him who labours in such a work. This is not all. When our work is done, and well done, the excitement which the employment had given us is gone, the spirits sink down, and there is a dreadful void in the mind. We feel as powerless as infancy till pushed to the exertion of our powers again ; even great success has its terrors. We fear that we shall never do so well again ; and know how churlishly the world receives from us that which will not bear a comparison with what we have given them before.

Yet these sufferings have their rewards. To bear up against ill health by a sudden and strong effort, to shake off low spirits, and drive away the mists which lie thick and heavy upon the mind, gives a new state of being to the soul cheerful as the light. To sit at home in our easy chair, and send our gay thoughts abroad, as it were, on wings to thousands—to imagine them laughing over the odd fancies and drolleries which had made us vain and happy in secret, multiplies and spreads our sympathies quietly and happily through the world. In this way, too, we can pour out before the world thoughts which had never been laid open even to a friend ; and make it feel our melancholy, and bear our griefs, while we still sit in the secret of our souls. The heart tells its story abroad, yet loses not its delicacy : it lays itself bare, but is still sensitive.

Industry necessary to the Attainment of Eloquence —
WARE.

THE history of the world is full of testimony to prove
how much depends upon industry ; not an eminent orator
has lived but is an example of it.   Yet, in contradiction to
all this, the almost universal feeling appears to be, that industry can effect nothing, that eminence is the result of
accident, and that every one must be content to remain just
what he may happen to be.   Thus multitudes, who come
forward as teachers and guides, suffer themselves to be satisfied with the most indifferent attainments, and a miserable
mediocrity, without so much as inquiring how they may
rise higher, much less making any attempt to rise.   For
any other art they would have served an apprenticeship,
and would be ashamed to practise it in public before they
had learned it.   If any one would sing, he attends a master, and is drilled in the very elementary principles; and
only after the most laborious process dares to exercise his
voice in public.   This he does, though he has scarce any
thing to learn but the mechanical execution of what lies
in sensible forms before the eye.   But the extempore speaker, who is to invent as well as to utter, to carry on an operation of the mind as well as to produce sound, enters upon the
work without preparatory discipline, and then wonders that
he fails !   If he were learning to play on the flute for public exhibition, what hours and days would he spend in giving facility to his fingers, and attaining the power of the
sweetest and most expressive execution !   If he were devoting himself to the organ, what months and years would
he labour, that he might know its compass, and be master
of its keys, and be able to draw out, at will, all its various
combinations of harmonious sound, and its full richness and
delicacy of expression !   And yet he will fancy that the
grandest, the most various and most expressive of all instruments, which the infinite Creator has fashioned by the union
of an intellectual soul with the powers of speech, may be
played upon without study or practice ; he comes to it a
mere uninstructed tyro, and thinks to manage all its stops,
and command the whole compass of its varied and com-

prehensive power! He finds himself a bungler in the attempt, is mortified at his failure, and settles it in his mind forever, that the attempt is vain.

Success in every art, whatever may be the natural talent, is always the reward of industry and pains. But the instances are many, of men of the finest natural genius, whose beginning has promised much, but who have degenerated wretchedly as they advanced, because they trusted to their gifts, and made no efforts to improve. That there have never been other men of equal endowments with Demosthenes and Cicero, none would venture to suppose; but who have so devoted themselves to their art, or become equal in excellence? If those great men had been content, like others, to continue as they began, and had never made their persevering efforts for improvement, what would their countries have benefited from their genius, or the world have known of their fame? They would have been lost in the undistinguished crowd that sunk to oblivion around them. Of how many more will the same remark prove true! What encouragement is thus given to the industrious! With such encouragement, how inexcusable is the negligence, which suffers the most interesting and important truths to seem heavy and dull, and fall ineffectual to the ground, through mere sluggishness in their delivery! How unworthy of one, who performs the high functions of a religious instructer, upon whom depend, in a great measure, the religious knowledge, and devotional sentiments, and final character, of many fellow-beings,— to imagine, that he can worthily discharge this great concern, by occasionally talking for an hour, he knows not now, and in a manner which he has taken no pains to render correct, impressive, and attractive; and which, simply through want of that command over himself, which study would give, is immethodical, verbose, inaccurate, feeble, trifling It has been said of the good preacher, that "truths divine come mended from his tongue." Alas! they come ruined and worthless from such a man as this. They lose that holy energy, by which they are to convert the soul and purify man for heaven, and sink, in interest and efficacy below the level of those principles, which govern the ordinary affairs of this lower world

Ingratitude towards the Deity.—APPLETON.

PERHAPS there is no crime which finds fewer advocates than ingratitude. Persons accused of this may deny the charge, but they never attempt to justify the disposition They never say that there is no obliquity and demerit in being unmindful of benefits. If a moral fitness is discern‐ible on any occasion, it is so on an occasion of favours be‐stowed and received. In proportion to these favours is the degree of demerit attached to ingratitude. Agreeable to this is the sentence so often quoted from Publius Syrus, " Omne dixeris maledictum, quum ingratum hominem dix‐eris."

With what feelings do we receive and enjoy favours bestowed by our Creator! Our dependence on him is ab‐solute and universal Existence is not more truly his gift, than are all those objects, which render existence valuable., To his munificence are we indebted for intellectual powers, and the means for their cultivation; for the sustenance daily provided; for the enjoyments derived from the ac‐tive and varying scenes of the day, and from the rest and tranquillity of the night.. His gifts are the relations and friends, whom we love, and from whose affection to us so considerable a part of the joy of life is derived. His are the showers which moisten, and the sun which warms the earth. From Him are the pleasures and animation of spring, and the riches of harvest—all, that satisfies the ap‐petite, supports or restores the animal system, gratifies the ear, or charms the eye. With what emotions, let it be asked, are all these objects viewed, and these blessings en‐joyed? Is it the habit of man to acknowledge God in his works, and to attribute all his pleasures and security of life to the Creator's munificence? Possession and prosperity are enjoyed not as a gift to the undeserving, but as the re‐sult of chance or good fortune, or as the merited reward of our own prudence and effort. Were gratitude a trait in the human character, it would be proportionate to obligation; and where much is received much would be acknowledged. In this the liveliest sense of obligation would be exhibited among the wealthy, and those whose prosperity had been long and uninterrupted. But do facts correspond to this supposition? Are God, his providence, and bounty, most sensibly and devoutly acknowledged by you, who feel no want, and are tried by no adversity? The truth is, our sense of obligation usually diminishes in proportion to the greatness and duration of blessings bestowed. A long course of prosperity renders us the more insensible and irreligious.

But on no subject is human ingratitude so remarkably apparent, as in regard to the Christian religion. I speak not of those who reject, but of those who believe Christianity, and who of course believe that " God so loved the world, as to give his only begotten Son, that whosoever believeth on him might not perish." Search all the records of every era and nation; look through the works of God so far as they are open to human inspection, and you find nothing which equally displays the riches of divine mercy. The Son of God died to save culprits from merited condemnation. But is this subject contemplated with interest, with joy, with astonishment? It is viewed with the most frigid indifference or heartfelt reluctance. The human mind, far from considering this as a favourite subject, flies from it, when occasionally presented.

Resistance to Oppression.—J. QUINCY, JUN.

To complain of the enormities of power, to expostulate with overgrown oppressors, hath in all ages been denominated sedition and faction; and to turn upon tyrants, treason and rebellion. But tyrants are rebels against the first laws of Heaven and society; to oppose their ravages is an instinct of nature—the inspiration of God in the heart of man. In the noble resistance which mankind make to exorbitant ambition and power, they always feel that divine afflatus, which, paramount to every thing human, causes

---

* This piece is extracted from " Observations on the Boston Port Bill," first published in 1774, and recently reprinted in connexion with the Life of Mr. Quincy, by his son.—ED.

4

them to consider the Lord of Hosts as their leader, and his angels as fellow-soldiers. Trumpets are to them joyful sounds, and the ensigns of war the banners of God. Their wounds are bound up in the oil of a good cause; sudden death is to them present martyrdom, and funeral obsequies resurrections to eternal honour and glory,—their widows and babes being received into the arms of a compassionate God, and their names enrolled among David's worthies :— greatest losses are to them greatest gains ; for they leave the troubles of their warfare to lie down on beds of eternal rest and felicity.

Lafayette in the French Revolution.—TICKNOR.

LAFAYETTE was, also, a prominent member of the States' General, which met in 1789, and assumed the name of the National Assembly. He proposed, in this body, a Declaration of Rights, not unlike our own, and it was under his influence, and while he was, for this very purpose, in the chair, that a decree was passed on the night of the 13th and 14th of July,—at the moment the Bastile was falling before the cannon of the populace,—which provided for the responsibility of ministers, and thus furnished one of the most important elements of a representative monarchy. Two days afterwards, he was appointed commander in chief of the National Guards of Paris, and thus was placed at the head of what was intended to be made, when it should be carried into all the departments, the effective military power of the realm, and what, under his wise management, soon became such.

His great military command, and his still greater personal influence, now brought him constantly in contact with the throne. His position, therefore, was extremely delicate and difficult, especially as the popular party in Paris, of which he was not so much the head as the idol, was already in a state of perilous excitement, and atrocious violences were beginning to be committed. The abhorrence of the queen was almost universal, and was excessive to a degree of which we can have no just idea. The

circumstance that the court lived at Versailles, sixteen
miles from Paris, and that the National Assembly was held
there, was another source of jealousy, irritation, and hatred on the part of the capital. The people of Paris, therefore, as a sign of opposition, had mounted their municipal
cockade of blue and red, whose effects were already becoming alarming. Lafayette, who was anxious about the
consequences of such a marked division, and who knew
how important are small means of conciliation, added to it,
on the 26th of July, the white of the royal cockade, and,
as he placed it in his own hat, amidst the acclamations of
the multitude, prophesied that it " would go round the
world ;" a prediction that is already more than half accomplished, since the tri-coloured cockade has been used
'for the ensign of emancipation in Spain, in Naples, in some
parts of South America, and in Greece.

Still, however, the tendency of every thing was to confusion and violence. The troubles of the times, too, rather
than a positive want of the means of subsistence, had
brought on a famine in the capital ; and the populace of
fauxbourgs, the most degraded certainly in France, having
assembled and armed themselves, determined to go to Versailles ; the greater part with a blind desire for vengeance
on the royal family, but others only with the purpose of
bringing the king from Versailles, and forcing him to reside in the more ancient, but scarcely habitable palace of
the Thuilleries, in the midst of Paris. The National
Guards clamoured to accompany this savage multitude.
Lafayette opposed their inclination ; the municipality of
Paris hesitated, but supported it ; he resisted nearly the
whole of the 5th of October, while the road to Versailles
was already thronged with an exasperated mob of above
a hundred thousand ferocious men and women, until, at
last, finding the multitude were armed, and even had cannon, he asked and received an order to march from the
competent authority, and set off at four o'clock in the afternoon, as one going to a post of imminent danger, which
it had clearly become his duty to occupy

He arrived at Versailles at ten o'clock at night, after
having been on horseback from before daylight in the
morning, and having made, during the whole interval, octo

at Paris and on the road, incredible exertions to control the multitude and calm the soldiers. "The Marquis de Lafayette at last entered the Château," says Madame de Staël, "and, passing through the apartment where we were, went to the king. We all pressed round him as if he were the master of events, and yet the popular party was already more powerful than its chief, and principles were yielding to factions, or rather were beginning to serve as their pretexts. M. de Lafayette's manner was perfectly calm; nobody ever saw it otherwise; but his delicacy suffered from the importance of the part he was called to act. He asked for the interior posts of the Château, in order that he might ensure their safety. Only the outer posts were granted to him." This refusal was not disrespectful to him who made the request. It was given simply because the etiquette of the court reserved the guard of the royal person and family to another body of men. Lafayette, therefore, answered for the National Guards, and for the posts committed to them; but he could answer for no more; and his pledge was faithfully and desperately redeemed.

Between two and three o'clock, the queen and the royal family went to bed. Lafayette, too, slept after the great fatigues of this fearful day. At half past four, a portion of the populace made their way into the palace by an obscure, interior passage, which had been overlooked, and which was not in that part of the Château intrusted to Lafayette. They were evidently led by persons who well knew the secret avenues. Mirabeau's name was afterwards strangely compromised in it, and the form of the infamous Duke of Orleans was repeatedly recognised on the great staircase, pointing the assassins the way to the queen's chamber. They easily found it. Two of her guards were cut down in an instant, and she made her escape almost naked. Lafayette immediately rushed in with the national troops, protected the guards from the brutal populace, and saved the lives of the royal family, which had so nearly been sacrificed to the etiquette of the monarchy.

The day dawned, as this fearful scene of guilt and bloodshed was passing in the magnificent palace, whose construction had exhausted the revenues of Louis Fourteenth, and which, for a century, had been the most splendid residence in Europe. As soon as it was light, the same furious multitude filled the space, which, from the rich materials of which it was formed, passed under the name of the Court of Marble. They called upon the king, in tones not to be mistaken, to go to Paris; and they called for the queen, who had but just escaped from their daggers, to come out upon the balcony. The king, after a short consultation with his ministers, announced his intention to set out for the capital; but Lafayette was afraid to trust the queen in the midst of the blood-thirsty multitude. He went to her, therefore, with respectful hesitation, and asked her if it were her intention to accompany the king to Paris. " Yes," she replied, " although I am aware of the danger." " Are you positively determined ?" " Yes, sir." " Condescend, then, to go out upon the balcony, and suffer me to attend you." " Without the king ?"—she replied, hesitating—" Have you observed the threats ?" " Yes, madam, I have; but dare to trust me." He led her out upon the balcony. It was a moment of great responsibility and great delicacy; but nothing, he felt assured, could be so dangerous as to permit her to set out for Paris, surrounded by that multitude, unless its feelings could be changed. The agitation, the tumult, the cries of the crowd, rendered it impossible that his voice should be heard. It was necessary, therefore, to address himself to the eye, and, turning towards the queen with that admirable presence of mind which never yet forsook him, and with that mingled grace and dignity, which were the peculiar inheritance of the ancient court of France, he simply kissed her hand before the vast multitude. An instant of silent astonishment followed, but the whole was immediately interpreted, and the air was rent with cries of " Long live the queen !" " Long live the general !" from the same fickle and cruel populace, that, only two hours before, had imbrued their hands in the blood of the guards who defended the life of this same queen.

4 *

Poeta nascitur, Orator fit.—MONTHLY ANTHOLOGY

POETRY is the frolic of invention, the dance of words, and the harmony of sounds. Oratory consists in a judicious disposition of arguments, a happy selection of terms, and a pleasing elocution. The object of poetry is to delight, that of oratory to persuade. Poetry is truth, but it is truth in her gayest and loveliest robes, and wit, flattery, hyperbole, and fable, are marshalled in her train. Oratory has a graver and more majestic port, and gains by slow advances and perseverance what the poet takes by suddenness of inspiration, and by surprise. Poetry requires genius; eloquence is within the reach of talent. Seriousness becomes one, sprightliness the other. The wittiest poets have been the shortest writers; but he is often the best orator, who has the strongest lungs, and the firmest legs. The poet sings for the approbation of the wise and the pleasure of the ingenious; the orator addresses the multitude, and the larger the number of ears, the better for his purpose; and he who can get the most votes most thoroughly understands his art. Bad verses are always abominable: but he is a good speaker who gains his cause. Bards are generally remarkable for generosity of nature; orators are as often notorious for their ambition. These enjoy most influence while alive; those live longest after death. Poets are not necessarily poor; for Theocritus and Anacreon, Horace and Lucian, Racine and Boileau, Pope and Addison, rolled in their carriages, and slept in palaces: yet it must be confessed, that most of the poetical tribe have rather feared the tap of the sheriff, than the damnation of critics. The poverty of a poet takes nothing from the richness and sweetness of his lines; while an orator's success is not infrequently promoted by his wealth. Nevertheless, were I poor, I would study eloquence, that I might be rich; had I riches, I would study poetry, that I might give a portion of immortality to both. Could I write no better than Blackmore, I would sometimes versify; but were I privileged to soar upon the daring wing of Dryden's muse, I would not keep my pinions continually spread.

Intellectual Qualities of Milton.—CHANNING.

IN speaking of the intellectual qualities of Milton, we may begin by observing that the very splendour of his poetic fame has tended to obscure or conceal the extent of his mind, and the variety of its energies and attainments. To many he seems only a poet, when in truth he was a profound scholar, a man of vast compass of thought, imbued thoroughly with all ancient and modern learning, and able to master, to mould, to impregnate with his own intellectual power, his great and various acquisitions. He had not learned the superficial doctrine of a later day, that poetry flourishes most in an uncultivated soil, and that imagination shapes its brightest visions from the mists of a superstitious age; and he had no dread of accumulating knowledge, lest he should oppress and smother his genius. He was conscious of that within him, which could quicken all knowledge, and wield it with ease and might; which could give freshness to old truths, and harmony to discordant thoughts; which could bind together, by living ties and mysterious affinities, the most remote discoveries; and rear fabrics of glory and beauty from the rude materials which other minds had collected. Milton had that universality which marks the highest order of intellect. Though accustomed, almost from infancy, to drink at the fountains of classical literature, he had nothing of the pedantry and fastidiousness, which disdain all other draughts. His healthy mind delighted in genius, in whatever soil, or in whatever age it has burst forth, and poured out its fulness. He understood too well the right, and dignity, and pride of creative imagination, to lay on it the laws of the Greek or Roman school. Parnassus was not to him the only holy ground of genius. He felt that poetry was a universal presence, Great minds were every where his kindred. He felt the enchantment of oriental fiction, surrendered himself to the strange creations of " Araby the blest," and delighted still more in the romantic spirit of chivalry, and in the tales of wonder in which it was imbodied. Accordingly, his poetry reminds us of the ocean, which adds to its own boundlessness contributions from all regions under heaven.

Nor was it only in the department of imagination, that his acquisitions were vast. He travelled over the whole field of knowledge, as far as it had then been explored. His various philological attainments were used to put him in possession of the wisdom stored in all countries where the intellect had been cultivated. The natural philosophy, metaphysics, ethics, history, theology and political science of his own and former times were familiar to him. Never was there a more unconfined mind; and we would cite Milton as a practical example of the benefits of that universal culture of intellect, which forms one distinction of our times, but which some dread as unfriendly to original thought. Let such remember, that mind is in its own nature diffusive. Its object is the universe, which is strictly one, or bound together by infinite connexions and correspondencies; and, accordingly, its natural progress is from one to another field of thought; and, wherever original power or creative genius exists, the mind, far from being distracted or oppressed by the variety of its acquisitions, will see more and more bearings, and hidden and beautiful analogies in all the objects of knowledge, will see mutual light shed from truth to truth, and will compel, as with a kingly power, whatever it understands to yield some tribute of proof, or illustration, or splendour, to whatever topic it would unfold.

National Recollections the Foundation of national Character.—EDWARD EVERETT.

AND how is the spirit of a free people to be formed, and animated, and cheered, but out of the store-house of its historic recollections? Are we to be eternally ringing the changes upon Marathon and Thermopylæ; and going back to read in obscure texts of Greek and Latin of the exemplars of patriotic virtue? I thank God that we can find them nearer home, in our own country, on our own soil;— that strains of the noblest sentiment that ever swelled in the breast of man, are breathing to us out of every page of our country's history, in the native eloquence of our mother tongue;—that the colonial and provincial councils of America exhibit to us models of the spirit and character, which gave Greece and Rome their name and their praise among the nations.   Here we ought to go for our instruction;—the lesson is plain, it is clear, it is applicable. When we go to ancient history, we are bewildered with the difference of manners and institutions.   We are willing to pay our tribute of applause to the memory of Leonidas, who fell nobly for his country in the face of his foe.   But when we trace him to his home, we are confounded at the reflection, that the same Spartan heroism, to which he sacrificed himself at Thermopylæ, would have led him to tear his own child, if it had happened to be a sickly babe,—the very object for which all that is kind and good in man rises up to plead,—from the bosom of its mother, and carry it out to be eaten by the wolves of Taygetus.   We feel a glow of admiration at the heroism displayed at Marathon, by the ten thousand champions of invaded Greece ; bu we cannot forget that the tenth part of the number were slaves, unchained from the work-shops and door-posts of their masters, to go and fight the battles of freedom.   I do not mean that these examples are to destroy the interest with which we read the history of ancient times; they possibly increase that interest by the very contrasts they exhibit.   But they do warn us, if we need the warning, to seek our great practical lessons of patriotism at home ; out of the exploits and sacrifices of which our own country is the theatre ; out of the characters of our own fathers. Them we know,—the high-souled, natural, unaffected, the citizen heroes.   We know what happy firesides they left for the cheerless camp.   We know with what pacific habits the dared the perils of the field.   There is no mystery, no romance, no madness, under the name of chivalry, about them.   It is all resolute, manly resistance for conscience' and liberty's sake, not merely of an overwhelming power, but of all the force of long-rooted habits and native love of order and peace.

Above all, their blood calls to us from the soil which we tread ; it beats in our veins ; it cries to us not merely in the thrilling words of one of the first victims in this cause,— " My sons, scorn to be slaves !"—but it cries with a still more moving eloquence—" My sons, forget not your fr

thers!" Fast, oh! too fast, with all our efforts to prevent
it, their precious memories are dying away. Notwithstanding our numerous written memorials, much of what is
known of those eventful times dwells but in the recollections of a few revered survivors, and with them is rapidly
perishing unrecorded and irretrievable. How many prudent counsels, conceived in perplexed times; how many
heart-stirring words, uttered when liberty was treason,
how many brave and heroic deeds, performed when the
halter, not the laurel, was the promised meed of patriotic
daring,—are already lost and forgotten in the graves of their
authors! How little do we,—although we have been permitted to hold converse with the venerable remnants of
that day,—how little do we know of their dark and anx-
.ous hours; of their secret meditations; of the hurried
and perilous events of the momentous struggle! And while
they are dropping around us like the leaves of autumn,
while scarce a week passes that does not call away some
member of the veteran ranks, already so sadly thinned,
shall we make no effort to hand down the traditions of their
day to our children; to pass the torch of liberty,—which
we received in all the splendour of its first enkindling,—
bright and flaming, to those who stand next us on the
line; so that, when we shall come to be gathered to the
lust where our fathers are laid, we may say to our sons
and our grandsons, "If we did not amass, we have not
squandered your inheritance of glory ?"

Extract from the Legend of Sleepy Hollow.—IRVING.

ON a fine autumnal morning, Ichabod, in pensive mood,
sat enthroned on a lofty stool, from whence he usually
watched all the concerns of his little literary realm. In
his hand he swayed a ferule, that sceptre of despotic power; the birch of justice reposed on three nails behind the
throne, a constant terror to evil doers; while on the desk before him might be seen sundry contraband articles and prohibited weapons, detected upon the persons of idle urchins; such
as half-munched apples, popguns, whirligigs, flycages, and

whole legions of rampant little paper game-cocks. Appa
rently there had been some act of justice recently inflicted, for his scholars were all busily intent upon their books,
or slyly whispering behind them, with one eye kept upon
the master; and a kind of buzzing stillness reigned
throughout the school-room. It was suddenly interrupted
by the appearance of a negro in tow-cloth jacket and trow
sers, a round-crowned fragment of a hat, like the cap of
Mercury, and mounted on a ragged, wild, half-broken colt,
which he managed with a rope, by way of halter. He
came clattering up to the school-door, with an invitation to
Ichabod to attend a merry-making, or " quilting frolic,"
to be held that evening at Mynheer Van Tassel's ; and, having delivered his message with that air of importance, and
effort of fine language, which a negro is apt to display on
petty embassies of the kind, he dashed over the brook, and
was seen scampering away up the hollow, full of the importance and hurry of his mission.

All was now bustle and hubbub in the late quiet school-
room. The scholars were hurried through their lessons
without stopping at trifles ; those who were nimble skip-
ped over half with impunity, and those who were tardy
had a smart application now and then in the rear, to quick-
en their speed, or help them over a tall word. Books were
thrown aside without being put away on the shelves ; ink-
stands were overturned, benches thrown down, and the
whole school was turned loose an hour before the usual
time ; bursting forth like a legion of young imps, yelping
and racketing about the green, in joy at their early emancipation.

The gallant Ichabod now spent at least an extra half-
hour at his toilet, brushing and furbishing up his best, and
indeed only, suit of rusty black, and arranging his looks by
a bit of broken looking-glass, that hung up in the school
house That he might make his appearance before his mistress in the true spirit of a cavalier, he borrowed a horse
from the farmer with whom he was domiciliated, a choleric old Dutchman, of the name of Hans Van Ripper, and,
thus gallantly mounted, issued forth like a knight errant
in quest of adventures.—But it is fit that I should, in the
true spirit of romantic story, give some account of the

looks and equipments of my hero and his steed. The animal he bestrode was a broken-down plough-horse, that had outlived almost every thing but his viciousness. He was gaunt and shagged, with an ewe neck, and a head like a hammer; his rusty mane and tail were tangled and knot. ted with burrs; one eye had lost its pupil, and was glaring and spectral, but the other had the gleam of a genuine devil in it. Still he must have had fire and mettle in his day, if we may judge from his name, which was Gunpowder. He had, in fact, been a favourite steed of his master's, the choleric Van Ripper, who was a furious rider, and had infused, very probably, some of his spirit into the animal; for, old and broken down as he looked, there was more of the lurking devil in him than in any young filly in the country.

Ichabod was a suitable figure for such a steed. He rode with short stirrups, which brought his knees nearly up to the pommel of the saddle; his sharp elbows stuck out like grasshoppers'; he carried his whip perpendicularly in his hand, like a sceptre, and, as his horse jogged on, the motion of his arms was not unlike the flapping of a pair of wings. A small wool hat rested on the top of his nose,— for so his scanty strip of a forehead might be called,—and the skirts of his black coat flirted out almost to the horse's tail. Such was the appearance of Ichabod and his steed, as he shambled out of the gate of Hans Van Ripper, and it was altogether such an apparition as is rarely to be met with in broad day-light.

It was, as I have said, a fine autumnal day, the sky was clear and serene, and nature wore that rich and golden livery, which we always associate with the idea of abundance. The forests had put on their sober brown and yellow, while some trees of the tenderer kind had been nipped by the frosts into brilliant dyes of orange, purple, and scarlet. Streaming files of wild ducks began to make their appearance high in the air; the bark of the squirrel might be heard from the groves of beech and hickory nuts, and the pensive whistle of the quail at intervals from the neighbouring stubble field.

The small birds were taking their farewell banquets. In the fulness of their revelry they fluttered, chirping and frolicking from bush to bush and tree to tree, capricious from the very abundance around them. There was the honest cock-robin, the favourite game of stripling sportsmen, with its loud, querulous note ; and the twitter-ing blackbirds flying in sable clouds ; and the golden-wing-el woodpecker, with his crimson crest, his broad black gor-get, and splendid plumage ; and the cedar bird, with its red-t'pped wings and yellow-tipped tail, and its little montero cap of feathers ; and the blue jay, that noisy coxcomb, in his gay light-blue coat and white under-clothes, screaming and chattering, nodding, and bobbing, and bowing, and pre-tending to be on good terms with every songster of the grove.

As Ichabod jogged slowly on his way, his eye, ever open to every symptom of culinary abundance, ranged with delight over the treasures of jolly autumn. On all sides he beheld vast store of apples, some hanging in oppressive opulence on the trees ; some gathered into baskets and bar-rels for the market ; others heaped up in rich piles for the cider-press. Farther on he beheld great fields of Indian corn, with its golden ears peeping from their leafy coverts, and holding out the promise of cakes and hasty puddings ; and the yellow pumpkins lying beneath them, turning up their fair round bellies to the sun, and giving ample pros-pects of the most luxurious pies ; and anon he passed the fragrant buckwheat fields, breathing the odour of the bee-hive, and, as he beheld them, soft anticipations stole over his mind of dainty slapjacks, well buttered, and garnished with honey or treacle, by the delicate little dimpled hand of Katrina Van Tassel.

Thus feeding his mind with many sweet thoughts and " sugared suppositions," he journeyed along the sides of a range of hills which look out upon some of the goodliest scenes of the mighty Hudson. The sun gradually wheel-ed his broad disk down into the west ; the wide bosom of the Tappan Zee lay motionless and glassy, excepting that, here and there, a gentle undulation waved and prolonged the blue shadow of the distant mountain. A few amber clouds floated in the sky, without a breath of air to move them. The horizon was of a fine golden tint, changing gradually into a pure apple green, and from that into the deep blue of the mid-heaven. A slanting ray lingered on the

5

woody crests of the precipices, that overhung some parts
of the river, giving greater depth to the dark gray and
purple of their rocky sides. A sloop was loitering in the
distance, dropping slowly down with the tide, her sail
hanging uselessly against the mast; and, as the reflection
of the sky gleamed along the still water, it seemed as if
the vessel was suspended in the air.

It was towards evening that Ichabod arrived at the castle of Heer Van Tassel, which he found thronged with the
pride and flower of the adjacent country Old farmers, a spare,
leatherned-faced race, in homespun coats and breeches, blue
stockings, huge shoes, and magnificent pewter buckles.
Their brisk, withered little dames, in close-crimped caps,
long-waisted gowns, homespun petticoats, with scissors and
pincushions, and gay calico pockets hanging on the outside.
Buxom lasses, almost as antiquated as their mothers, excepting where a straw hat, a fine riband, or perhaps a white
frock, gave symptoms of city innovations. The sons in short
square-skirted coats, with rows of stupendous brass buttons,
and their hair generally queued in the fashion of the times,
especially if they could procure an eelskin for the purpose,
it being esteemed throughout the country as a potent nour-
isher and strengthener of the hair.

Brom Bones, however, was the hero of the scene, having come to the gathering on his favourite steed Daredevil,
a creature, like himself, full of mettle and mischief, and
which no one but himself could manage. He was in fact
noted for preferring vicious animals, given to all kinds of
tricks, which kept the rider in constant risk of his neck,
for he held a tractable, wellbroken horse as unworthy a lad
of spirit.

Fain would I pause to dwell upon the world of charms
that burst upon the enraptured gaze of my hero as he entered the state parlour of Van Tassel's mansion : not those
of the bevy of buxom lasses, with their luxurious display of
red and white ; but the ample charms of a genuine Dutch
country tea-table in the sumptuous time of autumn. Such
heaped-up platters of cakes of various and almost indescribable kinds, known only to the experienced Dutch housewives ! There was the doughty dough-nut, the tender oly
koek, and the crisp and crumbling cruller, sweet cakes and

short cakes, ginger cakes and honey cakes, and the whole family of cakes. And then there were apple   es, and peach pies, and pumpkin pies ; besides slices of ham and smoked beef; and, moreover, delectable dishes of preserved plums, and peaches, and pears, and quinces; not to mention broiled shad and roasted chickens; together with bowls of milk and cream, all mingled higgledy-piggledy, pretty much as I have enumerated them, with the motherly tea-pot sending up its clouds of vapour from the midst. Heaven bless the mark! I want breath and time to discuss this banquet as it deserves, and am too eager to get on with my story. Happily, Ichabod Crane was not in so great a hurry as his historian, but did ample justice to every dainty.

Reflections on the Settlement of New England.
WEBSTER.

THE settlement of New England, by the colony which landed here on the twenty-second of December, sixteen hundred and twenty, although not the first European establish-ment in what now constitutes the United States, was yet so peculiar in its causes and character, and has been followed, and must still be followed, by such consequences, as to give it a high claim to lasting commemoration. On these causes and consequences, more than on its immediately at-tendant circumstances, its importance, as an historical event, depends. Great actions and striking occurrences, having excited a temporary admiration, often pass away and are forgotten, because they leave no lasting results, affecting the prosperity of communities. Such is frequently the for-tune of the most brilliant military achievements. Of the ten thousand battles which have been fought; of all the fields fertilized with carnage ; of the banners which have been bathed in blood; of the warriors who have hoped that they had risen from the field of conquest to a glory as bright and as durable as the stars, how few that continue long to interest mankind! The victory of yesterday is re-versed by the defeat of to-day ; the star of military glory rising like a meteor, like a meteor has fallen ; disgrace and disaster hang on the heels of conquest and renow—; victor and vanquished presently pass away to oblivion, and the world holds on its course, with the loss only of so many lives, and so much treasure.

But if this is frequently, or generally, the fortune of military achievements, it is not always so. There are enterprises, military as well as civil, that sometimes check the current of events, give a new turn to human affairs, and transmit their consequences through ages. We see their importance in their results, and call them great, because great things follow. There have been battles which have fixed the fate of nations. These come down to us in history with a solid and permanent influence, not created by a display of glittering armour, the rush of adverse battalions, the sinking and rising of pennons, the flight, the pursuit, and the victory; but by their effect in advancing or retarding human knowledge, in overthrowing or establishing despotism, in extending or destroying human happiness. When the traveller pauses on the plains of Marathon, what are the emotions which strongly agitate his breast? what is that glorious recollection that thrills through his frame, and suffuses his eyes? Not, I imagine, that Grecian skill and Grecian valour were here most signally displayed; but that Greece herself was saved. It is because to this spot, and to the event which has rendered it immortal, he refers all the succeeding glories of the republic. It is because, if that day had gone otherwise, Greece had perished. It is because he perceives that her philosophers and orators, her poets and painters, her sculptors and architects, her government and free institutions, point backward to Marathon, and that their future existence seems to have been suspended on the contingency, whether the Persian or Grecian banner should wave victorious in the beams of that day's setting sun. And, as his imagination kindles at the retrospect, he is transported back to the interesting moment; he counts the fearful odds of the contending hosts; his interest for the result overwhelms him; he trembles as if it were still uncertain, and seems to doubt whether he may consider Socrates and Plato, Demosthenes, Sophocles, and Phidias. as secure. yet, to himself and to the world.

"If we conquer,"—said the Athenian commander on the morning of that decisive day,—"if we conquer, we shall make Athens the greatest city of Greece." A prophecy how well fulfilled! "if God prosper us,"—might have been the more appropriate language of our fathers, when they landed upon this rock,—"if God prosper us, we shall here begin a work that shall last for ages; we shall plant here a new society, in the principles of the fullest liberty, and the purest religion; we shall subdue this wilderness which is before us; we shall fill this region of the great continent, which stretches almost from pole to pole, with civilization and Christianity; the temples of the true God shall rise where now ascends the smoke of idolatrous sacrifice; fields and gardens, the flowers of summer, and the waving and golden harvests of autumn, shall extend over a thousand hills, and stretch along a thousand valleys, never yet, since the creation, reclaimed to the use of civilized man. We shall whiten this coast with the canvass of a prosperous commerce; we shall stud the long and winding shore with a hundred cities. That which we sow in weakness shall be raised in strength. From our sincere, but houseless worship, there shall spring splendid temples to record God's goodness; from the simplicity of our social union, there shall arise wise and politic constitutions of government, full of the liberty which we ourselves bring and breathe; from our zeal for learning, institutions shall spring, which shall scatter the light of knowledge throughout the land, and, in time, paying back what they have borrowed, shall contribute their part to the great aggregate of human knowledge; and our descendants, through all generations, shall look back to this spot, and this hour, with unabated affection and regard."

Forest Scenery.—PAULDING.

By degrees, as custom reconciled me more and more to fasting and long rambles, I extended my excursions farther from home, and sometimes remained out all day without tasting food, or resting myself, except for a few minutes

5 *

upon the trunk of some decayed old tree or moss-covered rock. The country, though in a great degree in its native state of wildness, was full of romantic beauties. The Mohawk is one of the most charming of rivers, sometimes brawling among ragged rocks, or darting swiftly through long, narrow reaches, and here and there, as at the Little Falls, and again at the Cohoes, darting down high perpendicular rocks, in sheets of milk-white foam; but its general character is that of repose and quiet. It is no where so broad, but that rural objects and rural sounds may be seen and heard distinctly from one side to the other; and in many places the banks on either hand are composed of rich meadows, or *flats*, as they were denominated by the early Dutch settlers, so nearly on a level with the surface of the water, as to be almost identified with it at a distance, were it not for the rich fringe of water willows, that skirt it on either side, and mark the lines of separation. In these rich pastures may now be seen the lowing herds, half hidden in the luxuriant grass, and, a little farther on, out of the reach of the spring freshets, the comfortable farm-houses of many a sanguine country squire, who dreams of boundless wealth from the Grand Canal, and, in his admiration of the works of man, forgets the far greater beauty, grandeur, and utility of the works of his Maker. But I am to describe the scenery as it was in the days of my boyhood, when, like Nimrod, I was a mighty hunter before the Lord.

At the time I speak of, all that was to be seen was of the handy work of nature, except the little settlement, over which presided the patriarch Veeder. We were the advance guard of civilization, and a few steps beyond us was the region of primeval forests, composed of elms and maples, and oaks and pines, that seemed as if their seeds had been sown at the time of the deluge, and that they had been growing ever since. I have still a distinct recollection, I might almost say perception, of the gloom and damps which pervaded these chilling shades, where the summer sun never penetrated, and in whose recesses the very light was of a greenish hue. Here, especially along the little streams, many of which are now dried up by the opening of the earth to the sun-beams, every rock and piece of mouldering wood was wrapped in a carpet of green moss, fostered into more than velvet luxuriance by the everlasting damps, that, unlike the dews of heaven, fell all the day as well as all the night.   Here and there a flower reared its pale head among the rankness of the sunless vegetation of unsightly fungus, but it was without fragrance, and almost without life, for it withered as soon as plucked from the stem.   I do not remember ever to have heard a singing bird in these forests, except just on the outer skirts, fronting the south, where occasionally a robin chirped, or a thrush sung his evening chant.   These tiny choristers seem almost actuated by the vanity of human beings ; for I have observed they appear to take peculiar delight in the neighbourhood of the habitations of men, where they have listeners to their music.   They do not love to sing where there is no one to hear them.   The very insects of the wing seemed almost to have abandoned the gloomy solitude, to sport in the sunshine among the flowers.   Neither butterfly nor grasshopper abided there, and the honey-bee never came to equip himself in his yellow breeches.   He is the companion of the white man, and seems content to be his slave, to toil for him all the summer, only that he may be allowed the enjoyment of the refuse of his own labours in the winter.   To plunge into the recesses of these woods, was like descending into a cave under ground.   There was the coolness, the dampness, and the obscurity of twilight.   Yet custom made me love these solitudes, and many are the days I have spent among them, with my dog and gun, and no other guide but the sun in heaven and the moss on the north side of the trees.

Influence of Christianity in elevating the female Character.—J. G. CARTER.

THERE is one topic, intimately connected with the introduction and decline of Christianity, and subsequently with its revival in Europe, which the occasion strongly suggests, and which I cannot forbear briefly to touch upon.   I allude to the new and more interesting character assumed by wo-

man since those events. In the heathen world, and under
the Jewish dispensation, she was the slave of man. Christianity constituted her his companion. But, as our religion
gradually lost its power in the dark ages, she sunk down
again to her deep moral degradation. She was the first to
fall in the garden of Eden, and perhaps it was a judgment
upon her, that, when the whole human race was now low,
she sunk the lowest, and was the last to rise again to her
original consequence in the scale of being. The age of
·chivalry, indeed, exalted her to be an object of adoration.
But it was a profane adoration, not founded upon the respect
due to a being of immortal hopes and destinies as well as
man. This high character has been conceded to her at
a later period, as she has slowly attained the rank ordained
for her by Heaven. Although this change in the relation of
woman to man and to society is both an evidence and a consequence of an improvement in the human condition, yet now
her character is a cause operating to produce a still greater improvement. And if there be any one cause, to which
we may look with more confidence than to others, for hastening the approach of a more perfect state of society,
that cause is the elevated character of woman as displayed
in the full developement of all her moral and intellectual
powers. The conjugal confession of Eve to Adam,

> " God is thy law, thou mine ; to know no more
> Is woman's happiest knowledge and her praise,"

has grown to be obsolete. The influence of the female
character is now felt and acknowledged in all the relations
of her life. I speak not now of those distinguished women, who instruct their age through the public press ; nor
of those whose devout strains we take upon our lips when
we worship ; but of a much larger class ; of those whose
influence is felt in the relations of neighbour, fiiend, daughter, wife, mother. Who waits at the couch of the sick to
administer tender charities while life lingers, or to perform
the last acts of kindness when death comes ? Where shall
we look for those examples of friendship, that most adorn
our nature ; those abiding friendships, which trust even
when betrayed, and survive all changes of fortune ? Where
shall we find the brightest illustrations of filial piety?

Have you ever seen a daughter, herself, perhaps, timid and helpless, watching the decline of an aged parent, and holding out with heroic fortitude to anticipate his wishes to administer to his wants, and to sustain his tottering steps to the very borders of the grave?

But in no relation does woman exercise so deep an influence, both immediately and prospectively, as in that of mother. To her is committed the immortal treasure of the infant mind. Upon her devolves the care of the first stages of that course of discipline, which is to form, of a being perhaps the most frail and helpless in the world, the fearless ruler of animated creation, and the devout adorer of its great Creator. Her smiles call into exercise the first affections that spring up in our hearts. She cherishes and expands the earliest germs of our intellects She breathes over us her deepest devotions. She lifts our little hands, and teaches our little tongues to lisp in prayer. She watches over us, like a guardian angel, and protects us through all our helpless years, when we know not of her cares and her anxieties on our account. She follows us into the world of men, and lives in us, and blesses us, when she lives not otherwise upon the earth. What constitutes the centre of every home? Whither do our thoughts turn, when our feet are weary with wandering, and our hearts sick with disappointment? Where shall the truant and forgetful husband go for sympathy, unalloyed and without design, but to the bosom of her, who is ever ready and waiting to share in his adversity or his prosperity. And if there be a tribunal, where the sins and the follies of a froward child may hope for pardon and forgiveness this side heaven, that tribunal is the heart of a fond and devoted mother.

Necessity of a pure national Morality.—BEECHER.

THE crisis has come. By the people of this generation, by ourselves, probably, the amazing question is to be decided, whether the inheritance of our fathers shall be preserved or thrown away; whether our Sabbaths shall be a

delight or a loathing; whether the taverns, on that holy
day, shall be crowded with drunkards, or the sanctuary of
God with humble worshippers; whether riot and profane-
ness shall fill our streets, and poverty our dwellings, and
convicts our jails, and violence our land, or whether industry, and temperance, and righteousness, shall be the stability
of our times; whether mild laws shall receive the cheerful submission of freemen, or the iron rod of a tyrant compel the trembling homage of slaves. Be not deceived.
Human nature in this state is like human nature every
where. All actual difference in our favour is adventitious,
and the result of our laws, institutions, and habits. It is a
moral influence, which, with the blessing of God, has formed a state of society so eminently desirable. The same influence which formed it is indispensable to its preservation.
The rocks and hills of New England will remain till the
last conflagration. But let the Sabbath be profaned with
impunity, the worship of God be abandoned, the government and religious instruction of children neglected, and
the streams of intemperance be permitted to flow, and her
glory will depart. The wall of fire will no longer surround her, and the munition of rocks will no longer be her
defence.

If we neglect our duty, and suffer our laws and institutions to go down, we give them up forever. It is easy to
relax, easy to retreat; but impossible, when the abomina-
tion of desolation has once passed over New England, to
rear again the thrown-down altars, and gather again the
fragments, and build up the ruins of demolished institutions.
Another New England nor we nor our children shall ever
see, if this be destroyed. All is lost irretrievably when
the landmarks are once removed, and the bands which now
hold us are once broken. Such institutions and such a
state of society can be established only by such men as
our fathers were, and in such circumstances as they were
in. They could not have made a New England in Hol-
land; they made the attempt, but failed.

The hand that overturns our laws and temples is the
hand of death unbarring the gate of Pandemonium, and
letting loose upon our land the crimes and miseries of Hell.
If the Most High should stand aloof, and cast not a single

Ingredient into our cup of trembling, it would seem to be full of superlative wo. But he will not stand aloof. As we shall have begun an open controversy with him, he will contend openly with us. And never, since the earth stood, has it been so fearful a thing for nations to fall into the hands of the living God. The day of vengeance is at hand the day of judgment has come; the great earthquake which sinks Babylon is shaking the nations, and the waves of the mighty commotion are dashing upon every shore. Is this, then, a time to remove the foundations, when the earth itself is shaken? Is this a time to forfeit the protection of God, when the hearts of men are failing them for fear, and for looking after those things which are to come upon the earth? Is this a time to run upon his neck and the thick bosses of his buckler, when the nations are drinking blood, and fainting, and passing away in his wrath? Is this a time to throw away the shield of faith, when his arrows are drunk with the blood of the slain? to cut from the anchor of hope, when the clouds are collecting, and the sea and the waves are roaring, and thunders are uttering their voices, and lightnings blazing in the heavens, and the great hail is falling from heaven upon men, and every mountain, sea and island is fleeing in dismay from the face of an incensed God?

Value of religious Faith.—BUCKMINSTER.

WHO would look back upon the history of the world with the eye of incredulity, after having once read it with the eye of faith? To the man of faith it is the story of God's operations. To the unbeliever it is only the record of the strange sports of a race of agents as uncontrolled as they are unaccountable. To the man of faith every portion of history is part of a vast plan, conceived ages ago in the mind of Omnipotence, which has been fitted precisely to the period it was intended to occupy. The whole series of events forms a magnificent and symmetrical fabric to the eye of pious contemplation; and, though the dome be in the clouds, and the top, from its loftiness, be indiscerni-

ble to mortal vision, yet the foundations are so deep
and solid, that we are sure they are intended to support
something permanent and grand.   To the sceptic, all the
events of all the ages of the world are but a scattered
crowd of useless and indigested materials.   In his mind
all is darkness, all is incomprehensible.   The light of
prophecy illuminates not to him the obscurity of ancient
annals.   He sees in them neither design nor operation,
neither tendencies nor conclusions.   To him the wonderful
knowledge of one people is just as interesting as the desperate ignorance of another.   In the deliverance which
God has sometimes wrought for the oppressed, he sees
nothing but the fact; and in the oppression and decline of
haughty empires, nothing but the common accidents of national fortune.   Going about to account for events according to what he calls general laws, he never for a moment
considers, that all laws, whether physical, political or moral,
imply a legislator, and are contrived to serve some purpose.
Because he cannot always, by his short-sighted vision, discover the tendencies of the mighty events of which this
earth has been the theatre, he looks on the drama of existence around him as proceeding without a plan.   Is that
principle, then, of no importance, which raises man above
what his eyes see or his ears hear at present, and shows
him the vast chain of human events, fastened eternally to
the throne of God, and returning, after embracing the
universe, again to link itself to the footstool of Omnipotence ?

Would you know the value of this principle of faith to
the bereaved ?   Go, and follow a corpse to the grave.   See
the body deposited there, and hear the earth thrown in upon
all that remains of your friend.   Return now, if you will,
and brood over the lesson which your senses have given
you, and derive from it what consolation you can.   You
have learned nothing but an unconsoling fact.   No voice
of comfort issues from the tomb.   All is still there, and
blank, and lifeless, and has been so for ages.   You see
nothing but bodies dissolving and successively mingling
with the clods which cover them, the grass growing over
the spot, and the trees waving in sullen majesty over this
region of eternal silence.   And what is there more

Nothing.—Come, Faith, and people these deserts! Come, and reanimate these regions of forgetfulness! Mothers! take again your children to your arms, for they are living. Sons! your aged parents are coming forth in the vigour of regenerated years. Friends! behold, your dearest connexions are waiting to embrace you. The tombs are burst. Generations long since in slumbers are awakening. They are coming from the east and the west, from the north and from the south, to constitute the community of the blessed.

But it is not in the loss of friends alone, that faith furnishes consolations which are inestimable. With a man of faith not an affliction is lost, not a change is unimproved. He studies even his own history with pleasure, and finds it full of instruction. The dark passages of his life are illuminated with hope; and he sees, that although he has passed through many dreary defiles, yet they have opened at last into brighter regions of existence He recalls, with a species of wondering gratitude, periods of his life, when all its events seemed to conspire against him. Hemmed in by straitened circumstances, wearied with repeated blows of unexpected misfortunes, and exhausted with the painful anticipation of more, he recollects years, when the ordinary love of life could not have retained him in the world. Many a time he might have wished to lay down his being in disgust, had not something more than the senses provide us with, kept up the elasticity of his mind. He yet lives, and has found that light is sown for the righteous, and gladness for the upright in heart. The man of faith discovers some gracious purpose in every combination of circumstances. Wherever he finds himself, he knows that he has a destination—he has, therefore, a duty. Every event has, in his eye, a tendency and an aim. Nothing is accidental, nothing without purpose, nothing unattended with benevolent consequences. Every thing on earth is probationary, nothing ultimate. He is poor—perhaps his plans have, been defeated—he finds it difficult to provide for the exigencies of life—sickness is permitted to invade the quiet of his household—long confinement imprisons his activity, and cuts short the exertions on which so many depend—something apparently unlucky mars his best plans

6

—new failures and embarrassments among his friends present themselves, and throw additional obstruction in his way—the world look on and say, all these things are against him. Some wait coolly for the hour when he shall sink under the complicated embarrassments of his cruel fortune. Others, of a kinder spirit, regard him with compassion, and wonder how he can sustain such a variety of wo. A few there are, a very few, I fear, who can understand something of the serenity of his mind, and comprehend something of the nature of his fortitude. There are those, whose sympathetic piety can read and interpret the characters of resignation on his brow. There are those, in fine, who have felt the influence of faith.

In this influence there is nothing mysterious, nothing romantic, nothing of which the highest reason may be ashamed. It shows the Christian his God, in all the mild majesty of his parental character. It shows you God, disposing in still and benevolent wisdom the events of every individual's life, pressing the pious spirit with the weight of calamity to increase the elasticity of the mind, producing characters of unexpected worth by unexpected misfortune, invigorating certain virtues by peculiar probations, thus breaking the fetters which bind us to temporal things, and

> " From seeming evil still educing good,
> And better thence again, and better still,
> In infinite progression."

When the sun of the believer's hopes, according to common calculations, is set, to the eye of faith it is still visible. When much of the rest of the world is in darkness, the high ground of faith is illuminated with the brightness of religious consolation.

Come now, my incredulous friends, and follow me to the bed of the dying believer. Would you see in what peace a Christian can die ? Watch the last gleams of thought which stream from his dying eyes. Do you see any thing like apprehension ? The world, it is true, begins to shut in. The shadows of evening collect around his senses. A dark mist thickens, and rests upon the objects which have hitherto engaged his observation. The countenances of his friends

become more and more indistinct. The sweet expressions
of love and friendship are no longer intelligible. His ear
wakes no more at the well-known voice of his children,
an the soothing accents of tender affection die away unheard, upon his decaying senses. To him the spectacle
of human life is drawing to its close, and the curtain is
descending, which shuts out this earth, its actors, and its
scenes. He is no longer interested in all that is done under the sun. O! that I could now open to you the recesses
of his soul; that I could reveal to you the light, which
darts into the chambers of his understanding. He approaches that world which he has so long seen in faith.
The imagination now collects its diminished strength, and
the eye of faith opens wide. Friends! do not stand, thus
fixed in sorrow, around this bed of death. Why are you
so still and silent? Fear not to move—you cannot disturb
the last visions which enchant this holy spirit. Your lamentations break not in upon the songs of seraphs, which
inwrap his hearing in ecstasy. Crowd, if you choose,
around his couch—he heeds you not—already he sees the
spirits of the just advancing together to receive a kindred
soul. Press him not with importunities; urge him not
with alleviations. Think you he wants now these tones
of mortal voices—these material, these gross consolations?
No! He is going to add another to the myriads of the just,
that are every moment crowding into the portals of heav-
en! He is entering on a nobler life. He leaves you—he
leaves *you*, weeping children of mortality, to grope about
a little longer among the miseries and sensualities of a
worldly life. Already he cries to you from the regions of
bliss. Will you not join him there? Will you not taste the
sublime joys of faith? There are your predecessors in vlr
tue; there, too, are places left for your contemporaries.
There are seats for you in the assembly of the just made
perfect, in the innumerable company of angels, where is
Jesus, the mediator of the new covenant, and God, the
judge of all

Death of General Washington.—MARSHALL.

On Friday, the 13th of December, 1799, while attending to some improvements upon his estate, he was exposed to a slight rain, by which his neck and hair became wet. Unapprehensive of danger from this circumstance, he passed the afternoon in his usual manner; but in the night he was seized with an inflammatory affection of the windpipe. The disease commenced with a violent ague, accompanied with some pain in the upper and fore part of the throat, a sense of stricture in the same part, a cough, and a difficult, rather than a painful, deglutition, which were soon succeeded by a fever, and a quick and laborious respiration.

Believing bloodletting to be necessary, he procured a bleeder, who took from his arm twelve or fourteen ounces of blood; but he would not permit a messenger to be despatched for his family physician until the appearance of day. About eleven in the morning, Dr. Craik arrived; and, perceiving the extreme danger of the case, requested that two consulting physicians should be immediately sent for. The utmost exertions of medical skill were applied in vain. The powers of life were manifestly yielding to the force of the disorder; speaking, which was painful from the beginning, became almost impracticable; respiration became more and more contracted and imperfect; until half past eleven on Saturday night, when, retaining the full possession of his intellect, he expired without a struggle.

Believing, at the commencement of his complaint, as well as through every succeeding stage of it, that its conclusion would be mortal, he submitted to the exertions made for his recovery rather as a duty than from any expectation of their efficacy. Some hours before his death, after repeated efforts to be understood, he succeeded in expressing a desire that he might be permitted to die without interruption. After it became impossible to get any thing down his throat, he undressed himself, and went to bed, there to die. To his friend and physician, Dr. Craik, who sat on his bed, and took his head in his lap, he said with difficulty, "Doctor, I am dying, and have been dying for a long time; but I am not afraid to die."

During the short period of his illness, he economized his time in arranging, with the utmost serenity, those few concerns which required his attention, and anticipated his approaching dissolution with every demonstration of that equanimity, for which his life was so uniformly and singularly conspicuous.

The deep and wide-spreading grief, occasioned by this melancholy event, assembled a great concourse of people, for the purpose of paying the last tribute of respect to the first of Americans. On Wednesday, the 18th of December, attended by military honours and the ceremonies of religion his body was deposited in the family vault at Mount Vernon

So short was his illness, that, at the seat of government, the intelligence of his death preceded that of his indisposition. It was first communicated by a passenger in the stage to an acquaintance whom he met in the street, and the report quickly reached the house of representatives, which was then in session. The utmost dismay and affliction were displayed for a few minutes, after which a member stated in his place the melancholy information which had been received. This information, he said, was not certain, but there was too much reason to believe it true.

"After receiving intelligence," he added, "of a national calamity so heavy and afflicting, the house of representatives can be but ill fitted for public business." He therefore moved an adjournment. Both houses adjourned until the next day.

On the succeeding day, as soon as the orders were read, the same member addressed the chair, and afterwards offered the following resolutions :*

" Resolved, that this house will wait upon the president-in condolence of this mournful event.

" Resolved, that the speaker's chair be shrouded with black, and that the members and officers of the house wear black during the session.

" Resolved, that a committee, in conjunction with one from the senate, be appointed to consider on the most suit-

---

* These resolutions were prepared by General Lee, and offered by John Marshall, the future biographer of Washington. The last sentiment in them has been often quoted and admired.—Ed.

6 *

able manner of paying honour to the memory of the **Man**
first in war, first in peace, and first in the hearts of **his**
fellow-citizens "

The Lessons of Death.—NORTON.

WHEN such men are taken from us, we are made to feel
the instability of life, and the insecurity of the tenure by
which we hold its dearest blessings.   But this feeling will
be of little value, if it do not lead us to look beyond this world,
and if it be not thus connected with a strong sense of the
proper business of life,—to prepare ourselves for happiness
in that world, where there shall be no change but from
glory to glory.   It will be in vain for us to contemplate
such a character as we have been regarding, if we do not
feel that its foundation was in that religion, which teaches
every one of us to regard himself as created by God, to
be *an image of his own eternity.*   It will be in vain for
us to stand by the open grave of departed worth, if no
earthly passion grows cool, and no holy purpose gains
strength.

We are liable, in this world, to continual delusion ; to a
most extravagant over-estimate of the value of its objects.
With respect to many of our cares and pursuits, the sentiment expressed in the words of David must have borne
with all its truth and force upon the mind of every con-
siderate man in some moments, at least, of serious reflection : *Surely every one walketh in a vain show ; surely
they are disquieted in vain.*   The events of the next
month, or the next year, often assume in our eyes a most
disproportionate importance, and almost exclude from our
view all the other infinite variety of concerns and changes
which are to follow in the course of an immortal existence.
The whole happiness of our being seems sometimes to be
at stake upon the success of a plan, which, when we have
grown but a little older, we may regard with indifference.
These are subjects on which reason too commonly speaks
to us in vain.   But there is one lesson, which God sometimes gives us, that brings the truth home to our hearts

There is an admonition, which addresses itself directly to our feelings, and before which they bow in humility and tears. We can hardly watch the gradual decay of a man eminent for virtue and talents, and hear him uttering, with a voice that will soon be heard no more, the last expressions of piety and holy hope, without feeling that the delusions of life are losing their power over our minds. Its true purposes begin to appear to us in their proper distinctness. We are accompanying one, who is about to take his leave of present objects; to whom the things of this life, merely, are no longer of any interest or value. The eye, which is still turned to us in kindness, will, in a few days, be closed forever. The hand, by which ours is still pressed, will be motionless. The affections, which are still warm and vivid —they will not perish; but we shall know nothing of their exercise. We shall be cut off from all expressions and return of sympathy. He whom we love is taking leave of us for an undefined period of absence. We are placed with him on the verge between this world and the eternity into which he is entering; we look before us, and the objects of the latter rise to view, in all their vast and solemn magnificence.

There is, I well know, an anguish which may preclude this calmness of reflection and hope. Our resolution may be prostrated to the earth; for he, on whom we are accustomed to rely for strength and support, has been taken away. We return to the world, and there is bitterness in all it presents us; for every thing bears impressed upon it a remembrance of what we have lost. It has one, and but one, miserable consolation to offer :

> " That anguish will be wearied down, I know.
> What pang is permanent with man ? From th' highest,
> As from the vilest thing of every day,
> He learns to wean himself. For the strong hours
> Conquer him."

It is a consolation, which, offered in this naked and offensive form, we instinctively reject. Our recollections and our sorrows, blended as they are together, are far too dear to be parted with upon such terms. But God giveth not as the world giveth. There is a peace which comes from him, and brings healing to the heart. His religion would not have us forget, but cherish, our affections f＜ ｔｈｅ ｄｅａｄ for it makes known to us, that these affections sﾠall be immortal. It gradually takes away the bitterness ｏｆ ｏｕｒ recollections, and changes them into glorious hopes; for ｉ teaches us to regard the friend, who is with us ｎｏ longer, not as one whom we have lost on earth, but as one whom we shall meet, as an angel, in heaven.

———◆———

Character of Chief Justice Marshall.—WIRT.

THE chief justice of the United States is in his peﾠson tall, meager, emaciated; his muscles relaxed, and his joints so loosely connected, as not only to disqualify him, apparently, for any vigorous exertions of body, but to destroy every thing like elegance and harmony in his air and movements. Indeed, in his whole appearance and demeanour,—dress, attitudes, and gesture—sitting, standing, or walking,—he is as far removed from the idolized graces of Lord Chesterfield, as any other gentleman on earth. To continue the portrait: his head and face are small in proportion to his height; his complexion swarthy; the muscles of his face, being relaxed, give him the appearance of a man of fifty years of age, nor can he be much younger. His countenance has a faithful expression of great good-humour and hilarity; while his black eyes—that unerring index—possess an irradiating spirit, which proclaims the imperial powers of the mind that sits enthroned within.

This extraordinary man, without the aid of fancy, without the advantages of person, voice, attitude, gesture, or any of the ornaments of an orator, deserves to be considered as one of the most eloquent men in the world; if eloquence may be said to consist in the power of seizing the attention with irresistible force, and never permitting it to elude the grasp until the hearer has received the conviction which the speaker intends.

As to his person, it has already been described. His voice is dry and hard; his attitude, in his most effective orations, was often extremely awkward, as it was not unusual for him to stand with his left foot in advance; while all his

gesture proceeded from his right arm, and consisted merely in a vehement, perpendicular swing of it, from about
the elevation of his head to the bar, behind which he was
accustomed to stand.

As to Fancy, if she hold a seat in his mind at all, which
I very much doubt, his gigantic Genius tramples with disdain on all her flower-decked plats and blooming parterres.
How, then, you will ask, with a look of incredulous curiosity,—how is it possible that such a man can hold the attention of an audience enchained through a speech of even ordinary length? I will tell you.

He possesses one original, and almost supernatural faculty,—the faculty of developing a subject by a single glance
of his mind, and detecting at once the very point on which
every controversy depends. No matter what the question;
though ten times more knotty than " the gnarled oak," the
lightning of heaven is not more rapid nor more resistless
than his astonishing penetration. Nor does the exercise
of it seem to cost him an effort. On the contrary, it is as
easy as vision. I am persuaded that his eyes do not fly
over a landscape, and take in its various objects with more
promptitude and facility, than his mind embraces and ana-
lyzes the most complex subject.

Possessing while at the bar this intellectual elevation,
which enabled him to look down and comprehend the whole
ground at once, he determined, immediately, and without difficulty, on which side the question might be most advantageous-
ly approached and assailed. In a bad cause, his art consisted in
laying his premises so remotely from the point directly in
debate, or else in terms so general and specious, that the
hearer, seeing no consequence which could be drawn from
them, was just as willing to admit them as not ; but, his
premises once admitted, the demonstration, however distant, followed as certainly, as cogently. and as inevitably, as
any demonstration of Euclid.

All his eloquence consists in the apparently deep self-
conviction and emphatic earnestness of his manner; the
correspondent simplicity and energy of his style ; the close
and logical connexion of his thoughts ; and the easy gradations by which he opens his lights on the attentive minds
of his hearers.

The audience are never permitted to pause for a
moment.   There is no stopping to weave garlands of
flowers to be hung in festoons around a favourite argument
On the contrary, every sentence is progressive; every idea
sheds new light on the subject; the listener is kept perpetually in that sweetly pleasurable vibration, with which
the mind of man always receives new truths; the dawn
advances in easy but unremitting pace; the subject opens
gradually on the view; until, rising in high relief in all
its native colours and proportions, the argument is consummated by the conviction of the delighted hearer.

His political adversaries allege that he is a mere lawyer;
that his mind has been so long trammelled by judicial pre-
cedent, so long habituated to the quart and tierce of forensic digladiation, (as Dr. Johnson would probably have called it,) as to be unequal to the discussion of a great question of state.   Mr. Curran, in his defence of Rowan, seems
to have sanctioned the probability of such an effect from
such a cause, when he complains of his own mind as having been narrowed and circumscribed by a strict and technical adherence to established forms; but, in the next
breath, an astonishing burst of the grandest thought, and a
power of comprehension, to which there seems to be no
earthly limit, proves that his complaint, as it relates to himself, is entirely without foundation.

Indeed, if the objection to the chief justice mean any
thing more than that he has not had the same illumination
and exercise in matters of state as if he had devoted his
life to them, I am unwilling to admit it.   The force of a
cannon is the same, whether pointed at a rampart or a man
of war, although practice may have made the engineer
more expert in one case than in the other.   So it is clear
that practice may give a man a greater command over one
class of subjects than another; but the inherent energy
of his mind remains the same whithersoever it may be directed.   From this impression, I have never seen any
cause to wonder at what is called a universal genius: it
proves only that the man has applied a powerful mind
to a great variety of subjects, and pays a compliment rather
to his superior industry than his superior intellect.   I am
very certain that the gentleman of whom we are speaking

possesses the acumen which might constitute him a universal genius, according to the usual acceptation of that phrase.
But if he be the truant, which his warmest friends repre-
sent him to be, there is very little probability that he will
ever reach this distinction.

Moral Sublimity illustrated.—WAYLAND.

PHILOSOPHERS have speculated much concerning a process of sensation, which has commonly been denominated
the emotion of sublimity. Aware that, like any other simple feeling, it must be incapable of definition, they have
seldom attempted to define it ; but, content with remarking
the occasions on which it is excited, have told us that it
arises in general from the contemplation of whatever is
vast in nature, splendid in intellect, or lofty in morals : or,
to express the same idea somewhat varied, in the language
of a critic of antiquity, " That alone is truly sublime, of
which the conception is vast, the effect irresistible, and the
remembrance scarcely, if ever, to be erased."

But, although philosophers alone have written about this
emotion, they are far from being the only men who have
felt it. The untutored peasant, when he has seen the autumnal tempest collecting between the hills, and, as it advanced, enveloping in misty obscurity village and hamlet,
forest and meadow, has tasted the sublime in all its reality ;
and, whilst the thunder has rolled and the lightning flashed
around him, has exulted in the view of Nature moving
forth in her majesty. The untaught sailor-boy, listlessly
hearkening to the idle ripple of the moonlight wave, when on
a sudden he has thought upon the unfathomable abyss beneath him, and the wide waste of waters around him, and
the infinite expanse above him, has enjoyed to the full the
emotion of sublimity, whilst his inmost soul has trembled at the vastness of its own conceptions. But why
need I multiply illustrations from nature ? Who does not
recollect the emotion he has felt while surveying aught, in
the material world, of terror or of vastness ?

And this sensation is not produced by grandeur in material objects alone. It is also excited on most of those occasions in which we see man tasking to the uttermost the energies of his intellectual or moral nature. Through the long lapse of centuries, who, without emotion, has read of Leonidas and his three hundred's throwing themselves as a barrier before the myriads of Xerxes, and contending unto death for the liberties of Greece?

But we need not turn to classic story to find all that is great in human action; we find it in our own times, and in the history of our own country. Who is there of us that, even in the nursery, has not felt his spirit stir within him, when, with child-like wonder, he has listened to the story of Washington? And although the terms of the narrative were scarcely intelligible, yet the young soul kindled at the thought of one man's working out the delivery of a nation. And as our understanding, strengthened by age, was at last able to grasp the detail of this transaction, we saw that our infantile conceptions had fallen far short of its grandeur. Oh! if an American citizen ever exults in the contemplation of all that is sublime in human enterprise, it is when, bringing to mind the men who first conceived the idea of this nation's independence, he beholds them estimating the power of her oppressor, the resources of her citizens, deciding in their collected might that this nation should be free, and, through the long years of trial that ensued, never blenching from their purpose, but freely redeeming the pledge they had given, to consecrate to it "their lives, their fortunes, and their sacred honour."

> "Patriots have toiled, and, in their country's cause,
> Bled nobly, and their deeds, as they deserve,
> Receive proud recompense. We give in charge
> Their names to the sweet lyre. The historic Muse,
> Proud of her treasure, marches with it down
> To latest times: and Sculpture in her turn
> Gives bond, in stone and ever-during brass,
> To guard them, and immortalize her trust."

It is not in the field of patriotism alone that deeds have been achieved, to which history has awarded the palm of moral sublimity. There have lived men, in whom the name of patriot has been merged in that of philanthropist;

who, looking with an eye of compassion over the face of
the earth, have felt for the miseries of our race, and have
put forth their calm might to wipe off one blot from the
marred and stained escutcheon of human nature, to strike
off one form of suffering from the catalogue of human wo.
Such a man was Howard. Surveying our world like a
spirit of the blessed, he beheld the misery of the captive—
he heard the groaning of the prisoner. His determination
was fixed. He resolved, single-handed, to gauge and to
measure one form of unpitied, unheeded wretchedness, and,
bringing it out to the sunshine of public observation, to
work its utter extermination. And he well knew what this
undertaking would cost him. He knew what he had to hazard
from the infection of dungeons, to endure from the fatigues
of inhospitable travel, and to brook from the insolence of
legalized oppression. He knew that he was devoting himself to the altar of philanthropy, and he willingly devoted
himself. He had marked out his destiny, and he hasted
forward to its accomplishment, with an intensity, "which
the nature of the human mind forbade to be more, and the
character of the individual forbade to be less." . Thus he
commenced a new era in the history of benevolence. And
hence, the name of Howard will be associated with all that
is sublime in mercy, until the final consummation of all
things.

Such a man is Clarkson, who, looking abroad, beheld the
miseries of Africa, and, looking at home, saw his country
stained with her blood. We have seen him, laying aside
the vestments of the priesthood, consecrate himself to the
holy purpose of rescuing a continent from rapine and murder, and of erasing this one sin from the book of his nation's iniquities. We have seen him and his fellow phi-
lanthropists, for twenty years, never waver from their purpose. We have seen them persevere amidst neglect and
obloquy, and contempt, and persecution, until, the cry of the
oppressed having roused the sensibilities of the nation, the
"Island Empress" rose in her might, and said to this
foul traffic in human flesh, Thus far shalt thou go, and no
farther.

7

Eloquent Speech of Logan, Chief of the Mingoes.—
JEFFERSON.

I MAY challenge the whole orations of Demosthenes and
Cicero, and of any more eminent orator, if Europe has furnished more eminent, to produce a single passage superior
to the speech of Logan, a Mingo chief, to Lord Dunmore,
when governor of this state.*   And, as a testimony of their
talents in this line, I beg leave to introduce it, first stating
the incidents necessary for understanding it.

In the spring of the year 1774, a robbery was committed by some Indians on certain land adventurers on the
river of Ohio.   The whites in that quarter, according to their
custom, undertook to punish this outrage in a summary
way.   Captain Michael Cresap and a certain Daniel Great-
house, leading on these parties, surprised, at different times,
travelling and hunting parties of the Indians, having their
women and children with them, and murdered many.
Among these were unfortunately the family of Logan, a
chief celebrated in peace and war, and long distinguished
as the friend of the whites.   This unworthy return provoked
his vengeance.   He accordingly signalized himself in the war
which ensued.   In the autumn of the same year a decisive
battle was fought at the mouth of the Great Kanhaway, between the collected forces of the Shawanese, Mingoes, and
Delawares, and a detachment of the Virginia militia.   The
Indians were defeated, and sued for peace.   Logan, however, disdained to be seen among the suppliants.   But, lest
the sincerity of a treaty should be distrusted, from which
so distinguished a chief absented himself, he sent, by a
messenger, the following speech to be delivered to Lord
Dunmore.

"I appeal to any white man to say, if ever he entered
Logan's cabin hungry, and he gave him not meat ; if ever
he came cold and naked, and he clothed him not.   During
the course of the last long and bloody war, Logan remained
idle in his cabin, an advocate for peace.   Such was my
love for the whites, that my countrymen pointed as they
passed, and said, ' Logan is the friend of white men.'   I
had even thought to have lived with you, but for the inju

* Virginia

ries of one man. Colonel Cresap, the last spring, in cold blood, and unprovoked, murdered all the relations of Logan, not even sparing my women and children. There runs not a drop of my blood in the veins of any living creature. This called on me for revenge. I have sought it: I have killed many: I have fully glutted my vengeance. For my country, I rejoice at the beams of peace : but do not harbour a thought that mine is the joy of fear : Logan never felt fear: he will not turn on his heel to save his life. Who is there to mourn for Logan ? Not one."

Fox, Burke, and Pitt.—A. H. Everett.

If the views of the opposition in parliament, in regard to some very important subjects, have received an apparent confirmation from the final result of the measures that were pursued, the party can also boast the honour of reckoning upon its list of members some of the most distinguished statesmen that ever appeared in England or the world Not to mention those now living, who would do credit to any party or any nation, it may be sufficient to cite the illustrious names of Fox and Burke; names that are hardly to be paralleled in the records of eloquence, philosophy, and patriotism ; and which will only be more closely associated in the respect and veneration of future ages, on account of the personal schism which grew up between them, and which forms one of the most interesting parts of their history. Their difference was rather in regard to policy than to principle, both being warm and strenuous friends of liberty; and, when they differed, they were both partly right and partly wrong. That Burke was judicious and wise in discountenancing the too violent spirit of reform, which was then spreading through the nation, and threatening ruin to its institutions, and that Fox, in encouraging it, was rather influenced by a generous and unreflecting zeal for freedom, than by motives of sound policy, will now hardly be denied; and the time, perhaps, is not very distant, if it has not already arrived, when it will be admitted, with equal unanimity, that the policy of making war upon France.

whether for the purpose of crushing the principles of liber ty, or, at a subsequent period, of checking the developement of her power, was, throughout, not only unjust, but imprudent, and eminently un.brtunate for the ultimate interests of England; that Burke, by supporting this policy with his fervid and powerful eloquence, was unconsciously doing a serious injury to his country; and that the system of Fox and his friends and successors, in this point, was as politic and prudent as it was generous and humane. After thirty years of unheard-of exertion and unexampled success, the war seems to have ended by leaving an open field to the ambition of another state, infinitely more formidable and dangerous than France. It may be remarked, however, that this result does not appear to have been foreseen by the opposition any more than by the ministry. It has generally been the fault of the British statesmen, of all parties, to regard France merely as a rival state, instead of extending their views to the whole European system, of which France and England are only members, with interests almost wholly in unison.

Fox and Burke, if I may be allowed to dwell a little longer on so pleasing a theme as the characters of these illustrious statesmen, were not less distinguished for amiable personal qualities, and intellectual accomplishments, than for commanding eloquence and skill in political science. The friends of Fox dwell with enthusiasm and fond regret upon the cordiality of his manners and the unalloyed sweetness of his disposition. It is unfortunate that the pure lustre of these charming virtues was not graced by a sufficient regard to the dictates of private morality. Burke, on the contrary with an equally kind and social spirit, was a model of perfection in all the relations of domestic life ; his character being at once unsullied by the least stain of excess, and exempt from any shade of *rigorism* or defect of humour. While his private virtues made the happiness of his family and friends, his conversation was the charm and wonder of the loftiest minds and the most enlightened circles of society. He was the only man whom Dr. Johnson, a great master of conversation, admitted to be capable of tasking his powers. The only deduction from the uniform excellence of Burke is said to have been the small at

traction of his manner in public speaking, a point in which
Fox was also not particularly successful, but was reckon-
ed his superior.   It would be too rash for an ordinary observer to undertake to give to either of these two mighty
minds the palm of original superiority   It can hardly
be denied that that of Burke was better disciplined and
more accomplished ; and his intellectual reputation, being
better supported than that of Fox by written memorials,
will probably stand higher with posterity.   Had Fox been
permitted to finish the historical work which he had begun, he might, perhaps, have bequeathed to future ages
a literary monument, superior in dignity and lasting value
to any thing that remains from the pen of Burke.   Both
possessed a fine and cultivated taste for the beauties of art
and nature ; that of Fox seems to have been even more
poetical than his illustrious rival's ; but he has left no written proofs of it equal to the fine philosophical Essay on the
Sublime and Beautiful.   It is but poor praise of this elegant performance, to say that it is infinitely superior to the
essay of Longinus on the sublime, from which the hint
seems to have been taken, and which nothing but a blind
and ignorant admiration of antiquity could ever have exalted into a work of great merit.

A sagacious critic has advanced the opinion, that the
merit of Burke was almost wholly literary ; but I confess
I see little ground for this assertion, if literary excellence is here understood in any other sense than as an immediate result of the highest intellectual and moral endowments.   Such compositions as the writings of Burke suppose, no doubt, the fine taste, the command of language,
and the finished education, which are all supposed by every description of literary success.   But, in the present
state of society, these qualities are far from being uncommon ; and are possessed by thousands, who make no pretension to the eminence of Burke, in the same degree in
which they were by nim.   Such a writer as Cumberland,
for example, who stands infinitely below Burke on the
scale of intellect, may yet be regarded as his equal or superior in purely literary accomplishments, taken in this exclusive sense.   The style of Burke is undoubtedly one of
the most splendid forms, in which the English language

7 *

has ever been exhibited. It displays the happy and difficult union of all the richness and magnificence that good
taste admits, with a perfectly easy construction. In Burke,
we see the manly movement of a well-bred gentleman;
in Johnson, an equally profound and vigorous thinker, the
measured march of a grenadier. We forgive the great
moralist his stiff and cumbrous phrases, in return for
the rich stores of thought and poetry which they conceal;
but we admire in Burke, as in a fine antique statue, the
grace with which the large flowing robe adapts itself to
the majestic dignity of the person. But, with all his literary excellence, the peculiar merits of this great man were,
perhaps, the faculty of profound and philosophical thought,
and the moral courage which led him to disregard personal
inconvenience in the expression of his sentiments. Deep
thought is the informing soul, that every where sustains
and inspires the imposing grandeur of his eloquence. Even
in the Essay on the Sublime and Beautiful, the only work
of pure literature which he attempted, that is, the only one
which was not an immediate expression of his views on
public affairs, there is still the same richness of thought,
the same basis of "divine philosophy," to support the harmonious superstructure of the language. And the moral
courage, which formed so remarkable a feature in his
character, contributed not less essentially to his literary
success. It seems to be a law of nature, that the highest
degree of eloquence demands the union of the noblest
qualities of character as well as intellect. To think is the
highest exercise of the mind; to say what you think, the
boldest effort of moral courage ; and both these things are
required for a really powerful writer. Eloquence without
thoughts is a mere parade of words; and no man can express with spirit and vigour any thoughts but his own.
This was the secret of the eloquence of Rousseau, which
is not without a certain analogy in its forms to that of
Burke. The principal of the Jesuits' college one day inquired of him by what art he had been able to write so
well; " *I said what I thought*," replied the unceremonious
Genevan; conveying, in these few words, the bitterest satire on the system of the Jesuits, and the best explanation
of his own.

If, by the criticism above alluded to, it be meant that Burke, though an eloquent writer and profound thinker, was not an able practical statesman, the position may be more tenable, at least for the partisans of the school of Fox, but not, perhaps, ultimately more secure. To form correct conclusions in forms of practice, in opposition to the habitual current of one's opinions and prejudices, must be considered as the highest proof of practical ability; and this was done by Burke in regard to the French revolution. As a member of the opposition, and a uniform friend and supporter of liberal principles, he was led by all his habits of thinking, and by all his personal associations, to approve it; and to feel the same excessive desire to introduce its principles in England, which prevailed among his political friends. But he had sagacity enough to see the true interest of his country through the cloud of illusions and associations, and independence enough to proclaim his opinions, with the sacrifice of all his intimate connexions. This was at once the height of practical ability and disinterested patriotism. If he pushed his ideas to exaggeration in regard to foreign affairs, it was still the exaggeration of a system essentially correct in its domestic operation. He was rather a British than a European statesman; but the moment was so critical at home, that he may, perhaps, be excused for not seeing quite clearly what was right abroad; and it was also not unnatural that he should carry to excess the system to which he had sacrificed his prejudices and his friendships. That his system was not correct in all its parts may be easily admitted; but I think that, in supporting it, under the circumstances, he proved great practical ability; and what system was ever adopted, in which it was not possible, thirty years after, to point out faults?

By the side of these celebrated patriots arose another not less distinguished, though his name is hardly surrounded, in public opinion, with so many amiable and lofty associations; I mean the son of Chatham—" the pilot that weathered the storm!" Prejudice itself can hardly refuse to this statesman the praise of transcendent endowments, both intellectual and moral. He had the natural gift of a brilliant and easy elocution, great aptitude for despatch of business,

and a singular facility in seeing through, at a glance, and
developing with perfect clearness, the most intricate combinations of politics and finance. He possessed, moreover, a
firmness of purpose, and a determined confidence in his
own system, which finally ensured its success, and which
afford, perhaps, the strongest proofs he has given of the elevation of his character. It was no secondary statesman,
who could trust undauntedly to himself, when left, as it
were, alone in Europe, like the tragical Medea, abandoned
by all the world; and, in the confidence of his own resources, could renew his efforts with redoubled vigour. His
admirers will hardly venture to ascribe to him the enlarged
philosophy, or the warmth of heart, that belonged to his
illustrious colleagues and rivals. The conduct of public
affairs was the business of his life; and he neither knew
nor cared about any other matters. He was born and bred
to this; and if he was equal to it, he was also not above it.
Philosophy and friendship were to him, in the language of
the law, *surplusage;* as Calvinism was to the great Cu-
jas—*Nihil hoc ad edictum Prætoris.* And though political affairs are of a higher order, and of more extensive
interest, than any others, yet, when the conduct of them is
pursued mechanically, like a mere professional employment, it becomes, like other professions, a matter of routine
and drudgery. Thus, while Burke and Fox appear like
beings of a different class, descending from superior regions
to interest themselves in the welfare of mortals, Pitt presents himself to the mind as the first of mere politicians,
but still as a mere politician like the rest. His eloquence
is marked by the stamp of his character. It pursues a
clear and rapid course, neither falling below, nor rising
above, the elevation of his habitual themes. No attempt to
sound the depths of thought, or soar on the wings of fancy, still
less to touch the fine chords of feeling, but all $a + b$, an elegant solution of political problems very nearly in the manner of algebra. This profuse and interminable flow of words
is not in itself either a rare or remarkable endowment. It
is wholly a thing of habit, and is exercised by every village lawyer with various degrees of power and grace.
Lord Londonderry, though he wants the elegant correct-
ness of language, as well as the lofty talents of his great

predecessor, commands an equally ready and copious elocution. In the estimate of Mr. Pitt's powers, I have not
taken into account the errors of his foreign policy, because
an erroneous judgment is not always a proof of inferior
talents, but often only argues a false position. The misfortune of having countenanced and joined in the crusade
against the French, and the merit of having resisted the
spirit of revolution at home, belong alike to Pitt and to
Burke. The praise of a clearer and more generous view
of foreign politics is due to Fox ; though his plan is not always bottomed on the most enlarged system of European
relations, and although his glory is somewhat clouded by
his too precipitate zeal for political novelties at home.

Surprise and Destruction of the Pequod Indians.—
MISS SEDGWICK.

MAGAWISCA paused a few moments, sighed deeply,
and then began the recital of the last acts in the tragedy
of her people, the principal circumstances of which are de-
tailed in the chronicles of the times, by the witnesses of the
bloody scenes. " You know," she said, " our fortress-homes
were on the level summit of a hill. Thence we could see,
as far as the eye could stretch, our hunting-grounds, and our
gardens, which lay beneath us on the borders of a stream that
glided around our hill, and so near to it, that in the still nights
we could hear its gentle voice. Our fort and wigwams were
encompassed with a palisade, formed of young trees, and
branches interwoven and sharply pointed. No enemy's foot
had ever approached this nest, which the eagles of the tribe
had built for their mates and their young. Sassacus and my
father were both away on that dreadful night. They had
called a council of our chiefs, and old men ; our young
men had been out in their canoes, and, when they returned,
they had danced and feasted, and were now in deep sleep.
My mother was in her hut with her children, not sleeping;
for my brother Samoset had lingered behind his companions, and had not yet returned from the water-sport. The
warning spirit, that ever keeps its station at a mother's pil-

low, whispered that some evil was near; and my mother
bidding me lie still with the little ones, went forth in quest
of my brother.

"All the servants of the Great Spirit spoke to my mother's ear and eye of danger and death. The moon, as she
sunk behind the hills, appeared a ball of fire: strange lights
darted through the air; to my mother's eye they seemed
fiery arrows; to her ear the air was filled with death-
sighs.

"She had passed the palisade, and was descending the
hill, when she met old Cushmakin. "Do you know aught
of my boy?" she asked.

"Your boy is safe, and sleeps with his companions; he
returned by the Sassafras knoll; that way can only be
trodden by the strong-limbed and light-footed."

"My boy is safe," said my mother; "then tell me, for
thou art wise, and canst see quite through the dark future,
tell me, what evil is coming to our tribe?" She then described the omens she had seen. "I know not," said Cushmakin; "of late darkness hath spread over my soul, and all
is black there, as before those eyes, that the arrows of
death hath pierced; but tell me, Monoco, what see you
now in the fields of heaven?"

"Oh, now," said my mother, "I see nothing but the
blue depths and the watching stars. The spirits of the air
have ceased their moaning, and steal over my cheek like
an infant's breath. The water-spirits are rising, and will
soon spread their soft wings around the nest of our tribe."

"The boy sleeps safely," muttered the old man, "and I
have listened to the idle fear of a doting mother."

"I come not of a fearful race," said my mother.

"Nay, that I did not mean," replied Cushmakin; "but
the panther watching her young is fearful as a doe." The
night was far spent, and my mother bade him go home
with her, for our powwows have always a mat in the wigwam of their chief. "Nay," he said, "the day is near
and I am always abroad at the rising of the sun." It seemed that the first warm touch of the sun opened the eye of
the old man's soul, and he saw again the flushed hills, and
the shaded valleys, the sparkling waters, the green maize,
and the gray old rocks of our home. They were just pass-

ing the little gate of the palisade, when the old man's dog sprang from him with a fearful bark. A rushing sound was heard. "Owanox! Owanox! (the English! the English!") cried Cushmakin. My mother joined her voice to his, and in an instant the cry of alarm spread through the wigwams. The enemy were indeed upon us. They had surrounded the palisade, and opened their fire."

"Was it so sudden? Did they so rush on sleeping women and children?" asked Everell, who was unconsciously lending all his interest to the party of the narrator.

"Even so; they were guided to us by the traitor Wequash; he from whose bloody hand my mother had shielded the captive English maidens—he who had eaten from my father's dish, and slept on his mat. They were flanked by the cowardly Narragansetts, who shrunk from the sight of our tribe—who were pale as white men at the thought of Sassacus, and so feared him that, when his name was spoken, they were like an unstrung bow, and they said, ' He is all one God—no man can kill him.' These cowardly allies waited for the prey they dared not attack

"Then," said Everell, "as I have heard, our people had all the honour of the fight?"

"Honour! was it, Everell?—ye shall hear. Our warriors rushed forth to meet the foe; they surrounded the huts of their mothers, wives, sisters, children; they fought as if each man had a hundred lives, and would give each and all to redeem their homes. Oh! the dreadful fray, even now, rings in my ears! Those fearful guns, that we had never heard before—the shouts of your people—our own battle-yell—the piteous cries of the little children—the groans of our mothers, and, oh! worse—worse than all—the silence of those that could not speak.—The English fell back; they were driven to the palisade, some beyond it when their leader gave the cry to fire our huts, and led the way to my mother's. Samoset, the noble boy, defended the entrance with a princelike courage, till they struck him down; prostrate and bleeding, he again bent his bow, and had taken deadly aim at the English leader, when a sabre-blow severed his bow-string. Then was taken from our hearth-stone, where the English had been so often

warmed and cherished, the brand to consume our dwell
ings. They were covered with mats, and burnt like dried
straw. The enemy retreated without the palisade. In
vain did our warriors fight for a path by which we might
escape from the consuming fire ; they were beaten back ;
the fierce element gained on us ; the Narragansetts pressed on the English, howling like wolves for their prey
Some of our people threw themselves into the midst of the
crackling flames, and their courageous souls parted with
one shout of triumph ; others mounted the palisade, but
they were shot, and dropped like a flock of birds smitten by
the hunter's arrows. Thus did the strangers destroy, in
our own homes, hundreds of our tribe."

" And how did you escape in that dreadful hour, Magawisca ?—you were not then taken prisoners ?"

" No ; there was a rock at one extremity of our hut,
and beneath it a cavity, into which my mother crept, with
Oneco, myself, and the two little ones that afterwards perished. Our simple habitations were soon consumed ; we
heard the foe retiring, and, when the last sound had died
away, we came forth to a sight that made us lament to be
among the living. The sun was scarce an hour from his
rising, and yet in this brief space our homes had vanished
The bodies of our people were strewn about the smouldering ruin ; and all around the palisade lay the strong and
valiant warriors—cold—silent—powerless as the unformed
clay."

Magawisca paused ; she was overcome with the recollection of this scene of desolation. She looked upward
with an intent gaze, as if she held communion with an invisible being. " Spirit of my mother !" burst from her
lips—" oh ! that I could follow thee to that blessed land,
where I should no more dread the war-cry, nor the death-
knife." Everell dashed the gathering tears from his eyes,
and Magawisca proceeded in her narrative.

" While we all stood silent and motionless, we heard footsteps and cheerful voices. They came from my father and
Sassacus, and their band, returning from the friendly council. They approached on the side of the hill that was covered with a thicket of oaks, and their ruined homes at once
burst upon their view. Oh ! what horrid sounds then

pealed on the air! shouts of wailing, and cries of vengeance. Every eye was turned with suspicion and hatred
on my father. *He* had been the friend of the English;
he had counselled peace and alliance with them; *he* had
protected their traders; delivered the captives taken from
them, and restored them to their people : now his wife and
children alone were living, and they called him traitor. I
heard an angry murmur, and many hands were lifted to
strike the death-blow. He moved not—'Nay, nay,' cried
Sassacus, beating them off. 'Touch him not; his soul is
bright as the sun; sooner shall you darken that, than find
treason in his breast. If he hath shown the dove's heart
to the English, when he believed them friends, he will
show himself the fierce eagle, now he knows them enemies.
Touch him not, warriors; remember my blood runneth in
his veins.'

"From that moment my father was a changed man. He
neither spoke nor looked at his wife, or children; but
placing himself at the head of one band of the young men,
he shouted his war-cry, and then silently pursued the enemy. Sassacus went forth to assemble the tribe, and we
followed my mother to one of our villages."

"You did not tell me, Magawisca," said Everell, "how
Samoset perished; was he consumed in the flames, or shot
from the palisade ?"

"Neither—neither. He was reserved to whet my father's revenge to a still keener edge. He had forced a
passage through the English, and, hastily collecting a few
warriors, they pursued the enemy, sprung upon them from
a covert, and did so annoy them that the English turned,
and gave them battle. All fled save my brother, and him
they took prisoner. They told him they would spare his
life if he would guide them to our strong holds; he refused.
He had, Everell, lived but sixteen summers; he loved the
light of the sun even as we love it; his manly spirit was
tamed by wounds and weariness; his limbs were like a
bending reed, and his heart beat like a woman's; but the
fire of his soul burnt clear. Again they pressed him with
offers of life and reward; he faithfully refused, and with
one sabre-stroke they severed his head from his body."

8

Maga visca paused—she looked at Everell, and said with a bitter smile—" You English tell us, Everell, that the book of your law is better than that written on our hearts, for, ye say, it teaches mercy, compassion, forgiveness—if ye had such a law, and believed it, would ye thus have treated a captive boy ?"

Magawisca's reflecting mind suggested the most serious obstacle to the progress of the Christian religion, in all ages and under all circumstances; the contrariety between its divine principles and the conduct of its professors; which, instead of always being a medium for the light that emanates from our holy law, is too often the darkest cloud that obstructs the passage of its rays to the hearts of heathen men. Everell had been carefully instructed in the principles of his religion, and he felt Magawisca's relation to be an awkward comment on them, and her inquiry natural but, though he knew not what answer to make, he was sure there must be a good one, and, mentally resolving to refer the case to his mother, he begged Magawisca to proceed with her narrative.

" The fragments of our broken tribe," she said, " were collected, and some other small dependant tribes persuaded to join us. We were obliged to flee from the open grounds, and shelter ourselves in a dismal swamp. The English surrounded us; they sent in to us a messenger, and offered life and pardon to all who had not shed the blood of Englishmen. Our allies listened, and fled from us, as frightened birds fly from a falling tree. My father looked upon his warriors; they answered that look with their battle-shout. ' Tell your people,' said my father to the messenger, ' that we have shed and drank English blood, and that we will take nothing from them but death.' The messenger departed, and again returned with offers of pardon, if we would come forth, and lay our arrows and our tomahawks at the feet of the English. ' What say you, warriors ?' cried my father—' shall we take *pardon* from those who have burned your wives and children, and given your homes to the beasts of prey ?—who have robbed you of your hunting-grounds, and driven your canoes from their waters ?' A hundred arrows were pointed to the messenger. Enough—you have your answer,' said my father; and the messenger returned to announce the fate we had chosen."

"Where was Sassacus?—had he abandoned his people?" asked Everell.

"Abandoned them! No—his life was in theirs; but, accustomed to attack and victory, he could not bear to be thus driven like a fox to his hole. His soul was sick within him, and he was silent, and left all to my father. All day we heard the strokes of the English axes felling the trees that defended us, and, when night came, they had approached so near, that we could see the glimmering of their watch-lights through the branches of the trees. All night they were pouring in their bullets, alike on warriors, women, and children. Old Cushmakin was lying at my mother's feet, when he received a death-wound. Gasping for breath, he called on Sassacus and my father—'Stay not here,' he said; 'look not on your wives and children, but burst your prison bound; sound through the nations the cry of revenge! Linked together, ye shall drive the English into the sea. I speak the word of the Great Spirit —obey it!' While he was yet speaking, he stiffened in death. 'Obey him, warriors,' cried my mother; 'see,' she said, pointing to the mist that was now wrapping itself around the wood like a thick curtain—'see, our friends have come from the spirit-land to shelter you. Nay, look not on us—our hearts have been tender in the wigwam, but we can die before our enemies without a groan. Go forth and avenge us.'

"'Have we come to the counsel of old men and old women!' said Sassacus, in the bitterness of his spirit.

"'When women put down their womanish thoughts and counsel like men, they should be obeyed,' said my father 'Follow me, warriors.'

"They burst through the enclosure. We saw nothing more, but we heard the shout from the foe, as they issued from the wood—the momentary fierce encounter and the cry, 'They have escaped!' Then it was that my mother, who had listened with breathless silence, threw herself down on the mossy stones, and, laying her hot cheek to mine—'Oh, my children—my children!' she said, 'would that I could die for you! But fear not death—the blood of a hundred chieftains, that never knew fear, runneth in your veins. Hark, the enemy comes nearer and nearer. Now lift up your heads, my children, and show them that even the weak ones of our tribe are strong in soul.'

" We rose from the ground—all about sat women and children in family clusters, awaiting unmoved their fate. The English had penetrated the forest-screen, and were already on the little rising-ground where we had been intrenched. Death was dealt freely. None resisted—not a movement was made—not a voice lifted—not a sound escaped, save the wailings of the dying children.

" One of your soldiers knew my mother, and a command was given that her life and that of her children should be spared. A guard was stationed round us.

" You know that, after our tribe was thus cut off, we were taken, with a few other captives, to Boston. Some were sent to the Islands of the Sun, to bend their free limbs to bondage like your beasts of burden. There are among your people those who have not put out the light of the Great Spirit; they can remember a kindness, albeit done by an Indian; and when it was known to your sachems that the wife of Mononotto, once the protector and friend of your people, was a prisoner, they treated her with honour and gentleness. But her people were extinguished—her husband driven to distant forests—forced on earth to the misery of wicked souls—to wander without a home; her children were captives—and her heart was broken."

Character of Fisher Ames.—KIRKLAND.

MR. AMES, as a speaker and a writer, had the power to enlighten and persuade, to move, to please, to charm, to astonish. He united those decorations, which belong to fine talents, to that penetration and judgment, that designate an acute and solid mind. Many of his opinions had the authority of predictions fulfilled and fulfilling. He had the ability of investigation, and, where it was necessary, did investigate with patient attention, going through a series of observation and deduction, and tracing the links which connect one truth with another. When the result of his researches was exhibited in discourse, the steps of a logical process were in some measure concealed by the colouring of rhetoric. Minute calculation and dry details were employments, however, the least adapted to his peculiar construction of mind. It was easy and delightful for him to illustrate by a picture, but painful and laborious to prove by a diagram. It was the prerogative of his mind to discern by a glance, so rapid as to seem intuition, those truths which common capacities struggle hard to apprehend; and it was the part of his eloquence to display, expand and enforce them.

His imagination was a distinguishing feature of his mind. Prolific grand, sportive, original, it gave him the command of nature and of art, and enabled him to vary the disposition and the dress of his ideas without end. Now it assembled most pleasing images, adorned with all that is soft and beautiful; and now rose in the storm, wielding the elements, and flashing in the most awful splendours. Very few men have produced more original combinations. He presented resemblances and contrasts, which none saw before, but all admitted to be just and striking. In delicate and powerful wit he was pre-eminent.

The exercise of these talents and accomplishments was guided and exalted by a sublime morality and the spirit of rational piety, was modelled by much good taste, and prompted by an ardent heart.

He was more adapted to the senate than the bar. His speeches in congress, always respectable, were many of them excellent, abounding in argument and sentiment, having all the necessary information, embellished with rhetorical beauties, and animated by patriotic fires.

So much of the skill and address of the orator do they exhibit, that, though he had little regard to the rules of the art, they are perhaps fair examples of the leading precepts for the several parts of an oration. In debates on important questions, he generally waited before he spoke till the discussion had proceeded at some length, when he was sure to notice every argument that had been offered. He was sometimes in a minority, when he well considered the

S *

temper of a majority in a republican assembly, impatient of contradiction, refutation, or detection, claiming to be allowed sincere in their convictions, and disinterested in their views. He was not unsuccessful in uniting the prudence and conciliation, necessary in parliamentary speaking, with lawful freedom in debate, and an effectual use of those sharp and massy weapons, which his talents supplied, and which his frankness and zeal prompted him to employ.

He did not systematically study the exterior graces of speaking, but his attitude was erect and easy, his gestures manly and forcible, his intonations varied and expressive, his articulation distinct, and his whole manner animated and natural. His written compositions, it will be perceived, have that glow and vivacity which belong to his speeches.

All the other efforts of his mind, however, were probably exceeded by his powers in conversation. He appeared among his friends with an illuminated face, and, with peculiar amenity and captivating kindness, displayed all the playful felicity of his wit, the force of his intellect, and the fertility of his imagination.

On the kind or degree of excellence which criticism may concede or deny to Mr. Ames's productions, we do not undertake with accurate discrimination to determine. He was undoubtedly rather actuated by the genius of oratory, than disciplined by the precepts of rhetoric; was more intent on exciting attention and interest, and producing effect, than securing the praise of skill in the artifice of composition. Hence critics may be dissatisfied, yet hearers charmed. The abundance of materials, the energy and quickness of conception, the inexhaustible fertility of mind, which he possessed, as they did not require, so they forbade, a rigid adherence to artificial guides, in the disposition and employment of his intellectual stores. To a certain extent, such a speaker and writer may claim to be his own authority.

Image crowded upon image in his mind, yet he is not chargeable with affectation in the use of figurative language; his tropes are evidently prompted by imagination, and not forced into service. Their novelty and variety create constant surprise and delight. But they are perhaps too lavishly employed. The fancy of his hearers is sometimes overplied with stimulus, and the importance of the thought liable to be concealed in the multitude and beauty of the metaphors. His condensation of expression may be thought to produce occasional abruptness. He aimed rather at the terseness, strength, and vivacity of the short sentence, than at the dignity of the full and flowing period. His style is conspicuous for sententious brevity, for antithesis and point. Single ideas appear with so much prominence, that the connexion of the several parts of his discourse is not always obvious to the common mind, and the aggregate impression of the composition is not always completely obtained. In these respects, where his peculiar excellences came near to defects, he is rather to be admired than imitated.

Mr. Ames, though trusting much to his native resources, did by no means neglect to apply the labours of others to his own use. His early love of books he retained and cherished through the whole of his life. He was particularly fond of ethical studies; but he went more deeply into history than any other branch of learning. Here he sought the principles of legislation, the science of politics, the causes of the rise and decline of nations, and the characters and passions of men acting in public affairs. He read Herodotus, Thucydides, Livy, Tacitus, Plutarch, and the modern historians of Greece and Rome. The English history he studied with much care. Hence he possessed a great fund of historical knowledge, always at command, both for conversation and writing. He contemplated the character of Cicero as an orator and statesman with fervent admiration.

He never ceased to be a lover of the poets. Homer, in Pope, he often perused; and he read Virgil in the original, within two years of his death, with increased delight. His knowledge of the French enabled him to read their authors, though not to speak their language. He was accustomed to read the Scriptures, not only as containing a system of truth and duty, but as displaying, in their poetical parts, all that is sublime, animated and affecting in composition

His learning seldom appeared as such, but was interwoven with his thoughts, and became his own.

In public speaking he trusted much to excitement, and did little more in his closet than draw the outlines of his speech, and reflect on it till he had received deeply the impressions he intended to make; depending for the turns and figures of language, illustrations and modes of appeal to the passions, on his imagination and feelings at the time. This excitement continued when the cause had ceased to operate. After debate his mind was agitated, like the ocean after a storm, and his nerves were like the shrouds of a ship, torn by the tempest. He brought his mind much in contact with the minds of others, ever pleased to converse on subjects of public interest, and seizing every hint that might be useful to him in writing for the instruction of his fellow-citizens. He justly thought that persons below him in capacity might have good ideas, which he might employ in the correction and improvement of his own. His attention was always awake to grasp the materials that came to him from every source. A constant labour was going on in his mind. He never sunk from an elevated tone of thought and action, nor suffered his faculties to slumber in indolence. The circumstances of the times, in which he was called to act, contributed to elicit his powers, and supply fuel to his genius. The greatest interests were subjects of debate. When he was in the national legislature, the spirit of party did not tie the hands of the public functionaries; and questions, on which depended the peace or war, the safety or danger, the freedom or dishonour, of the country, might be greatly influenced by the counsels and efforts of a single patriot.

Mr. Ames's character as a patriot rests on the highest and firmest ground. He loved his country with equal purity and fervour. This affection was the spring of all his efforts to promote her welfare. The glory of being a benefactor to a great people he could not despise, but justly valued. He was covetous of the fame purchased by desert; but he was above ambition; and popularity, except as an instrument of public service, weighed nothing in the balance by which he estimated good and evil. Had he sought power only, he would have devoted himself to that

COMMON-PLACE BOOK OF PROSE.

party, in whose gift he foresaw it would be placed. His
first election, though highly flattering, was equally un-
sought and unexpected, and his acceptance of it interrupted his chosen plan of life. It obliged him to sacrifice the
advantages of a profession, which he needed, and placed in
uncertainty his prospects of realizing the enjoyments of
domestic life, which he considered the highest species of
happiness. But he found himself at the disposal of others,
and did not so much choose, as acquiesce, in his destination
to the national legislature.

The objects of religion presented themselves with a
strong interest to his mind. The relation of the world to
its Author, and of this life to a retributory scene in another,
could not be contemplated by him without the greatest solemnity. The religious sense was, in his view, essential
n the constitution of man. He placed a full reliance on
the divine origin of Christianity. If there ever was a time
in his life when the light of revelation shone dimly upon
his understanding, he did not rashly close his mind against
clearer vision; for he was more fearful of mistakes to the
disadvantage of a system, which he saw to be excellent
and benign, than of prepossessions in its favour. He felt
it his duty and interest to inquire, and discover on the side
of faith, a fulness of evidence little short of demonstration.
At about thirty-five he made a public profession of his faith
in the Christian religion, and was a regular attendant on
its services. In regard to articles of belief, his conviction
was confined to those leading principles, about which
Christians have little diversity of opinion. Subtile questions of theology, from various causes often agitated, but
never determined, he neither pretended nor desired to investigate, satisfied that they related to points uncertain or
unimportant. He loved to view religion on the practical
side, as designed to operate, by a few simple and grand
truths, on the affections, actions and habits of men. His
conversation and behaviour evinced the sincerity of his religious impressions. No levity upon these subjects ever
escaped his lips; but his manner of recurring to them in
conversation indicated reverence and feeling. The sublime,
the affecting character of Christ, he never mentioned without emotion.

He was gratefully sensible of the peculiar felicity of his domestic life. In his beloved home his sickness found all the alleviation, that a judicious and unwearied tenderness could minister ; and his intervals of health a succession of every pleasing enjoyment and heartfelt satisfaction. The complacency of his looks, the sweetness of his tones, his mild and often playful manner of imparting instruction, evinced his extreme delight in the society of his family, who felt that they derived from him their chief happiness, and found in his conversation and example a constant excitement to noble and virtuous conduct. As a husband and father, he was all that is provident, kind, exemplary. He was riveted in the regards of those who were in his service. He felt all the ties of kindred. The delicacy, the ardour, and constancy, with which he cherished his friends, his readiness to the offices of good neighbourhood, and his propensity to contrive and execute plans of public improvement, formed traits in his character, each of remarkable strength. He cultivated friendship by an active and punctual correspondence, which made the number of his letters very great, and which are not less excellent than numerous.

Mr. Ames in person a little exceeded the middle height, was well proportioned, and remarkably erect. His features were regular, his aspect respectable and pleasing, his eye expressive of benignity and intelligence. In his manners he was easy, affable, cordial, inviting confidence, yet inspiring respect. He had that refined spirit of society, which observes the forms of real, but not studied politeness, and paid a most delicate regard to the propriety of conversation and behaviour.

Reflections on the Death of Adams and Jefferson.—
SERGEANT.

TIME in its course has produced a striking epoch in the history of our favoured country; and, as if to mark with peculiar emphasis this interesting stage of our national existence, it comes to us accompanied with incidents calculated to make a powerful and lasting impression. The dawn of the fiftieth anniversary of independence beamed upon two venerable and illustrious citizens, to whom, under Providence, a nation acknowledged itself greatly indebted for the event which the day was set apart to commemorate. The one was the author, the other was "the ablest advocate," of that solemn assertion of right, that heroic defiance of unjust power, which, in the midst of difficulty and danger, proclaimed the determination to assume a separate and equal station among the powers of the earth, and declared to the world the causes which impelled to this decision. Both had stood by their country with unabated ardour and unwavering fortitude, through every vicissitude of her fortune, until the "glorious day" of her final triumph crowned their labours and their sacrifices with complete success. With equal solicitude, and with equal warmth of patriotic affection, they devoted their great faculties, which had been employed in vindicating the rights of their country, to construct for her, upon deep and strong foundations, the solid edifice of social order, and of civil and religious freedom. They had both held the highest public employment, and were distinguished by the highest honours the nation could confer. Arrived at an age when nature seems to demand repose, each had retired to the spot from which the public exigencies had first called him,—his public labours ended, his work accomplished, his country prosperous and happy,— there to indulge in the blessed retrospect of a well-spent life, and await that period which comes to all ;—but not to await it in idleness or indifference. The same spirit of active benevolence, which made the meridian of their lives resplendent with glory, continued to shed its lustre upon their evening path. Still intent upon doing good, still devoted to the great cause of human happiness and improvement, neither of these illustrious men relaxed in his exertions. They seemed only to concentrate their energy, as age and increasing infirmity contracted the circle of action, bestowing, without ostentation, their latest efforts upon the state and neighbourhood in which they resided. There, with patriarchal simplicity, they lived, the objects of a nation's grateful remembrance and affection; the living records of a nation's history ; the charm of an age which

they delighted, adorned and instructed by their vivid
sketches of times that are past; and, as it were, the imbodied spirit of the revolution itself, in all its purity and
force, diffusing its wholesome influence through the generations that have succeeded, rebuking every sinister design, and invigorating every manly and virtuous resolution.

The Jubilee came,—the great national commemoration
of a nation's birth,—the fiftieth year of deliverance from
a foreign rule, wrought out by exertions, and sufferings, and
sacrifices of the patriots of the revolution. It found these
illustrious and venerable men, full of honours and full of
years, animated with the proud recollection of the times
in which they had borne so distinguished a part, and cheered by the beneficent and expanding influence of their
patriotic labours. The eyes of a nation were turned towards them with affection and reverence. They heard the
first song of triumph on that memorable day. As the
voice of millions of freemen rose in gratitude and joy, they
both sunk gently to rest, and their spirits departed in the
midst of the swelling chorus of national enthusiasm.

Death has thus placed his seal upon the lives of these
two eminent men with impressive solemnity. A gracious
Providence, whose favours have been so often manifested
in mercy to our country, has been pleased to allow them
an unusual length of time, and an uncommon continuance
of their extraordinary faculties. They have been, as it
were, united in death; and they have both, in a most signal manner, been associated in the great event which
they so largely contributed to produce. Henceforward the
names of Jefferson and Adams can never be separated from
the Declaration of Independence. Whilst that venerated
instrument shall continue to exist, as long as its sacred
spirit shall dwell with the people of this nation, or the free
institutions that have grown out of it be preserved and
respected, so long will our children, and our children's children, to the latest generation, bless the names of these our
illustrious benefactors, and cherish their memory with reve-
rential respect. The Jubilee, at each return, will bring
back, with renovated force, the lives and the deaths of these
distinguished men; and History, with the simple pencil of

Truth, sketching the wonderful coincidence, will, for once at least, set at defiance all the powers of poetry and romance.

Indolence.—DENNIE.

' How long wilt thou sleep, O sluggard? When wilt thou arise out of sleep?''

NOT until you have had another nap, you reply; not till there has been a little more folding of the hands!

Various philosophers and naturalists have attempted to define man. I never was satisfied with their labours: absurd to pronounce him a two-legged, unfeathered animal, when it is obvious he is a *sleepy* one. In this world there is business enough for every individual: a sparkling sky over his head to admire, a soil under his feet to till, and innumerable objects, useful and pleasant, to choose. But such in general is the provoking indolence of our species, that the lives of many, if impartially journalized, might be truly said to have consisted of a series of slumbers. Some men are infested with day dreams, as well as by visions of the night: they travel a certain insipid round, like the blind horse of the mill, and, as Bolingbroke observes, perhaps beget others to do the like after them. They may sometimes open their eyes a little, but they are soon dimmed by some lazy fog; they may sometimes stretch a limb, but its efforts are soon palsied by procrastination. Yawning, amid tobacco fumes, they seem to have no hopes, except that their bed will soon be made, and no fears, except that their slumbers will be broken by business clamouring at the door.

How tender and affectionate is the reproachful question of Solomon, in the text, "When wilt thou arise out of sleep?" The Jewish prince, whom we know to be an active one, from the temple which he erected and the books which he composed, saw, when he cast his eyes around the city, half his subjects asleep. Though in many a wise proverb he had warned them of the baneful effects of in-

9

dolence, they were deaf to his charming voice, and blind
to his noble example. The men servants and the maid
servants, whom he had hired, nodded over their domestic
duties in the royal kitchen, and when, in the vineyards he
had planted, he looked for grapes, lo, they brought forth
wild grapes, for the vintager was drowsy.

At the present time, few Solomons exist to preach against
pillows, and never was there more occasion for a sermon.
Our country being at peace, not a drum is heard to rouse
the slothful. But, though we are exempted from the tumults and vicissitudes of war, we should remember that
there are many posts of duty, if not of danger, and at these
we should vigilantly stand. If we will stretch the hand
of exertion, means to acquire competent wealth, and honest
fame, abound, and when such ends are in view, how shameful
to close our eyes! He who surveys the paths of active life,
will find them so numerous and long, that he will feel the
necessity of early rising, and late taking rest, to accomplish
so much travel. He who pants for the shade of speculation,
will find that literature cannot flourish in the bowers of indolence and monkish gloom. Much midnight oil must be
consumed, and innumerable pages examined, by him whose
object is to be really wise. Few hours has that man to
sleep, and not one to loiter, who has many coffers of wealth
to fill, or many cells in his memory to store.

Among the various men, whom I see in the course of my
pilgrimage through this world, I cannot frequently find
those who are broad awake. Sloth, a powerful magician,
mutters a witching spell, and deluded mortals tamely suffer
this drowsy being to bind a fillet over their eyes. All
their activity is employed in turning themselves like the
door on a rusty hinge, and all the noise they make in the
world is a snore. When I see one, designed by nature for
noble purposes, indolently declining the privilege, and, heed-
less, like Esau, bartering the birthright, for what is of less
worth than his red pottage of lentils,—for liberty to sit still
and lie quietly,—I think I see, not a man, but an oyster
The drone in society, like that fish on our shores, might as
well be sunken in the mud, and enclosed in a shell, as
stretched on a couch, or seated in a chimney-corner

The season is now approaching fast, when some of the most plausible excuses for a *little more sleep* must fail. Enervated by indulgence, the slothful are of all men most impatient of cold, and they deem it never more intense than in the morning. But the last bitter month has rolled away, and now, could I persuade to the experiment, the sluggard may discover that he may toss off the bed-quilt, and try the air of *early* day, without being congealed! He may be assured that sleep is a very stupid employment, and differs very little from death, except in duration. He may receive it implicitly, upon the faith both of the physician and the preacher, that morning is friendly to the health and the heart; and if the idler is so manacled by the chains of habit, that he can, at first, do no more, he will do wisely and well to inhale pure air, to watch the rising sun, and mark the magnificence of nature.

Escape of Harvey Birch and Captain Wharton.—
COOPER.

THE road which it was necessary for the pedler and the English captain to travel, in order to reach the shelter of the hills, lay, for half a mile, in full view from the door of the building, that had so recently been the prison of the latter; running for the whole distance over the rich plain, that spreads to the very foot of the mountains, which here rise in a nearly perpendicular ascent from their bases; it then turned short to the right, and was obliged to follow the windings of nature, as it won its way into the bosom of the Highlands.

To preserve the supposed difference in their stations, Harvey rode a short distance ahead of his companion, and maintained the sober, dignified pace, that was suited to his assumed character. On their right, the regiment of foot, that we have already mentioned, lay in tents; and the sentinels, who guarded their encampment, were to be seen moving, with measured tread, under the skirts of the hills themselves The first impulse of Henry was, certainly, to urge the beast he rode to his greatest speed at once, and

by a coup-de-main, not only to accomplish his escape, bu
relieve himself from the torturing suspense of his situation
But the forward movement that the youth made for this
purpose was instantly checked by the pedler.

" Hold up !" he cried, dexterously reining his own horse
across the path of the other; " would you ruin us both ?
Fall into the place of a black following his master. Did
you not see their blooded chargers, all saddled and bridled,
standing in the sun before the house ? How 'ong do you
think that miserable Dutch horse you are on would hold
his speed, if pursued by the Virginians ? Every foot that
we can gain without giving the alarm, counts us a day
in our lives. Ride steadily after me, and on no account
look back. They are as subtle as foxes, ay, and as ravenous for blood as wolves."

Henry reluctantly restrained his impatience, and followed the direction of the pedler. His imagination, however,
continually alarmed him with the fancied sounds of pursuit ;
though Birch, who occasionally looked back under the pretence of addressing his companion, assured him that all
continued quiet and peaceful.

" But," said Henry, " it will not be possible for Cæsar
to remain long undiscovered : had we not better put our
horses to the gallop ? and, by the time they can reflect on
the cause of our flight, we can reach the corner of the
woods."

" Ah ! you little know them, Captain Wharton," returned the pedler ; " there is a sergeant at this moment looking after us, as if he thought all was not right ; the keen-
eyed fellow watches me like a tiger laying in wait for his
leap ; when I stood on the horse block, he half suspected
something was wrong ; nay, check your beast ; we must
let the animals walk a little, for he is laying his hand on
the pommel of his saddle ; if he mounts now, we are
gone. The foot soldiers could reach us with their muskets."

" What does he do ?" asked Henry, reining his horse to
a walk, but, at the same time, pressing his heels into the
animal's sides, to be in readiness for a spring.

" He turns from his charger, and looks the other way.
Now trot on gently ; not so fast. not so fast ; observe the

sentinel in the field a little ahead of us; he eyes us keenly."

"Never mind the footman," said Henry impatiently; "he can do nothing but shoot us; whereas these dragoons may make me a captive again. Surely, Harvey, there are horsemen moving down the road behind us. Do you see nothing particular?"

"Humph!" ejaculated the pedler; "there is something particular, indeed, to be seen behind the thicket on your left; turn your head a little, and you may see and profit by it too.".

Henry eagerly seized his permisson to look aside, and his blood curdled to the heart as he observed they were passing a gallows, that had unquestionably been erected for his own execution. He turned his face from the sight in undisguised horror.

"There is a warning to be prudent in that bit of wood," said the pedler, in that sententious manner that he often adopted.

"It is a terrific sight indeed!" cried Henry, for a moment veiling his face with his hands, as if to drive a vision from before him.

The pedler moved his body partly around, and spoke with energetic but gloomy bitterness—"and yet, Captain Wharton, you see it when the setting sun shines full upon you; the air you breathe is clear, and fresh from the hills before you. Every step that you take leaves that hated gallows behind; and every dark hollow, and every shapeless rock in the mountains, offers you a hiding-place from the vengeance of your enemies. But I have seen the gibbet raised, when no place of refuge offered. Twice have I been buried in dungeons, where, fettered and in chains, I have passed nights in torture, looking forward to the morning's dawn that was to light me to a death of infamy. The sweat has started from limbs that seemed already drained of their moisture, and if I ventured to the hole, that admitted air through grates of iron, to look out upon the smiles of nature, which God has bestowed for the meanest of his creatures, the gibbet has glared before my eyes, like an evil conscience, harrowing the soul of a dying man. Four times have I been in their power, besides this last; but—twice—twice did I think that my hour had come. It is hard to die at the best,

9 *

Captain Wharton; but to spend your last moments alone,
and unpitied, to know that none near you so much as think
of the fate that is to you the closing of all that is earthly
to think that in a few hours you are to be led from the
gloom—which, as you dwell on what follows, becomes dear
to you—to the face of day, and there to meet all eyes
upon you, as if you were a wild beast; and to lose sight of
every thing amidst the jeers and scoffs of your fellow creatures;—that, Captain Wharton, that indeed is to die."

Henry listened in amazement, as his companion uttered
this speech with a vehemence altogether new to him,
both seemed to have forgotten their danger and their disguises, as he cried—

" What! were you ever so near death as that?"

" Have I not been the hunted beast of these hills for
three years past?" resumed Harvey; " and once they even
led me to the foot of the gallows itself, and I escaped only
by an alarm from the royal troops. Had they been a quarter of an hour later, I must have died. There was I placed,
in the midst of unfeeling men, and gaping women and
children, as a monster to be cursed. When I would pray
to God, my ears were insulted with the history of my crimes;
and when, in all that multitude, I looked around for a single face that showed me any pity, I could find none—no,
not even one—all cursed me as a wretch who would sell
his country for gold. The sun was brighter to my eyes
than common—but then it was the last time I should see
it. The fields were gay and pleasant, and every thing seemed as if this world was a kind of heaven. Oh! how sweet
life was to me at that moment! 'Twas a dreadful hour,
Captain Wharton, and such as you have never known. You
have friends to feel for you; but I had none but a father
to mourn my loss when he might hear of it; there was no
pity, no consolation near to soothe my anguish. Every
thing seemed to have deserted me,—I even thought that
He had forgotten that I lived."

" What! did you feel that God had forsaken you, Harvey?" cried the youth, with strong sympathy

" God never forsakes his servants," returned Birch, with
reverence, and exhibiting naturally a devotion that hitherto
he had only assumed.

" And who did you mean by He ?"

The pedler raised himself in his saddle to the stiff and upright posture that was suited to the outward appearance. The look of fire, that, for a short time, glowed upon his countenance, disappeared in the solemn lines of unbending self-abasement, and, speaking as if addressing a negro, he replied—

" In heaven, there is no distinction of colour, my brother; therefore you have a precious charge within you, that you must hereafter render an account of,"—dropping his voice; " this is the last sentinel near the road; look not. back, as you value your life."

Henry remembered his situation, and instantly assumed the humble demeanour of his adopted character.   The unaccountable energy of the pedler's manner was soon forgotten in the sense of his own immediate danger; and with the recollection of his critical situation returned all the uneasiness that he had momentarily forgotten.

" What see you, Harvey ?" he cried, observing the pedler to gaze towards the building they had left, with ominous interest; " what see you at the house ?"

" That which bodes no good to us," returned the pretended priest. " Throw aside the mask and wig—you will need all your senses without much delay—throw them in the road : there are none before us that I dread, but there are those behind us, who will give us a fearful race."

" Nay, then," cried the captain, casting the implements of his disguise into the highway, " let us improve our time to the utmost; we want a full quarter to the turn; why not push for it at once ?"

" Be cool—they are in alarm, but they will not mount without an officer, unless they see us fly—now he comes— he moves to the stables—trot briskly—a dozen are in their saddles, but the officer stops to tighten his girths—they hope to steal a march upon us—he is mounted—now ride, Captain Wharton, for your life, and keep at my heels. If you quit me you will be lost."

A second request was unnecessary. The instant that Harvey put his horse to his speed, Captain Wharton was at his heels, urging the miserable animal that he rode to the ntmost. Birch had selected the beast on which he rode and, although vastly inferior to the high-fed and blooded chargers of the dragoons, still it was much superior to the little pony that had been thought good enough to carry Cæsar Thompson on an errand. A very few jumps convinced the captain that his companion was fast leaving him, and a fearful glance that he threw behind informed the fugitive that his enemies were as speedily approaching. With that abandonment that makes misery doubly grievous, when it is to be supported alone, Henry called aloud to the pedler not to desert him. Harvey instantly drew up, and suffered his companion to run along-side of his own horse. The cocked hat and wig of the pedler fell from his head the moment that his steed began to move briskly, and this developement of their disguise, as it might be termed, was witnessed by the dragoons, who announced their observation by a boisterous shout, that seemed to be uttered in the very ears of the fugitives—so loud was the cry, and so short the distance between them.

" Had we not better leave our horses," said Henry, "and make for the hills across the fields on our left ?—the fence will stop our pursuers."

"'That way lies the gallows," returned the pedler— " these fellows go three feet to our two, and would mind them fences no more than we do these ruts ; but it is a short quarter to the turn, and there are two roads behind the wood. They may stand to choose until they can take the track, and we shall gain a little upon them there."

" But this miserable horse is blown already," cried Henry, urging his beast with the end of his bridle, at the same time that Harvey aided his efforts by applying the lash of a heavy riding whip that he carried ; " he will never stand it for half a mile further."

" A quarter will do—a quarter will do," said the pedler ; " a single quarter will save us, if you follow my directions."

Somewhat cheered by the cool and confident manner of his companion, Henry continued silently urging his horse forward. A few moments brought them to the desired turn, and, as they doubled round a point of low under-brush, the fugitives caught a glimpse of their pursuers scattered

along the highway. Mason and the sergeant, being better
mounted than the rest of the party, were much nearer to
their heels than even the pedler thought could be possible.

At the foot of the hills, and for some distance up the
dark valley that wound among the mountains, a thick underwood of saplings had been suffered to shoot up, when
the heavier growth was felled for the sake of fuel. At
the sight of this cover, Henry again urged the pedler to
dismount, and to plunge into the woods; but his request
was promptly refused. The two roads before mentioned
met at a very sharp angle, at a short distance from the turn,
and both were circuitous, so that but little of either could
be seen at a time. The pedler took the one which led to
the left, but held it only a moment, for, on reaching a partial opening in the thicket, he darted across the right hand
path, and led the way up a steep ascent, which lay directly before them. This manœuvre saved them. On reaching
the fork, the dragoons followed the track, and passed the
spot where the fugitives had crossed to the other road, before they missed the marks of the footsteps. Their loud
cries were heard by Henry and the pedler, as their wearied and breathless animals toiled up the hill, ordering their
comrades in the rear to ride in the right direction. The
captain again proposed to leave their horses, and dash into
the thicket.

"Not yet—not yet," said Birch in a low voice ; the road
falls from the top of this hill as steep as it rises—first let
us gain the top." While speaking they reached the desired summit, and both threw themselves from their horses.
Henry plunged into the thick underwood, which covered
the side of the mountain for some distance above them. Harvey stopped to give each of their beasts a few severe blows
of his whip, that drove them headlong down the path on
the other side of the eminence, and then followed his example.

The pedler entered the thicket with a little caution,
and avoided, as much as possible, rustling or breaking the
branches in his way. There was but time only to shelter
his person from view, when a dragoon led up the ascent,
and, on reaching the height he cried aloud—

" I saw one of their horses turning the hill this min
ute."

" Drive on—spur forward, my lads," shouted Mason
" give the Englishman quarter, but cut down the pedlor,
and make an end of him."

Henry felt his companion gripe his arm hard, as he listened in a great tremour to this cry, which was followed by
the passage of a dozen horsemen, with a vigour and speed
that showed too plainly how little security their over-tired
steeds could have afforded them.

" Now," said the pedler, rising from his cover to recon-
noitre, and standing for a moment in suspense, " all that we
gain is clear gain ; for, as we go up, they go down. Let us
be stirring."

" But will they not follow us, and surround this mountain ?" said Henry, rising, and imitating the laboured but
rapid progress of his companion ; " remember they have
foot as well as horse, and at any rate we shall starve in the
hills."

" Fear nothing, Captain Wharton," returned the pedler
with confidence ; " this is not the mountain that I would
be on, but necessity has made me a dexterous pilot among
these hills.   I will lead you where no man will dare to follow.   See, the sun is already setting behind the tops of the
western mountains, and it will be two hours to the rising
of the moon.   Who, think you, will follow us far, on
a November night, among these rocks and precipices ?"

" But listen !" exclaimed Henry ; " the dragoons are
shouting to each other—they miss us already."

" Come to the point of this rock, and you may see them,"
said Harvey, composedly setting himself down to rest. "Nay,
they can see us—notice, they are pointing up with their
fingers.   There ! one has fired his pistol, but the distance
is too great for even a musket to carry upwards."

" They will pursue us," cried the impatient Henry ;
" let us be moving."

" They will not think of such a thing," returned the
pedler, picking the chickerberries that grew on the thin
soil where he sat, and very deliberately chewing them,
leaves and all, to refresl his mouth. " What progress

could they make here, in their boots and spurs, with their long swords, or even pistols? No, no—they may go back and turn out the foot · but the horse pass through these defiles, when they can keep the saddle, with fear and trembling. Come, follow me, Captain Wharton; we have a troublesome march before us, but I will bring you where none will think of venturing this night."

So saying, they both arose, and were soon hid from view amongst the rocks and caverns of the mountain.

Scenery in the Notch of the White Mountains.— DWIGHT.

THE Notch of the White Mountains is a phrase appropriated to a very narrow defile, extending two miles in length between two huge cliffs apparently rent asunder by some vast convulsion of nature. This convulsion was, in my own view, that of the deluge. There are here, and throughout New England, no eminent proofs of volcanic violence, nor any strong exhibitions of the power of earthquakes. Nor has history recorded any earthquake or volcano in other countries, of sufficient efficacy to produce the phenomena of this place. The objects rent asunder are too great, the ruin is too vast and too complete, to have been accomplished by these agents. The change appears to have been effected when the surface of the earth extensively subsided; when countries and continents assumed a new face; and a general commotion of the elements produced a disruption of some mountains, and merged others beneath the common level of desolation. Nothing less than this will account for the sundering of a long range of great rocks, or rather of vast mountains; or for the existing evidences of the immense force, by which the rupture was effected.

The entrance of the chasm is formed by two rocks standing perpendicularly at the distance of twenty-two feet from each other; one about twenty feet in height, the other about twelve. Half of the space is occupied by the brook mentioned as the head stream of the Saco; the other half

by the road. The stream is lost and invisible beneath a
mass of fragments, partly blown out of the road, and partly thrown down by some great convulsion.

When we entered the Notch, we were struck with the
wild and solemn appearance of every thing before us. The
scale, on which all the objects in view were formed, was
the scale of grandeur only. The rocks, rude and ragged
in a manner rarely paralleled, were fashioned and piled by
a hand operating only in the boldest and most irregular manner. As we advanced, these appearances increased rapidly.
Huge masses of granite, of every abrupt form, and hoary
with a moss, which seemed the product of ages, recalling
to the mind the *saxum vetustum* of Virgil, speedily rose
to a mountainous height. Before us the view widened
fast to the south-east. Behind us, it closed almost instanta-
neously, and presented nothing to the eye but an impassa-
ble barrier of mountains.

About half a mile from the entrance of the chasm, we
saw, in full view, the most beautiful cascade, perhaps, in
the world. It issued from a mountain on the right, about
eight hundred feet above the subjacent valley, and at the
distance from us of about two miles. The stream ran over
a series of rocks almost perpendicular, with a course so
little broken as to preserve the appearance of a uniform
current; and yet so far disturbed as to be perfectly white.
The sun shown with the clearest splendour, from a station
in the heavens the most advantageous to our prospect;
and the cascade glittered down the vast steep, like a stream
of burnished silver.

At the distance of three quarters of a mile from the entrance, we passed a brook, known in this region by the
name of *the flume;* from the strong resemblance to that
object exhibited by the channel, which it has worn for a
considerable length in a bed of rocks; the sides being perpendicular to the bottom. This elegant piece of water we determined to examine farther; and, alighting from our horses,
walked up the acclivity perhaps a furlong. The stream fell
from a height of two hundred and forty or two hundred and
fifty feet over three precipices; the second receding a small
distance from the front of the first, and the third from that
of the second. Down the first and second it fell in a sin-

gte current; and down the third in three, which united
their streams at the bottom in a fine basin, formed by the
hand of nature in the rocks immediately beneath us. It is
impossible for a brook of this size to be modelled into more
diversified or more delightful forms ; or for a cascade to descend over precipices more happily fitted to finish its beauty. The cliffs, together with a level at their foot, furnished a considerable opening, surrounded by the forest. The
sunbeams, penetrating through the trees, painted here a
great variety of fine images of light, and edged an equally
numerous and diversified collection of shadows ; both dancing on the waters, and alternately silvering and obscuring
their course. Purer water was never seen. Exclusively
of its murmurs, the world around us was solemn and silent.
Every thing assumed the character of enchantment; and, had
I been educated in the Grecian mythology, I should scarcely have been surprised to find an assemblage of Dryads,
Naiads and Oreades, sporting on the little plain below our
feet. The purity of this water was discernible, not only by
its limpid appearance, and its taste, but from several other
circumstances. Its course is wholly over hard granite ; and
the rocks and the stones in its bed and at its side, instead of
being covered with adventitious substances, were washed
perfectly clean ; and, by their neat appearance, added not a
little to the beauty of the scenery.

From this spot the mountains speedily began to open
with increased majesty ; and, in several instances, rose to
a perpendicular height little less than a mile. The bosom
of both ranges was overspread, in all the inferior regions,
by a mixture of evergreens with trees, whose leaves are
deciduous. The annual foliage had been already changed
by the frost. Of the effects of this change it is, perhaps,
impossible for an inhabitant of Great Britain, as I have
been assured by several foreigners, to form an adequate
conception, without visiting an American forest. When I
was a youth, I remarked that Thomson had entirely omitted in his Seasons this fine part of autumnal imagery.
Upon inquiring of an English gentleman the probable cause
of the omission, he informed me that no such scenery
existed in Great Britain. In this country, it is often among
the most splendi. beauties of nature All the leaves on
10

trees, which are not evergreens, are, by the first severe frost,
changed from their verdure towards the perfection of that
colour which they are capable of ultimately assuming,
through yellow, orange and red, to a pretty deep brown.
As the frost affects different trees, and different leaves of the
same tree, in very different degrees, a vast multitude of
tinctures are commonly found on those of a single tree,
and always on those of a grove or forest. These colours
also, in all their varieties, are generally full; and, in many
instances, are among the most exquisite, which are found
in the regions of nature.. Different sorts of trees are susceptible of different degrees of this beauty. Among them
the maple is pre-eminently distinguished by the prodigious
varieties, the finished beauty, and the intense lustre of its
hues; varying through all the dyes between a rich green
and the most perfect crimson, or, more definitely, the red
of the prismatic image.

There is, however, a sensible difference in the beauty of
this appearance of nature in different parts of the country,
even when the forest trees are the same. I have seen no
tract where its splendour was so highly finished, as in the
region which surrounds Lancaster for a distance of thirty
miles. The colours are more varied and more intense;
and the numerous evergreens furnish, in their deep hues,
the best groundwork of the picture.

I have remarked, that the annual foliage on the semoun-
tains had been already changed by the frost. Of course, the
darkness of the evergreens was finely illumined by the
brilliant yellow of the birch, the beech and the cherry,
and the more brilliant orange and crimson of the maple.
The effect of this universal diffusion of gay and splendid
light was, to render the preponderating deep green more
solemn. The mind, encircled by this scenery, irresistibly
remembered that the light was the light of decay, autumnal and melancholy. The dark was the gloom of evening,
approximating to night. Over the whole, the azure of the
sky cast a deep, misty blue; blending, towards the summit,
every other hue, and predominating over all.

As the eye ascended these steeps, the light decayed, and
gradually ceased. On the inferior summits rose crowns of
conical firs and spruces. On the superior eminences, the

trees, growing less and less, yielded to the chilling atmosphere, and marked the limit of forest vegetation. Above,
the surface was covered with a mass of shrubs, terminating,
at a still higher elevation, in a shroud of dark-coloured
moss.

As we passed onward through this singular valley, occasional torrents, formed by the rains and dissolving snows at
the close of winter, had left behind them, in many places,
perpetual monuments of their progress, in perpendicular,
narrow and irregular paths of immense length, where they
had washed the precipices naked and white, from the summit of the mountain to the base.   Wide and deep chasms
also met the eye, both on the summits and the sides; and
strongly impressed the imagination with the thought, that
a hand of immeasurable power had rent asunder the solid
rocks, and tumbled them into the subjacent valley.   Over
all, hoary cliffs, rising with proud supremacy, frowned awfully on the world below, and finished the landscape.

By our side, the Saco was alternately visible and lost,
and increased, almost at every step, by the junction of
tributary streams.   Its course was a perpetual cascade;
and with its sprightly murmurs furnished the only contrast
to the scenery around us.

Exalted Character of Poetry.—CHANNING.

By those who are accustomed to speak of poetry as light
reading, Milton's eminence in this sphere may be considered only as giving him a high rank among the contributors
to public amusement.   Not so thought Milton.   Of all
God's gifts of intellect, he esteemed poetical intellect the
most transcendent.   He esteemed it in himself as a kind of
inspiration, and wrote his great works with the conscious
dignity of a prophet.   We agree with Milton in his estimate of poetry.   It seems to us the divinest of all arts; for
it is the breathing or expression of that principle or sentiment, which is deepest and sublimest in human nature ; we
mean, of that thirst or aspiration, to which no mind is wholly a stranger for something purer and lovelier, something

more powerful, lofty and thrilling, than ordinary and rea
life affords.—No doctrine is more common among Christians than that of man's immortal‡‡ ; but it is not so generally understood, that the germs or principles of his whole
future being are *now* wrapped up in his soul, as the rudi-
ments of the future plant in the seed. As a necessary result of this constitution, the soul, possessed and moved by
these mighty though infant energies, is perpetually stretching beyond what is present and visible, struggling against
the bounds of its earthly prison-house, and seeking relief
and joy in imaginings of unseen and ideal being. This view
of our nature, which has never been fully developed, and
which goes farther towards explaining the contradictions
of human life than all others, carries us to the very foundation and sources of poetry. He, who cannot interpret by
his own consciousness what we now have said, wants the
true key to works of Genius. He has not penetrated those
secret recesses of the soul, where Poetry is born and nourished, and inhales immortal vigour, and wings herself for
her heavenward flight.—In an intellectual nature, framed
for progress and for higher modes of being, there must be
creative energies, power of original and ever-growing
thought; and poetry is the form in which these energies
are chiefly manifested. It is the glorious prerogative of
this art, that it " makes all things new" for the gratification of a divine instinct. It indeed finds its elements in
what it actually sees and experiences in the worlds of matter and mind; but it combines and blends these into new
forms, and according to new affinities; breaks down, if
we may so say, the distinctions and bounds of nature; imparts to material objects life, and sentiment, and emotion,
and invests the mind with the powers and splendours of the
outward creation; describes the surrounding universe in
the colours which the passions throw over it, and depicts
the mind in those modes of repose or agitation, of tenderness or sublime emotion, which manifest its thirst for a
more powerful and joyful existence. To a man of a literal
and prosaic character, the mind may seem lawless in its
workings; but it observes higher laws than it transgresses,—
the laws of the immortal intellect; it is trying and developing
its best faculties; and, in the objects which it describes

or the emotions which it awakens, anticipates those states of progressive power, splendour, beauty and happiness, for which it was created.

We accordingly believe that poetry, far from injuring society, is one of the great instruments of its refinement and exaltation. It lifts the mind above ordinary life, gives it a respite from depressing cares, and awakens the consciousness of its affinity with what is pure and noble. In its legitimate and highest efforts, it has the same tendency and aim with Christianity; that is, to spiritualize our nature. True, poetry has been made the instrument of vice, the pander of bad passions; but when genius thus stoops, it dims its fires, and parts with much of its power; and even when Poetry is enslaved to licentiousness and misanthropy, she cannot wholly forget her true vocation. Strains of pure feeling, touches of tenderness, images of innocent happiness, sympathies with what is good in our nature, bursts of scorn or indignation at the hollowness of the world, passages true to our moral nature, often escape in an immoral work, and show us how hard it is for a gifted spirit to divorce itself wholly from what is good.—Poetry has a natural alliance with our best affections. It delights in the beauty and sublimity of outward nature and of the soul. It indeed portrays with terrible energy the excesses of the passions, but they are passions which show a mighty nature, which are full of power, which command awe, and excite a deep though shuddering sympathy. Its great tendency and purpose is, to carry the mind beyond and above the beaten, dusty, weary walks of ordinary life; to lift it into a purer element, and to breathe into it more profound and generous emotion. It reveals to us the loveliness of nature, brings back the freshness of youthful feeling, revives the relish of simple pleasures, keeps unquenched the enthusiasm which warmed the spring-time of our being, refines youthful love, strengthens our interest in human nature by vivid delineations of its tenderest and loftiest feelings, spreads our sympathies over all classes of society, knits us by new ties with universal being, and, through the brightness of its prophetic visions, helps faith to lay hold on the future life.

10 *

We are aware that it is objected to poetry, that it gives wrong views, and excites false expectations of life, peoples the mind with shadows and illusions, and builds up imagina tion on the ruins of wisdom. That there is a wisdom, against which poetry wars,—the wisdom of the senses, which makes physical comfort and gratification the supreme good, and wealth the chief interest of life,—we do not deny; nor do we deem it the least service which poetry renders to mankind, that it redeems them from the thraldom of this earthborn prudence. But, passing over this topic, we would observe, that the complaint against poetry as abounding in illusion and deception is, in the main, groundless. In many poems there is more of truth than in many histories and philosophic theories. The fictions of genius are often the vehicles of the sublimest verities, and its flashes often open new regions of thought, and throw new light on the mysteries of our being. In poetry the letter is falsehood, but the spirit is often profoundest wisdom. And if truth thus dwells in the boldest fictions of the poet, much more may it be expected in his delineations of life; for the present life, which is the first stage of the immortal mind abounds in the materials of poetry, and it is the highest office of the bard to detect this divine element among the grosser pleasures and labours of our earthly being. The present life is not wholly prosaic, precise, tame and finite. To the gifted eye it abounds in the poetic. The affections which spread beyond ourselves, and stretch far into futurity; the workings of mighty passions, which seem to arm the soul with an almost superhuman energy; the innocent and irrepressible joy of infancy; the bloom, and buoyancy, and dazzling hopes of youth; the throbbings of the heart when it first wakes to love, and dreams of a happiness too vast for earth; woman, with her beauty, and grace, and gentleness, and fulness of feeling, and depth of affection, and her blushes of purity, and the tones and looks which only a mother's heart can inspire;—these are all poetical. It is not true that the poet paints a life which does not exist. He only extracts and concentrates, as it were, life's ethereal essence, arrests and condenses its volatile fragrance brings together its scattered beauties, and prolongs its more refined but evanescent joys; and in this he does well; for it is good to feel that life is not wholly usurped by cares for subsistence and physical gratifications, but admits, in measures which may be indefinitely enlarged, sentiments and delights worthy of a higher being. This power of poetry to refine our views of life and happiness, is more and more needed as society advances. It is needed to withstand the encroachments of heartless and artificial manners, which make civilization so tame and uninteresting. It is needed to counteract the tendency of physical science, which, being now sought, not, as formerly, for intellectual gratification, but for multiplying bodily comforts, requires a new developement of imagination, taste and poetry, to preserve men from sinking into an earthly, material, epicurean life.

Our remarks in vindication of poetry have extended beyond our original design. They have had a higher aim than to assert the dignity of Milton as a poet, and that is, to endear and recommend this divine art to all who reverence, and would cultivate and refine their nature.

Eloquent Appeal in Favour of the Greeks.—North American Review.*

There is an individual, who sits on no throne, in whose veins no aristocratic blood runs, who derives no influence from amassed or inherited wealth, but who, by the simple supremacy of mind, exercises, at this moment, a political sway, as mighty as that of Napoleon at the zenith of his power. Indebted for his own brilliant position to the liberality of the age, which is shaking off the fetters of ancient prejudices, this literal ruler by the grace of God can feel no deference for most of the maxims, by which the

---

* The article, from which this extract is taken, is ascribed to the pen of the Hon. Edward Everett. Little did its author imagine, while thus eloquently apostrophizing the prime minister of England, that he was so soon to be withdrawn by the mysterious hand of the Almighty from that wide sphere of power and benevolence, to which the "liberality of the age" had exalted him.—Ed

neutrality of England in the wars of Grecian liberty is justified. How devoutly is it to be wished, that the pure and undying glory of restoring another civilized region to the family of Christendom, could present itself in vision to the mind of this fortunate statesman; that, turning from his fond but magnificent boast, that he had called into existence a new world in the Indies, he would appropriate to himself the immortal fame, which could not be gainsaid, of having recalled to life the fairest region of Europe. He has but to speak the word within the narrow walls of St. Stephen's, and the sultan trembles on his throne. He has but to speak the word, and all the poor scruples and hypocritical sophistries of the continental cabinets vanish into air. Let him then abandon the paltry chase of a few ragamuffin Portuguese malecontents, and follow a game, which is worthy of himself and the people whose organ he is. Let him pronounce the sentence of expulsion from Europe of the cruel and barbarous despotism, which has so long oppressed it. The whole civilized world will applaud and sanction the decree; he will alleviate an amount of human suffering, he will work out a sum of human good, which the revolutions of ages scarcely put it within the reach of men, or governments, to avert or effect. He will encircle his plebeian temples with a wreath of fame, compared with which the diadem of the monarch whom he serves is worthless dross.

* * * * * * * * * * * * *

At all events, there they are, a gallant race, struggling, single-handed, for independence; an extraordinary spectacle to the world! With scarcely a government of their own, and without the assistance of any established power, they have waged, for six years, a fearfully contested war against one of the great empires of the earth. When Mr. Canning lately held out the menace of war against those continental nations who should violently interfere with the English system, he sought to render the menace more alarming, by calling it "a war of opinions," in which the discontented of every other country would rally against their own government under the banners of Great Britain. On this menace, which, considering the quarter from whence it

proceeds, comes with somewhat of a revolutionary and dis-
organizing tone, we have now no comment to make.   The
war now raging in Greece is, in a much higher and better
sense, a war of opinion which has actually begun ; and in
which the unarrayed, the unofficial, and, we had almost
said, the individual efforts and charities of the friends of
liberty throughout Christendom are combatting, and thus
far successfully, the barbarous hosts of the Turk.   Deserted as they have been by the governments to whom they
naturally looked for aid ; by Russia, who tamely sees the
head of the Russian church hung up at the door of his own
cathedral ; by England, the champion of liberal principles
in Europe, and the protectress of the Ionian Isles ; by the
Holy Alliance, that takes no umbrage at the debarkation
of army after army of swarthy infidels on the shores of a
Christian country ;—the Greeks have still been cheered
and sustained by the sympathy of the civilized world. Gallant volunteers have crowded to their assistance, and some
of the best blood in Europe has been shed in their defence.
Liberal contributions of money have been sent to them
across the globe ; and, while we write these sentences, supplies are despatched to them from various parts of our own
country, sufficient to avert the horrors of famine for
another season.   The direct effect of these contributions,
great as it is, (and it is this which has enabled the Greeks
to hold out thus far,) is not its best operation.   We live in
an age of moral influences.   Greece, in these various acts,
feels herself incorporated into the family of civilized nations ; raised out of the prison-house of a cruel and besotted despotism, into the community of enlightened states
Let an individual fall in with and be assailed by a superior
force in the lonely desert, on the solitary ocean, or beneath
the cover of darkness, and his heart sinks within him, as
he receives blow after blow, and feels his strength wasting
in the unwitnessed and uncheered struggle : but let the
sound of human voices swell upon his ear, or a friendly
sail draw nigh, and life and hope revive within his bosom.
Nor is human nature different in its operation in the large
masses of men.   Can any one doubt, that, if the Greeks,
instead of being placed where they are, on a renowned
arena, in sight of the civilized world,—visited, aided, ap

plaude.! as they have been, from one extreme of Christen
dom to the other,—had been surrounded by barbarism, secluded in the interior of the Turkish empire, without a
medium of communication with the world, they would
have been swept away in a single campaign? They would
have been crushed; they would have been trampled into
the dust; and the Tartars, that returned from the massacre, would have brought the first tidings of their struggle.
This is our encouragement to persevere in calling the attention of the public to this subject. It is a warfare in
which we all are or ought to be enlisted. It *is* a war of
opinion, and of feeling, and of humanity. It is a great war
of public sentiment; not conflicting (as it is commonly
called to do) merely with public sentiment operating in an
opposite direction, but with a powerful, barbarous, and despotic government. The strength and efficacy of the public sentiment of the civilized world are now, therefore, to
be put to the test on a large scale, and upon a most momentous issue. It is now to be seen whether mankind,
that is, its civilized portion,—whether enlightened Europe
and enlightened America will stand by, and behold a civilized Christian people massacred *en masse;* whether a
people that cultivate the arts which we cultivate,—that
enter into friendly intercourse with us,—that send their
children to our schools,—that translate and read our historians, philosophers and moralists,—that live by the same
rule of faith, and die in the hope of the same Saviour, shall
be allowed to be hewn down to the earth in our sight, by a
savage horde of Ethiopians and Turks. For ourselves, we
do not believe it. An inward assurance tells us that it
cannot be. Such an atrocity never has happened in human affairs, and will not now be permitted. As the horrid
catastrophe draws near, if draw near it must, the Christian
governments will awaken from their apathy. If governments remain enchained by reasons of state, the common
feeling of humanity among men will burst out, in some effectual interference. And if this fail, why should not
Providence graciously interpose, to prevent the extinction
of the only people, in whose churches the New Testament
is used in the original tongue? Is it not a pertinent subject of inquiry with those, who administer the religious

charities of this and other Christian countries, whether the entire cause of the diffusion of the Gospel is not more closely connected with the event of the struggle in Greece, than with any thing else, in any part of the world? Is not the question whether Greece and her islands shall be Christian or Mahometan, a more important question than any other, in the decision of which we have the remotest agency? Might not a well-devised and active concert among the Christian charitable societies in Europe and America, for the sake of rescuing this Christian people, present the most auspicious prospect of success, and form an organization adequate to the importance and sacredness of the object? And can any man, who has humanity, liberty, or Christianity at heart, feel justified in forbearing to give his voice, his aid, his sympathy, to this cause, in any way in which it is practicable to advance it.

Small as are the numbers of the Greeks, and limited as is their country, it may be safely said, that there has not, since the last Turkish invasion of Europe, been waged a war, of which the results, in the worst event, could have been so calamitous, as it must be allowed by every reflecting mind, that the subjugation and consequent extirpation of the Greeks would be. The wars that are waged between the states of Christendom, generally grow out of disputed titles of princes, or state quarrels between the governments. Serious changes no doubt take place, as these wars may be decided one way or the other. Nations, formerly well governed, may come under an arbitrary sway; or a despotic be exchanged for a milder government. But, inasmuch as victor and vanquished belong to the same civilized family; and the social condition, the standard of morality, and the received code of public law, are substantially the same in all the nations of Europe; no irreparable disaster to the cause of humanity itself can ensue from any war, in which they may be engaged with each other Had Napoleon, for instance, succeeded in invading and conquering England, (and this is probably the strongest case that could be put,) after the first calamities of invasion and conquest were past, which must in all cases be much the same, no worse evils would probably have esulted to the cause of humanity, than the restoration of

the Catholic religion as the religion of the state, the introduction of the civil law in place of the common law, and
the general exclusion of the English nobility and gentry
from offices of power and profit; an exclusion, which
the English government itself, since the year 1688, has
enforced towards the Catholic families, among which are
some of the oldest and richest in the kingdom. Whereas,
should the Turks prevail in the present contest, an amal-
gamation of victor and vanquished would be as impracticable now, as when Greece was first conquered by the
Ottoman power. The possession of the country has been
promised to the Bey of Egypt, as the reward of his services
in effecting its conquest. The men-at-arms have already
been doomed to military execution of the most cruel kind,
and the women and children would be sold into Asiatic and
African bondage.

We are not left to collect this merely from the known
maxims of Turkish warfare, nor the menaces which have
repeatedly been made by the Porte, but we see it exem-
plified in the island of Scio. On the soil of Greece, thus
swept of its present population, will be settled the Egyptian
and Turkish troops, by whom it shall have been subdued.
Thus will have been cut off, obliterated from the map of
Europe, and annihilated by the operation of whatever is
most barbarous and terrific in the military practice of the
Turkish government, an entire people; one of those distinct social families, into which Providence collects the sons
of men. In them will perish the descendants of ancestors,
toward whom we all profess a reverence; who carry, in
the language they speak, the proof of their national identity. In them will be exterminated a people apt and pre-
disposed for all the improvements of civilized life; a people connected with the rest of Europe by every moral and
intellectual association, and capable of being reared up into
a prosperous and cultivated state. Finally; in them will
perish one whole Christian people; and that the first that
embraced Christianity; churches actually founded by the
apostles in person, churches, for whose direct instruction a
considerable part of the New Testament was composed,
after abiding all the storms of eighteen centuries, and surviving so many vicissitudes, are now at length to be

razed; and, in the place of all this, an uncivilized Mahometan horde is to be established upon the ruins. We say it is a most momentous alternative. *Interest humani generis.* The character of the age is concerned. The impending evil is tremendous. To preserve the faith of certain old treaties, concluded we forget when, the parliament of England decides by acclamation to send an army into Portugal and Spain, because Spain has patronised the disaffection of the Portuguese ultra-royalists. To prevent a change in the governments of Piedmont, Naples and Spain, Austria and France invade those countries with large armies. Can those great powers look tamely on, and see the ruin of their Christian brethren consummated in Greece? Is there a faded parchment in the diplomatic archives of London or Lisbon, that binds the English government more imperiously than the great original obligation to rescue an entire Christian people from the cimeter? Can statesmen, who profess to be, who are, influenced by the rules of a chaste and lofty public morality, justify their sanguinary wars with Ashantees and Burmans, and find reasons of duty for shaking the petty thrones of the interior of Africa, and allow an African satrap to strew the plains of Attica with bloody ashes?

If they can, and if they will, then let the friends of liberty, humanity, and religion, take up this cause, as one that concerns them, all and each, in his capacity as a Christian and a man. Let them make strong the public sentiment on this subject, and it will prevail. Let them remember what ere now has been done, by the perseverance and resolution of small societies, and even individual men. Let them remember how small a company of adventurers, unpatronised, scarcely tolerated by their government, succeeded in laying the foundations of this our happy country beyond a mighty ocean. Let them recollect, that it was one fixed impression, cherished and pursued in the heat of an humble and friendless mariner, through long years of fruitless solicitation and fainting hope, to which it is owing, that these vast American continents are made a part of the heritage of civilized man. Let them recollect that, in the same generation, one poor monk dismembered the great ecclesiastical empire of Europe. Let them bear

11

in mind, that it was a hermit who roused the nations of
Europe in mass, to engage in an expedition against the
common enemy of Chistendom ; an expedition, wild indeed,
and unjustifiable, according to our better lights, but lawful
and meritorious in those who embarked in it.   Let them,
in a word, never forget, that when, on those lovely islands
and once happy shores, over which a dark cloud of destruction now hangs, the foundations of the Christian church
were first laid, it was by the hands of private, obscure and
persecuted individuals.   It was the people, the humblest
of the people, that took up the Gospel, in defiance of all
the patronage, the power, and the laws of the government.
Why should not Christianity be sustained in the same country, and by the same means by which it was originally established ?   If, as we believe, it is the strong and decided
sentiment of the civilized world, that the cause of the
Greeks is a good cause, and that they ought not to be allowed to perish, it cannot be that this sentiment will remain inoperative.   The very existence of this sentiment
is a tower of strength.   It will make itself felt by a thousand manifestations.   It will be heard in our senates and
our pulpits ; it will be echoed from our firesides.   Does
any one doubt the cause of America was mightily strengthened and animated by the voices of the friends of liberty
in the British parliament ?   Were not the speeches of
Chatham and Burke worth a triumphant battle to our fathers ?   And can any one doubt that the Grecian patriots
will hold out, so long as the Christian world will cheer
them with its sanction ?

Let, then, the public mind be disabused of the prejudices
which mislead it on this question.   Let it not be operated
upon by tales of piracies at sea, and factions on land ; evils,
which belong not to Greeks, but to human nature.   Let
the means of propagating authentic intelligence of the progress of the revolution be multiplied.   Let its well-wishers
and its well-hopers declare themselves in the cause.   Let
the tide of pious and Christian charity be turned into this
broad and thirsty channel.   Let every ardent and high-
spirited young man, who has an independent subsistence
of two or three hundred dollars a year, embark personally
in the cause, and aspire to that crown of glory, never yet

were except by him who so lately triumphed in the hearts
of the entire millions of Americans.   Let this be done,
and Greece is safe.

Death of Josiah Quincy, Jun.—J. Quincy.

AFTER being five weeks at sea, the wished-for shore
yet at a distance, he became convinced that his fate was
inevitable,—and prepared to submit himself to the will of
Heaven with heroic calmness and Christian resignation.
Under the pressure of disease, and amidst the daily sinking of nature, his friends, his family, and, above all, his
country, predominated in his affections.   He repeatedly
said to the seaman on whose attentions he was chiefly dependant, that he had but one desire and one prayer, which
was, that he might live long enough to have an interview
with Samuel Adams or Joseph Warren ;—that granted, he
should die content.   This wish of the patriot's heart,
Heaven, in its inscrutable wisdom, did not grant.

As he drew towards his native shore, the crisis he had
so long foreseen arrived.   The battle of Lexington was
fought.   According to his predictions, " his countrymen
scaled their faith and constancy to their liberties with their
blood."   But he lived not to hear the event of that glorious day.

While yet the ship was three days' sail from land, exhausted by disease, and perceiving his last hour approach,
he called the seaman to the side of his birth, and, being
himself too weak to write, dictated to him a letter full of
the most interesting and affecting communications to his
family and nearest friends.   This letter still exists
among his papers, in the rude hand-writing of an illiterate
sailor.

* * * * * * * * * * * * *

Such is the last notice of the close of the life of Josiah
Quincy, Jun.   On the 26th of April, 1775, within sight of
that beloved country, which he was not permitted to reach·
neither supported by the kindness of friendship, nor cheered by the voice of affection, he expired ;—not, indeed, as

a few weeks afterwards did his friend and co-patriot Warren, in battle, on a field ever-memorable and glorious; but
in solitude, amidst suffering, without associate and without
witness; yet breathing forth a dying sigh for his country,
desiring to live only to perform towards her a last and signal service

A few hours after his death, the ship, with his lifeless
remains, entered the harbour of Gloucester, Cape Ann.

His arrival had been anticipated with anxious solicitude,
and the intelligence of his death was received with an universal sorrow. By his family and immediate friends, the
event was mourned as the extinction of their brightest
hope. His contemporaries, faithful to his virtues, and
deeply sensible of his services, early associated his name
with these most honoured and most beloved of the period
in which he lived. It was his lot to compress events and
exertions sufficient for a long life within the compass of a
few short years. To live forever in the hearts of his countrymen, and, by labour and virtue, to become immortal in
the memory of future times, were the strong passions of
his soul. That he was prohibited from filling the great
sphere of usefulness, for which his intellectual powers
seemed adapted and destined, is less a subject of regret,
than it is of joy and gratitude that he was permitted, in so
short a time, to perform so noble a part, and that to his
desire has been granted so large a portion of that imperishable meed, which, beyond all earthly reward, was the object of his search and solicitude.

Danger of Delay in Religion.—BUCKMINSTER

IT has been most acutely and justly observed, that all
resolutions to repent at a future time are necessarily in-
sincere, and must be a mere deception; because they imply a preference of a man's present habits and conduct,
they imply, that he is really unwilling to change them,
and that nothing but necessity would lead him to make any
attempt of the kind. But let us suppose the expected leisure for repentance to have arrived; the avaricious or

fraudulent dealer to have attained that competency, which is to secure him from want; the profligate and debauched to have passed the slippery season of youth, and to be established in life; the gamester, by one successful throw, to have recovered his desperate finances; the dissipated and luxurious to have secured a peaceful retreat for the remainder of his days;—to each of these the long anticipated hour of amendment, the opportune leisure for religion, has at length arrived; but where, alas! is the disposition! where the necessary strength of resolution! How rare, and, I had almost said, how miraculous, is the instance of a change!

The danger of delay, even if we suppose this uncertain leisure and inclination to be secured, is inconceivably heightened, when we consider, further, the nature of repentance. It is a settled change of the disposition from vice to virtue, discovered in the gradual improvement of the life. It is not a fleeting wish, a vapoury sigh, a lengthened groan. Neither is it a twinge of remorse, a flutter of fear, nor any temporary and partial resolution. The habits of a sinner have been long in forming. They have acquired a strength, which is not to be broken by a blow. The labour of a day will not build up a virtuous habit on the ruins of an old and vicious character. You, then, who have deferred, from year to year, the relinquishment of a vice; you, if such there be, who, while the wrinkles are gathering in your foreheads, are still dissatisfied with yourselves, remember, that amendment is a slow and laborious process. Can you be too assiduous, too fearful, when you consider how short the opportunity, and how much is required to complete the work of reformation, and to establish the dominion of virtue?

It is impossible to dismiss this subject without considering a common topic,—the inefficacy of a death-bed repentance. It is to be feared that charity, which hopeth and believeth all things, has sometimes discovered more of generous credulity, than of well-founded hope, when it has laid great stress, and built much consolation, on the casual expressions and faint sighs of dying men. Far be it from us to excite suspicion or recall anxiety in the breast of surviving friendship, or to throw a new shade of terror

11 *

over the valley of death; but better, far better, were it
for a thousand breasts to be pierced with temporary anguish,
and a new ho.ror be added to the dreary passage of the
grave, than that one soul be lost to heaven by the delusive
expectation of effectual repentance in a dying hour. For,
as we have repeatedly asked, what is effectual repentance ?
Can it be supposed, that, where the vigour of life has been
spent in the establishment of vicious propensities; where
all the vivacity of youth, all the soberness of manhood, and
all the leisure of old age, have been given to the service
of sin ; where vice has been growing with the growth, and
strengthening with the strength ; where it has spread out
with the limbs of the stripling, and become rigid with the
fibres of the aged; can it, I say, be supposed, that the labours of such a life are to be overthrown by one last exertion of a mind impaired with disease, by the convulsive
exercise of an affrighted spirit, and by the inarticulate and
feeble sounds of an expiring breath ? Repentance consists
not in one or more acts of contrition; it is a permanent
change of the disposition. Those dispositions and habits
of mind, which you bring to your dying bed, you will
carry with you to another world. These habits are the
dying dress of the soul. They are the grave-clothes,
in which it must come forth, at the last, to meet the sentence of an impartial Judge. If they were filthy, they
will be filthy still. The washing of baptismal water will
not, at that hour, cleanse the spots of the soul. The confession of sins, which have never been removed, will not
furnish the conscience with an answer towards God. The
reception of the elements will not, then, infuse a principle
of spiritual life, any more than unconsecrated bread and
wine will infuse health into the limbs, on which the cold
cramps of death have already collected. Say not, that you
have discarded such superstitious expectations. You have
not discarded them, while you defer any thing to that hour;
while you venture to rely on any thing but the mercy of
God toward a heart, holy, sincere, and sanctified ; a heart,
which loves heaven for its purity, and God for his goodness.
If, in this solemn hour, the soul of an habitual and inveterate offender be prepared for the residence of pure and
spotless spirits, it can be only by a sovereign and miracu

lous interposition of Omnipotence. His power we pretend
not to limit. He can wash the sooty Ethiop white, and
cause the spots on the leopard's skin to disappear. We
presume not to fathom the counsels of his will ; but this we
will venture to assert, that if, at the last hour of the sinner's life, the power of God ever interposes to snatch him
from his ruin, such interposition will never be disclosed to
the curiosity of man. For, if it should once be believed,
that the rewards of heaven can be obtained by such an instantaneous and miraculous change at the last hour of life,
all our ideas of moral probation, and of the connexion between character here, and condition hereafter, are loose
unstable, and groundless ; the nature and the laws of God's
moral government are made at once inexplicable ; our ex-
hortations are useless, our experience false, and the whole
apparatus of Gospel means and motives becomes a cumbrous
and unnecessary provision.

What, then, is the great conclusion, which we should
deduce from all that we have said of the nature of habit,
and the difficulty of repentance ? It is this : Behold, now
is the accepted time, now is the day of salvation. If you
are young, you cannot begin too soon ; if you are old, you
may begin too late. Age, says the proverb, strips us of
every thing, even of resolution. To-morrow we shall be
older ; to-morrow, indeed, Death may fix his seal forever
on our characters. It is a seal which can never be broken,
till the voice of the Son of man shall burst the tombs,
which enclose us. If, then, we leave this place, sensible
of a propensity which ought to be restrained, of a lust
which ought to be exterminated, of a habit which ought
to be broken, and rashly defer the hour of amendment,
consider, I beseech you, it may, perhaps, be merciful in
God to refuse us another opportunity. It may be a gracious method of preventing an abuse, which will only ag-
gravate the retribution, which awaits the impenitent. Make
haste, then, and delay not to keep the commandments of
God ; of that God, who has no pleasure in the death of the
wicked, but that the wicked turn from his way, and live

Scenes in Philadelphia during the Prevalence of the Yellow Fever, in 1793.—C. B. Brown.

My thoughts were called away from pursuing these inquiries by a rumour, which had gradually swelled to formidable dimensions ; and which, at length, reached us in our quiet retreats. The city, we were told, was involved in confusion and panic ; for a pestilential disease had begun its destructive progress. Magistrates and citizens were flying to the country. The numbers of the sick multiplied beyond all example ; even in the pest-affected cities of the Levant. The malady was malignant and unsparing.

The usual occupations and amusements of life were at an end. Terror had exterminated all the sentiments of nature. Wives were deserted by husbands, and children by parents. Some had shut themselves in their houses, and debarred themselves from all communication with the rest of mankind. The consternation of others had destroyed their understanding, and their misguided steps hurried them into the midst of the danger which they had previously laboured to shun. Men were seized by this disease in the streets ; passengers fled from them ; entrance into their own dwellings was denied to them ; they perished in the public ways.

The chambers of disease were deserted, and the sick left to die of negligence. None could be found to remove the lifeless bodies. Their remains, suffered to decay by piecemeal, filled the air with deadly exhalations, and added tenfold to the devastation.

Such was the tale, distorted and diversified a thousand ways, by the credulity and exaggeration of the tellers. At first I listened to the story with indifference or mirth. Methought it was confuted by its own extravagance. The enormity and variety of such an evil made it unworthy to be believed. I expected that every new day would detect the absurdity and fallacy of such representations. Every new day, however, added to the number of witnesses, and the consistency of the tale, till, at length, it was not possible to withhold my faith.

This rumour was of a nature to absorb and suspend the whole soul. A certain sublimity is connected with enormous

dangers, that imparts to our consternation or our pity a tinc-
ture of the pleasing.   This, at least, may be experienced
by those who are beyond the verge of peril.   My own person was exposed to no hazard.   I had leisure to conjure
up terrific images, and to personate the witnesses and suf-
ferers of this calamity.   This employment was not enjoin-
ed upon me by necessity, but was ardently pursued, and
must therefore have been recommended by some nameless
charm.

   Others were very differently affected.   As often as the
tale was embellished with new incidents, or enforced by
new testimony, the hearer grew pale, his breath was stifled
by inquietudes, his blood was chilled, and his stomach was
bereaved of its usual energies.   A temporary indisposition
was produced in many.   Some were haunted by a melancholy bordering upon madness, and some, in consequence
of sleepless panics, for which no cause could be assigned,
and for which no opiates could be found, were attacked by
lingering or mortal diseases.

* * * * * * * * * * * * * *

   In proportion as I drew near the city, the tokens of its
calamitous condition became more apparent.   Every farm-
house was filled with supernumerary tenants; fugitives from
home, and haunting the skirts of the road, eager to detail
every passenger with inquiries after news.   The passengers were numerous; for the tide of emigration was by no
means exhausted.   Some were on foot, bearing in their
countenances the tokens of their recent terror, and filled
with mournful reflections on the forlornness of their state.
Few had secured to themselves an asylum; some were
without the means of paying for victuals or lodging for the
coming night; others, who were not thus destitute, yet
knew not whither to apply for entertainment, every house
being already overstocked with inhabitants, or barring its
inhospitable doors at their approach.

   Families of weeping mothers, and dismayed children,
attended with a few pieces of indispensable furniture, were
carried in vehicles of every form.   The parent or husband
had perished; and the price of some moveable, or the pit-
tance handed forth by public charity, had been expended

to purchase the means of retiring from this theatre of disasters; though uncertain and hopeless of accommodation in the neighbouring districts.

Between these and the fugitives whom curiosity had led to the road, dialogues frequently took place, to which I was suffered to listen. From every mouth the tale of sorrow was repeated with new aggravations. Pictures of their own distress, or of that of their neighbours, were exhibited in all the hues which imagination can annex to pestilence and poverty.

My preconceptions of the evil now appeared to have fallen short of the truth. The dangers into which I was rushing seemed more numerous and imminent than I had previously imagined. I wavered not in my purpose. A panic crept to my heart, which more vehement exertions were necessary to subdue or control; but I harboured not a momentary doubt that the course which I had taken was prescribed by duty. There was no difficulty or reluctance in proceeding. All for which my efforts were demanded was, to walk in this path without tumult or alarm.

Various circumstances had hindered me from setting out upon this journey as early as was proper. My frequent pauses, to listen to the narratives of travellers, contributed likewise to procrastination. The sun had nearly set before I reached the precincts of the city. I pursued the track which I had formerly taken, and entered High Street after night-fall. Instead of equipages and a throng of passengers, the voice of levity and glee, which I had formerly observed, and which the mildness of the season would, at other times, have produced, I found nothing but a dreary solitude.

The market-place, and each side of this magnificent avenue were illuminated, as before, by lamps; but between the verge of Schuylkill and the heart of the city, I met not more than a dozen figures; and these were ghost-like, wrapped in cloaks, from behind which they cast upon me glances of wonder and suspicion; and, as I approached, changed their course, to avoid touching me. Their clothes were sprinkled with vinegar; and their nostrils defended from contagion by some powerful perfume.

I cast a look upon the houses, which I recollected to have formerly been, at this hour, brilliant with lights, resounding with lively voices, and thronged with busy faces. Now, they were closed, above and below; dark, and without tokens of being inhabited. From the upper windows of some, a gleam sometimes fell upon the pavement I was traversing, and showed that their tenants had not fled, but were secluded or disabled.

These tokens were new, and awakened all my panics. Death seemed to hover over this scene, and I dreaded that the floating pestilence had already lighted on my frame. I had scarcely overcome these tremours, when I approached a house, the door of which was opened, and before which stood a vehicle, which I presently recognised to be a *hearse.*

The driver was seated on it. I stood still to mark his visage, and to observe the course which he proposed to take. Presently a coffin, borne by two men, issued from the house. The driver was a negro, but his companions were white. Their features were marked by ferocious indifference to danger or pity. One of them, as he assisted in thrusting the coffin into the cavity provided for it, said, " I'll be damned if I think the poor dog was quite dead. It was'nt the *fever* that ailed him, but the sight of the girl and her mother on the floor. I wonder how they all got into that room. What carried them there ?"

The other surlily muttered, " Their legs, to be sure."

" But what should they hug together in one room for ?"

" To save us trouble, to be sure."

" And I thank them with all my heart; but damn it, it was'nt right to put him in his coffin before the breath was fairly gone. I thought the last look he gave me, told me to stay a few minutes "

" Pshaw : He could not live. The sooner dead the better for him, as well as for us. Did you mark how he eyed us, when we carried away his wife and daughter ? I never cried in my life, since I was knee-high, but curse me if I ever felt in better tune for the business than just then. Hey !" continued he, looking up, and observing me standing a few paces distant, and listening to their discourse, " What's wanted ? Any body dead ?"

I stayed not to answer or parley, but hurried forward
My joints trembled, and cold drops stood on my forehead
I was ashamed of my own infirmity; and, by vigorous ef
forts of my reason, regained some degree of composure
The evening had now advanced, and it behooved me to pro
cure accommodation at some of the inns.

These were easily distinguished by their *signs*, but many
were without inhabitants. At length I lighted upon one, the
hall of which was open, and the windows lifted. After
knocking for some time, a young girl appeared, with many
marks of distress. In answer to my question, she answered
that both her parents were sick, and that they could receive no one. I inquired, in vain, for any other tavern at
which strangers might be accommodated. She knew of
none such; and left me, on some one's calling to her from
above, in the midst of my embarrassment. After a moment's pause, I returned, discomforted and perplexed, to
the street.

I proceeded, in a considerable degree, at random. At
length I reached a spacious building in Fourth Street, which
the sign-post showed me to be an inn. I knocked loudly
and often at the door. At length a female opened the
window of the second story, and in a tone of peevishness
demanded what I wanted. I told her that I wanted
lodging.

" Go hunt for it somewhere else," said she ; " you'll find
none here." I began to expostulate ; but she shut the
window with quickness, and left me to my own reflections.

I began now to feel some regret at the journey I had
taken. Never, in the depth of caverns or forests, was I
equally conscious of loneliness. I was surrounded by the
habitations of men; but I was destitute of associate or
friend. I had money, but a horse shelter, or a morsel of
food, could not be purchased. I came for the purpose of
relieving others, but stood in the utmost need myself
Even in health my condition was helpless and forlorn;
but what would become of me, should this fatal malady
be contracted? To hope that an asylum would be afforded to a sick man, which was denied to one in health, was
unreasonable

Importance of Knowledge to the Mechanic.—
G. B. EMERSON.

LET us imagine for a moment the condition of an individual, who has not advanced beyond the merest elements
of knowledge, who understands nothing of the principles
even of his own art, and inquire what change will be
wrought in his feelings, his hopes, and happiness, in all
that makes up the character, by the gradual inpouring of
knowledge. He has now the capacity of thought, but it
is a barren faculty, never nourished by the food of the
mind, and never rising above the poor objects of sense.
Labour and rest, the hope of mere animal enjoyment,
or the fear of want, the care of providing covering and
food, make up the whole sum of his existence. Such
a man may be industrious, but he cannot love labour, for
it is not relieved by the excitement of improving or changing the processes of his art, nor cheered by the hope of a
better condition. When released from labour, he does not
rejoice, for mere idleness is not enjoyment; and he has no
book, no lesson of science, no play of the mind, no interesting pursuit, to give a zest to the hour of leisure. Home
has few charms for him; he has little taste for the quiet,
the social converse, and exchange of feeling and thought,
the innocent enjoyments that ought to dwell there. Society has little to interest him, for he has no sympathy for
the pleasures or pursuits, the cares or troubles of others,
to whom he cannot feel nor perceive his bonds of relation-
ship. All of life is but a poor boon for such a man; and
happy for himself and for mankind, if the few ties that hold
him to this negative existence be not broken. Happy for
him if that best and surest friend of man, that messenger
of good news from Heaven to the poorest wretch on earth,
Religion, bringing the fear of God, appear to save him.
Without her to support, should temptation assail him, what
an easy victim would he fall to vice or crime! How little
would be necessary to overturn his ill-balanced principles,
and throw him grovelling in intemperance, or send him
abroad on the ocean or the highway, an enemy to himself
and his kind!

12

But let the light of science fall upon that man ; open to him the fountain of knowledge ; a few principles of philosophy enter his mind, and awaken the dormant power of thought ; he begins to look upon his art with an altered eye. It ceases to be a dark mechanical process, which he cannot understand ; he regards it as an object of inquiry, and begins to penetrate the reasons, and acquire a new mastery over his own instruments. He finds other and better modes of doing what he had done before, blindly and without interest, a thousand times. He learns to profit by the experience of others, and ventures upon untried paths Difficulties, which before would have stopped him at the outset, receive a ready solution from some luminous principle of science. He gains new knowledge and new skill, and can improve the quality of his manufacture, while he shortens the process, and diminishes his own labour. Then labour becomes sweet to him ; it is accompanied by the consciousness of increasing power ; it is leading him forward to a higher place among his fellow men. Relaxation, too, is sweet to him, as it enables him to add to his intellectual stores, and to mature, by undisturbed meditation, the plans and conceptions of the hour of labour. His home has acquired a new charm ; for he is become a man of thought, and feels and enjoys the peace and seclusion of that sacred retreat ; and he carries thither the honest complacency which is the companion of well-earned success. There, too, bright visions of the future sphere open upon him, and excite a kindly feeling towards those who are to share in his prosperity. Thus his mind and heart expand together. He has become an intelligent being, and, while he has learnt to esteem himself, he has also learnt to live no longer for himself alone. Society opens like a new world to him , he looks upon his fellow-creatures with interest and sympathy, and feels that he has a place in their affections and respect. Temptations assail him in vain. He is armed by high and pure thoughts. He takes a wider view of his relations with the beings about and above him. He welcomes every generous virtue that adorns and dignifies the human character. He delights in the exercise of reason—he glories in the consciousness and the hope of immortality.

Humorous Description of the Custom of Whitewash ing.—FRANCIS HOPKINSON.*

MY wish is to give you some account of the people of these new States, but I am far from being qualified for the purpose, having as yet seen little more than the cities of New York and Philadelphia. I have discovered but few national singularities among them. Their customs and manners are nearly the same with those of England, which they have long been used to copy. For, previous to the revolution, the Americans were from their infancy taught to look up to the English as patterns of perfection in all things. I have observed, however, one custom, which, for aught I know, is peculiar to this country: an account of it will serve to fill up the remainder of this sheet. and may afford you some amusement.

When a young couple are about to enter into the matrimonial state, a never-failing article in the marriage treaty is, that the lady shall have and enjoy the free and unmolested exercise of the rights of *whitewashing*, with all its ceremonials, privileges and appurtenances. A young woman would forego the most advantageous connexion, and even disappoint the warmest wish of her heart, rather than resign the invaluable right. You would wonder what this privilege of *whitewashing* is :—I will endeavour to give you some idea of the ceremony, as I have seen it performed.

There is no season of the year, in which the lady may not claim her privilege, if she pleases ; but the latter end of May is most generally fixed upon for the purpose. The attentive husband may judge by certain prognostics when the storm is nigh at hand. When the lady is unusually fretful, finds fault with the servants, is discontented with the children, and complains much of the filthiness of every thing about her —these are signs which ought not to be neglected ; yet they are not decisive, as they sometimes come on and go off again without producing any further effect. But

* This piece has been incorrectly ascribed to the pen of Dr. Franklin. Hopkinson possessed much of that ease and humour, which have rendered the writings of the former so universally admired.—Ed

if, when the husband rises in the morning, he should observe in the yard a wheelbarrow with a quantity of lime
in it, or should see certain buckets with lime dissolved in
water, there is then no time to be lost; he immediately
locks up the apartment or closet where his papers or his
private property are kept, and, putting the key in his pocket,
betakes himself to flight: for a husband, however beloved,
becomes a perfect nuisance during this season of female
rage; his authority is superseded, his commission is suspended, and the very scullion, who cleans the brasses in
the kitchen, becomes of more consideration and importance
than him.   He has nothing for it but to abdicate, and run
from an evil which he can neither prevent nor mollify.

The husband gone, the ceremony begins.   The walls
are in a few minutes stripped of their furniture; paintings,
prints and looking-glasses lie in a huddled heap about the
floors; the curtains are torn from the testers, the beds
crammed into the windows; chairs and tables, bedsteads
and cradles crowd the yard; and the garden fence bends
beneath the weight of carpets, blankets, cloth cloaks, old
coats and ragged breeches.   Here may be seen the lumber
of the kitchen, forming a dark and confused mass; for the
foreground of the picture, gridirons and frying-pans, rusty
shovels and broken tongs, spits and pots, and the fractured
remains of rush-bottomed chairs.   There, a closet has dis-
gorged its bowels, cracked tumblers, broken wine-glasses,
phials of forgotten physic, papers of unknown powders,
seeds and dried herbs, handfuls of old corks, tops of teapots
and stoppers of departed decanters;—from the rag hole in
the garret to the rat hole in the cellar, no place escapes un-
rummaged.   It would seem as if the day of general doom
was come, and the utensils of the house were dragged forth
to judgment.   In this tempest the words of Lear naturally
present themselves, and might, with some alteration, be
made strictly applicable:

> ————————" Let the great gods,
> That keep this dreadful pudder o'er our heads,
> Find out their enemies now.   Tremble, thou wretch,
> That hast within thee undivulged crimes
> Unwhipp'd of Justice! ——
> ————————Close pent-up Guilt,
> Raise your concealing continents, and ask
> These dreadful summoners grace!"

This ceremony completed, and the house thoroughly evacuated, the next operation is to smear the walls and ceilings of every room and closet with brushes dipped in a solution of lime, called *whitewash ;* to pour buckets of water over every floor, and scratch all the partitions and wainscots with rough brushes wet with soap-suds, and dipped in stone-cutter's sand. The windows by no means escape the general deluge. A servant scrambles out upon the penthouse, at the risk of her neck, and, with a mug in her hand and a bucket within reach, she dashes away innumerable gallons of water against the glass panes, to the great annoyance of passengers in the street.

I have been told, that an action at law was once brought against one of these water-nymphs, by a person who had a new suit of clothes spoiled by this operation ; but, after a long argument, it was determined by the whole court, that the action would not lie, inasmuch as the defendant was in the exercise of a legal right, and not answerable for the consequences ; and so the poor gentleman was doubly non-suited ; for he lost not only his suit of clothes but his suit at law.

These smearings and scratchings, washings and dashings, being duly performed, the next ceremony is to cleanse and replace the distracted furniture. You may have seen a house-raising, or a ship-launch, when all the hands within reach are collected together; recollect, if you can, the hurry, bustle, confusion and noise of such a scene, and you will have some idea of this cleaning match. The misfortune is, that the sole object is to make things clean ; it matters not how many useful, ornamental or valuable articles are mutilated, or suffer death under the operation ; a mahogany chair and carved frame undergo the same discipline ; they are to be made clean at all events ; but their preservation is not worthy of attention. For instance, a fine large engraving is laid flat upon the floor ; smaller prints are piled upon it, and the superincumbent weight cracks the glasses of the lower tier ; but this is of no consequence. A valuable picture is placed leaning against the sharp corner of a table ; others are made to lean against that, until the pressure of the whole forces the corner of the table through the canvass of the first. The frame and

12 *

glass of a fine print are to be cleaned; the spirit and oil used on this occasion are suffered to leak through and spoil the engraving; no matter, if the glass is clean, and the frame shine, it is sufficient; the rest is not worthy of consideration. An able mathematician has made an accurate calculation founded on long experience, and has discovered that the losses and destruction incident to two whitewashings are equal to one removal, and three removals equal to one fire.

The cleaning frolic over, matters begin to resume their pristine appearance. The storm abates, and all would be well again, but it is impossible that so great a convulsion, in so small a community, should not produce some further effects. For two or three weeks after the operation, the family are usually afflicted with sore throats or sore eyes, occasioned by the caustic quality of the lime, or with severe colds from the exhalations of wet floors or damp walls.

I know a gentleman, who was fond of accounting for every thing in a philosophical way. He considers this, which I have called a custom, as a real periodical disease peculiar to the climate. His train of reasoning is ingenious and whimsical, but I am not at leisure to give you the detail. The result was, that he found the distemper to be incurable; but, after much study, he conceived he had discovered a method to divert the evil he could not subdue. For this purpose he caused a small building, about twelve feet square, to be erected in his garden, and furnished with some ordinary chairs and tables; and a few prints of the cheapest sort were hung against the walls. His hope was, that, when the whitewashing frenzy seized the females of his family, they might repair to this apartment, and scrub and smear and scour to their hearts' content; and so spend the violence of the disease in this outpost, while he enjoyed himself in quiet at head-quarters. But the experiment did not answer his expectation; it was impossible it should, since a principal part of the gratification consists in the lady's having an uncontrolled right to torment her husband at least once a year, and to turn him out of doors and take the reins of government into her own hands.

There is a much better contrivance than this of the philosopher, which is, to cover the walls of the house with paper : this is generally done ; and, though it cannot abolish, it at least shortens, the period of female dominion. The paper is decorated with flowers of various fancies, and made so ornamental, that the women have admitted the fashion without perceiving the design.

There is also another alleviation of the husband's distress ; he generally has the privilege of a small room or closet for his books and papers, the key of which he is allowed to keep. This is considered as a privileged place, and stands like the land of Goshen amid the plagues of Egypt. But then he must be extremely cautious, and ever on his guard ; for should he inadvertently go abroad and leave the key in his door, the housemaid, who is always on the watch for such an opportunity, immediately enters in triumph with buckets, brooms and brushes ; takes possession of the premises, and forthwith puts all his books and papers *to rights*—to his utter confusion, and sometimes serious detriment. For instance :

A gentleman was sued by the executors of a tradesman, in a charge found against him in the deceased's books, to the amount of thirty pounds. The defendant was strongly impressed with the idea, that he had discharged the debt and taken a receipt ; but, as the transaction was of long standing, he knew not where to find the receipt. The suit went on in course, and the time approached when judgment would be obtained against him. He then sat seriously down to examine a large bundle of old papers, which he had untied and displayed on a table for that purpose. In the midst of his search, he was suddenly called away on business of importance ;—he forgot to lock the door of his room. The housemaid, who had been long looking out for such an opportunity, immediately entered with the usual implements, and with great alacrity fell to cleaning the room, and putting things *to rights*. The first object that struck her eye was the confused situation of the papers on the table ; these were without delay bundled together as so many dirty knives and forks ; but in the action, a small piece of paper fell unnoticed on the floor, which happened to be the very receipt in question : as it had no very resp c..ble appearance, it was soon after swept out with the common dirt of the room, and carried in the rubbish-pan into the yard. The tradesman had neglected to enter the credit in his book; the defendant could find nothing to obviate the charge, and so judgment went against him for the debt and costs. A fortnight after the whole was settled and the money paid, one of the children found the receipt among the rubbish in the yard.

There is another custom, peculiar to the city of Philadelphia, and nearly allied to the former. I mean, that of washing the pavement before the doors every Saturday evening. I at first took this to be a regulation of the police; but, on further inquiry, find it is a religious rite preparatory to the Sabbath; and is, I believe, the only religious rite, in which the numerous sectaries of this city perfectly agree. The ceremony begins about sunset, and continues till about ten or eleven at night. It is very difficult for a stranger to walk the streets on those evenings; he runs a continual risk of having a bucket of dirty water thrown against his legs; but a Philadelphian born is so much accustomed to the danger, that he avoids it with surprising dexterity. It is from this circumstance that a Philadelphian may be known any where by his gait. The streets of New York are paved with rough stones; these indeed are not washed, but the dirt is so thoroughly swept from before the doors, that the stones stand up sharp and prominent, to the great inconvenience of those who are not accustomed to so rough a path. But habit reconciles every thing. It is diverting enough to see a Philadelphian at New York, he walks the streets with as much painful caution as if his toes were covered with corns, or his feet lamed with the gout; while a New Yorker, as little approving the plain masonry of Philadelphia, shuffles along the pavement like a parrot on a mahogany table.

It must be acknowledged, that the ablutions I have mentioned are attended with no small inconvenience; but the women would not be induced, on any consideration, to resign their privilege. Notwithstanding this, I can give you the strongest assurances that the women of America make the most faithful wives and the most attentive mothers in the world; and I am sure you will join me in opinion that if a married man is made miserable only *one* week in a whole year, he will have no great cause to complain of the matrimonial bond.

May you die among your Kindred.—GREENWOOD. .

IT is a sad thing to feel that we must die away from our home. Tell not the invalid who is yearning after his distant country, that the atmosphere around him is soft; that the gales are filled with balm, and the flowers are springing from the green earth ;—he knows that the softest air to his heart would be the air which hangs over his native land ; that more grateful than all the gales of the south, would breathe the low whispers of anxious affection ; that the very icicles clinging to his own caves, and the snow beating against his own windows, would be far more pleasant to his eyes, than the bloom and verdure which only more forcibly remind him how far he is from that one spot which is dearer to him than the world beside. He may, indeed, find estimable friends, who will do all in their power to promote his comfort and assuage his pains ; but they cannot supply the place of the long known and long loved ; they cannot read as in a book the mute language of his face ; they have not learned to wait upon his habits, and anticipate his wants, and he has not learned to communicate, without hesitation, all his wishes, impressions, and thoughts, to them. He feels that he is a stranger ; and a more desolate feeling than that could not visit his soul.— How much is expressed by that form of oriental benediction, *May you die among your kindred!*

Description of a Death Scene.—MISS FRANCIS.

GRACE, agitated by these events, and her slight form daily becoming more shadowy, seemed like a celestial spirit, which having performed its mission on earth, melts into a misty wreath, then disappears forever. Hers had always

been the kind of beauty that is eloquence, though it speaks
not. The love she inspired was like that of some fair infant,
which we would fain clasp to our hearts in its guileless beauty; and when it repays our fondness with a cherub smile, its
angelic influence rouses all that there is of heaven within
he soul. Deep compassion was now added to these emotions;
and wherever she moved, the eye of pity greeted her, as it
would some wounded bird, nestling to the heart in its timid
loveliness. Every one who knew her felt the influence
of her exceeding purity and deep pathos of character; but
very few had penetrated into its recesses, and discovered
its hidden treasures. Melody was there, but it was too
plaintive, too delicate in its combination, to be produced by
an unskilful hand. The coarsest minds felt its witching effect, though they could not define its origin;—like the servant mentioned by Addison, who drew the bow across every
string of her master's violin, and then complained that she
could not, for her life, find where the tune was secreted.

Souls of this fine mould keep the fountain of love sealed
deep within its caverns; and to one only is access ever
granted. Miss Osborne's affection had been tranquil on
the surface,—but it was as deep as it was pure. It was a
pool which had granted its healing influence to one, but
could never repeat the miracle, though an angel should
trouble its waters. Assuredly he that could mix death in
the cup of love which he offered to one so young, so fair,
and so true, was guilty as the priest who administered
poison in the holy eucharist.

Lucretia, now an inmate of the family, read to her, supported her across the chamber, and watched her brief, gentle slumbers with an intense interest, painfully tinged with
self-reproach. She was the cause of this premature decay,—innocent, indeed, but still the cause. Under such
circumstances, the conscience is morbid in its sensibility,—
unreasonable in its acuteness; and the smiles and forgiveness of those we have injured, tear and scorch it like burning pincers. Yet there was one who suffered even more
than Lucretia,—though he was never conscious of giving
one moment's pain to the object of his earliest affection.
During the winter, every leisure moment which Doctor
Willard's numerous avocations allowed him, was spent in

Miss Osborne's sick chamber ; and every tone, every look of his went to her heart with a thrilling expression, which seemed to say, " Would I could die for thee ! Oh! would to God I could die for thee !"

Thus pillowed on the arm of Friendship, and watched over by the eye of Love, Grace languidly awaited the return of spring ; and, when May did arrive, wasted as she was, she seemed to enjoy its pure breath and sunny smile. Alas ! that the month, which dances around the flowery earth with such mirthful step and beaming glance, should call so many victims of consumption to their last home ! Towards the close of this delightful season, the invalid, bolstered in her chair, and surrounded by her affectionate family, was seated at the window, watching the declining sun. There was deep silence for a long while ;—as if her friends feared that a breath might scare the flitting soul from its earthly habitation. Henry and Lucretia sat on either side, pressing her hands in mournful tenderness ; Doctor Willard leaned over her chair and looked up to the unclouded sky, as if he reproached it for mocking him with brightness ; and her father watched the hectic flush upon her cheek with the firmness of Abraham, when he offered his only son upon the altar. Oh! how would the heart of that aged sufferer have rejoiced within him, could he too have exchanged the victim !

She had asked Lucretia to place Somerville's rose on the window beside her. One solitary blossom was on it ; and she reached forth her weak hand to pluck it ; but its leaves scattered beneath her trembling touch. She looked up to Lucretia with an expression, which her friend could never forget,—and one cold tear slowly glided down her pallid cheek. Gently as a mother kisses her sleeping babe, Doctor Willard brushed it away ; and, turning hastily to conceal his quivering lip, he clasped Henry's hand with convulsive energy as he whispered, " Oh! God of mercies, how willingly would I have wiped away all tears from her eyes ? '

There is something peculiarly impressive in manly grief. The eye of woman overflows as readily as her heart ; but when waters gush from the rock, we feel that they are extorted by no gentle blow

The invalid looked at him with affectionate regret, as if she thought it a crime not to love such endearing kindness; and every one present made a powerful effort to suppress painful, suffocating emotion.—Lucretia had a bunch of purple violets fastened in her girdle,—and with a forced smile she placed them in the hands of her dying friend. She looked at them a moment with a sort of abstracted attention, and an expression strangely unearthly, as she said, " I have thought that wild flowers might be the alphabet of angels,—whereby they write on hills and fields mysterious truths, which it is not given our fallen nature to understand. What think you, dear father ?"

" I think, my beloved child, that the truths we do comprehend are enough to support us through all our trials."

The confidence of the Christian was strong within him, when he spoke ; but he looked on his dying daughter, the only image of a wife dearly beloved,—and nature prevailed. He covered his eyes, and shook his white hairs mournfully, as he added, " God in his mercy grant, that we may find them sufficient in this dreadful struggle." All was again still,—still, in that chamber of death. The birds sung as sweetly as if there was no such thing as discord in the habitations of man ; and the blue sky was as bright as if earth were a stranger to ruin, and the human soul knew not of desolation. Twilight advanced, unmindful that weeping eyes watched her majestic and varied beauty. The silvery clouds, that composed her train, were fast sinking into a gorgeous column of gold and purple. It seemed as if celestial spirits were hovering around their mighty pavilion of light, and pressing the verge of the horizon with their glittering sandals.

Amid the rich variegated heaps of vapour, was one spot of clear bright cerulean. The deeply coloured and heavy masses that surrounded it, gave it the effect of distance ; so that it seemed like a portion of the inner heaven. Grace fixed her earnest gaze upon it, as a weary traveller does upon an Oasis in the desert. That awful lustre which the soul beams forth at its parting was in her eye, as she said, " I could almost fancy there are happy faces looking down to welcome me."

"It is very beautiful," said Lucretia in a subdued tone.
"It is such a sky as you loved to look upon, dear Grace."

"It is such an one as we loved," she answered. "There
was a time when it would have made me very happy; but
—my thoughts are now beyond it."

Her voice grew faint, and there was a quick gasp,—as
if the rush of memory was too powerful for her weak
frame

Doctor Willard hastily prepared a cordial, and offered
it to her lips. Those lips were white and motionless; her
long, fair eyelashes drooped, but trembled not.—He placed
his hand on her side;—the heart that had loved so well,
and endured so much, throbbed its last.

The Rose.—Mrs. Sigourney.

I saw a rose perfect in beauty; it rested gracefully
upon its stalk, and its perfume filled the air. Many stopped
to gaze upon it, many bowed to taste its fragrance, and its
owner hung over it with delight. I passed it again, and behold it was gone—its stem was leafless—its root had withered; the enclosure which surrounded it was broken down.
The spoiler had been there; he saw that many admired it;
he knew it was dear to him who planted it, and beside it he
had no other plant to love. Yet he snatched it secretly
from the hand that cherished it; he wore it on his bosom
till it hung its head and faded, and, when he saw that its
glory was departed, he flung it rudely away. But it left a
thorn in his bosom, and vainly did he seek to extract it;
for now it pierces the spoiler, even in his hour of mirth.
And when I saw that no man, who had loved the beauty
of the rose, gathered again its scattered leaves, or bound
up the stalk which the hands of violence had broken, I
looked earnestly at the spot where it grew, and my soul
received instruction. And I said, Let her who is full
of beauty and admiration, sitting like the queen of flowers in majesty among the daughters of women, let her
watch lest vanity enter her heart, beguiling her to rest

13

proudly upon her own strength; let her remember that she standeth upon slippery places, "and be not high minded, but fear"

---

*Influence of Female Character.—*THACHER.

THE influence of woman on the intellectual character of the community, may not seem so great and obvious as upon its civilization and manners. One reason is, that hitherto such influence has seldom been exerted in the most direct way of gaining celebrity—the writing of books. In our own age, indeed, this has almost ceased to be the case, and, if we should inquire for those persons, whose writings for the last half century have produced the most practical and enduring effects, prejudice itself must confess, that the name of more than one illustrious woman would adorn the catalogue.

That the society and influence of woman has often prompted and refined the efforts of genius, may be granted by the most zealous advocate for the superiority of our sex. From the hallowed retreats of the Port Royal issued the immortal writings of Pascal, Nicole and Racine; and the heavenly muse of Cowper had its inspiration nourished almost exclusively in the society of females. But, whatever may be thought of the influence of the sex in these particulars, there is one point of view in which it is undeniably great and important. The mother of your children is necessarily their first instructer. It is her task to watch over and assist their dawning faculties in their first expansion. And can it be of light importance in what manner this task is performed? Will it have no influence on the future mental character of the child, whether the first lights, which enter its understanding, are received from wisdom or folly? Are there no bad mental habits, no lasting biases, no dangerous associations, no deep-seated prejudices, which can be communicated from the mother, the fondest object of the affection and veneration of the child? In fine, do the opinions of the age take no direction and no colouring from the modes of thinking which prevail among one half of the minds that exist on earth? Unless you are willing to say that an incalculably great amount of mental power is utterly wasted and thrown away; or else, with a Turkish arrogance and brutality, to deny that woman shares with you in the possession of a reasoning and immortal mind; you must acknowledge the vast importance of the influence, which the female sex exerts on the intellectual character of the community.

But it is in its moral effects on the mind and the heart of man, that the influence of woman is most powerful and important. In the diversity of tastes, habits, inclinations and pursuits of the two sexes, is found a most beneficent provision for controlling the force and extravagance of human passions. The objects which most strongly seize and stimulate the mind of man, rarely act at the same time and with equal power on the mind of woman. While he delights in enterprise and action, and the exercise of the stronger energies of the soul, she is led to engage in calmer pursuits, and seek for gentler enjoyments. While he is summoned into the wide and busy theatre of a contentious world, where the love of power and the love of gain, in all their innumerable forms, occupy and tyrannise over the soul, she is walking in a more peaceful sphere; and though I say not that these passions are always unfelt by her, ye they lead her to the pursuit of very different objects. The current, if it draws its waters in both from the same source, moves with her not only in a narrower stream, and less impetuous tide, but sets also in a different direction. Hence it is that the influence of the society of woman is almost always to soften the violence of those impulses, which would otherwise act with so constant and fatal an influence on the soul of man. The domestic fireside is the great guardian of society against the excesses of human passions. When man, after his intercourse with the world, where, alas! he finds so much to inflame him with a feverous anxiety for wealth and distinction, retires at evening to the bosom of his family, he finds there a repose for his tormenting cares. He finds something to bring him back to human sympathies. The tenderness of his wife and the caresses of his children introduce a new train of softer thoughts and gentler feelings. He is reminded of

what constitutes the real felicity of man ; and, while his
neart expands itself to the influence of the simple and intimate delights of the domestic circle, the demons of avarice and ambition, if not exorcised from his breast, at least
for a time, relax their grasp.   How deplorable would be the
consequence if all these were reversed; and woman, instead of checking the violence of these passions, were to
employ her blandishments and charms to add fuel to their
rage !   How much wider would become the empire of
guilt !   What a portentous and intolerable amount would
be added to the sum of the crimes and miseries of the human race !

But the influence of the female character on the virtue
of man, is not seen merely in restraining and softening the
violence of human passions.   To her is mainly committed
the task of pouring into the opening mind of infancy its
first impressions of duty, and of stamping on its susceptible
heart the first image of its God.   Who will not confess the
influence of a mother in forming the heart of a child ?   What
man is there who cannot trace the origin of many of the best
maxims of his life to the lips of her who gave him birth ?
How wide, how lasting, how sacred is that part of woman's
influence !   Who that thinks of it, who that ascribes any
moral effect to education, who that believes that any good
may be produced, or any evil prevented by it can need
any arguments to prove the importance of the character
and capacity of her, who gives its earliest bias to the infant mind ?

There is yet another mode, by which woman may exert a powerful influence on the virtue of a community.   It
rests with her, in a pre-eminent degree, to give tone and
elevation to the moral character of the age, by deciding
the degree of virtue that shall be necessary to afford a
passport to her society.   The extent of this influence has
perhaps never been fully tried ; and, if the character of
our sex is not better, it is to be confessed that it is in no
trifling degree to be ascribed to the fault of yours.   If all
the favour of woman were given only to the good ; if it
were known that the charms and attractions of beauty, and
wisdom, and wit, were reserved only for the pure.; if, in
one word, something of a similar rigour were exerted to

exclude the profligate and abandoned of our sex from your society, as is shown to those, who have fallen from virtue in your own,—how much would be done to reenforce the motives to moral purity among us, and impress on the minds of all a reverence for the sanctity and obligations of virtue !

The influence of woman on the moral sentiments of society is intimately connected with her influence on its religious character ; for religion and a pure and elevated morality must ever stand in the relation to each other of effect and cause. The heart of woman is formed for the abode of Christian truth ; and for reasons alike honourable to her character and to that of the Gospel. From the nature of Christianity this must be so. The foundation of evangelical religion is laid in a deep and constant sense of the invisible presence, providence and influence of an invisible Spirit, who claims the adoration, reverence, gratitude and love of his creatures. By man, busied as he is in the cares, and absorbed in the pursuits of the world, this great truth is, alas! too often and too easily forgotten and disregarded ; while woman, less engrossed by occupation, more " at leisure to be good," led often by her duties to retirement, at a distance from many temptations, and endued with an imagination more easily excited and raised than man's, is better prepared to admit and cherish, and be affected by, this solemn and glorious acknowledgment of a God.

Again ; the Gospel reveals to us a Saviour, invested with little of that brilliant and dazzling glory, with which conquest and success would array him in the eyes of proud and aspiring man ; but rather as a meek and magnanimous sufferer, clothed in all the mild and passive graces, all the sympathy with human wo, all the compassion for human frailty, all the benevolent interest in human welfare, which the heart of woman is formed to love ; together with all that solemn and supernatural dignity, which the heart of woman is formed peculiarly to feel and to reverence. To obey the commands, and aspire to imitate the peculiar virtues, of such a being, must always be more natural and easy for her than for man.

13 *

So, too, it is with that future life which the Gospel un
veils, where all that is dark and doubtful in this shall be
explained; where penitence shall be forgiven, and faith
and virtue accepted; where the tear of sorrow shall be
dried, the wounded bosom of bereavement be healed;
where love and joy shall be unclouded and immortal.   To
these high and holy visions of faith I trust that man is not
always insensible; but the superior sensibility of woman,
as it makes her feel more deeply the emptiness and wants
of human existence here, so it makes her welcome with
more deep and ardent emotions the glad tidings of salvation,
the thought of communion with God, the hope of the purity, happiness and peace of another and a better world.

In this peculiar susceptibility of religion in the female
character, who does not discern a proof of the benignant
care of Heaven of the best interest of man? How wise
it is, that she, whose instructions and example must have
so powerful an influence on the infant mind, should be
formed to own and cherish the most sublime and important
of truths! The vestal flame of piety, lighted up by Heaven
in the breast of woman, diffuses its light and warmth over
the world;—and dark would be the world if it should ever
be extinguished and lost.

Character of James Monroe.*—WIRT.

In his stature, he is about the middle height of men,
rather firmly set, with nothing further remarkable in his
person, except his muscular compactness, and apparent
ability to endure labour.   His countenance, when grave,
has rather the expression of sternness and irascibility: a
smile, however, (and a smile is not unusual with him in a
social circle,) lights it up to very high advantage, and gives
t a most impressive and engaging air of suavity and benevolence.   Judging merely from his countenance, he is
between the ages of forty-five and fifty years.   His dress

---

* From " Letters of the British Spy," first published in 1806.

and personal appearance are those of a plain and modest gentleman.   He is a man of soft, polite, and even assiduous attentions ; but these, although they are always well timed, judicious, and evidently the offspring of an obliging and philanthropic temper, are never performed with the striking and captivating graces of a Marlborough or a Bolingbroke.   To be plain, there is often in his manner an inartificial and even an awkward simplicity, which, while t provokes the smile of a more polished person, forces him to the opinion, that Mr. Monroe is a man of a most sincere and artless soul.

Nature has given him a mind neither rapid nor rich ; and, therefore, he cannot shine on a subject which is entirely new to him.   But, to compensate him for this, he is endued with a spirit of restless and generous emulation, a judgment solid, strong and clear, and a habit of application, which no difficulties can shake, no labours tire.   With these aids, simply, he has qualified himself for the first honours of this country ; and presents a most happy illustration of the truth of the maxim, *Quisque, suæ fortunæ faber*.   For his emulation has urged him to perpetual and unremitting inquiry · his patient and unwearied industry has concentrated before him all the lights which others have thrown on the subjects of his consideration, together with all those which his own mind, by repeated efforts, is enabled to strike ; while his sober, steady and faithful judgment has saved him from the common error of more quick and brilliant geniuses—the too hasty adoption of specious, but false conclusions.

These qualities render him a safe and an able counsellor.   And by their constant exertion he has amassed a store of knowledge, which, having passed seven times through the crucible, is almost as highly corrected as human knowledge can be ; and which certainly may be much more safely relied on, than the spontaneous and luxuriant growth of a more fertile, but less chastened mind,—" a wild, where weeds and flowers promiscuous shoot."   Having engaged very early, first in the life of a soldier, then of a statesman. then of a laborious practitioner of the law, and finally again of a politician, his intellectual operations have been almost entirely confined to juridical and political topics

Indeed, it is easy to perceive, that the mind of a man engaged in so active a life must possess more native supple-
ness, versatility and vigour, than that of Mr. Monroe, to be
able to make an advantageous tour of the sciences in the
rare interval of importunate duties.   It is possible that the
early habit of contemplating subjects as expanded as the
earth itself, with all the relative interests of the great nations thereof, may have inspired him with an indifference,
perhaps an inaptitude, for mere points of literature.   Al-
gernon Sydney has said, that he deems all studies unwor
thy the serious regard of a man, except the study of the
principles of just government ; and Mr. Monroe, perhaps,
concurs with our countryman in this as well as in his other
principles.   Whatever may have been the occasion, his
acquaintance with the fine arts is certainly very limited
and superficial ; but, making allowances for his bias towards
republicanism, he is a profound and even an eloquent statesman.

Knowing him to be attached to that political party, who,
by their opponents, are sometimes called democrats, sometimes jacobins ; and aware also that he was a man of warm
and even ardent temper, I dreaded much, when I first entered his company, that I should have been shocked and
disgusted with the narrow, virulent, and rancorous invectives of party animosity.   How agreeably, how delightfully,
was I disappointed !   Not one sentiment of intolerance
polluted his lips.   On the contrary, whether they be the
offspring of rational induction, of the habit of surveying
men and things on a great scale, of native magnanimity,
or of a combination of all those causes, his principles, as
far as they were exhibited to me, were forbearing, liberal,
widely extended, and great.   As the elevated ground
which he already holds has been gained merely by the
lint of application ; as every new step which he mounts
becomes a mean of increasing his powers still further, by
opening a wider horizon to his view, and thus stimulating
his enterprise afresh, re-invigorating his habits, multiplying
the materials, and extending the range, of his knowledge,
it would be no matter of surprise to me, if before his death
the world should see him at the head of the American administration.   So much for the governor of the common-

wealth of Virginia.—a living, an honorable, an illustrious
monument of self-created eminence, worth and greatness!

The Stout Gentleman.   A Stage-coach Romance.—
IRVING

It was a rainy Sunday in the gloomy month of November. I had been detained, in the course of a journey, by
a slight indisposition, from which I was recovering ; but I
was still feverish, and was obliged to keep within doors
all day, in an inn of the small town of Derby. A wet
Sunday in a country inn—whoever has had the luck to ex
perience one can alone judge of my situation. The rain
pattered against the casements ; the bells tolled for church
with a melancholy sound. I went to the windows in quest
of something to amuse the eye ; but it seemed as if I had
been placed completely out of the reach of all amusement.
The windows of my bed-room looked out among tiled roofs
and stacks of chimneys, while those of my sitting-room
commanded a full view of the stable-yard. I know of
nothing more calculated to make a man sick of this world
than a stable-yard on a rainy day. The place was littered
with straw, that had been kicked about by travellers ar
stable-boys. In one corner was a stagnant pool of water
surrounding an island of muck ; there were several half
drowned fowls, crowded together under a cart, among
which was a miserable crest-fallen cock, drenched out of
all life and spirit, his drooping tail matted, as it were, into
a single feather, along which the water trickled from his
back ; near the cart was a half-dozing cow, chewing the
cud, and standing patiently to be rained on, with wreaths
of vapour rising from her reeking hide ; a wall-eyed horse,
tired of the loneliness of the stable, was poking his spectral head out of a window, with the rain dripping on it
from the eaves ; an unhappy cur, chained to a dog-house
hard by, uttered something every now and then between
a bark and a yelp ; a drab of a kitchen wench tramped
backwards and forwards through the yard in pattens, looking as sulky as the weather itself ; every thing, in short

was comfortless and forlorn, excepting a crew of hard-drink-
ing ducks, assembled like boon companions round a puddle,
and making a riotous noise over their liquor.

I was lonely and listless, and wanted amusement. My
room soon became insupportable : I abandoned it, and sought
what is technically called the travellers' room. This is a
public room set apart at most inns for the accommodation
of a class of wayfarers, called travellers, or riders,—a kind
of commercial knights-errant, who are incessantly scouring the kingdom in gigs, on horseback, or by coach. They
are the only successors that I know of, at the present day,
to the knights-errant of yore. They lead the same kind
of roving, adventurous life, only changing the lance for a
driving-whip, the buckler for a pattern-card, and the coat
of mail for an upper-Benjamin. Instead of vindicating
the charms of peerless beauty, they rove about, spreading
the fame and standing of some substantial tradesman or
manufacturer, and are ready at any time to bargain in his
name ; it being the fashion now-a-days to trade instead of
fight with one another. As the room of the hostel, in the
good old fighting times, would be hung round at night
with the armour of way-worn warriors—such as coats of
mail, falchions and yawning helmets ; so the travellers'
room is garnished with the harnessing of their successors,—
with box-coats, whips of all kinds, spurs, gaiters, and oil-
cloth covered hats.

I was in hopes of finding some of these worthies to talk
with, but was disappointed. There were, indeed, two or
three in the room ; but I could make nothing of them-
One was just finishing his breakfast, quarrelling with his
bread and butter, and huffing the waiter ; another buttoned on a pair of gaiters, with many execrations at Boots for
not having cleaned his shoes well ; a third sat drumming
on the table with his fingers, and looking at the rain as it
streamed down the window-glass ; they all appeared infected with the weather, and disappeared, one after the
other, without exchanging a word.

I sauntered to the window, and stood gazing at the people picking their way to church, with petticoats hoisted
mid-leg high, and dripping umbrellas. The bell ceased to
toll, and the streets became silent. I then amused myself

with watching the daughters of a tradesman opposite, who, being confined to the house for fear of wetting their Sunday finery, played off their charms at the front windows to fascinate the chance tenants of the inn. They at length were summoned away by a vigilant, vinegar-faced mother and I had nothing further from without to amuse me.

What was I to do to pass away the long-lived day? I was sadly nervous and lonely; and every thing about an inn seems calculated to make a dull day ten times duller: old newspapers, smelling of beer and tobacco smoke, and which I had already read half a dozen times; good-for-nothing books, that were worse than rainy weather. I bored myself to death with an old volume of the Lady's Magazine. I read all the common-place names of ambitious travellers scrawled on the panes of glass; the eternal families of the Smiths and the Browns, and the Jacksons and the Johnsons, and all the other sons; and I deciphered several scraps of fatiguing inn-window poetry, which I have met with in all parts of the world.

The day continued lowering and gloomy; the slovenly, ragged, spongy clouds drifted heavily along; there was no variety even in the rain; it was one dull, continued, monotonous patter—patter—patter, except that now and then I was enlivened by the idea of a brisk shower, from the rattling of the drops upon a passing umbrella.

It was quite refreshing (if I may be allowed a hackneyed phrase of the day) when, in the course of the morning, a horn blew, and a stage-coach whirled through the street, with outside passengers stuck all over it, cowering under cotton umbrellas, and seethed together, and reeking with the steams of wet box-coats and upper Benjamins. The sound brought out from their lurking-places a crew of vagabond boys and vagabond dogs, and the carroty-headed hostler, and that non-descript animal yclept Boots, and all the other vagabond race that infest the purlieus of an inn: but the bustle was transient; the coach again whirled on its way, and boy and dog, and hostler and Boots, all slunk back again to their holes; the street again became silent, and the rain continued to rain on. In fact there was no hope of its clearing up: the barometer pointed to rainy weather; mine hostess' tortoise-shell cat sat by the fire

washing her face, and rubbing her paws over her ears
and, on referring to the almanac, I found a direful prediction stretching from the top of the page to the bottom,
through the whole month, "Expect—much—rain—about
—this—time."

I was dreadfully hipped. The hours seemed as if they
would never creep by. The very ticking of the clock became irksome. At length the stillness of the house was
interrupted by the ringing of a bell. Shortly after, I heard
the voice of a waiter at the bar,—" The stout gentleman in
No. 13 wants his breakfast. Tea and bread and butter,
with ham and eggs; the eggs not to be too much done."
In such a situation as mine, every incident was of importance. Here was a subject of speculation presented to my
mind ; and ample exercise for my imagination. I am prone
to paint pictures to myself, and on this occasion I had some
materials to work upon. Had the guest up stairs been mentioned as Mr. Smith, or Mr. Brown, or Mr. Jackson, or
merely as " the gentleman in No. 13," it would have been
a perfect blank to me ; I should have thought nothing of
it ; but " the stout gentleman !"—the very name had
something in it of the picturesque. It at once gave the
size ; it imbodied the personage to my mind's eye, and my
fancy did the rest. He was stout, or, as some term it,
lusty ; in all probability, therefore, he was advanced in
life, some people expanding as they grow old. By his
breakfasting rather late, and in his own room, he must be
a man accustomed to live at his ease, and above the necessity of early rising ; no doubt a round, rosy, lusty old gentleman.

There was another violent ringing; the stout gentleman
was impatient for his breakfast. He was evidently a man
of importance ; " well to do in the world ;" accustomed to
be promptly waited upon ; of a keen appetite, and a little
cross when hungry. " Perhaps," thought I, " he may be
some London alderman ; or who knows but he may be a
member of parliament."

The breakfast was sent up, and there was a short interval of silence ; he was doubtless making the tea. Presently
there was a violent ringing, and, before it could be answered,
another ringing still more violent. " Bless me ! what a

choleric old gentleman!" The waiter came down in a huff. The butter was rancid; the eggs were overdone; the ham too salt. The stout gentleman was evidently nice in his eating; one of those who eat and growl, and keep the waiter on the trot, and live in a state militant with the household. The hostess got into a fume. I should observe that she was a brisk, coquettish woman; a little of a shrew, and something of a slammerkin, but very pretty withal; with a nincompoop for a husband, as shrews are apt to have. She rated the servants roundly, for their negligence in sending up so bad a breakfast, but said not a word against the stout gentleman; by which I clearly perceived that he must be a man of consequence, entitled to make a noise, and to give trouble at a country inn. Other eggs and ham, and bread and butter, were sent up. They appeared to be more graciously received; at least there was no further complaint. I had not made many turns about the travellers' room, when there was another ringing. Shortly afterwards there was a stir and an inquest about the house. The stout gentleman wanted the Times or Chronicle newspaper. I set him down therefore for a whig; or rather, from his being so absolute and lordly where he had a chance, I suspected him of being a radical. Hunt, I had heard, was a large man; "Who knows," thought I, " but it is Hunt himself?"

My curiosity began to be awakened. I inquired of the waiter, who was this stout gentleman, that was making all this stir; but I could get no information. Nobody seemed to know his name. The landlords of bustling inns seldom trouble their heads about the names or occupations of transient guests. The colour of the coat, the shape or size of the person, is enough to suggest a travelling name. It is either the tall gentleman, or the short gentleman, or the gentleman in black, or the gentleman in snuff colour, or, as in the present instance, the stout gentleman: a designation of the kind once hit on, answers every purpose, and saves all further inquiry.—Rain—rain—rain! pitiless, ceaseless rain! No such thing as putting a foot out of doors, and no occupation or amusement within. By and by I heard some one walking over head. It was in the stout gentleman's room. He evidently was a large man, by the heaviness of his tread; and an old man, from his wearing

14

such creaking soles. " He is doubtless," thought I, " some rich old square-toes, of regular habits, and is now taking exercise after breakfast."

I had to go to work at this picture again, and to pain him entirely different. I now set him down for one of those stout gentlemen, that are frequently met with, swaggering about the doors of country inns : moist, merry fellows, in Belcher handkerchiefs, whose bulk is a little assisted by malt liquors : men who have seen the world, and been sworn at High-gate ; who are used to tavern life ; up to all the tricks of tapsters, and knowing in the ways of sinful publicans ; free livers on a small scale, who are prod igal within the compass of a guinea ; who call all the waiters by name, tousle the maids, gossip with the landlady at the bar, and prose over a pint of port, or a glass of negus after dinner. The morning wore away in forming of these and similar surmises. As fast as I wove one system of belief, some movement of the unknown would completely overthrow it, and throw all my thoughts again into confusion. Such are the solitary operations of a feverish mind I was, as I have said, extremely nervous ; and the continual meditation on the concerns of this invisible personage began to have its effect. Dinner time came. I hoped the stout gentleman might dine in the travellers' room, and that I might at length get a view of his person ; but no, he had dinner served in his own room. What could be the meaning of this solitude and mystery ? He could not be a radical ; there was something too aristocratical in thus keeping himself apart from the rest of the world, and condemning himself to his own dull company through a rainy day. And then, too, he lived too well for a discontented politician. He seemed to expatiate on a variety of dishes, and to sit over his wine like a jolly friend of good living. Indeed, my doubts on this head were soon at an end ; for he could not have finished his first bottle, before I could faintly hear him humming a tune ; and, on listening, I found it to be " God save the King." 'Twas plain, then, he was no radical, but a faithful subject ; one that grew loyal over his bottle, and was ready to stand by King and Constitution when he could stand by nothing else. But who could he be ? My conjectures began to run wild. Was

he not some person of distinction travelling *incog.* ? "Who
knows ?" said I, at my wit's end ; " it may be one of the
royal family, for aught I know, for they are all stout gentlemen !" The weather continued rainy. The mysterious
unknown kept his room, and, as far as I could judge, his
chair, for I did not hear him move. In the mean time, as
the day advanced, the travellers' room began to be frequented. Some, who had just arrived, came in buttoned up in
box-coats ; others came home, who had been dispersed
about the town. Some took their dinners, and some their
tea. Had I been in a different mood, I should have found
entertainment in studying this peculiar class of men. There
were two, especially, who were regular wags of the road,
and up to all the standing jokes of travellers. They had
a thousand sly things to say to the waiting maid, whom
they called Louisa and Ethelinda, and a dozen other fine
names, changing the name every time, and chuckling
amazingly at their own waggery. My mind, however,
had become completely engrossed by the stout gentleman
He had kept my fancy in chase during a long day, and it
was not now to be diverted from the scent.

The evening gradually wore away ; the travellers read
the papers two or three times over ; some drew round the
fire, and told long stories about their horses, about their adventures, their overturns and breakings down. They discussed the credit of different merchants and different inns.
And the two wags told several choice anecdotes of pretty
chambermaids and landladies. All this passed as they were
quietly taking what they called their night-caps, that is to
say, strong glasses of brandy and water and sugar, or some
other mixture of the kind, after which they, one after
another, rang for Boots and the chambermaid, and walked
off to bed in old shoes cut down into marvellously uncomfortable slippers. There was only one man left—a short-
legged, long-bodied, plethoric fellow, with a very large,
sandy head. He sat by himself with a glass of port-wine
negus and a spoon ; sipping and stirring, and meditating
and sipping, until nothing was left but the spoon. He
gradually fell asleep, but upright in his chair, with the
empty glass standing before him ; and the candle seemed
to fall asleep too, for the wick grew long, and black, and

cabbaged at the end, and dimmed the little light that remained in the chamber. The gloom that now prevailed
was contagious. Around hung the shapeless and almost
spectral box-coats of the travellers, long since buried in
deep sleep. I only heard the ticking of the clock, with
the deep-drawn breathings of the sleeping toper, and the
drippings of the rain,—drop—drop—drop,—from the eaves
of the house. The church bells chimed midnight. All at
once the stout gentleman began to walk over head, pacing
slowly backwards and forwards. There was something extremely awful in all this, especially to one in my state of
nerves,—these ghastly great-coats, these guttural breath
ings, and the creaking footsteps of this mysterious gentleman. His steps grew fainter and fainter, and at length
died away. I could bear it no longer. I was wound up
to the desperation of a hero of romance. " Be he who or
what he may," said I to myself, " I'll have a sight of
him !" I seized a chamber-candle, and hurried up to No
13. The door stood ajar. I hesitated,—I entered. The
room was deserted. There stood a large broad-bottomed
elbow-chair at a table, on which was an empty tumbler,
and a Times newspaper ; and the room smelt powerfully
of Stilton cheese. The mysterious stranger had evidently
just retired. I turned off, sorely disappointed, to my room,
which had been changed to the front of the house. As I
went along the corridor, I saw a large pair of boots, with
dirty, waxed tops, standing at the door of a bed-chamber.
They doubtless belonged to the unknown ; but it would
not do to disturb so redoubtable a person in his den. He
might discharge a pistol, or something worse, at my head.
I went to bed, therefore, and lay awake half the night in
a terribly nervous state, and, even when I fell asleep, I
was still haunted by the idea of the stout gentleman and
his wax-topped boots.

　　I slept rather late the next morning, and was awakened
by some stir or bustle in the house, which I could not at
first comprehend ; until, getting more awake, I found there
was a mail coach starting from the door. Suddenly there
was a cry from below, " The gentleman has forgotten his
umbrella ! look for the gentleman's umbrella in No. 13 !"
I heard an immediate scampering of a chambermaid along

the passage, and a shrill reply as she ran, " Here it is,
here's the gentleman's umbrella !"   The mysterious stranger was, then, on the point of setting off.   This was the
only chance I could ever have of knowing him.   1 sprang
out of bed, scrambled to the window, snatched aside the
curtains, and just caught a glimpse at the rear of a person,
getting in at the coach-door.   The skirts of a brown coat
parted behind, and gave me a full view of the broad disk
of a pair of drab breeches.   The door closed.   "All
right !" was the word,—the coach whirled off,—and that
was all I ever saw of the stout gentleman.

Patriotism and Eloquence of John Adams.—WEBSTER

HE possessed a bold spirit, which disregarded danger,
and a sanguine reliance on the goodness of the cause and
the virtues of the people, which led him to overlook all
obstacles.   His character, too, had been formed in troubled
times.   He had been rocked in the early storms of the controversy, and had acquired a decision and a hardihood,
proportioned to the severity of the discipline which he had
undergone.

He not only loved the American cause devoutly, but
had studied and understood it.   He had tried his powers,
on the questions which it involved, often, and in various
ways ; and had brought to their consideration wha'ever
of argument or illustration the history of his own country,
the history of England, or the stores of ancient or of legal
learning could furnish.   Every grievance enumerated in
the long catalogue of the Declaration, had been the subject of his discussion, and the object of his remonstrance
and reprobation.   From 1760, the colonies, the rights of
the colonies, the liberties of the colonies, and the wrongs
inflicted on the colonies, had engaged his constant attention ; and it has surprised those, who have had the opportunity of observing, with what full remembrance. and with
what prompt recollection, he could refer, in his extreme
old age, to every act of parliament affecting the colonies,
distinguishing and stating their respective titles, sections
14 *

and provisions; and to all the colonial memorials, remon
strances and petitions, with whatever else belonged to the
intimate and exact history of the times, from that year to
1775. It was, in his own judgment, between these years,
that the American people came to a full understanding
and thorough knowledge of their rights, and to a fixed resolution of maintaining them; and, bearing himself an active part in all important transactions, the controversy with
England being then, in effect, the business of his life, facts,
dates and particulars made an impression which was never
effaced. He was prepared, therefore, by education and
discipline, as well as by natural talent and natural temper-
ament, for the part which he was now to act.

The eloquence of Mr. Adams resembled his general
character, and formed, indeed, a part of it. It was bold,
manly and energetic; and such the crisis required.
When public bodies are to be addressed on momentous occasions, when great interests are at stake, and strong passions excited, nothing is valuable in speech, further than it
is connected with high intellectual and moral endowments
Clearness, force and earnestness are the qualities which
produce conviction. True eloquence, indeed, does not
consist in speech. It cannot be brought from far. Labour
and learning may toil for it, but they will toil in vain.
Words and phrases may be marshalled in every way, but
they cannot compass it. It must exist in the man, in the
subject, and in the occasion. Affected passion, intense expression, the pomp of declamation, all may aspire after it—
they cannot reach it. It comes, if it come at all, like the
outbreaking of a fountain from the earth, or the bursting
forth of volcanic fires, with spontaneous, original, native
force. The graces taught in the schools, the costly ornaments, and studied contrivances of speech, shock and disgust men, when their own lives, and the fate of their
wives, their children, and their country, hang on the decision of the hour. Then words have lost their power,
rhetoric is vain, and all elaborate oratory contemptible.
Even genius itself then feels rebuked, and subdued, as in
the presence of higher qualities. Then patriotism is eloquent; then self-devotion is eloquent. The clear conception, out-running the deductions of logic, the high purpose,

the firm resolve, the dauntless spirit, speaking on the tongue, beaming from the eye, informing every feature, and urging the whole man onward, right onward to his object—this, this is eloquence; or, rather, it is something greater and higher than all eloquence—it is action, noble, sublime, godlike action.

In July, 1776, the controversy had passed the stage of argument. An appeal had been made to force, and opposing armies were in the field. Congress, then, was to decide whether the tie, which had so long bound us to the parent State, was to be severed at once, and severed forever. All the colonies had signified their resolution to abide by this decision, and the people looked for it with the most intense anxiety. And surely, fellow-citizens, never, never were men called to a more important political deliberation. If we contemplate it from the point where they then stood, no question could be more full of interest; if we look at it now, and judge of its importance by its effects, it appears in still greater magnitude.

Let us, then, bring before us the assembly, which was about to decide a question thus big with the fate of empire. Let us open their doors, and look in upon their deliberations Let us survey the anxious and care-worn countenances, let us hear the firm-toned voices, of this band of patriots.

Hancock presides over the solemn sitting; and one of those not yet prepared to pronounce for absolute independence, is on the floor, and is urging his reasons for dissenting from the Declaration.

* * * * * * * * * * * *

It was for Mr. Adams to reply to arguments like these. We know his opinions, and we know his character. He would commence with his accustomed directness and earnestness.

" Sink or swim, live or die, survive or perish, I give my hand, and my heart, to this vote. It is true, indeed, that, in the beginning, we aimed not at independence. But there's a Divinity which shapes our ends. The injustice of England has driven us to arms; and, blinded to her own interest, for our good, she has obstinately persisted, till independence is now within our grasp. We have but

reach forth to it, and it is ours. Why then should we de
fer the Declaration ? Is any man so weak as now to hope
for a reconciliation with England, which shall leave either
safety to the country and its liberties, or safety to his own
life, and his own honour ? Are not you, sir, who sit in that
chair, is not he, our venerable colleague near you, are you
not both already the proscribed and predestined objects of
punishment and of vengeance ? Cut off from all hope of
royal clemency, what are you, what can you be, while
the power of England remains, but outlaws ? If we postpone independence, do we mean to carry on, or to give up
the war ? Do we mean to submit to the measures of parliament, Boston port-bill and all ? Do we mean to submit,
and consent that we ourselves shall be ground to powder,
and our country and its rights trodden down in the dust ?
I know we do not mean to submit. We never shall submit. Do we intend to violate that most solemn obligation
ever entered into by men, that plighting, before God, of
our sacred honour to Washington, when, putting him forth
to incur the dangers of war, as well as the political hazards of the times, we promised to adhere to him, in every
extremity, with our fortunes and our lives ? I know there
is not a man here, who would not rather see a general
conflagration sweep over the land, or an earthquake sink
it, than one jot or tittle of that plighted faith fall to the
ground. For myself, having, twelve months ago, in this
place, moved you that George Washington be appointed
commander of the forces, raised or to be raised, for defence
of American liberty, may my right hand forget her cunning, and my tongue cleave to the roof of my mouth, if
I hesitate or waver, in the support I give him. The war,
then, must go on. We must fight it through. And if the
war must go on, why put off longer the Declaration of Independence ? That measure will strengthen us. It will
give us character abroad. The nations will then treat with
us, which they never can do while we acknowledge ourselves subjects, in arms against our sovereign. Nay, I
maintain that England herself will sooner treat for peace
with us on the footing of independence, than consent, by
repealing her acts, to acknowledge that her whole conduct
towards us has been a course of injustice and oppression

Her pride will be less wounded, by submitting to that course of things which now predestinates our independence, than by yielding the points in controversy to her rebellious subjects. The former she would regard as the result of fortune ; the latter she would feel as her own deep disgrace. Why then, why then, sir, do we not, as soon as possible, change this from a civil to a national war ? And, since we must fight it through, why not put ourselves in a state to enjoy all the benefits of victory, if we gain the victory ?

"If we fail, it can be no worse for us. But we shall not fail. The cause will raise up armies; the cause will create navies. The people, the people, if we are true to them, will carry us, and will carry themselves, gloriously through this struggle. I care not how fickle other people have been found. I know the people of these colonies, and I know that resistance to British aggression is deep and settled in their hearts, and cannot be eradicated. Every colony, indeed, has expressed its willingness to follow, if we but take the lead. Sir, the Declaration will inspire the people with increased courage. Instead of a long and bloody war for restoration of privileges, for redress of grievances, for chartered immunities, held under a British king, set before them the glorious object of entire independence, and it will breathe into them anew the breath of life. Read this Declaration at the head of the army every sword will be drawn from its scabbard, and the solemn vow uttered, to maintain it, or to perish on the bed of honour. Publish it from the pulpit; religion will approve it, and the love of religious liberty will cling round it, resolved to stand with it, or fall with it. Send it to the public halls; proclaim it there ; let them hear it, who heard the first roar of the enemy's cannon ; let them see it, who saw their brothers and their sons fall on the field of Bunker Hill, and in the streets of Lexington and Concord, and the very walls will cry out in its support.

"Sir, I know the uncertainty of human affairs, but I see, I see clearly, through this day's business. You and I indeed, may rue it. We may not live to the time when this Declaration shall be made good. We may die ; die, colonists ; die, slaves ; die, it may be, ignominiously, and on the scaffold. Be it so. Be it so. If it be the pleasure

of Heaven that my country shall require the poor offering
of my life, the victim shall be ready, at the appointed hour
of sacrifice, come when that hour may.   But, while I do
live, let me have a country, or at least the hope of a country, and that a free country.

"But, whatever may be our fate, be assured, be assured,
that this Declaration will stand.   It may cost treasure, and
it may cost blood ; but it will stand, and it will richly compensate for both.   Through the thick gloom of the present,
I see the brightness of the future, as the sun in heaven
We shall make this a glorious, an immortal day.   When
we are in our graves, our children will honour it.   They
will celebrate it with thanksgiving, with festivity, with
bonfires and illuminations.   On its annual return they will
shed tears, copious, gushing tears, not of subjection and
slavery, not of agony and distress, but of exultation, of
gratitude, and of joy.   Sir, before God, I believe the hour
is come.   My judgment approves this measure, and my
whole heart is in it.   All that I have, and all that I am,
and all that I hope in this life, I am now ready here to
stake upon it; and I leave off, as I begun, that, live or die,
survive or perish, I am for the Declaration.   It is my living sentiment, and, by the blessing of God, it shall be my
dying sentiment—independence *now ;* and INDEPEN-
DENCE FOREVER !"

Description of the Speedwell Mine in England —
SILLIMAN.

WE entered a wooden door, placed in the side of a hill
and descended one hundred and six stone steps, laid like
those of a set of cellar stairs.   The passage was regularly
arched with brick, and was in all respects convenient.

Having reached the bottom of the steps, we found a
handsome vaulted passage cut through solid limestone.
The light of our candles discovered that it extended hori-
zontally into the mountain, and its floor was covered with an
unruffled expanse of water, four feet deep.   The entrance
of this passage was perfectly similar in form to the mouth

of a common oven, only it was much larger. Its breadth,
by my estimation, was about five feet at the water's surface, and its height four or five feet, reckoning from the
same place.

On this unexpected, and to me, at that moment, *incomprehensible* canal, we found launched a large, clean and
convenient boat.

We embarked, and pulled ourselves along, by taking
hold of wooden pegs, fixed for that purpose in the walls.
Our progress was through a passage wholly artificial, it
having been all blasted and hewn out of the solid rock.
You will readily believe that this adventure was a delightful recreation. I never felt more forcibly the power of
contrast. Instead of crawling through a narrow, dirty passage, we were now pleasantly embarked, and were pushing along into I knew not what solitary regions of this rude
earth, over an expanse as serene as summer seas. We
had not the odours nor the silken sails of Cleopatra's barge,
but we excelled her in melody of sound, and distinctness
of echo; for, when, in the gayety of my spirits, I began
to sing, the boatman soon gave me to understand that no
one should sing in his mountain, without his permission;
and, before I had uttered three notes, he broke forth in
such a strain, that I was contented to listen, and yield the
palm without a contest.

His voice, which was strong, clear and melodious, made
all those silent regions ring; the long, vaulted passage
augmented the effect; echo answered with great distinctness, and had the genii of the mountain been there, they
would doubtless have taken passage with us, and hearken-
ed to the song. In the mean time we began to hear the
sound of a distant water-fall, which grew louder and louder, as we advanced under the mountain, till it increased
to such a roaring noise that the boatman could no longer
be heard. In this manner we went on, a quarter of a mile,
till we arrived in a vast cavern formed there by nature.
The miners, as they were blasting the rocks, at the time
when they were forming the vaulted passage, accidentally
opened their way into this cavern. Here I discovered how
the canal was supplied with water;—I found that it communicated with a river running through the cavern at

right angles with the arched passage, and falling down a precipice twenty-five feet into a dark abyss.

After crossing the river, the arched way is continued a quarter of a mile farther, on the other side, making in the whole half a mile from the entrance. The end of the arch is six hundred feet below the summit of the mountain. When it is considered that all this was effected by mere dint of hewing and blasting, it must be pronounced a stupendous performance. It took eleven years of constant labour to effect it. In the mean time the fortune of the adventurer was consumed, without any discovery of ore, except a very little lead, and, to this day, this great work remains only a wonderful monument of human labour and perseverance.

During the whole period of five years that they continued this work, after they crossed the cavern, they threw the rubbish into the abyss, and it has not sensibly filled it up.

They have contrived to increase the effect of the cataract by fixing a gate along the ledge of rocks over which the river falls. This gate is raised by a lever, and then the whole mass of water in the vaulted passage, as well as that in the river, presses forward towards the cataract. I ascended a ladder made by pieces of timber fixed in the sides of the cavern, and, with the aid of a candle elevated on a pole, I could discover no top; my guide assured me that none had been found, although they had ascended very high. This cavern is, without exception, the most grand and solemn place that I have ever seen. When you view me as in the centre of a mountain, in the midst of a void, where the regularity of the walls looks like some vast rotunda: when you think of a river as flowing across the bottom of this cavern, and falling abruptly into a profound abyss, with the stunning noise of a cataract; when you imagine. that, by the light of a fire-work of gun-powder, played off on purpose to render this darkness visible, the foam of the cataract is illuminated even down to the surface of the water in the abyss. and the rays emitted by the livid blaze of this preparation are reflected along the dripping walls of the cavern till they are lost in the darker regions above. you will not wonder that such a scene should seize on my

whole soul, and fill me with awe and astonishment, causing me to exclaim, as I involuntarily did, *Marvellous are
thy works, Lord God Almighty!*

After ascending from the navigation mine, I attempted
to go up the front of one of the mountains, with the double
purpose of obtaining a view of the valley from an elevated
point, and of reaching the ancient castle. But my labour
proved fruitless; the mountain, which from the valley
seemed not difficult to ascend, proved to be exceedingly
steep. I toiled on, two thirds of the way up, and finding
it steeper and steeper, and still resolved not to relinquish
my purpose; in the mean time it grew dark, with the decay of twilight, and I was suddenly enveloped in mist and
rain; the steep side of the mountain became very slippery;
I fell frequently, and, at length, a deep and abrupt chasm,
torn by the floods, completely arrested my progress, and
compelled me to make the best of my way down, which I
did with no small difficulty. In the midst of darkness and
rain, I reached the Castle-Inn, completely drenched, and
exhausted with fatigue.

Effects of the modern Diffusion of Knowledge.—
WAYLAND.

In consequence of this general diffusion of intelligence,
nations are becoming vastly better acquainted with the
physical, moral and political conditions of each other.
Whatever of any moment is transacted in the legislative
assemblies of one country is now very soon known, not
merely to the rulers, but also to the people, of every other
country. Nay, an interesting occurrence of any nature
cannot transpire in an insignificant town of Europe or
America, without finding its way, through the medium of
the national journals, to the eyes and ears of all Christendom. Every man must now be in a considerable degree
a spectator of the doings of the world, or he is soon very
far in the rear of the intelligence of the day. Indeed, he
has only to read a respectable newspaper, and he may
informed of the discoveries in the arts, the disc

15

the senates, and the bearings of public opinion all over the world.

The reasons of all this may chiefly be found in that increased desire of information, which characterizes the mass of society in the present age. Intelligence of every kind, and specially political information, has become an article of profit; and when once this is the case, there can be no doubt that it will be abundantly supplied. Besides this, it is important to remark, that the art of navigation has been within a few years materially improved, and commercial relations have become vastly more extensive. The establishment of packet ships between the two continents has brought London and Paris as near to us as Pittsburgh and New Orleans. There is every reason to believe, that, within the next half century, steam navigation will render communication between the ports of Europe and America as frequent, and almost as regular, as that by ordinary mails. The commercial houses of every nation are establishing their agencies in the principal cities of every other nation, and thus binding together the people by every tie of interest; while at the same time they are furnishing innumerable channels, by which information may be circulated among every class of the community.

Hence it is, that the moral influence which nations are exerting upon each other, is greater than it has been at any antecedent period in the history of the world. The institutions of our country are becoming known, almost of necessity, to every other country. Knowledge provokes to comparison, and comparison leads to reflection. The fact that others are happier than themselves prompts men to inquire whence this difference proceeds, and how their own melioration may be accomplished. By simply looking upon a free people, an oppressed people instinctively feel that they have inalienable rights, and they will never afterwards be at rest, until the enjoyment of these rights is guarantied to them. Thus one form of government, which in any pre-eminent degree promotes the happiness of man, is gradually but irresistibly disseminating the principles of its constitution, and, from the very fact of its existence, calling into being those trains of thought, which must in the end revolutionize every government within the sphere of its influence, under which the people are oppressed.

And thus is it that the field, in which mind may labour, has now become wide as the limits of civilization. A doc trine advanced by one man, if it have any claim to interest, is soon known to every other man. The movement of one intellect now sets in motion the intellects of millions. We may now calculate upon effects, not upon a state or a people, but upon the melting, amalgamating mass of human nature. Man is now the instrument which genius wields at its will; it touches a chord of the human heart, and nations vibrate in unison. And thus he who can rivet the attention of a community upon an elementary principle hitherto neglected in politics or morals, or who can bring an acknowledged principle to bear upon an existing abuse, may, by his own intellectual might, with only the assistance of the press, transform the institutions of an empire or a world.

In many respects the nations of Christendom collectively are becoming somewhat analogous to our own Federal Republic. Antiquated distinctions are breaking away, and local animosities are subsiding. The common people of different countries are knowing each other better, esteeming each other more, and attaching themselves to each other by various manifestations of reciprocal good will. It is true, every nation has still its separate boundaries, and its individual interests; but the freedom of commercial intercourse is allowing those interests to adjust themselves to each other, and thus rendering the causes of collision of vastly less frequent occurrence. Local questions are becoming of less, and general questions of greater importance. Thanks be to God, men have at last begun to understand the rights, and feel for the wrongs, of each other. Mountains interposed do not so much make enemies of nations. Let the trumpet of alarm be sounded, and its notes are now heard by every nation, whether of Europe or America. Let a voice, borne on the feeblest breeze, tell that the rights of man are in danger, and it floats over valley and mountain, across continent and ocean, until it has vibrated on the ear of the remotest dweller in Christendom. Let the arm of oppression be raised to crush the feeblest nation on earth, and there will be heard every where, if not the shout of defiance, at least the deep-toned murmur of implacable displeasure. It is the cry of aggrieved, insulted, much-abused man. It is Human Nature waking in her might from the slumber of ages, shaking herself from the dust of antiquated institutions, girding herself for the combat, and going forth conquering and to conquer; and wo unto the man, wo unto the dynasty, wo unto the party, and wo unto the policy, on whom shall fall the scath of her blighting indignation.

The Love of human Estimation.—BUCKMINSTER.

Is it true that a passion of such powerful and various operation, as that we have now been considering, is no where recommended 'n Scripture as a motive of action? Are we no where referred to the opinion of the world, no where expostulated with from a regard to reputation? Are there no appeals made by any of the messengers of God's will to our sense of shame, to our pride, to our ambition, to our vanity? Certain it is that such appeals are at least rarely to be met with. Our Saviour, indeed, seems to have thought it hazardous, in any degree, to encourage a regard to the opinion of the world as a motive to action, because, however advantageous might be its operation in some instances, where a higher principle was wanting, still the most casual recommendation of a sentiment so natural, so seducing, and so universal, would have been liable to perpetual misconstruction and abuse.

Indeed, no man can read the discourses of our Saviour, or of his apostles, without observing how utterly they are at war with the spirit of self-aggrandizement. Perhaps, however, you may expect, that I should refer you to examples where this temper is clearly censured or punished. What think you, then, of the history of Herod Agrippa? "On a set day," says the historian, "Herod, arrayed in royal apparel, sat upon his throne, and made an oration unto the people. And the people gave a shout, saying, It is the voice of a god, and not of a man. And immediately the angel of the Lord smote him, because he gave not God the glory ; and he was eaten of worms, and gave up the ghost." I make no comments on this story. It is too sol emn. Think only, if such was the punishment of a man for accepting the idolatrous flattery offered him, can they be guiltless in the eyes of Heaven, who cannot live but upon the honey of adulation, and whose whole life is but a continual series of contrivances to gain the favour of the multitude, a continual preference of the glory of themselves to the glory of their Creator ? Is not this example of the requisitions of the Gospel sufficient ? Read then the dreadful woes denounced against the Jewish rulers, not merely because they did not receive our Saviour, nor merely because they were continually meditating his destruction; but because they did all their works to be seen of men.

But as nothing, perhaps, is gained in point of practical improvement, by pushing these principles of indifference to the world to an extreme, or in declaiming indiscriminately against any prevailing sentiment of extensive influence, before we consider the restrictions under which the love of fame should be laid in the mind of a Christian, we will, as we proposed, endeavour to ascertain, and candidly to allow, all those advantages, which may result from this regard to the opinion of others, when more pure and evangelical motives are either wanting or not sufficiently established.

Here, then, we will allow, that much of the real as well as fictitious excellence, which has adorned the world, may be traced, in some degree, to the principle of emulation. We allow, that it calls forth the energies of the young mind ; that it matures in our colleges and schools some of the earliest products of youthful capacity ; and that it offers incalculable aid to the lessons and to the discipline of instructers. When we look at our libraries, we can hardly find a volume, which does not, in a measure, owe its appearance to the love of fame. When we gaze on the ruins of ancient magnificence, or the rare remains of ancient skill, we are obliged to confess, that we owe these to the influence of emulation. Nay, more, when we read the lives of great men, and are lost in wonder at their astonishing intellectual supremacy, we are compelled to acknowledge, that for this we are partly indebted to the love

15 *

of fame. We acknowledge, also, that it often supplies successfully the place of nobler motives ; and that, notwithstanding the evils which grow out of its abuse, the world would suffer from its utter extinction. For the weight of public opinion is sometimes thrown into the scale of truth. We know that the popular sentiment will sometimes control the tyranny of the powerful, and counteract the influence of wealth ; that it restrains sometimes the madness of lust, and sometimes the cunning of malevolence. We are also sensible, that the influence of a regard to reputation is often favourable to the improvement of social intercourse. To a deference to the world's opinion, and to a love of its good will, are we to attribute much of that politeness and propriety, which are discoverable in manners, and much of that courtesy, which, by habitual observance, sheds perhaps, at length, a favourable influence on the disposition. It is this, which brings down the haughty to condescension, and softens the rough into gentleness. It is this which sometimes checks the offensiveness of vanity, and moderates the excess of selfishness. It causes thousands to appear kind, who would otherwise be rude,—and honourable, who would otherwise be base.

These genial effects upon the intercourse of society are sufficient to induce us to retain the love of human estimation in the number of lawful motives. It was probably a view of some of these influences partially supplying the place of real benevolence, which induced the apostle sometimes to recommend a regard to human opinion. He advises the Roman converts to " provide things honourable in the eyes of all men." To the Philippians, after recommending all things honest, just, pure, and lovely, he ventures also to add " whatsoever things are of good report." Nay, more : he says not only, " if there be any virtue," but " if there be any praise, think on these things." We believe this is the most decisive testimony of approbation, which can be gathered from the Scripture. We will add, also, in favour of the useful operation of this universal passion, that it perhaps cannot be completely engaged, like all the other passions, on the side of vice. For the highest degree of moral depravity is consistent only with an utter insensibility to the opinion of the world ; and we are willing to believe, also, that, were it not for this, the form and profession of Christianity would be more frequently outraged than it now is, by those who secretly detest it.

And now, after all these acknowledgments, what new merit is conceded to our favourite passion? After it has done its utmost, it can only quicken the energies of the mind, restrain sometimes the other passions, afford occasional aid to the cause of order and propriety, soften some of the asperities of social intercourse, and perhaps keep the sinner from open and hardened profligacy. But it cannot purify the affections, melt the hardness of the heart, and break its selfishness, or elevate its desires to the region of purity and peace.

We have seen that this regard to human estimation, though a principle of universal, I had almost said of infinite influence, is confined to very narrow limits in the Gospel of Christ. Is there nothing, then, provided to supply the place of so powerful an agent in the formation of the human character? Is there nothing left to awaken the ambition of the Christian, to rouse him from sloth and universal indifference, to call forth the energies of his mind, and to urge him forward in the career of holiness? Yes; if we will listen to the language of an apostle, whose history proclaims that his passions were not asleep, that his emulation was not quenched by the profession of Christianity, and whose spirit ever glowed with a most divine enthusiasm,—I say, if we listen to him, we shall find that there is enough to stimulate all the faculties of the soul, and, finally, to satiate the most burning thirst of glory. Yes, " eye hath not seen, nor ear heard, nor hath it entered into the heart of man to conceive, the things which God hath prepared for them that love him." Yes, our whole progress here, through all the varieties of honour and of dishonour, of evil report and of good report, is a spectacle to angels and to men. We are coming into " an innumerable company of angels, and to the spirits of the just made perfect, and to Jesus, the Mediator of the new covenant, and to God, the Judge of all." These have been the spectators of our course, and from such we are to receive glory, and honour, and immortality.

*Extract from an Address on retiring from the public Service of the United States of America.—*WASH-INGTON.

IN looking forward to the moment which is intended to terminate the career of my public life, my feelings do not permit me to suspend the deep acknowledgment of that debt of gratitude which I owe to my beloved country, for the many honours it has conferred upon me ; still more for the steadfast confidence with which it has supported me ; and for the opportunities I have thence enjoyed of manifesting my inviolable attachment, by services faithful and persevering, though in usefulness unequal to my zeal If benefits have resulted to our country from these services, let it always be remembered to your praise, as an instructive example in our annals, that, under circumstances in which the passions, agitated in every direction, were liable to mislead, amidst appearances somewhat dubious, vicissitudes of fortune often discouraging, in situations in which not unfrequently want of success has countenanced the spirit of criticism,—the constancy of your support was the essential prop of the efforts, and a guarantee of the plans, by which they were effected. Profoundly penetrated with this idea, I shall carry it with me to my grave, as a strong incitement to unceasing prayers, that Heaven may continue to you the choicest tokens of its beneficence ; that your union and brotherly affection may be perpetual ; that the free constitution, which is the work of your hands, may be sacredly maintained ; that its administration, in every department, may be stamped with wisdom and virtue ; that, in fine, the happiness of the people of these States, under the auspices of liberty, may be made complete, by so careful a preservation, and so prudent a use, of this blessing, as will acquire to them the glory of recommending it to the applause, the affection, and adoption, of every nation which is yet a stranger to it.

Here, perhaps, I ought to stop. But a solicitude for your welfare, which cannot end but with my life, and the apprehension of danger, natural to that solicitude, urge me.

on an occasion like the present, to offer to your solemn
contemplation, and to recommend to your frequent review,
some sentiments, which are the result of much reflection,
of no inconsiderable observation, and which appear to me
all-important to the permanence of your felicity.as a people. These will be offered to you with the more freedom,
as you can only see in them the disinterested warnings
of a parting friend, who can possibly have no motive to bias
his counsel. Nor can I forget, as an encouragement to it,
your indulgent reception of my sentiments on a former,
and not dissimilar occasion.

* * * * * * * * * * * (* *

Of all the dispositions and habits which lead to political
prosperity, religion and morality are indispensable supports
In vain would that man claim the tribute of patriotism,
who should labour to subvert these great pillars of human
happiness—these firmest props of the duties of men and
citizens. The mere politician, equally with the pious man,
ought to respect and to cherish them. A volume could not
trace all their connexions with private and public felicity.
Let it simply be asked, where is the security for property,
for reputation, for life, if the sense of religious obligation
desert the oaths, which are the instruments of investigation in courts of justice ? And let us with caution indulge
the supposition, that morality can be maintained without
religion. Whatever may be conceded to the influence of
refined education on minds of peculiar structure, reason
and experience both forbid us to expect that national
morality can prevail in exclusion of religious principles.

It is substantially true, that virtue or morality is a necessary spring of popular government. The rule, indeed,
extends with more or less force to every species of free
government. Who, that is a sincere friend to it, can look
with indifference upon attempts to shake the foundation of
the fabric ?

Promote, then, as an object of primary importance,
institutions for the general diffusion of knowledge. In
proportion as the structure of a government gives force to
public opinion, it is essential that public opinion should be
enlightened.

Observe good faith and justice towards all nations; cultivate peace and harmony with all; religion and morality
enjoin this conduct; and can it be that good policy does not
equally enjoin it? It will be worthy of a free, enlightened, and, at no distant period, a great nation, to give to
mankind the magnanimous and too novel example of a people always guided by an exalted justice and benevolence
Who can doubt, that, in the course of time and things, the
fruits of such a plan would richly repay any temporary
advantages which might be lost by a steady adherence to
it? Can it be, that Providence has not connected the permanent felicity of a nation with its virtue? The experiment, at least, is recommended by every sentiment which
ennobles human nature. Alas! is it rendered impossible by
its vices?

* * * * * * * * * * * * *

In offering to you, my countrymen, these counsels of an
old and affectionate friend, I dare not hope they will make
the strong and lasting impression I could wish; that they
will control the usual current of the passions, or prevent
our nation from running the course which has hitherto
marked the destiny of empires. But if I may even flatter
myself that they may be productive of some partial benefit, some occasional good; that they may now and then
recur, to moderate the fury of party spirit, to warn against
the mischiefs of foreign intrigue, to guard against the im-
postures of pretended patriotism; this hope will be a full
recompense for that solicitude for your welfare, by which
they have been dictated.

How far, in the discharge of my official duties, I have
been guided by the principles which have been delineated,
the public records and other evidences of my conduct
must witness to you and the world. To myself the assurance of my own conscience is, that I have at least
BELIEVED myself to be guided by them.

Though, in reviewing the incidents of my administration,
I am unconscious of intentional error, I am nevertheless
too sensible of my defects not to think it probable that I
may have committed many errors. Whatever they may
be, I fervently beseech the Almighty to avert and mitigate

the evils to which they may tend.   I shall also carry with
me the hope, that my country will never cease to view
them with indulgence ; and that, after forty-five years of
my life dedicated to its service with an upright zeal, the
faults of incompetent abilities will be consigned to oblivion,
as myself must soon be to the mansions of rest.

Relying on its kindness in this, as in other things, and
actuated by that fervent love towards it, which is so natural to a man who views in it the native soil of himself
and his progenitors for several generations, I anticipate
with pleasing expectation that retreat, in which I promise
myself to realize, without alloy, the sweet enjoyment of
partaking, in the midst of my fellow citizens, the benign
influence of good laws under a free government,—the ever
favourite object of my heart,—and the happy reward, as I
trust, of our mutual cares, labours, and dangers.

United States, September 17th, 1796.

---

*Speech over the Grave of Black Buffaloe, Chief of the
Teton Tribe of Indians.*—BIG ELK MAHA CHIEF

Do not grieve.   Misfortunes will happen to the wisest
and best men.   Death will come, and always comes out of
season.   It is the command of the Great Spirit, and all
nations and people must obey.   What has passed, and cannot be prevented, should not be grieved for.   Be not
discouraged or displeased, then, that, in visiting your father
here, you have lost your chief.   A misfortune of this kind
may never again befall you ; but this would have attended
you, perhaps, at your own village.   Five times have I
visited this land, and never returned with sorrow or pain.
Misfortunes do not flourish particularly in our path.   They
grow every where.   What a misfortune for me, that I
could not have died this day, instead of the chief that lies
before us !   The trifling loss my nation would have sustained in my death, would have been doubly paid for by
the honours of my burial.   They would have wiped off
every thing like regret.   Instead of being covered with a
cloud of sorrow, my warriors would have felt the sunshine

of joy in their hearts. To me it would have been a most glorious occurrence. Hereafter, when I die at home, instead of a noble grave and a grand procession—the rolling music and the thundering cannon—with a flag waving at my head,—I shall be wrapt in a robe—an old robe per-haps—and hoisted on a slender scaffold to the whistling winds, soon to be blown to the earth—my flesh to be de-voured by the wolves, and my bones rattled on the plain by the wild beasts.

Chief of the soldiers*—your labours have not been in vain. Your attention shall not be forgotten. My nation shall know the respect that is paid over the dead. When I return I will echo the sound of your guns.

Speech of Ho-na-yu-wus, or Farmer's Brother.

THE sachems, chiefs, and warriors of the Seneca nation to the sachems and chiefs assembled about the great council-fire of the state of New York.

Brothers—As you are once more assembled in council for the purpose of doing honour to yourselves and justice to your country, we, your brothers, the sachems, chiefs, and warriors of the Seneca nation, request you to open your ears, and give attention to our voice and wishes.

Brothers—You will recollect the late contest between you and your father, the great king of England. This contest threw the inhabitants of this whole island into a great tumult and commotion, like a raging whirlwind, which tears up the trees, and tosses to and fro the leaves, so that no one knows from whence they come, or when they will fall.

Brothers—This whirlwind was so directed by the Great Spirit above, as to throw into our arms two of your infant children, Jasper Parrish and Horatio Jones. We adopted them into our families, and made them our children. We loved them and nourished them. They lived with us many years. At length the Great Spirit spoke to the

---

* Colonel Miller.

whirlwind—and it was still.* A clear and uninterrupted sky appeared. The path of peace was opened, and the chain of friendship was once more made bright. Then these, our adopted children, left us to seek their relations. We wished them to remain among us, and promised, if they would return and live in our country, to give each of them a seat of land for them and their children to sit down upon.

Brothers—They have returned, and have for several years past been serviceable to us as interpreters. We still feel our hearts beat with affection for them, and now wish to fulfil the promise we made them, and to reward them for their services. We have therefore made up our minds to give them a seat of two square miles of land lying on the outlet of Lake Erie, about three miles below Black Rock.

Brothers—We have now made known to you our minds. We expect and earnestly request, that you will permit our friends to receive this our gift, and will make the same good to them, according to the laws and customs of your nation.

Brothers—Why should you hesitate to make our minds easy with regard to this our request? To you it is but a little thing; and have you not complied with the request, and confirmed the gift, of our brothers the Oneidas, the Onondagas, and Cayugas, to their interpreters? and shall we ask, and not be heard?

Brothers—We send you this our speech, to which we expect your answer before the breaking up of your great council-fire.

Abdication of Napoleon, and Retirement of Lafayette.—
TICKNOR.

At last, on the 21st of June, Bonaparte arrived from Waterloo, a defeated and a desperate man. He was already determined to dissolve the representative body, and, assuming the whole dictatorship of the country, play at least one deep and bloody game for power and success. Some of his council, and among the rest Regnault de St

---

* God said, Let here be light; and there was light.

16

Jean d'Angely, who were opposed to this violent measure, informed Lafayette that it would be taken instantly, and that in two hours the chamber of representatives would cease to exist. There was, of course, not a moment left for consultation or advice; the emperor or the chamber must fall that morning. As soon, therefore, as the session was opened, Lafayette, with the same clear courage, and in the same spirit of self-devotion, with which he had stood at the bar of the national assembly in 1792, immediately ascended the tribune, for the first time for twenty years, and said these few words; which, assuredly, would have been his death warrant, if he had not been supported in them by the assembly he addressed :

"When, after an interval of many years, I raise a voice, which the friends of free institutions will still recognise, I feel myself called upon to speak to you only of the dangers of the country, which you alone have now the power to save. Sinister intimations have been heard; they are unfortunately confirmed. This, therefore, is the momen for us to gather round the ancient tri-coloured standard; the standard of '89; the standard of freedom, of equal rights, and of public order. Permit, then, gentlemen, a veteran in this sacred cause, one who has always been a stranger to the spirit of faction, to offer you a few preparatory resolutions, whose absolute necessity, I trust, you feel as I do."

These resolutions declared the chamber to be in permanent session, and all attempts to dissolve it, high treason; and they also called for the four principal ministers to come to the chamber and explain the state of affairs. Bonaparte is said to have been much agitated when word was brought him simply that Lafayette was in the tribune; and his fears were certainly not ill founded; for these resolutions, which were at once adopted, both by the representatives and the peers, substantially divested him of his power, and left him merely a factious and dangerous individual in the midst of a distracted state.

He hesitated during the whole day as to the course he should pursue; but, at last, hoping that the eloquence of Lucien, which had saved him on the 18th Brumaire, might be found no less effectual now, he sent him, with three other ministers to the chamber, just at the beginning of the evening; having first obtained a vote that all should pass in secret session   It was certainly a most perilous crisis. Reports were spread abroad that the populace of the fauxbourgs had been excited, and were arming themselves. It was believed, too, with no little probability, that Bonaparte would march against the chamber, as he had formerly marched against the council of five hundred, and disperse them at the point of the bayonet.   At all events, it was a contest for existence, and no man could feel his life safe.

At this moment Lucien rose, and, in the doubtful and gloomy light which two vast torches shed through the hall, and over the pale and anxious features of the members, made a partial exposition of the state of affairs, and the projects and hopes he still entertained.   A deep and painful silence followed.   At length Mr. Jay, well known above twenty years ago in Boston, under the assumed name of Renaud, as a teacher of the French language, and an able writer in one of the public newspapers of that city, ascended the tribune, and, in a long and vehement speech of great eloquence, exposed the dangers of the country, and ended by proposing to send a deputation to the emperor, demanding his abdication.   Lucien immediately followed.   He never showed more power, or a more impassioned eloquence.   His purpose was to prove that France was still devoted to the emperor, and that its resources were still equal to a contest with the allies.   " It is not Napoleon," he cried, " that is attacked ; it is the French people.   And a proposition is now made to this people to abandon their emperor ; to expose the French nation, before the tribunal of the world, to a severe judgment on its levity and inconstancy.   No, sir, the honour of this nation shall never be so compromised!"   On hearing these words, Lafayette rose.   He did not go to the tribune, but spoke, contrary to rule and custom, from his place. His manner was perfectly calm, but marked with the very spirit of rebuke ; and he addressed himself, not to the president, but directly to Lucien : " The assertion, which has just been uttered, is a calumny.   Who shall dare to accuse the French nation of inconstancy to the emperor Napoleon '   That nation had followed his bloody footsteps through the sands of Egypt, and through the wastes of Russia; over fifty fields of battle; in disaster as faithfully as in victory; and it is for having thus devotedly followed him, that we now mourn the blood of three millions of Frenchmen." These few words made an impression on the assembly, which could not be mistaken; and, as Lafayette ended, Lucien himself bowed respectfully to him, and, without resuming his speech, sat down.

It was determined to appoint a deputation of five members from each chamber, to meet the grand council of the ministers, and deliberate in committee on the measures to be taken. This body sat during the night, under the presidency of Cambaceres, arch-chancellor of the empire Lafayette moved, that a deputation should be sent to Napoleon, demanding his abdication. The arch-chancellor refused to put the motion, but it was as much decided as if it had been formally carried. The next morning, June 22d, the emperor sent in his abdication, and Lafayette was on the committee that went to the Thuilleries to thank him for it on behalf of the nation.

A crude, provisional government was now established by the two chambers, which lasted only a few days, and whose principal measure was the sending a deputation to the allied powers, of which Lafayette was the head, to endeavour to stop the invasion of France. This of course failed, as had been foreseen; Paris surrendered on the 3d of July, and what remained of the representative government, which Bonaparte had created for his own purposes, but which Lafayette had turned against him, was soon afterwards dissolved. Its doors were found guarded on the morning of the 8th, but by what authority has never been known; and the members met at Lafayette's house, entered their formal protest, and went quietly to their own homes

Lafayette retired immediately to La Grange, from which, in fact, he had been only a month absent, and resumed at once his agricultural employments. There, in the midst of a family of above twenty children and grand children, who all look up to him as their patriarchal chief, he lives in a simple and sincere happiness, rarely granted to those who have borne such a leading part in the troubles and sufferings of a great period of political revolution. In.

1817, he has been twice elected to the chamber of depu·
ties, and in all his votes has shown himself constant to his
ancient principles. When the ministry proposed to establish a censorship of the press, he resisted them in an able
speech; but Lafayette was never a factious man, and
therefore he has never made any further opposition to the
present order of things in France, than his conscience and
his official place required. That he does not approve the
present constitution of the monarchy, or the political principles and management of the existing government, his
votes as a deputy, and his whole life, plainly show; and
that his steady and temperate opposition is matter of serious
anxiety to the family now on the throne is apparent, from
their conduct towards him during the last nine years, and
their management of the public press since he has been in
this country. If he chose to make himself a tribune of the
people, he might at any moment become formidable; but
he trusts rather to the progress of general intelligence and
political wisdom throughout the nation, which he feels
sure will at last bring his oountry to the practically free
government, he has always been ready to sacrifice his life
to purchase for it. To this great result he looks forward,
as Madame de Stael has well said of him, with the entire
confidence a pious man enjoys in a future life; but when
he feels anxious and impatient to hasten onward to it, he
finds a wisdom tempered by long experience stirring within
him, which warns him, in the beautiful language of Milton, that "they also serve, who only stand and wait"

Extract from "Hyperion."[*]—Josiah Quincy, Jun.

When I reflect on the exalted character of the
antient Britons, on the fortitude of our illustrious prede-

---

[*] The first part of this extract was published in the Boston Gazette
in September, 1767, on receiving information of threatening import from
England; the remainder appeared in October, 1768, when British
troops had landed in Boston, and taken possession of Faneuil Hall
under circumstances intended to inspire the people 'o alarm an ,
terror.—Ed.

16 *

tessors, on the noble struggles of the late memorable
period, and from these reflections, when, by a natural
transition, I contemplate the gloomy aspect of the present
day, my heart is alternately torn with doubt and hope,
despondency and terror.   Can the true, generous magnanimity of British heroes be entirely lost in their degenerate progeny?   Is the genius of liberty, which so late
inflamed our bosoms, fled forever?

An attentive observer of the deportment of some particular persons in this metropolis would be apt to imagine, that
the grand point was gained; that the spirit of the people
was entirely broken to the yoke; that all America was
subjugated to bondage.   Already the minions of power in
fancy fatten and grow wanton on the spoils of the land.
They insolently toss the head, and put on the air of con-
temptuous disdain.   In the imaginary possession of lord-
ships and dominions, these potentates and powers dare tell
us, that our only hope is to crouch, to cower under, and to
kiss, the iron rod of oppression.   Precious sample of the
meek and lowly temper of those who are destined to be our
lords and masters!

Be not deceived, my countrymen.   Believe not these
venal hirelings, when they would cajole you by their sub-
tilties into submission, or frighten you by their vapourings
into compliance.   When they strive to flatter you by the
terms "moderation and prudence," tell them that calmness
and deliberation are to guide the judgment; courage and
intrepidity command the action.   When they endeavour to
make us "perceive our inability to oppose our mother
country," let us boldly answer;—In defence of our civil
and religious rights, we dare oppose the world; with the
God of armies on our side, even the God who fought our
fathers' battles, we fear not the hour of trial, though the
hosts of our enemies should cover the field like locusts.
If this be enthusiasm, we will live and die enthusiasts.

Blandishments will not fascinate us, nor will threats of
a "halter" intimidate.   For, under God, we are determined, that wheresoever, whensoever, or howsoever we
shall be called to make our exit, we will die freemen
Well do we know that all the regalia of this world cannot
dignify the death of a villain. nor diminish the ignominy,

with which a slave shall quit existence. Neither can it
taint the unblemished honour of a son of freedom, though
he should make his departure on the already prepared gibbet, or be dragged to the newly erected scaffold for execution. With the plaudits of his conscience he will go off
the stage. A crown of joy and immortality shall be his
reward. The history of his life his children shall venerate. The virtues of their sire shall excite their emulation.

* * * * * * * * * * * * * *

If there ever was a time, this is the hour, for America: s
to rouse themselves, and exert every ability. Their all is
at a hazard, and the die of fate spins doubtful. In vain
do we talk of magnanimity and heroism, in vain do we
trace a descent from the worthies of the earth, if we inherit
not the spirit of our ancestors. Who is he that boasteth
of his patriotism? Has he vanquished luxury, and subdued the worldly pride of his heart? Is he not still drinking the poisonous draught, and rolling the sweet morsel
under his tongue? He who cannot conquer the little vanity of his heart, and deny the delicacy of a debauched
palate, let him lay his hand upon his mouth, and his mouth
in the dust.

Now is the time for this people to summon every aid,
human and divine ; to exhibit every moral virtue, and call
forth every Christian grace. The wisdom of the serpent,
the innocence of the dove, and the intrepidity of the lion,
with the blessing of God, will yet save us from the jaws
of destruction.

Where is the boasted liberty of Englishmen, if property
may be disposed of, charters suspended, assemblies dissolved, and every valued right annihilated, at the uncontrol-
lable will of an external power? Does not every man, who
feels one ethereal spark yet glowing in his bosom, find his
indignation kindle at the bare imagination of such wrongs?
What would be our sentiments were this imagination realized.

Did the blood of the ancient Britons swell our veins, did
the spirit of our forefathers inhabit our breasts, should we
hesitate a moment in preferring death to a miserable exis-

ence in bondage? Did we reflect on their toils, their dangers, their fiery trials, the thought would inspire unconquerable courage.

Who has the front to ask, Wherefore do you complain? Who dares assert, that every thing worth living for is not lost, when a nation is enslaved? Are not pensioners, stipendiaries and salary-men, unknown before, hourly multiplying upon us, to riot in the spoils of miserable America? Does not every eastern gale waft us some new insect, even of that devouring kind, which eat up every green thing? Is not the bread taken out of the children's mouths and given unto the dogs? Are not our estates given to corrupt sycophants, without a design, or even a pretence, of soliciting our assent; and our lives put into the hands of those whose tender mercies are cruelties? Has not an authority in a distant land, in the most public manner, proclaimed a right of disposing of *the all* of Americans? In short, what have we to lose? What have we to fear? Are not our distresses more than we can bear? And, to finish all, are not our cities, in a time of profound peace, filled with standing armies, to preclude from us that last solace of the wretched—to open their mouths in complaint, and send forth their cries in bitterness of heart?

But is there no ray of hope? Is not Great Britain inhabited by the children of those renowned barons, who waded through seas of crimson gore to establish their liberty? and will they not allow us, their fellow-men, to enjoy that freedom which we claim from nature, which is confirmed by our constitution, and which they pretend so highly to value? Were a tyrant to conquer us, the chains of slavery, when opposition should become useless, might be supportable; but to be shackled by Englishmen,—by our equals,—is not to be borne. By the sweat of our brow we earn the little we possess; from nature we derive the common rights of man; and by charter we claim the liberties of Britons. Shall we, dare we, pusillanimously surrender our birthright? Is the obligation to our fathers discharged? Is the debt we owe posterity paid? Answer me, thou coward, who hidest thyself in the hour of trial; If there is no reward in this life, no prize of glory in the next, capable of animating thy dastard soul, think and

tremble, thou miscreant! at the whips and stripes thy
master shall lash thee with on earth,—and the flames and
scorpions thy second master shall torment thee with here
after!

Oh, my countrymen! what will our children say, when
they read the history of these times, should they find that
we tamely gave away, without one noble struggle, the
most invaluable of earthly blessings! As they drag the
galling chain, will they not execrate us? If we have any
respect for things sacred, any regard to the dearest treasure on earth; if we have one tender sentiment for posterity; if we would not be despised by the whole world ;—
let us, in the most open, solemn manner, and with determined fortitude, swear—We will die, if we cannot live
freemen!

Be not lulled, my countrymen, with vain imaginations
or idle fancies. To hope for the protection of Heaven,
without doing our duty, and exerting ourselves as becomes
men, is to mock the Deity. Wherefore had man his reason,
if it were not to direct him? wherefore his strength, if it
be not his protection? To banish folly and luxury, correct
vice and immorality, and stand immoveable in the freedom
in which we are free indeed, is eminently the duty of each
individual at this day. When this is done, we may ration-
ally hope for an answer to our prayers—for the whole
counsel of God, and the invincible armour of the Almighty.

However righteous our cause, we cannot, in this period
of the world, expect a miraculous salvation. Heaven will
undoubtedly assist us if we act like men; but to expect
protection from above, while we are enervated by luxury,
and slothful in the exertion of those abilities, with which
we are endued, is an expectation vain and foolish. With
the smiles of Heaven, virtue, unanimity and firmness will
ensure success. While we have equity, justice and God
on our side, Tyranny, spiritual or temporal, shall never
ride triumphant in a land inhabited by Englishmen.

The Sabbath in New England.—Miss Sedgwick.

THE observance of the Sabbath began with the Puri
tans, as it still does with a great portion of their descendants, on Saturday night. At the going down of the sun
on Saturday, all temporal affairs were suspended; and so
zealously did our fathers maintain the letter, as well as the
spirit of the law, that, according to a vulgar tradition in
Connecticut, no beer was brewed in the latter part of the
week, lest it should presume to *work* on Sunday.

It must be confessed, that the tendency of the age is to
laxity; and so rapidly is the wholesome strictness of primitive times abating, that, should some antiquary, fifty years
hence, in exploring his garret rubbish, chance to cast his
eye on our humble pages, he may be surprised to learn,
that, even now, the Sabbath is observed, in the interior of
New England, with an almost Judaical severity.

On Saturday afternoon an uncommon bustle is apparent.
The great class of procrastinators are hurrying to and fro
to complete the lagging business of the week. The good
mothers, like Burns' matron, are plying their needles,
making " auld claes look amaist as weel's the new ;" while
the domestics, or *help*, (we prefer the national descriptive
term,) are wielding, with might and main, their brooms and
mops, to make all *tidy* for the Sabbath.

As the day declines, the hum of labour dies away, and,
after the sun is set, perfect stillness reigns in every well-
ordered household, and not a foot-fall is heard in the village
street.   It cannot be denied, that even the most scriptu-
ral, missing the excitement of their ordinary occupations,
anticipate their usual bed-time. The obvious inference
from this fact is skilfully avoided by certain ingenious
reasoners, who allege, that the constitution was originally

---

* This description is executed with admirable truth and humour;
yet it has, we fear, in these times of disregard to the sacredness of the
institution, a slight tendency to make the ancient strict observance of
the Sabbath appear somewhat ridiculous.   It is not to be regretted, that
the austerity and gloom, which pervaded the character of the Puritans,
has entirely disappeared ;—but it *is* to be regretted, that so much, which
was truly religious, should have fled along with it.—ED

so organized, as to require an extra quantity of sleep on every seventh night. We recommend it to the curious to inquire, how this peculiarity was adjusted, when the first day of the week was changed from Saturday to Sunday.

The Sabbath morning is as peaceful as the first hallowed day. Not a human sound is heard without the dwellings, and, but for the lowing of the herds, the crowing of the cocks, and the gossiping of the birds, animal life would seem to be extinct, till, at the bidding of the church-going bell, the old and young issue from their habitations, and, with solemn demeanor, bend their measured steps to the *meeting-house ;*—the families of the minister, the squire, the doctor, the merchants, the modest gentry of the village, and the mechanic and labourer, all arrayed in their best, all meeting on even ground, and all with that consciousness of independence and equality, which breaks down the pride of the rich, and rescues the poor from servility, envy, and discontent. If a morning salutation is reciprocated, it is in a suppressed voice ; and if, perchance, nature, in some reckless urchin, burst forth in laughter— "My dear, you forget it's Sunday," is the ever ready reproof.

Though every face wears a solemn aspect, yet we once chanced to see even a deacon's muscles relaxed by the wit of a neighbour, and heard him allege, in a half-deprecating, half-laughing voice, "The squire is so droll, that a body must laugh, though it be Sabbath-day."

The farmer's ample wagon, and the little one-horse vehicle, bring in all who reside at an inconvenient walking distance,—that is to say, in our riding community, half a mile from the church. It is a pleasing sight, to those who love to note the happy peculiarities of their own land, to see the farmers' daughters, blooming, intelligent, well-bred, pouring out of these homely coaches, with their nice white gowns, prunel shoes, Leghorn hats, fans and parasols, and the spruce young men, with their plaited ruffles, blue coats, and yellow buttons. The whole community meet as one religious family, to offer their devotions at the common altar. If there is an outlaw from the society,— a luckless wight, whose vagrant taste has never been subdued,—he may be seen stealing along the margin of some

little brook, far away from the condemning observatio
and troublesome admonitions of his fellows.

Towards the close of the day, or (to borrow a phrase descriptive of his feelings, who first used it) "when the Sab
bath begins to *abate*," the children cluster about the windows. Their eyes wander from their catechisms to the
western sky, and, though it seems to them as if the sun
would never disappear, his broad disk does slowly sink behind the mountain ; and, while his last ray still lingers on
the eastern summits, merry voices break forth, and the
ground resounds with bounding footsteps. The village
belle arrays herself for her twilight walk ; the boys gather
on " the green ;" the lads and girls throng to the " singing
school ;" while some coy maiden lingers at home, awaiting
her expected suitor; and all enter upon the pleasures of
the evening with as keen a relish as if the day had been a
preparatory penance.

Description of the Capture of a Whale.—COOPER.

THE cockswain cast a cool glance at the crests of foam
that were breaking over the tops of the billows within a
few yards of where their boat was riding, and called aloud
to his men—

" Pull a stroke or two ; away with her into dark
water."

The drop of the oars resembled the movements of a nice
machine, and the light boat skimmed along the water like
a duck, that approaches to the very brink of some imminent
danger, and then avoids it at the most critical moment, apparently without an effort. While this necessary movement was making, Barnstable arose, and surveyed the cliffs
with keen eyes, and then, turning once more in disappointment from his search, he said—

" Pull more from the land, and let her run down, at an
easy stroke, to the schooner. Keep a lookout at the cliffs,
boys; it is possible that they are stowed in some of the
holes in the rocks, for it's no daylight business they
are on."

The order was promptly obeyed, and they had glided along for near a mile in this manner, in the most profound silence, when suddenly the stillness was broken by a heavy rush of air, and a dash of water, seemingly at no great distance from them.

"By heaven! Tom," cried Barnstable, starting, "there is the blow of a whale."

"Ay, ay, sir," returned the cockswain, with undisturbed composure; "here is his spout, not half a mile to seaward; the easterly gale has driven the creater to leeward, and he begins to find himself in shoal water. He's been sleeping, while he should have been working to windward!"

"The fellow takes it coolly, too! he's in no hurry to get an offing."

"I rather conclude, sir," said the cockswain, rolling over his tobacco in his mouth very composedly, while his little sunken eyes began to twinkle with pleasure at the sight, "the gentleman has lost his reckoning, and don't know which way to head, to take himself back into blue water."

"'Tis a fin-back!" exclaimed the lieutenant; "he will soon make head-way, and be off."

"No, sir, 'tis a right whale," answered Tom; "I saw his spout; he threw up a pair of as pretty rainbows as a Christian would wish to look at. He's a raal oil-butt, that fellow!"

Barnstable laughed, turned himself away from the tempting sight, and tried to look at the cliffs; and then unconsciously bent his eyes again on the sluggish animal, who was throwing his huge carcass at times for many feet from the water, in idle gambols. The temptation for sport, and the recollection of his early habits, at length prevailed over his anxiety in behalf of his friends, and the young officer inquired of his cockswain—

"Is there any whale-line in the boat to make fast to that harpoon which you bear about with you in fair weather or foul?"

"I never trust the boat from the schooner without part of a shot, sir," returned the cockswain; "there is something nateral in the sight of a tub to my old eyes."

17

Barnstable looked at his watch, and again at the cliffs,
when he exclaimed in joyous tones—

" Give strong way, my hearties!   There seems nothing
better to be done ; let us have a stroke of a harpoon at tha
impudent rascal."

The men shouted spontaneously, and the old cockswain
suffered his solemn visage to relax into a small laugh, while
the whale-boat sprang forward like a courser for the goal.
During the few minutes they were pulling towards their
game, long Tom arose from his crouching attitude in the
stern sheets, and transferred his huge frame to the bows
of the boat, where he made such preparation to strike the
whale as the occasion required.   The tub, containing about
half of a whale-line, was placed at the feet of Barnstable,
who had been preparing an oar to steer with, in place of
the rudder, which was unshipped in order that, if necessary, the boat might be whirled round when not advancing.

Their approach was utterly unnoticed by the monster
of the deep, who continued to amuse himself with throwing the water in two circular spouts high into the air, occasionally flourishing the broad flukes of his tail with graceful but terrific force, until the hardy seamen were within
a few hundred feet of him, when he suddenly cast his head
downwards, and, without an apparent effort, reared his immense body for many feet above the water, waving his tail
violently, and producing a whizzing noise, that sounded
like the rushing of winds.   The cockswain stood erect,
poising his harpoon, ready for the blow ; but, when he
beheld the creature assume this formidable attitude, he
waved his hand to his commander, who instantly signed to
his men to cease rowing.   In this situation the sportsmen
rested a few moments, while the whale struck several
blows on the water in rapid succession, the noise of which
re-echoed along the cliffs, like the hollow reports of so
many cannon.   After this wanton exhibition of his territe
strength, the monster sunk again into his native element
and slowly disappeared from the eyes of his pursuers.

" Which way did he head, Tom ?" cried Barnstable, the
moment the whale was out of sight.

"Pretty much up and down, sir," returned the cock-swain, whose eye was gradually brightening with the ex citement of the sport; "he'll soon run his nose against the bottom, if he stands long on that course, and will be glad to get another snuff of pure air; send her a few fath-oms to starboard, sir, and I promise we shall not be out of his track."

The conjecture of the experienced old seaman proved true, for in a few minutes the water broke near them, and another spout was cast into the air, when the huge animal rushed for half his length in the same direction, and fell on the sea with a turbulence and foam equal to that, which is produced by the launching of a vessel, for the first time, into its proper element. After this evolution, the whale rolled heavily, and seemed to rest from further efforts.

His slightest movements were closely watched by Barn-stable and his cockswain, and, when he was in a state of comparative rest, the former gave a signal to his crew to ply their oars once more. A few long and vigorous strokes sent the boat directly up to the broadside of the whale, with its bows pointing towards one of the fins, which was at times, as the animal yielded sluggishly to the action of the waves, exposed to view. The cockswain poised his harpoon with much precision, and then darted it from him with a violence that buried the iron in the body of their foe. The instant the blow was made, long Tom shouted with singular earnestness—

"Starn all!"

"Stern all!" echoed Barnstable; when the obedient seamen, by united efforts, forced the boat in a backward direction, beyond the reach of any blow from their formi-dable antagonist. The alarmed animal, however, meditated no such resistance; ignorant of his own power, and of the insignificance of his enemies, he sought refuge in flight. One moment of stupid surprise succeeded the entrance of the iron, when he cast his huge tail into the air with a vi-olence that threw the sea around him into increased com-motion, and then disappeared, with the quickness of light-ning, amid a cloud of foam

"Snub him!" shouted Barnstable; "hold on, Tom; he rises already."

"Ay, ay, sir," replied the composed cockswain, seizing the line which was running out of the boat with a velocity that rendered such a manœuvre rather hazardous, and causing it to yield more gradually round the large loggerhead, that was placed in the bows of the boat for that purpose. Presently the line stretched forward, and, rising to the surface with tremulous vibrations, it indicated the direction in which the animal might be expected to re-appear. Barnstable had cast the bows of the boat towards that point, before the terrified and wounded victim rose once more to the surface, whose time was, however, no longer wasted in his sports, but who cast the waters aside as he forced his way, with prodigious velocity, along their surface. The boat was dragged violently in his wake, and cut through the billows with a terrific rapidity, that at moments appeared to bury the slight fabric in the ocean. When long Tom beheld his victim throwing his spouts on high again, he pointed with exultation to the jetting fluid, which was streaked with the deep red of blood, and cried—

"Ay, I've touched the fellow's life! It must be more than two foot of blubber that stops my iron from reaching the life of any whale that ever sculled the ocean!"

"I believe you have saved yourself the trouble of using the bayonet you have rigged for a lance," said his commander, who entered into the sport with all the ardour of one, whose youth had been chiefly passed in such pursuits; "feel your line, Master Coffin; can we haul alongside of our enemy? I like not the course he is steering, as he tows us from the schooner."

"'Tis the creater's way, sir," said the cockswain; "you know they need the air in their nostrils when they run, the same as a man; but lay hold, boys, and let us haul up to him"

The seamen now seized their whale-line, and slowly drew their boat to within a few feet of the tail of the fish, whose progress became sensibly less rapid as he grew weak with the loss of blood. In a few minutes he stopped running, and appeared to roll uneasily on the water, as if suffering the agony of death.

"Shall we pull in and finish him, Tom?" cried Barnstable; "a few sets from your bayonet would do it."

The cockswain stood examining his game with cool discretion, and replied to this interrogatory—

"No, sir, no—he's going into his flurry; there's no occasion for disgra·ing ourselves by using a soldier's weapon in taking a wha ɔ. Starn off, sir, starn off! the creater's in his flurry!"

The warning of the prudent cockswain was promptly obeyed, and the boat cautiously drew off to a distance, leaving to the animal a clear space while under its dying agonies. From a state of perfect rest, the terrible monster threw its tail on high as when in sport, but its blows were trebled in rapidity and violence, till all was hid from view by a pyramid of foam, that was deeply dyed with blood. The roarings of the fish were like the bellowings of a herd of bulls, and, to one who was ignorant of the fact, it would have appeared as if a thousand monsters were engaged in deadly combat behind the bloody mist that obstructed the view. Gradually these effects subsided, and, when the discoloured water again settled down to the long and regular swell of the ocean, the fish was seen exhausted, and yielding passively to its fate. As life departed, the enormous black mass rolled to one side, and when the white and glistening skin of the belly became apparent, the seamen well knew that their victory was achieved.

Lake George.—CLUB-ROOM.

"It was a still
And calmy bay, on the one side sheltered
With the brode shadow of an hoarie hill;
On the other side an high rock toured still."

* * * * * * * * * * * * * *

"Waiting to pass, he saw whereas did swim
Along the shore, as swift as glaunce of eye,
A little gondelay, bedecked trim,
With boughs and arbours woven cunningly,
That like a little forest seemed outwardly;
And therein sat a lady fresh and faire."

FAERIE QUEENE.

IF any of my readers have ever visited these transparent waters, and have wound their way among the thousand little woody islands which sprinkle their surface from Fort

17 *

George to the Falls of Ticonderoga, they may have remark ed, just beyond Bolton, at the bottom of a beautiful inlet, or bay, formed by two craggy promontories of the western shore, a small dwelling-house, upon which the fingers of Time seem to have wrought more ruinously than man, in the pride of his dominion, is accustomed to allow them. It stands lone and desolate. Storms have shattered its roof, and wild shrubs have already sprung up in dark profusion over its avenues; while the white-columned portico, which was wont to look so cheering to the eye of the passenger, has put on the damp and mouldering garment of decay.

Some years ago business led me to the Canadian frontier by that route. I travelled alone in a light wagon. A part of the road, which was extremely rugged, stretched along the bold shore of the lake; sometimes winding up the craggy side of the mountain, and sometimes running close to the precipice, which, from the height of two or three hundred feet, flung its huge and dusky shadow into the mirror beneath. As I was anxious to reach my inn before night-fall, and blue mists were already beginning to gather upon the lake, I quickened the pace of my horse wherever the smoothness of the road would permit. I had just passed a young foot-traveller, and was turning a sharp corner formed by a rock shelving out of the mountain's side, when my horse started suddenly, and, carrying the wheel of my wagon over a fallen fragment, dashed me to the ground. I fell near the edge of the cliff, where its surface was already considerably inclined. I seized upon a small projection of the rock. It loosened, and gave way under my grasp. I slipped downward, and found not even a bramble within reach, when I felt myself suddenly stayed by I knew not what. It was the young man I had just passed, who sprang forward, and, not without imminent hazard of fol- lowing me in my fall, caught the skirt of my coat at the instant I was rolling over the brink. Supporting himself by the frail bough of a dwarf-oak which grew a little above, he held me hanging by a thread over " the dark valley of the shadow of death." The fragment which I had loos- ened fell, and the sullen splash of the water which re- ceived it just reached my ear. From that moment I be came insensible.

On recovery I found myself on a bed. Three or four faces were bending over me with expressions of the deepest concern, and a beautiful girl was bathing my temples. I looked her my thanks—it was all I could. Presently the door opened, and a voice anxiously asked—" How is he ?—will he live ?" " Hush !" she replied, in a low whisper, " He is well enough to hear you." It was my young preserver, who entered, and brought with him the doctor of the neighbouring village. It were tedious to detail all the symptoms of inward injury, and prognostics of impending fever, which were found about me by this rustic son of Æsculapius. Let it suffice that my limbs were pronounced unbroken, though badly bruised—that I submitted quietly to remedies, which I had not strength to resist —in short, that I was well enough in a few days, in spite of all circumstance of delay, to enjoy the society of the kind friends who attended me, and the beauties of their romantic residence.

The name of my host was Burton—a robust and well-looking man, just entering life's downward path. He was by birth an Englishman, and had been a soldier in his youth—served in America during our revolutionary war— was taken prisoner, with many of his countrymen, at Ticonderoga—fell in love with a young woman in that neighbourhood, whom he married soon after the declaration of peace—and, having acquired a competent fortune in merchandise, hastened to indulge an Englishman's taste for rural pursuits in this delightful spot.

Mary Burton, his only daughter, was a beautiful girl just turned of eighteen; adorned with all the sensibilities of her sex ; and, if she wanted the accomplishments of a fine lady, she had that, which more than compensates for them all—uniform simplicity and gayety of heart. It was she whom I first discovered among the group standing about me, watching with tender anxiety the earliest symptoms of returning life

But my readers would perhaps know something of my youthful preserver. He was not of the Burton family, though constantly with them. His name was Arthur Murray. Of good parentage and liberal attainments, a boyish romance first led him to that neighbourhood ; for his con tinuance there, you have perhaps already guessed that something might be attributed to the charms of Mary But ton. The old folks looked with pleasure on the growing attachment between them, and had recently granted a glad consent to their union.

The only other inmates of the parlour were two rosy-cheeked boys, many years younger, yet constant companions of the kind-hearted Arthur. Nor let me exclude from the family roll, Rover, the large Newfoundland dog, who was allowed to participate in most of the family pleasures.

It was an uncommonly happy circle. Separated from the rest of mankind—unsullied by the cold, selfish pleasures of the city—the absorbing cares of avarice and pride—home was their world ;—they indulged not a wish beyond "the happy valley," but lived peaceful and contented, with all the sympathies of life wrapped up in the little compass of a few loving hearts. If this be seclusion, who would exchange it for the refined vanities of fashion—the turmoils of interest and ambition—the modish sensibilities which wear the semblance of feeling, and obliterate the feeling itself!

And then the scenery about them was so exquisitely touching! In the freshness of the dawn, I used to delight, with Rover only by my side, to climb the neighbouring hill, and catch the first ruddy tint that gleamed upon the lake—and at noon to stretch myself in some shady recess, and watch the white sail, now lost behind the bold headland, now gliding among the trees, and now cutting the clear expanse of water—or, in the stillness of night, broken only by the moan of the sad whip-poor-will, and the fret of waters, to muse upon the wildness of the scene, and commune with unearthly forms, which seemed to be flitting in the moonbeam ;—but, most of all, I delighted, on a fine afternoon, to join the little family party, in Arthur's pleasure-boat, sailing from island to island, each beauty presenting itself in ever new and varying lights, and the sweet, artless song of Mary, who seemed to be the fairy spirit of the lake, warbling in my ear. And I would not, even now, mingled as my recollections are with melancholy and sorrow, I would not, for any earthly good, suffer the memory of this delicious period to fade upon the tablet of my heart. It was one of the few, few green and sunny spots, which lie scattered over the dark waste of time.

But the day at length arrived, when the imperious calls of business—that perpetual intruder on the poetry of life—must tear me from the friends and scenes which I so dearly loved. I had already lingered much longer on the hospitality of the Burtons than necessity required; and I know not when I should have left them, had I waited till either my own inclination, or their friendly importunities, had ceased. I bade adieu—but not without a willing promise to visit them once more on my return.

About three weeks elapsed. I had despatched my business, and was returning homeward light-hearted and free, when, after toiling up a long and dusty hill, I caught sight again, at a few miles' distance, of the green, refreshing valley, and the pure crystal within it. My pulse beat high with expectation. My horse had not forgotten the hospitality of the Burtons, and we rapidly approached these well-remembered scenes. As I descended the last hill, and some time before I reached the house, Rover came bounding along, with every demonstration of joy, to welcome my return. Upon entering, the domestics, who were making ready their evening repast, informed me, that the whole family had gone upon the water in Arthur's pleasure-boat.

Taking Rover with me, I strayed down to the neighbourhood of their landing-place, and seated myself on a cliff, which overlooked the lake. The waters of Lake George are peculiarly transparent. I have often looked out of a boat upon its pebbly bed, and thought I might easily have waded to the shore, when in truth my oar's length could not reach the bottom. It was from this singular beauty, as well as the *tout ensemble* of witching scenery about it, that the Indians, who formerly inhabited the adjacent territories, believed the bosom of the lake to be the abode of the Great Spirit; and the French priests, who came to convert them, infected with the superstition of the place, named it the Holy Water; and, either imagining it to be uncommonly pure, or else believing it to be really endowed with a peculiar sanctity, used to send vessels filled with it to their native country, to be used in the sacred

rites of their church. This afternoon was remarkably
calm and cloudless. The opposite shore hung in the water with such truth and life of expression, that it looked
like the scenery of another world, calmer and more lovely
than our own.

Presently, however, a breeze sprung from the east. The
smooth surface just curled beneath its kiss ; and, in a short
time, I observed the full sail of the pleasure-boat emerging
at no great distance from behind a little knoll, that had
concealed it. It was shaping its homeward course. The
sun was fast declining towards the western mountain—upon
whose summit was piled a thick mass of snowy clouds.
Every thing promised a glorious sunset.

I sat wrapped in the dream of expectation, measuring
the long ripple which the boat left upon the lake, and thinking, within myself, whether they could reach home before
dusk. I turned towards the sun, to judge from his height
how many minutes the light of day had yet to live. I was
immediately struck by the uncommon richness of the white
fleece, which was rolling itself, volume upon volume, into
a thousand wild, fantastic shapes. At the same moment, a
small black cloud seemed suddenly to grow out of the mountain. As it rose, it swelled, and spread itself, like a pall,
over the rich mass of vapours, effacing one by one the
beauties of the gorgeous spectacle. The wind freshened
from the east—but the thunder-cloud still steered against
it, and sailed on, in sullen majesty, like some dusky spirit,
regardless of the opposing element. The sun was obscured,
and a cold shade thrown over the lake. The leaves rustled
through the forest with a noise like the long roll of the
ocean on some distant beach, and a dull, low moaning seemed to move upon the waters. All nature portended one of
those tremendous storms, which there, in seasons of the
profoundest calm, pour in a moment out of the hollows of
the surrounding mountains. I looked back anxiously for
my friends. Their bark had neared the bay, and was still
gallantly cleaving the waves. I thought I could distinguish Arthur at the helm, proudly steering his little treasure, fearful but for those whom he loved dearer than life.
I waved my handkerchief, and 't was answered. Rover

stood just below me, snuffing the air, and wagging his tail in silent expectation.

The heavens were now completely overcast—the thunders rolled heavily, nearer and nearer, and big round drops splashed here and there upon the water. Presently there was a blinding flash, and an explosion shaking the cliff to its very root. The long, broken peal, that followed, reverberated from crag to crag, and died away in the far distance. There was a momentary pause ;—the gates of heaven were loosed, and the water fell in sheets, as if another lake were emptying itself from the sky. I could just discern the little bark through the thick rain. In spite of the fury of the storm, it gained its way, and had already reached the entrance to its harbour. A few moments more, and it was safe. While I was yet looking at it, a sudden gust of wind rushed out of the west. The boat stopped for an instant, as if fixed to the spot—and then, with a slight tremulous motion, settled into the waves.

Rover, who sat watching its progress from a point beneath, set up a wild howl, and dashed into the water. I instinctively followed, leaping from point to point—slipping among the rocks—catching at weeds and briers, which sprang out of the crevices—nor was it till I stood upon the very margin of the lake, that I reflected on the rashness of my design ;—I was wholly unable to swim. Rover, however, bore him stoutly from the shore, and had almost reached the spot ; but not a trace of the vessel could be seen. The torrents of rain ceased, and I could now clearly descry a human figure emerging from the waves—it was Arthur—and he dragged after him, from the bottom, the dear object, who clung to him when they sunk. Rover now reached them, and, with all the sagacity of his tribe, seizing the long tresses of Mary in his mouth, so as to lift her head out of the water, bore her triumphantly toward the shore. Arthur swam by her side. I could only wait for them on the shore. They were now within a few yards of land, when Arthur's strength began to fail. Poor Arthur sunk. He rose again—made a few feeble strokes —and the waters again covered him ;—he rose—endeavoured to speak, cast a mournful look upon Mary—folded his arms—and sunk,—forever. A few noiseless bubbles struggled to the surface, and his spirit mingled with the air.

Those who have stood by the bed-side of a dying brother, and watched the last faint struggle with death,—the cold damps gathering upon the brow—the fixing eye—the convulsive gasp—without the power to repress a single groan,—have felt all that was labouring in my heart. He was a fellow being—a friend—my benefactor—and he sunk within a few feet of me into a watery grave.

But it was no time to indulge the selfishness of sorrow. Rover had come to land, with the body of his mistress pale and cold. I took it up, and bore it to the house. The servants were in a state of distraction; it was with difficulty I could persuade them to use necessary means for the recovery of the unfortunate Mary. After much labour, she began to breathe, and a few deep groans marked the unwillingness with which life returned to its deserted tenement. Good God, thought I, what a cruelty do I not commit in restoring this wretched maid to a desolate existence! Surely she had better, far better, die—and sleep quietly in her grave, than revive to see a few more miserable years, parentless—brotherless—alone—not a friend on earth to alleviate the sorrows of life. I almost repented what I had done. Yet what right had I to sit in judgment on the mysteries of Providence? It has pleased God to interpose miraculously for her preservation:—let not man attempt to thwart his just, inscrutable designs!

We redoubled our efforts. In a little time she seemed partially to have recovered her senses. She looked wildly round, and, extending her feeble hand towards mine, cried, with a faint voice, "Arthur!" I pressed her hand—my heart was too full to speak. Alas! she did not know the touch —but, fixing her glazed eye upon me, repeated the name of Arthur. " It is not Arthur," said I—and the tears gushed as I spoke. " Oh where is he?—where are they all?"— and then, as if the memory of what had passed had suddenly flashed upon her mind, she shrieked out, and fell senseless away. I could restrain my feelings no longer, but, leaving her in the charge of the weeping domestics, hurried out of the room

The storm, which had wreaked its fury, was dissipated
as suddenly as it arose. I determined to walk abroad, and
see if I could calm the violence of my feelings in the still
moonlight. I passed through the parlour. There the repast was spread, and the chairs were standing round the
hospitable board, for those who could never fill them again.
I strayed down to the margin of the lake. The faithful
Rover was still swimming about, and whining piteously
over the fatal spot. Wherever I went, at every turn, something arose to refresh the horror of the scene.

Mary recovered to linger a few years a miserable maniac ;—

> " Though health and bloom returned, the delicate chain
> Of thought, once tangled, never cleared again."

She was sensible, however, a few moments before she died
—thanked the kind domestics, who had never left her—
and begged to be buried at the bottom of the garden, beneath an arbour which Arthur had reared.   Her injunction
was obeyed—and a small tombstone may yet be found there
under the long grass, bearing this simple inscription—

> " Poor Mary Burton rests beneath this stone ;
> God suffereth not his saints to live alone."

———◆———

Hypochondriasis and its Remedies.—RUSH.

THE extremes of low and high spirits, which occur in
the same person at different times, are happily illustrated by the following case : A physician in one of the cities
of Italy was once consulted by a gentleman, who was much
distressed by a paroxysm of this intermitting state of hy-
pochondriasm. He advised him to seek relief in convivial
company, and recommended him in particular to find out
a gentleman of the name of Cardini, who kept all the tables in the city, to which he was occasionally invited, in a
roar of laughter. " Alas! sir," said the patient, with a
heavy sigh, " I am that Cardini." Many such characters,
alternately marked by high and low spirits, are to be found
in all the cities in the world.

18

But there are sometimes flashes of apparent cheerfulness and even of mirth, in the intervals of this disease, which are accompanied with latent depression of mind. This appears to have been the case in Cowper, who knew all its symptoms by sad experience. Hence, in one of his letters to Mr. Hayley, he says, " I am cheerful upon paper, but the most distressed of all creatures." It was probably in one of these opposite states of mind, that he wrote his humorous ballad of John Gilpin.

In proportion as the hypochondriac disease advances, the symptoms of the hysteria, which are generally combined with it in its first stage, disappear, and all the systems in which the disease is seated acquire an uniformly torpid or irritable state. The remissions and intermissions which have been described cease, and even the transient blaze of cheerfulness, which now and then escapes from a heart smothered with anguish, is seen no more. The distress now becomes constant. " Clouds return after every rain." Not a ray of comfort glimmers upon the soul in any of the prospects or retrospects of life. " All is now darkness without and within." These poignant words were once uttered by a patient of mine with peculiar emphasis, while labouring under this stage of the disease. Neither nature nor art now possess a single beauty, nor music or poetry a single charm. The two latter often give pain, and sometimes offence. In vain do love and friendship, and domestic affection, offer sympathy or relief to the mind in this awful situation. Even the consolations of religion are rejected, or heard with silence and indifference. Night no longer affords a respite from misery. It is passed in distracting wakefulness, or in dreams more terrible than waking thoughts; nor does the light of the sun chase away a single distressing idea   " I rise in the morning," says Cowper, in a letter to Mr. Hayley, " like an infernal frog out of Acheron, covered with the ooze and mud of melancholy." No change of place is wished for, that promises any alleviation of suffering. " Could I be translated to paradise," says the same elegant historian of his own sorrows, in a letter to Lady Hesketh, " unless I could leave my body behind me. my melancholy would cleave to me there."

Can any thing be anticipated more dreadful than universal madness? and yet I once attended a lady in this city,
whose sufferings from low spirits were of such a nature,
that she ardently wished she might lose her reason, in order
thereby to be relieved from the horror of her thoughts.
This state of mind was not new in this disease. Shakspeare
has described it in the following lines, in his inimitable history of all the forms of derangement, in the tragedy of
King Lear. They are as truly philosophical as they are
poetical.

> ————————" Better I were distract ;
> So should my thoughts be sever'd from my griefs,
> And woes, by wrong imaginations, lose
> The knowledge of themselves "

A pleasant season, a fine day, and even the morning sun,
often suspend the disease. Cowper bears witness to the
truth of this remark, in one of his letters to Mr. Hayley.
" I rise," says he, " cheerless and distressed, and brighten
as the sun goes on."

Dr. Burton, in his Anatomy of Melancholy, delivers the
following direction for its cure : " Be not idle ; be not solitary." Dr. Johnson has improved this advice by the following commentary upon it : " When you are idle be not
solitary ; and when you are solitary be not idle." The
illustrious Spinola, upon hearing of the death of a friend,
inquired of what disease he died. " Of having nothing to
do," said the person who mentioned it. " Enough," said
Spinola, " to kill a general." Not only the want of employment, but the want of care, often increases as well as
brings on this disease.

Concerts, evening parties, and the society of the ladies, to
gentlemen affected with this disease, have been useful. Of
the efficacy of the last, Mr. Green has happily said,

> " With speech so sweet, so sweet a mien,
> They excommunicate the spleen."

Those amusements should be preferre', which, while
they interest the mind, afford exercise to the body.
The chase, shooting, playing at quoits, are all useful for
this purpose. The words of the poet, Mr. Green, upon

this subject, deserve to be committed to memory by a
physicians :

> " To cure the mind's wrong bias, spleen,
> Some recommend the bowling-green ;
> Some, hilly walks ; all, exercise ;
> Fling but a stone—the giant dies."

Chess, checkers, cards, and even push-pin, should be preferred to idleness, when the weather forbids exercise in
the open air.   The theatre has often been resorted to, to
remove fits of low spirits ; and it is a singular fact, that a
tragedy oftener dissipates them than a comedy.   The remedy, though distressing to persons with healthy minds, is
like the temperature of cold water to persons benumbed
with frost ; it is exactly proportioned to the excitability of
their minds, and it not only abstracts their attention from
themselves, but even revives their spirits.   Mirth, or even
cheerfulness, when employed as remedies in low spirits,
are like hot water to a frozen limb.   They are disproportioned to the excitability of the mind, and, instead of elevating, never fail to increase its depression, or to irritate it.
Cowper could not bear to hear his humorous story of John
Gilpin read to him in his paroxysms of this disease.   It was
to his heavy heart what Solomon happily compares to the
conflict produced by pouring vinegar upon nitre, or, in other
words, upon an alkaline salt.

   Certain objects distinguished for their beauty or grandeur
often afford relief in this disease.   Cowper experienced a
transient elevation of spirits from contemplating the ocean
from the house of his friend Mr. Hayley ; and the unfortunate Mrs. Robinson soothed the gloom of her mind, by
viewing the dashing of the waves of the same sublime object, in the light of the moon, at Brighton.   Certain animals suspend the anguish of mind of this disease, by their
innocence, ingenuity or sports.   Cowper sometimes found
relief in playing with three tame hares, and in observing
a number of leeches to rise and fall in a glass with the
changes of the weather.   The poet says,—

> " Laugh and be well.   Monkeys have been
> Extreme good doctors for the spleen
> And kitten—if the humour hit—
> Has harlequin'd away the fit "

The famous Luther was cheered under his fits of low spirits, by listening to the prattle, and observing the sports and innocent countenances, of young children. The tone of their voices is probably a source of a part of the relief derived from their company. Cowper was always exhilarated by conversing with Mr. Hayley's son, only because he was pleased with the soft and musical tones of his voice.

Music has often afforded great relief in this disease. Luther, who was sorely afflicted with it, has left the following testimony in favour of the art: " Next to Theology, I give the highest place to music, for thereby all anger is forgotten ; the devil, also melancholy, and many tribulations and evil thoughts are driven away." For the same reason that tragedies afford more relief than comedies, plaintive tunes are more useful than such as are of a sprightly nature. I attended a citizen of Philadelphia occasionally in paroxysms of this disease, who informed me that he was cured of one of them, by hearing the Old Hundred psalm tune sung in a country church. His disorder, he said, instantly left him in a flood of tears. Dr Cardan always felt a suspension of the anguish of his mind from the same cause ; and Cowper tells his friend, in one of his letters, that he was "relieved as soon as his troubles gushed from his eyes."

Climate and Scenery of New England.—TUDOR.

THE position of our confinent, and the course of the winds, will always give us an unequal climate, and one abounding in contrasts. In the latitude of 508, on the northwest coast of America, the weather is milder even than in the same parallel in Europe ;—the wind, three quarters of the year, comes off the Pacific : in the same latitude on the eastern side, the country is hardly worth inhabiting, under the dreary length of cold, produced by the succession of winds across a frozen continent. The wind and the sun, too, often carry on the contest here, which they exerted on the poor traveller in the fable ; and we are in doubt to which we shall yield. The changes that cultivation and

18 *

planetary influence, if there be such a thing, can create are very gradual. It seems to be a general opinion, that the cold is more broken now. The totals of heat and cold may be nearly the same as they were fifty years ago. The winters particularly have commenced later. The autumn is warmer and the spring colder. We are still subject to the same caprices; a flight of snow in May, a frost in June, and sometimes in every month in the year; and Æolus indulges his servants in stranger freaks and extravagances here than elsewhere; yet the severe cold seldom sets in before January; the snow is less and later, and, on the sea coast, does not, on an average, afford more than a month's sleighing.

These contrasts in our climate occasion some very picturesque effects,—some that would be considered phenomena by persons unaccustomed to them. It blends together the circumstances of very distant regions in Europe. Thus, when the earth lies buried in a deep covering of snow, in Europe, the clime is so far to the north, that the sun rises but little above the horizon, and his daily visit is a very short one;—his feeble rays hardly illumine a chilly sky, that harmonizes with the dreary waste it covers: but here, the same surface reflects a dazzling brilliancy from rays that strike at the same angle, at which they do the dome of St. Peter's. The plains of Siberia and the *Campagna di Roma* are here combined;—we have the snow of the one and the sun of the other at the same period. While his rays in the month of March are expanding the flowers and blossoms at Albano and Tivoli, they are here falling on a wide, uninterrupted covering of snow,—producing a dazzling brilliancy that is almost insupportable. A moonlight at this season is equally remarkable, and its effects can be more easily endured. Our moon is nearly the same with that moon of Naples, which Carracioli told the king of England was "superior to his majesty's sun." When this surface of spotless snow is shone upon by this moon at its full, and reflects back its beams, the light indeed is not that of day, but it takes away all appearance of night;—the witch and the spectre would shrink from its exposure:

> "It is not night,—'tis but the daylight sick ;
> It looks a little paler "

On the sea coast, the winters are milder, but the obnoxious east winds are more severely felt in the spring, than they are in the interior. The whole coast of Massachusetts Bay is remarkably exposed to their influence Some compensation, however, is derived for their harshness and virulence in the spring, by their refreshing and salutary breezes in the summer, when they frequently allay the sultry heat, and prevent it from becoming oppressive. Although a district favourably situated will enjoy an average of climate two or three degrees better than those in its neighbourhood, yet, generally, the progress of the climate is pretty regular as you follow the coast of the United States from north-east to south-west. I am induced to think, that our great rivers have some connexion with the gradations of climate; that every large river you pass makes a difference of two or three degrees in the averages of the thermometer. The position of mountains will affect the climate essentially; but these rivers, whose course upwards is northerly, will still, in general, be lines of demarcation.

One of the most agreeable peculiarities in our climate, is a period in the autumn called the Indian Summer. It happens in October, commencing a few days earlier or later, as the season may be. The temperature is delightful, and the weather differing in its character from that of any other season. The air is filled with a slight haze, like smoke, which some suppose it to be; the wind is south-west, and there is a vernal softness in the atmosphere; yet the different altitude of the sun from what it has in the summer, makes it, in other respects, very unlike that season. This singular occurrence in our climate seems to be to summer, what a vivid recollection of past joys is to the reality. The Indians have some pleasing superstitions respecting it. "They believe it is caused by a wind, which comes immediately from the court of their great and benevolent god Cautantowwit, or the south-western god, the god that is superior to all other beings, who sends them every blessing which they enjoy, and to whom the souls of their fathers go after their decease."

In connexion with our climate, the appearance of our atmosphere may be considered. The lover of picturesque

beauty will find this a fruitful source of it. The same in
equalities will be found here, that take place in the measure of heat and cold, and an equal number of contrasts and
varieties. We have many of those days, when a murky
vapourishness is diffused through the air, dimming the lustre of the sun, and producing just such tones of light and
colour as would be marked, in the calendar of Newfoundland or the Hebrides, for a bright, fair day. We have
again others, in which even the transparency and purity
of the tropics, and all the glowing mellow hues of Greece
and Naples are blended together, to shed a hue of paradise on every object. I have already spoken of the intense
brilliancy of a winter moonlight, when the air has a polar
temperature; the same brilliancy and a greater clearness are
often found in the month of June, and sometimes in July,
with the warmth of the equator. There are, occasionally, in
the summer and autumn, such magical effects of light, such
a universal tone of colouring, that the very air seems tinged;
and an aspect of such harmonious splendour is thrown over
every object, that the attention of the most indifferent is
awakened, and the lovers of the beautiful in nature enjoy
the most lively delight. These are the kinds of tints, which
even the matchless pencil of Claude vainly endeavoured
to imitate. They occur a few times every year, a little
before sunset, under a particular state of the air and position of the clouds. These beautiful appearances are not
so frequent, indeed, here, as they are at Naples; all those
warm and delicate colours, which we see in Neapolitan
pictures, occur there more often; but I have frequently
seen the hills on the south of Boston exhibiting, towards
sunset, the same exquisite hues, which Vesuvius more frequently presents, and which the Neapolitans, in their paintings of it, always adopt. The vivid beauty, which I now
speak of, is rare and transient; but we often enjoy the
charms of a transparent atmosphere, where objects stand
in bold relief, and even distant ones will present all their
hues and angles, clear and sharp, from the deep distant sky,
as on the shores of Greece; and we gaze at sunset on gorgeous skies, where all the magnificence, that form and colour can combine, is accumulated to enrapture the eye, and
render description hopeless.

The scenery of this country will have struck you at
once, as very different from that of Europe. This difference is partly intrinsic, and partly accidental,—arising out
of the kinds and degrees of cultivation. The most obvious
and extensive view, in which it differs, is the redundancy
of forest. A vast forest, to a person who had never seen
one, would excite almost as strong sensations, as the sight
of the ocean to him who beheld it for the first time ;
and in both cases a long continuance of the prospect becomes tiresome. From some of our hills, the spectator
looks over an expanse of woods bounded by the horizon,
and slightly chequered by cultivation. The view is grand
and imposing at first, but will be more agreeable, and afford
more lasting pleasure, when the relative proportions of wood
and open ground are reversed. The most cultivated parts
of these States approach nearest to some of the most covered in England, that are not an actual forest. We have
nothing like the Downs on your southern coast,—and fatiguing as an eternal forest may be, it is less so than those
dreary wastes, as destitute of objects as the mountain
swell of the ocean. We have still so much wood, that, even
in the oldest cultivated parts of the country, it is difficult
to find a panoramic view of any extent, where some patches
of the native forest are not to be found. I know of but
one exception, which is from the steeple of the church in
Ipswich, in Essex, Massachusetts. This is one of the oldest
towns ; the prospect will put you in mind of the scenery
of your own country ;—I need not add, that it is a very
pleasing one, and will repay you for the slight trouble of
ascending the steeple.

The trees, though there are too many of them, at least
in masses, must please the eye of an European, from their
variety and beauty, as well as novelty. The richness of
our trees and shrubs has always excited the admiration of
botanists and the lovers of landscape gardening. There
can be nothing nobler than the appearance of some of the
oaks and beeches in England, and the walnuts and chest-
nuts in France and Italy. The vast size of these spreading
trees is only surpassed by some of our sycamores on the
banks of the Ohio. Our oaks may sometimes be seen of
the same size,—and the towering white pine and hemlock

reach a height, that I had never seen attained by trees in
Europe ;—but, for grandeur of appearance, we must rely,
in the first instance, on the American elm, that has been
planted for ornament. Its colour, its form, and its size,
place it much before the European elm; it is one of our
most majestic trees. There are many varieties of it very
distinct,—yet not so numerous as of the oaks, walnuts and
some others. Of the former, you know, we have between
thirty and forty different species, and a great number of
species exist of all our principal trees. This variety, in the
hands of taste, would be made productive of the highest
effects in ornamental planting, of which you may find more
specimens in your own country than in this, though only
a part of our riches in this way have been transplanted by
your gardeners. You will remark the fresh and healthy
look of our forest, as well as fruit trees, compared with
those of all the northern parts of Europe. The humidity
of that atmosphere nourishes the mosses, and a green coat-
ing over the trunks and branches, that give the aspect of
disease and decay. You will often observe the clean and
smooth bark of our trees of all kinds : among the forest
trees, particularly the walnut, maple, beech, birch, &c. will
be entirely free from moss or rust of any kind,—and their
trunks form fine contrasts with the leaves. You will have
too much of forest in this country to go in pursuit of one
but, should you happen to visit Nashawn, one of the Elizabeth Islands, you will see the most beautiful insulated forest in the United States, with less of that ragged, lank look,
which our native forests commonly present, from the trees
struggling with each other for the light, and running up to
great height, with few or no branches; but this one exhibits
the tufted, rounded masses, which are found in the groves
of your parks.

I will mention a peculiarity, which you will witness in
autumn, that will affect a lover of landscape scenery, like
yourself, on seeing it the first time, with surprise as well
as delight. The rich and mellow tints of the forest, at that
season of the year, have often furnished subjects for the
poet and the painter in Europe; but it will hardly prepare
you for the sights our woods exhibit. I have never seen
a representation of them attempted in painting; it would

probably be grotesque. Besides all the shades of brown
and green, which you have in European trees, there are
the most brilliant and glaring colours,—bright yellow, and
scarlet for instance,—not merely on single leaves, but in
masses of whole trees, with all their foliage thus tinged.
I do not know that it has ever been accounted for; it may
perhaps be owing to the frosts coming earlier here than in
Europe, and falling on the leaves while the sap is yet copious, before they have begun to dry up and fall off. However this may be, the colouring is wonderful; the walnut
is turned to the brightest yellow, the maple to scarlet, &c.
Our trees put on this harlequin dress about the first of
October. I leave to your imagination, which can never
reach the reality, to fancy the appearance of such scenes
as you may behold at this season. A cloudless sky, and
transparent atmosphere, a clear blue lake, with meadows
of light, delicate green, backed by hills and dales of those
party-coloured, gorgeous forests, are often combined, to form
the most enchanting views.

First and Second Death.—GREENWOOD.

THE first death is the death of the body; the quenching
of that undiscovered spark, which warms and animates the
human frame; the return of our dust to the earth as it
was; the event which happeneth unto all men; "the
sentence of the Lord over all flesh." We cannot prevent
it. Like birth, it is inevitable. Helplessly, and without
our own will, we open our eyes at first to the light of day;
and then, by an equal necessity, we lie down to sleep,
some at this hour, some at the next, on the lap of our
mother. This death is an ordinance of God. It was
intended for our benefit; and can do us no essential harm.
It disturbs not the welfare of the soul; it touches not the
life of the spirit.

The second death is more awful and momentous. It is
the death of that which the first death left alive. It is the
death of reputation, the death of love, the death of happiness, the exile of the soul It has no connexion with the

first death, for its causes are all engendered in the h͏ͅe ot the body. Unlike the first, it is a death which all men dc not die. Unlike the first, it is a death from which there is a way of escape. And yet there are more who are terrified with the first death, unimportant as it is, than there are who fear the second, though it includes every wo. And almost all men attempt to fly from the first, though they know it to be impossible ; while few take pains to avoid the last, though it is within their ability to do so.

The first death, then, is invested with complete power over all men. It withers human strength, it respects not human authority. Rank is not exempt from it, art cannot elude, riches cannot bribe, eloquence cannot soften, nor can even virtue overcome it. But with that second and far more dreadful death, it is not so. There are those over whom it hath no power. Any one may join their number. There is no mystery, no hardship, in the terms of the blessed exemption. All may read, all may comply with them. They arise from the nature of the second death. For as nothing but vice and disobedience towards God can affect the life of the spirit, and invest the second death with its power, so it is righteousness only, and the healthful fruits of religion, which can defy and render it powerless. " In the way of righteousness there is life, and in the pathway thereof there is no death." So little is the first death considered, and so little account of it is made, in many parts of Scripture, that we are told, in some of its sublimest strains, that the believer in Jesus, the true Christian, " shall never die." Goodness carries with it the eternal principles of life, deeply engrafted into its constitution ; so that it cannot lose it, nor part with it. It is the good, the benevolent, the pious, and the pure, to whom life is promised ; and on such " the second death has no power."

In the sight of men they die ; and so far there is indeed but one event to the righteous and the wicked. But this is only the first, the corporeal death ; and in all essential respects they live.

Posthumous Influence of the Wise and Good.—Norton.

The relations between man and man cease not with life The dead leave behind them their memory, their exam. ple, and the effects of their actions. Their influence stil abides with us. Their names and characters dwell in our thoughts and hearts. We live and commune with them in their writings. We enjoy the benefit of their labours. Our institutions have been founded by them. We are surrounded by the works of the dead. Our knowledge and our arts are the fruit of their toil. Our minds have been formed by their instructions. We are most intimately connected with them by a thousand dependencies. Those whom we have loved in life are still objects of our deepest and holiest affections. Their power over us remains They are with us in our solitary walks; and their voices speak to our hearts in the silence of midnight. Their image is impressed upon our dearest recollections, and our most sacred hopes. They form an essential part of our treasure laid up in heaven. For, above all, we are separated from them but for a little time. We are soon to be united with them. If we follow in the path of those we have loved, we too shall soon join the innumerable company of the spirits of just men made perfect. Our affections and our hopes are not buried in the dust, to which we commit the poor remains of mortality. The blessed retain their remembrance and their love for us in heaven; and we will cherish our remembrance and our love for them while on earth.

Creatures of imitation and sympathy as we are, we look around us for ⁿ pport and countenance even in our virtues. We recur for them, most securely, to the examples of the dead. There is a degree of insecurity and uncertainty about living worth. The stamp has not yet been put upon it, which precludes all change, and seals it up as a just object of admiration for future times. There is no service which a man of commanding intellect can render his fellow creatures better than that of leaving behind him an unspotted example. If he do not confer upon them this benefit; if he leave a character dark with vices in the

19

sight of God, but dazzling with shining qualities in the
view of men; it may be that all his other services had
better have been forborne, and he had passed inactive and
unnoticed through life. It is a dictate of wisdom, therefore, as well as feeling, when a man, eminent for his virtues and talents, has been taken away, to collect the riches
of his goodness, and add them to the treasury of human
improvement. The true Christian *liveth not for himself,
and dieth not for himself;* and it is thus, in one respect,
that he dieth not for himself.

Difficulties encountered by the Federal Convention.
MADISON.

AMONG the difficulties encountered by the convention,
a very important one must have lain, in combining the
requisite stability and energy in government, with the
inviolable attention due to liberty, and to the republican
form. Without substantially accomplishing this part of
their undertaking, they would have very imperfectly fulfilled the object of their appointment, or the expectation
of the public; yet, that it could not easily be accomplished,
will be denied by no one, who is unwilling to betray his
ignorance on the subject. Energy in government is
essential to that security against external and internal
danger, and to that prompt and salutary execution of the
laws, which enter into the very definition of good government. Stability in government is essential to national
character, and to the advantages annexed to it, as well as
to that repose and confidence in the minds of the people,
which are among the chief blessings of civil society. An
irregular and mutable legislation is not more an evil in
itself, than it is odious to the people; and it may be pronounced with assurance, that the people in this country,
enlightened as they are with regard to the nature, and
interested, as the great body of them are, in the effects
of good government, will never be satisfied till some
remedy be applied to the vicissitudes and uncertainties,
which characterize the state administrations. On compar-

ing, however, these valuable ingredients with the vital principles of liberty, we must perceive, at once, the difficulty of mingling them together in their due proportions. The genius of republican liberty seems to demand, on the one side, not only that all power should be derived from the people, but that those intrusted with it should be kept in dependence on the people, by a short duration of their appointments ; and that, even during this short period, the trust should be placed not in a few, but in a number of hands.   Stability, on the contrary, requires that the hands in which power is lodged should remain for a length of time the same.   A frequent change of men will result from a frequent return of elections ; and a frequent change of measures from a frequent change of men ; whilst energy in government requires not only a certain duration of power, but the execution of it by a single person.

Not less arduous must have been the task of marking the proper line of partition between the authority of the general, and that of the state governments.   Every man will be sensible of this difficulty, in proportion as he has been accustomed to contemplate and discriminate objects, extensive and complicated in their nature.   The faculties of the mind itself have never yet been distinguished and defined, with satisfactory precision, by all the efforts of the most acute and metaphysical philosophers.   Sense, perception, judgment, desire, volition, memory, imagination, are found to be separated by such delicate shades and minute gradations, that their boundaries have eluded the most subtile investigations, and remain a pregnant source of ingenious disquisition and controversy.   The boundaries between the great kingdoms of nature, and, still more, between the various provinces and lesser proportions into which they are subdivided, afford another illustration of the same important truth.   The most sagacious and laborious naturalists have never yet succeeded in tracing, with certainty, the line which separates the district of vegetable life from the neighbouring region of unorganized matter, or which marks the termination of the former, and the commencement of the animal empire.   A still greater obscurity lies in the distinctive characters, by which the object in each of these great departments of nature have been arranged and assorted.

When we pass from the works of nature, in which all the delineations are perfectly accurate, and appear to be otherwise only from the imperfection of the eye which surveys them, to the institutions of man, in which the obscurity arises as well from the object itself, as from the organ by which it is contemplated, we must perceive the necessity of moderating still further our expectations and hopes from the efforts of human sagacity. Experience has instructed us, that no skill in the science of government has yet been able to discriminate and define, with sufficient certainty, its three great provinces, the legislative, the executive, and the judiciary ; or even the privileges and powers of the different legislative branches. Questions daily occur, in the course of practice, which prove the obscurity that reigns over these subjects, and which puzzle the greatest adepts in political science.

Besides the obscurity arising from the complexity of objects, and the imperfection of the human faculties, the medium through which the conceptions of men are conveyed to each other, adds a fresh embarrassment. The use of words is to express ideas. Perspicuity, therefore, requires not only that the ideas should be distinctly formed, but that they should be expressed by words distinctively and exclusively appropriated to them. But no language is so copious as to supply words and phrases for every complex idea, or so correct as not to include many equivocally denoting different ideas. Hence it must happen, that, however accurately objects may be discriminated in themselves, and however accurately the discrimination may be considered, the definition of them may be rendered inaccurate by the inaccuracy of the terms in which it is delivered. And this unavoidable inaccuracy must be greater or less, according to the complexity and novelty of the objects defined. When the Almighty himself condescends to address mankind in their own language, his meaning, luminous as it must be, is rendered dim and doubtful by the cloudy medium through which it is communicated.

Here, then, are three sources of vague and incorrect definitions;—indistinctness of the object, imperfection of the organ of perception, inadequateness of the vehicle of ideas. Any one of these must produce a certain degree of obscurity. The convention, in delineating the boundary between the federal and state jurisdictions, must have experienced the full effect of them all.

Would it be wonderful if, under the pressure of all these difficulties, the convention should have been forced into some deviations from that artificial structure and regular symmetry, which an abstract view of the subject might lead an ingenious theorist to bestow on a constitution planned in his closet or in his imagination? The real wonder is, that so many difficulties should have been surmounted; and surmounted with unanimity almost as unprecedented as it must have been unexpected. It is impossible for any man of candour to reflect on this circumstance without partaking of the astonishment. It is impossible for the man of pious reflection not to perceive in it the finger of that Almighty Hand, which has been so frequently and signally extended to our relief in the critical stages of the revolution.

Reflections on the Battle of Lexington.—EDWARD EVERETT.

IT was one of those great days, one of those elemental occasions in the world's affairs, when the people rise and act for themselves. Some organization and preparation had been made; but, from the nature of the case, with scarce any effect on the events of that day. It may be doubted, whether there was an efficient order given the whole day to any body of men as large as a regiment. It was the people, in their first capacity, as citizens and as freemen, starting from their beds at midnight, from their firesides, and their fields, to take their own cause into their own hands. Such a spectacle is the height of the moral sublime; when the want of every thing is fully made up by the spirit of the cause; and the soul within stands in place of discipline, organization, resources. In the prodigious

19 *

efforts of a veteran army, beneath the dazzling splendour
of their array, there is something revolting to the reflecting
mind.   The ranks are filled with the desperate, the
mercenary, the depraved ; an iron slavery, by the name
of subordination, merges the free will of one hundred
thousand men in the unqualified despotism of one ; the
humanity, mercy, and remorse, which scarce ever desert the individual bosom, are sounds without a meaning
to that fearful, ravenous, irrational monster of prey, a
mercenary army.   It is hard to say who are most to be
commiserated, the wretched people on whom it is let loose,
or the still more wretched people whose substance has
been sucked out, to nourish it into strength and fury.   But
in the efforts of the people, of the people struggling for
their rights, moving not in organized, disciplined masses,
but in their spontaneous action, man for man, and heart for
heart,—though I like not war, nor any of its works,—there
is something glorious.   They can then move forward
without orders, act together without combination, and brave
the flaming lines of battle, without entrenchments to cover,
or walls to shield them.   No dissolute camp has worn off
from the feelings of the youthful soldier the freshness of
that home, where his mother and his sisters sit waiting,
with tearful eyes and aching hearts, to hear good news
from the wars; no long service in the ranks of the con-
queror has turned the veteran's heart into marble ; their
valor springs not from recklessness, from habit, from indifference to the preservation of a life, knit by no pledges to
the life of others; but in the strength and spirit of the cause
alone they act, they contend, they bleed.   In this they conquer.   The people always conquer.   They always must conquer.   Armies may be defeated ; kings may be overthrown,
and new dynasties imposed by foreign arms on an ignorant
and slavish race, that care not in what language the covenant of their subjection runs, nor in whose name the deed
of their barter and sale is made out.   But the people never
invade , and, when they rise against the invader, are never
subdued.   If they are driven from the plains, they fly to
the mountains.   Steep rocks and everlasting hills are their
castles ; the tangled, pathless thicket their palisado ; and
nature,—God,—is their ally.   Now he overwhelms the

nos s of their enemies beneath his drifting mountains of
san.; now he buries them beneath an atmosphere of falling
snows; he lets loose his tempests on their fleets; he puts
a folly into their counsels, a madness into the hearts of
their leaders; and he never gave, and never will give, a full
and final triumph over a virtuous, gallant people, resolved
to be free.

Purpose of the Monument on Bunker Hill.—WEBSTER.

WE know that the record of illustrious actions is most
safely deposited in the universal remembrance of mankind.
We know, that if we could cause this structure to ascend,
not only till it reached the skies, but till it pierced them,
its broad surfaces could still contain but part of that, which,
in an age of knowledge, hath already been spread over the
earth, and which History charges herself with making
known to all future times.   We know that no inscription,
on entablatures less broad than the earth itself, can carry
information of the events we commemorate where it has
not already gone; and that no structure, which shall not
outlive the duration of letters and knowledge among men,
can prolong the memorial.   But our object is, by this edifice, to show our deep sense of the value and importance
of the achievements of our ancestors; and, by presenting
this work of gratitude to the eye, to keep alive similar
sentiments, and to foster a constant regard to the principles
of the revolution.   Human beings are composed not of reason only, but of imagination also, and sentiment; and that
is neither wasted nor misapplied, which is appropriated to
the purpose of giving right direction to sentiments, and
opening proper springs of feeling in the heart.

Let it not be supposed that our object is to perpetuate
national hostility, or even to cherish a mere military spirit.
It is higher, purer, nobler.   We consecrate our work to
the spirit of national independence, and we wish that the
light of peace may rest upon it forever.   We rear a memorial of our conviction of that unmeasured benefit, which
has been conferred on our land, and of the happy influences,

which have been produced, by the same events, on the general interests of mankind. We come, as Americans, to mark a spot, which must be forever dear to us, and our posterity. We wish, that whosoever, in all coming time, shall turn his eye hither, may behold that the place is not undistinguished where the first great battle of the revolution was fought. We wish, that this structure may proclaim the magnitude and importance of that event to every class and every age. We wish, that infancy may learn the purpose of its erection from maternal lips, and that weary and withered age may behold it, and be solaced by the recollections which it suggests. We wish, that labor may look up here, and be proud, in the midst of its toil. We wish, that, in those days of disaster, which, as they come upon all nations, must be expected to come on us also, desponding patriotism may turn its eyes hither, and be assured that the foundations of our national power still stand strong. We wish, that this column, rising towards heaven among the pointed spires of so many temples dedicated to God, may contribute also to produce, in all minds, a pious feeling of dependence and gratitude. We wish, finally, that the last object on the sight of him who leaves his native shore, and the first to gladden his who revisits it, may be something which shall remind him of the liberty and glory of his country. Let it rise, till it meet the sun in his coming ; let the earliest light of morning gild it, and parting day linger and play upon its summit.

Albums and the Alps.—BUCKMINSTER.

You find, in some of the rudest passes in the Alps, homely inns, which public beneficence has erected for the convenience of the weary and benighted traveller. In most of these inns albums are kept to record the names of those, whose curiosity has led them into these regions of barrenness, and the album is not unfrequently the only book in the house. In the album of the Grand Chartreuse, Gray, on his way to Geneva, recorded his deathless name, and left that exquisite Latin ode, beginning, "O ! tu severi

religio loci ;" an ode which is indeed " pure nectar." It
is curious to observe in these books the differences of national character. The Englishman usually writes his name
only, without explanation or comment. The Frenchman
records something of his feelings, destination, or business ;
commonly adding a line of poetry, an epigram, or some
exclamation of pleasure or disgust. The German leaves a
long dissertation upon the state of the roads, the accommodations, &c., detailing at full length whence he came and
whither he is going, through long pages of crabbed
writing.

In one of the highest regions of the Swiss Alps, after a
day of excessive labour in reaching the summit of our
journey, near those thrones erected ages ago for the majesty of Nature, we stopped, fatigued and dispirited, on a
spot destined to eternal barrenness, where we found one of
these rude but hospitable inns open to receive us. There
was not another human habitation within many miles. All
the soil, which we could see, had been brought thither, and
placed carefully round the cottage, to nourish a few cabbages
and lettuces. There were some goats, which supplied the
cottagers with milk ; a few fowls lived in the house ; and
the greatest luxuries of the place were new-made cheeses,
and some wild Alpine mutton, the rare provision of the traveller. Yet here Nature had thrown off the veil, and
appeared in all her sublimity. Summits of bare granite
rose all around us. The snow-clad tops of distant Alps
seemed to chill the moon-beams that lighted on them;
and we felt all the charms of the picturesque, mingled
with the awe inspired by unchangeable grandeur. We
seemed to have reached the original elevations of the
globe, o'ertopping forever the tumults, the vices and the
miseries of ordinary existence, far out of hearing of the
murmurs of a busy world, which discord ravages, and
luxury corrupts. We asked for the album, and a large
folio was brought to us, almost filled with the scrawls of
every nation on earth that could write. Instantly our
fatigue was forgotten, and the evening passed away pleasantly in the entertainment which this book afforded us.
I copied the following French couplet :

> " Dans ces sauvages lieux tout orgueil s'humanise ,
> Dieu s'y montre plus grand ; l'homme s'y pulverise !
>   "Signed,
>   " p. ed. trénir."

I wish I could preserve the elegance, as well as the con
densed sentiment of the original

> Still are these rugged realms ; e'en pride is hushed ;
> God seems more grand ; man crumbles into dust

Interview with Robert Southey.—GRISCOM.

ON alighting at Keswick, I inquired for the house of
Robert Southey ; for it is in this poetic region that the
laureate has fixed his residence ; remote from the confusion
and irritations of the metropolis ; but holding a daily intercourse, by the rapid conveyance of the mail, with that
great fountain of intelligence, and deriving all that he may
wish from the prolific stores of Paternoster-Row. His
house is situated on an eminence, with a fine prospect
before it ; a plain and unimposing, but comfortable mansion. I was introduced to him in his library up stairs, and
was met with an ease and politeness, which distinguished
at once the man of kind feeling, of good sense, and good
society. He has still an air of youthfulness in his countenance, and his manners are lively and animated.

There are few men, I should presume, in England, who
are spending their lives more classically, in a more agreeable literary retirement, than Robert Southey. His library
occupies several rooms. The fertility of his mind, and the
activity of his researches, appear to leave him at no loss in
the selection of a subject for the employment of his genius ; and the different productions of his pen are too well
known to need any remarks from me upon their various
merits. His early life was spent in Bristol. It was in
that neighbourhood that Coleridge,* Lovell, and himself, all

---

* The youthful enthusiasm, which dictated this romantic idea, is a
beautifully referred to in an essay in the first volume of " The Friend,'
by Coleridge ; whose prose writings should be more extensively known
in this country than they are.—ED

fellow commoners at Oxford, attached themselves to three sisters of a respectable family, whom they married ; and, in the ardour of youthful anticipation, and with those high-wrought notions of worldly happiness, which always have much more of poetry than of sober judgment in them, they resolved, with their wives, to embark for the United States, to settle themselves in a retired spot on the banks of the Susquehannah, there to plant an Arcadia, and there to spend a life of primitive simplicity and Elysian enjoyment. Happily for their comfort, and the credit of English litera-ture, the scheme was given up.

Southey is about forty-five years of age. His person is of the middle size, and his looks and manners are indic-ative of frankness and amiableness of character. In the same house, but in separate apartments, the two sisters of his wife, the widow of Lovell, and the wife of Coleridge, the poet, also reside. The former of these two, who lost her husband soon after her marriage, has employed herself in instructing the daughters of her brother-in-law. Cole-ridge lives, I believe, altogether in London ; the separation from his wife arising more from his eccentricities and sin-gularities than from any breach of family agreement. His two sons remain with their mother, and I have understood that Southey, with a liberality that does him the highest honour, takes upon himself the responsibility of their edu-cation, and the utmost harmony prevails in the family.

In rising to take leave, after an hour of delightful con-versation, Southey proposed to walk with me on the mar-gin of the lake. We had a charming ramble of half a mile along a path which presented, at various points, beau-tiful views of the Derwent-water. This end of the lake is diversified with islands, some of which are adorned with elegant mansions. Boats, neatly painted, and adapted to excursions of pleasure, are kept by many of the inhab-itants of Keswick. The grounds, through which we walked, belonged formerly to the Earl of Derwent-water; but, becoming confiscated to the crown, they were appro-priated to the support of Greenwich Hospital, to the funds of which they still contribute. We walked to a point which gave us a view of the southern termination of the lake, and the entrance of Borrowdale. The scenery is wild and beautiful, reminding me of Lake George in .our own state, but more subdued and enriched by cultivation Skiddaw, one of the highest mountains in Cumberland, rises a little to the north of Keswick. Its summit is about three thousand feet above the level of the sea, equalling, in point of elevation, the highest peak of the High-lands, through which the Hudson passes, just below Newburgh. Southey informed me that he had made an excursion to the top of this mountain with Sir Humphrey Davy. Near the summit the latter discovered a mineral of rare occurrence, (if I recollect rightly, the chiastolite,) found only in clay-slate, which appears to be the prevailing formation of this mountain.—Our walk along the Derwent having extended as far as my limited time would admit, we returned to one of the village inns, where I parted with a person, whose conversation and suavity of manners, more than the poetry and the prose, which have placed him among the most prominent of living authors, have left an impression which I shall delight in cherishing.

Christmas.—Irving.

There is nothing in England that exercises a more delightful spell over my imagination than the lingerings of the holyday customs and rural games of former times. They recall the pictures my fancy used to draw in the May-morning of my life, when as yet I only knew the world through books, and believed it to be all that poets had painted ; and they bring with them the flavour of those honest days of yore, in which, perhaps with equal fallacy, I am apt to think the world was more home-bred, social, and joyous, than at present. I regret to say, that they are daily growing more and more faint, being gradually worn away by time, but still more obliterated by modern fashion. They resemble those picturesque morsels of Gothic architecture, which we see crumbling in various parts of the country, partly dilapidated by the waste of ages, and partly lost in the additions and alterations of latter days. Poetry, however, clings with cherishing fond

ness about the rural game and holyday revel, from which
it has derived so many of its themes—as the ivy winds its
rich foliage about the gothic arch and mouldering tower,
gratefully repaying their support, by clasping together
their tottering remains, and, as it were, embalming them
in verdure.

Of all the old festivals, however, that of Christmas awakens the strongest and most heart-felt associations. There
is a tone of sacred and solemn feeling, that blends with our
conviviality, and lifts the spirit to a state of hallowed and
elevated enjoyment. The services of the church about
this season are extremely tender and inspiring. They
dwell on the beautiful story of the origin of our faith, and
the pastoral scenes that accompanied its announcement.
They gradually increase in fervour and pathos during the
season of Advent, until they break forth in full jubilee on
the morning that brought peace and good-will to men. I
do not know a grander effect of music on the moral feelings, than to hear the full choir and the pealing organ
performing a Christmas anthem in a cathedral, and filling
every part of the vast pile with triumphant harmony.

It is a beautiful arrangement, also, derived from days of
yore, that this festival, which commemorates the announcement of the religion of peace and love, has been made the
season for gathering together of family connexions, and
drawing closer again those bands of kindred hearts, which
the cares and pleasures and sorrows of the world are continually operating to cast loose ; of calling back the children of a family who have launched forth in life, and wan-
dered widely asunder, once more to assemble about the
paternal hearth, that rallying place of the affections, there
to grow young and loving again among the endearing
mementos of childhood.

There is something in the very season of the year, that
gives a charm to the festivity of Christmas. At other
times we derive a great portion of our pleasures from the
beauties of nature. Our feelings sally forth, and dissipate
themselves over the sunny landscape, and we " live abroad
and every where." The song of the bird, the murmur of
the stream, the breathing fragrance of spring, the soft
voluptuousness of summer, the golden pomp of autumn,

20

earth, with its mantle of refreshing green, and heaven
with its deep, delicious blue, and its cloudy magnificence,
all fill us with mute but exquisite delight, and we revel in
the luxury of mere sensation. But in the depth of win
ter, when Nature lies despoiled of every charm, and
wrapped in her shroud of sheeted snow, we turn for our
gratifications to moral sources. The dreariness and desolation of the landscape, the short, gloomy days, and dark-
some nights, while they circumscribe our wanderings, shut
in our feelings, also, from rambling abroad, and make us
more keenly disposed for the pleasures of the social circle.
Our thoughts are more concentrated; our friendly sympathies more aroused. We feel more sensibly the charm of
each other's society, and are brought more closely together by dependence on each other for enjoyment. Heart
calleth unto heart, and we draw our pleasures from· the
deep wells of living kindness, which lie in the deep recesses
of our bosoms, and which, when resorted to, furnish forth
the pure element of domestic felicity. The pitchy gloom
without makes the heart dilate on entering the room filled
with the glow and warmth of the evening fire. The ruddy
blaze diffuses an artificial summer and sunshine through
the room, and lights up each countenance into a kindlier
welcome. Where does the honest face of hospitality
expand into a broader and more cordial smile—where is
the shy glance of love more sweetly eloquent—than by the
winter fire-side? And, as the hollow blast of wintry wind
rushes through the hall, claps the distant door, whistles
about the casement, and rumbles down the chimney, what
can be more grateful than that feeling of sober and sheltered security, with which we look round upon the comfortable chamber, and the scene of domestic hilarity?

Declaration of American Independence.—JEFFERSON.

WHEN, in the course of human events, it becomes
necessary for one people to dissolve the political bands
which have connected them with another, and to assume,
among the powers of the earth, the separate and equal sta-

tion, to which the laws of nature and of nature's God entitle them, a decent respect to the opinions of mankind requires that they should declare the causes which impel them to the separation.

We hold these truths to be self-evident:—that all men are created equal; that they are endowed by their Creator with certain unalienable rights, that among these are life, liberty, and the pursuit of happiness; that, to secure these rights, governments are instituted among men, deriving their just powers from the consent of the governed; that, whenever any form of government becomes destructive of these ends, it is the right of the people to alter or to abolish it, and to institute a new government, laying its foundation on such principles, and organizing its powers in such form, as to them shall seem most likely to effect their safety and happiness. Prudence, indeed, will dictate, that govern ments long established should not be changed for light and transient causes; and, accordingly, all experience hath shown, that mankind are more disposed to suffer, while evils are sufferable, than to right themselves by abolishing the forms to which they are accustomed. But when a long train of abuses and usurpations, pursuing invariably the same object, evinces a design to reduce them under absolute despotism, it is their right, it is their duty, to throw off such government, and to provide new guards for their future security. Such has been the patient suffer-ance of these colonies, and such is now the necessity which constrains them to alter their former systems of government. The history of the present king of Great Britain is a history of repeated injuries and usurpations, all having in direct object the establishment of an absolute tyranny over these states. To prove this, let facts be sub-mitted to a candid world.

He has refused his assent to laws the most wholesome and necessary for the public good. He has forbidden his governors to pass laws of immediate and pressing impor-tance, unless suspended in their operation till his assent should be obtained; and, when so suspended, he has utterly neglected to attend to them He has refused to pass other laws for the accommodation of large districts of people, unless those people would relinquish the right of representation in the legislature—a right inestimable to them, and formidable to tyrants only. He has called together legislative bodies, at places unusual, uncomfortable, and distant from the depositories of their public records, for the sole purpose of fatiguing them into compliance with his measures. He has dissolved representatives houses, repeatedly, for opposing, with manly firmness, his invasions on the rights of the people. He has refused, for a long time after such dissolutions, to cause others to be elected ; whereby the legislative powers, incapable of annihilation, have returned to the people at large for their exercise ; the state remaining, in the mean time, exposed to all the danger of invasion from without, and convulsions within. He has endeavoured to prevent the population of these states ; for that purpose obstructing the laws for naturalization of foreigners ; refusing to pass others, to encourage their migration hither, and raising the conditions of new appropriations of lands. He has obstructed the administration of justice, by refusing his assent to laws for establishing judiciary powers. He has made judges dependent on his will, alone, for the tenure of their offices, and the amount and payment of their salaries. He has erected a multitude of new offices, and sent hither swarms of officers to harass our people, and eat out their substance. He has kept among us, in times of peace, standing armies, without the consent of our legislatures. He has affected to render the military independent of, and superior to, the civil power. He has combined with others to subject us to a jurisdiction foreign to our constitution, and unacknowledged by our laws ; giving his assent to their acts of pretended legislation,—for quartering large bodies of armed troops among us ; for protecting them, by a mock trial, from punishment for any murders which they should commit on the inhabitants of these states ; for cutting off our trade with all parts of the world ; for imposing taxes on us without our consent ; for depriving us, in many cases, of the benefits of trial by jury ; for transporting us beyond seas, to be tried for pretended offences : for abolishing the free system of English laws in a neighbouring province, establishing therein an arbitrary government, and enlarging its boundaries so as to render it at once an example, and fit instrument.

for introducing the same absolute rule into these colonies; for taking away our charters, abolishing our most valuable laws, and altering fundamentally the forms of our governments; for suspending our own legislatures, and declaring themselves invested with power to legislate for us in all cases whatsoever. He has abdicated government here, by declaring us out of his protection, and waging war against us. He has plundered our seas, ravaged our coasts, burned our towns, and destroyed the lives of our people. He is at this time transporting large armies of foreign mercenaries, to complete the work of death, desolation, and tyranny, already begun, with circumstances of cruelty and perfidy, scarcely paralleled in the most barbarous ages, and totally unworthy the head of a civilized nation. He has constrained our fellow-citizens, taken captive on the high seas, to bear arms against their country, to become the executioners of their friends and brethren, or to fall themselves by their hands. He has excited domestic insurrections amongst us, and has endeavoured to bring on the inhabitants of our frontiers the merciless Indian savages, whose known rule of warfare is, an undistinguished destruction of all ages, sexes, and conditions.

In every stage of these oppressions, we have petitioned for redress in the most humble terms. Our repeated petitions have been answered only by repeated injury. A prince, whose character is thus marked by every act which may define a tyrant, is unfit to be the ruler of a free people.—Nor have we been wanting in attention to our British brethren. We have warned them, from time to time, of attempts made by their legislature to extend an unwarrantable jurisdiction over us. We have reminded them of the circumstances of our emigration and settlement here. We have appealed to their native justice and magnanimity, and we have conjured them, by the ties of our common kindred, to disavow these usurpations, which would inevitably interrupt our connexions and correspondence. They, too have been deaf to the voice of justice and of consanguinity We must therefore acquiesce in the necessity which denounces our separation; and hold them, as we hold the rest of mankind,—enemies in war,—in peace, friends.

20 *

We, therefore, the representatives of the United States
of America, in general congress assembled, appealing to
the Supreme Judge of the world for the rectitude of our
ntentions, do, in the name and by the authority of the good
people of these colonies, solemnly publish and declare, that
these united colonies are, and of right ought to be, free and
independent states; that they are absolved from all allegiance to the British crown, and that all political connexion between them and the state of Great Britain is, and
ought to be, totally dissolved; and that, as free and independent states, they have full power to levy war, conclude
peace, contract alliances, establish commerce, and to do all
other acts and things which independent states may of
right do. And for the support of this Declaration, with
a firm reliance on the protection of Divine Providence,
we mutually pledge to each other our lives, our fortunes,
and our sacred honour.

Mementos of the Instability of human Existence.— FITCH.

WE have such a memento in the fact, that others, who
have been sharing with us in our privileges, are constant-
y leaving the world.   They who dwell with us in the city
of our residence on earth—beings of immortality—are
constantly bidding us adieu, and entering into eternity. All
our privileges thus become associated with the memory of
former companions, who once had their abode below. They
dwelled with us but a few days, they scarcely made themselves known to us, when they gave the farewell look,
pressed the parting hand, bade adieu, and entered on an
abode in eternity.   The tolling bell, the mournful procession, the grave of their relics, the erected monument, signalized their departure; and now all around the city of our
abode are the traces of their former presence, reminding us
of our having no continuing residence here.   We look back
at the days they passed with us before they entered into
eternity, and they appear to us but a hand breadth; and,
from their dwelling in eternity, we seem to hear them say,

as we miss them from the scenes in which they once mingled with us, that these are scenes where pilgrims to eter.
nity tarry but a day.   When in the habitations where they
once dwelt with us, or in the streets where they walked with
us, or the sanctuary to which they went with us in company,
or at the mercy-seat where they once bent with us the knee
of devotion, or by the Scriptures before which they once
listened with us to the words of Jesus Christ, we look for
them, but they are gone ; the place which they once occupied at our side is vacant ; they are far from us in their
eternal dwelling ; and the places where we once knew
them are now so many mementos, that here we ourselves
have no continuing city.

We have another continual memento of this fact, in the
advancement we are constantly making ourselves towards
eternity.   Every thing in the city of our residence on
earth reminds us, that we are never stationary in it, but are
always advancing towards the period of our final departure.
We have entered into a scene of divine wonders, but we
cannot delay to spend our existence here in gazing upon
them ; we are constantly in motion, urging our way through
them to an eternal dwelling.   Each breaking morn, each
radiant noon, each shadowy eve, as they pass by us, make
no tarrying, but pass us never more to return.   The joc-
und Spring, Summer, with his swarms of life, Autumn,
with her golden harvest, Winter, with his icy sceptre and
his snowy robes, as each year they pass us, are in constant
motion, and, while we greet them, take their leave of us
forever.   Each changing scene of life arrests our minds,
enlists our feelings ; then takes its final leave of us, the
sons of eternity.   Creeping infancy, merry boyhood, aspiring youth, industrious manhood, decrepit age, we meet
in swift succession ; just greet, and bid adieu for eternity.
In the midst of all the privileges of our city here below,
do our advancing steps towards the eternal world serve
constantly to remind us, that here we have no permanent
dwelling.   The aggregate of days that have passed by us,
the yearly seasons, the scenes of life, and periods of age,
since we came into possession of our privileges,—since we
first knew our dwellings, walked our streets, and entered
our sanctuaries, and heard the words of God, —are so many

advances towards eternity; and tell, as they thicken on
the path we leave, how soon we reach the close of our pilgrimage, and enter upon unknown worlds.

We have another constant memento of the fact, again, in
our inability of prolonging our continuance in the world.
We have constant notices around us of our frailty, and inability to continue to ourselves our present privileges for the
future. Even in the city of our privileges below, do we
see ourselves hurried on, by an unseen hand we cannot
control; the almighty Guide who conducts us seems unwilling we should stay; the God of our spirits, who goes
with us, designs we should have our settled dwelling in
eternity; and soon he will bring us to the gates of the
city, and, at the bidding we cannot resist, must we take
our leave of it for eternity. Around us, every thing is be-
tokening his design of our departure and our inability to
prolong our stay. The frail hold we take of every earthly
possession tells that our grasp on none is for eternity. We
are hurried on from object to object, before we can call
any thing ours. We meet friends, but, while we cling
to them, the unseen hand of Providence tears us away
from their embrace. Beauty we would linger here to admire, but, while we look, the grace of the fashion of it
perisheth. Power just takes us by the hand, and bids us
adieu to greet a successor. Fame crowns us with her
wreath, but, while we feel the rising flush of joy, she
plucks it off to sport with others. Wealth comes to feast
us, and roll us in his car of pleasures, and, while accepting
his proposals, he dismisses us to tempt some other pilgrims
on their way to eternity. The unseen hand of Providence
thus tears us away from object after object, to show that
here is not our rest, and that our hold on earth is frail and
giving way. Around the city of our habitation, too, are
the messengers he sends to warn us of this approaching
departure. Decay stands with tottering limbs and feeble
breath, and lisps to us, with dying life, that we draw nigh
the gates of our habitation, and soon will leave it for eternal worlds. Diseases—busy messengers—fly here and
there, to tell us of our frail abode, and whisper in our ears
" eternity." Death, armed with resistless power, stands
with his commissions, and their unknown dates, to lead us

out of our residence below, and bar on us its gates forever Every where in the city of our abode are we reminded that we have not the power to prolong our stay in it, and that soon we shall leave its privileges, its dwellings, its streets, its sanctuaries, its Scriptures, its busy throng, for eternity.

There is another means reminding us constantly of his fact,—*the voice of God.* In the city of our habitation below, God has published his glories, his statutes, his offers of pardon and assistance, for our use as sojourners here, who are passing to eternity. He, the infinite Being, who is from everlasting to everlasting himself, has conferred on us an existence, that is to continue and grow up by the side of his, through everlasting ages. He has beheld us, in the first stages of our being here, engaged in unrighteous rebellion against his authority, and bent on neglect of his glories; and, moved with pity, sent his everlasting Son to atone for our guilt, and to call us to repentance, and his Holy Spirit to indite his will, and influence us to obedience. In our habitation we have his word; here temples are erected for his service; a day is appointed by him for men to assemble; ministers commissioned to teach; and they who love his name speak to one another and to their fellow-men of his designs. Wherever we go, then, the voice of God is reaching us, and re-echoing the truth, that we are beings whose final dwelling-place is eternity, and who have here no continuing city. The Bible, wherever it meets our eye, reiterates the voice of God, that we must die and rise again in other worlds. In each reproof of conscience, his awful voice is heard to speak a reckoning day in eternity. In each act we do for God or for his kingdom here, his voice of love whispers of eternal joys. Each revolving Sabbath, with its pealing bells, and open sanctuaries, and solemn rites, bears on its hours his voice, that warns us of an abode in heaven or hell. Each sermon is the call he makes to hear his voice to-day. In each season of prayer we hear him say, that we have not reached our home— that we are pilgrims here. From the throne of glory, on which he will sit in judgment, and assign us our dwelling in eternity, the Saviour now sends down the voice of me-

nition; and, while it rolls round the world we dwell in, ten
thousand messengers echo back the voice to our ears, that
" here we have no continuing city."

Description of the Preaching of Whitfield.—
MISS FRANCIS.

THERE was nothing in the appearance of this extraordinary man, which would lead you to suppose that a Felix
could tremble before him. " He was something above
the middle stature, well proportioned, and remarkable for
a native gracefulness of manner. His complexion was very
fair, his features regular, and his dark blue eyes small and
lively : in recovering from the measles, he had contracted
a squint with one of them ; but this peculiarity rather rendered the expression of his countenance more remember-
able, than in any degree lessened the effect of its uncommon sweetness. His voice excelled, both in melody and
compass ; and its fine modulations were happily accompanied by that grace of action, which he possessed in an eminent degree, and which has been said to be the chief
requisite for an orator." To have seen him when he first
commenced, one would have thought him any thing but
enthusiastic and glowing; but, as he proceeded, his heart
warmed with his subject, and his manner became impetuous and animated, till, forgetful of every thing around him,
he seemed to kneel at the throne of Jehovah, and to be
seech in agony for his fellow-beings.

After he had finished his prayer, he knelt for a long
time in profound silence ; and so powerfully had it affected
the most heartless of his audience, that a stillness like that
of the tomb pervaded the whole house. Before he commenced his sermon, long, darkening columns crowded the
bright, sunny sky of the morning, and swept their dull
shadows over the building, in fearful augury of the storm.

His text was, " Strive to enter in at the strait gate ; for
many, I say unto you, shall seek to enter in, and shall not
be able." " See that emblem of human life," said he,
pointing to a shadow that was flitting across the floor. " It

passed for a moment, and concealed the brightness of heaven from our view ;—but it is gone. And where will ye be, my hearers, when your lives have passed away like that dark cloud ? Oh, my dear friends, I see thousands sitting attentive, with their eyes fixed on the poor, unworthy preacher. In a few days, we shall all meet at the judgment-seat of Christ. We shall form a part of that vast assembly that will gather before the throne ; and every eye will behold the judge. With a voice whose call you must abide and answer, he will inquire whether on earth ye strove to enter in at the strait gate ; whether you were supremely devoted to God ; whether your hearts were absorbed in him. My blood runs cold when I think how many of you will then seek to enter in, and shall not be able. Oh, what plea can you make before the Judge of the whole earth ? Can you say it has been your whole endeavour to mortify the flesh, with its affections and lusts ? that your life has been one long effort to do the will of God ? No! you must answer, I made myself easy in the world by flattering myself that all would end well ; but I have deceived my own soul, and am lost.

" You, O false and hollow Christian, of what avail will it be that you have done many things ; that you have read much in the sacred word ; that you have made long prayers ; that you have attended religious duties, and appeared holy in the eyes of men ? What will all this be, if, instead of loving Him supremely, you have been supposing you should exalt yourself in heaven by acts really polluted and unholy ?

" And you, rich man, wherefore do you hoard your silver ? wherefore count the price you have received for him whom you every day crucify in your love of gain ? Why, that, when you are too poor to buy a drop of cold water, your beloved son may be rolled to hell in his chariot pillowed and cushioned around him."

His eye gradually lighted up, as he proceeded, till, towards the close, it seemed to sparkle with celestial fire.

" Oh, sinners !" he exclaimed, " by all your hopes of happiness, I beseech you to repent. Let not the wrath of God be awakened. Let not the fires of eternity be kindled against you. See there !" said he, pointing to the

lightning, which played on the corner of the pulpit—" 'Tis
a glance from the angry eye of Jehovah! Hark!" continued he, raising his finger in a listening attitude, as the
distant thunder grew louder and louder, and broke in one
tremendous crash over the building. "It was the voice
of the Almighty as he passed by in his anger!"

As the sound died away, he covered his face with his
hands, and knelt beside his pulpit, apparently lost in inward
and intense prayer. The storm passed rapidly away, and
the sun, bursting forth in his might, threw across the heavens a magnificent arch of peace. Rising, and pointing to
the beautiful object, he exclaimed, "Look upon the rainbow, and praise him that made it. Very beautiful it is in
the brightness thereof. It compasseth the heavens about
with glory; and the hands of the Most High have bend-
ed it."

The effect was astonishing. Even Somerville shaded
his eyes when he pointed to the lightning, and knelt as he
listened to the approaching thunder; while the deep sensibility of Grace, and the thoughtless vivacity of Lucretia, yielded to the powerful excitement in an unrestrained
burst of tears. "Who could resist such eloquence?" said
Lucretia, as they mingled with the departing throng.

Anecdote of Dr. Chauncy.—TUDOR.

DR. COOPER, who was a man of accomplished manners,
and fond of society, was able, by the aid of his fine talents,
to dispense with some of the severe study that others engaged in. This, however, did not escape the envy and
malice of the world, and it was said, in a kind of petulant
and absurd exaggeration, that he used to walk to the south-
end of a Saturday, and, if he saw a man riding into town
in a black coat, would stop, and ask him to preach the
next day. Dr. Chauncy was a close student, very absent,
and very irritable. On these traits in the character of the
two clergymen, a servant of Dr. Chauncy laid a scheme
for obtaining a particular object from his master. Scipio
went into his master's study one morning to receive some

directions, which the doctor having given, resumed his writing, but the servant still remained. The master, looking up a few minutes afterwards, and supposing he had just come in, said, " Scipio, what do you want ?" " I want a new coat, massa." " Well, go to Mrs. Chauncy, and tell her to give you one of my old coats;" and was again absorbed in his studies. The servant remained fixed. After a while, the doctor, turning his eyes that way, saw him again, as if for the first time, and said, " What do you want, Scip. ?" " I want a new coat, massa." " Well, go to my wife, and ask her to give you one of my old coats;" and fell to writing once more. Scipio remained in the same posture. After a few moments, the doctor looked towards him, and repeated the former question, " Scipio, what do you want ?" " I want a new coat, massa." It now flashed over the doctor's mind, that there was something of repetition in this dialogue. " Why, have I not told you before to ask Mrs. Chauncy to give you one ? get away." " Yes, massa, but I no want a black coat." " Not want a black coat ! why not ?" " Why, massa,—I 'fraid to tell you,— but I don't want a black coat." " What's the reason you don't want a black coat ? tell me directly." " O! massa, I don't want a black coat, but I 'fraid to tell the reason, you so passionate." " You rascal ! will you tell me the reason ?" " O! massa, I'm sure you be angry." " If I had my cane here, you villain, I'd break your bones : will you tell me what you mean ?" " I 'fraid to tell you, massa ; I know you be angry." The doctor's impatience was now highly irritated, and Scipio, perceiving, by his glance at the tongs, that he might find a substitute for the cane, and that he was sufficiently excited, said, " Well, massa, you make me tell, but I know you be angry—I 'fraid, massa, if I wear another black coat, Dr. Cooper ask me to preach for him !" This unexpected termination realized the servant's calculation ; his irritated master burst into a laugh,—" Go, you rascal, get my hat and cane, and tell Mrs. Chauncy she may give you a coat of any colour a red one if you choose." Away went the negro to his mistress, and the doctor to tell the story to his friend, Dr. Cooper.

21

Effects of a Dissolution of the Federal Union.—
HAMILTON.

ASSUMING it, therefore, as an established truth, that,
in case of disunion, the several states, or such combinations
of them as might happen to be formed out of the wreck of
the general confederacy, would be subject to those vicissitudes of peace and war, of friendship and enmity with each
other, which have fallen to the lot of all other nations not
united under one government, let us enter into a concise
detail of some of the consequences that would attend such
a situation.

War between the states, in the first periods of their separate existence, would be accompanied with much greater
distresses than it commonly is in those countries where
regular military establishments have long obtained. The
disciplined armies always kept on foot on the continent of
Europe, though they bear a malignant aspect to liberty and
economy, have, notwithstanding, been productive of the
singular advantage of rendering sudden conquests impracticable, and of preventing that rapid desolation, which used
to mark the progress of war prior to their introduction. The
art of fortification has contributed to the same ends. The
nations of Europe are encircled with chains of fortified
places, which mutually obstruct invasion. Campaigns are
wasted in reducing two or three fortified garrisons, to gain
admittance into an enemy's country. Similar impediments occur at every step, to exhaust the strength, and
delay the progress, of an invader. Formerly, an invading
army would penetrate into the heart of a neighbouring
country almost as soon as intelligence of its approach could
be received ; but now, a comparatively small force of disciplined troops, acting on the defensive, with the aid of posts,
is able to impede, and finally to frustrate, the purposes of
one much more considerable. The history of war in tha
quarter of the globe is no longer a history of nations sub
dued, and empires overturned ; but of towns taken and re-
taken, of battles that decide nothing, of retreats more beneficial than victories, of much effort and little acquisition.

In this country the scene would be altogether reversed. The jealousy of military establishments would postpone them as long as possible. The want of fortifications, leaving the frontier of one state open to another, would facilitate inroads. The populous states would with little difficulty overrun their less populous neighbours. Conquests would be as easy to be made as difficult to be retained. War, therefore, would be desultory and predatory. Plunder and devastation ever march in the train of irregulars. The calamities of individuals would ever make the principal figure in events, and would characterize our exploits.

This picture is not too highly wrought; though, I confess, it would not long remain a just one. Safety from external danger is the most powerful director of national conduct   Even the ardent love of liberty will, after a time, give way to its dictates. The violent destruction of life and property incident to war, the continual effort and alarm attendant on a state of continual danger, will compel nations the most attached to liberty to resort for repose and security to institutions, which have a tendency to destroy their civil and political rights. To be more safe, they, at length, become willing to run the risk of being less free. The institutions chiefly alluded to are STANDING ARMIES, and the corresponding appendages of military establishments. Standing armies, it is said, are not provided against in the new constitution ; and it is thence inferred that they would exist under it. This inference, from the very form of the proposition, is, at best, problematical and uncertain But standing armies, it may be replied, must inevitably result from a dissolution of the confederacy. Frequent war and constant apprehension, which require a state of as constant preparation, will infallibly produce them. The weaker states or confederacies would first have recourse to them, to put themselves on an equality with their more potent neighbours. They would endeavour to supply the inferiority of population and resources by a more regular and effective system of defence,—by disciplined troops, and by fortifications. They would, at the same time, be obliged to strengthen the executive arm of government ; in doing which their constitutions would require a progressive direction towards monarchy. It is the nature of war t' ir crease the executive, at the expense of the legislative authority.

The expedients, which have been mentioned, would soon give the states, or confederacies, that made use of them, a superiority over their neighbours. Small states, or states of less natural strength, under vigorous governments, and with the assistance of disciplined armies, have often triumphed over large states, or states of greater natural strength, which have been destitute of these advantages. Neither the pride nor the safety of the important states, or confederacies, would permit them long to submit to this mortifying and adventitious superiority. They would quickly resort to means similar to those by which it had been effected, to reinstate themselves in their lost pre-eminence. Thus we should, in a little time, see established in every part of this country the same engines of despotism, which have been the scourge of the old world. This, at least, would be the natural course of things; and our reasonings will be likely to be just, in proportion as they are accommodated to this standard. These are not vague inferences deduced from speculative defects in a constitution, the whole power of which is lodged in the hands of the people, or their representatives and delegates; they are solid conclusions, drawn from the natural and necessary progress of human affairs.

* * * * * * * * * * * * *

If we are wise enough to preserve the union, we may for ages enjoy an advantage similar to that of an insulated situation. Europe is at a great distance from us. Her colonies in our vicinity will be likely to continue too much disproportioned in strength to be able to give us any dangerous annoyance. Extensive military establishments cannot, in this position, be necessary to our security. But, if we should be disunited, and the integral parts should either remain separated, or, which is most probable, should be thrown together into two or three confederacies, we should be, in a short course of time, in the predicament of the continental powers of Europe. Our liberties would be a prey to the means of defending ourselves against the ambition and jealousy of each other.

This is an idea not superficial or futile, but solid and weighty. It deserves the most serious and mature consideration of every prudent and honest man, of whatever party. If such men will make a firm and solemn pause, and meditate dispassionately on its importance; if they will contemplate it in all its attitudes, and trace it to all its consequences, they will not hesitate to part with trivial objections to a constitution, the rejection of which would, in all probability, put a final period to the union. The airy phantoms, that now flit before the distempered imaginations of some of its adversaries, would then quickly give place to more substantial prospects of dangers, real, certain, and extremely formidable

———

Sports on New Year's day.—PAULDING.

"Cold and raw the north win ds blow,
    Bleak in the morning early
All the hills are covered witn snow,
    And winter's now come fairly."

WINTER, with silver locks and sparkling icicles, now gradually approached, under cover of his north-west winds, his pelting storms, cold, frosty mornings, and bitter, freezing nights. And here we will take occasion to express our obligations to the popular author of the PIONEERS, for the pleasure we have derived from his happy delineations of the progress of our seasons, and the successive changes which mark their course. All that remember their youthful days in the country, and look back with tender, melancholy enjoyment upon their slippery gambols on the ice, their Christmas pies, and nut-crackings by the cheerful fireside, will read his pages with a gratified spirit, and thank him heartily for having refreshed their memory with the half-effaced recollections of scenes and manners, labours and delights, which, in the progress of Time, and the changes which every where mark his course, will, in some future age, perhaps, live only in the touches of his pen. If, in the course of our history, we should chance to dwell upon scenes somewhat similar to those he de

21 *

scribes, or to mark the varying tints of our seasons with
a sameness of colouring, let us not be stigmatized with
oorrowing from him, since it is next to impossible to be
true to nature, without seeming to have his sketches in our
eye.

The holydays, those wintry blessings, which cheer the
heart of young and old, and give to the gloomy depths of
winter the life and spirit of laughing, jolly spring, were
now near at hand.   The chopping-knife gave token of good-
ly minced pies, and the bustle of the kitchen afforded shrewd
indications of what was coming by and by.   The celebra-
tion of the new year, it is well known, came originally
from the northern nations of Europe, who still keep up
many of the practices, amusements, and enjoyments, known
to their ancestors.   The Heer Piper valued himself upon
being a genuine northern man, and, consequently, held the
winter holydays in special favour and affection.   In addition to this hereditary attachment to ancient customs, it was
shrewdly suspected, that his zeal in celebrating these good
old sports was not a little quickened, in consequence of his
mortal antagonist, William Penn, having hinted, in the
course of their controversy, that the practice of keeping
holydays savoured not only of Popery, but paganism.

Before the Heer consented to sanction the projects of
Dominie Kanttwell for abolishing sports and ballads, he
stipulated for full liberty, on the part of himself and his
people of Elsingburgh, to eat, drink, sing and frolic as much
as they liked, during the winter holydays.   In fact, the
Dominie made no particular opposition to this suspension
of his blue-laws, being somewhat addicted to good eating
and drinking, whenever the occasion justified ; that is to
say, whenever such accidents came in his way.

It had long been the custom with Governor Piper to
usher in the new year with a grand supper, to which the
Dominie, the members of the council, and certain of the
most respectable burghers, were always bidden.   This
year, he determined to see the old year out, and the new
one in, as the phrase was, having just heard of a great victory gained by the Bulwark of the Protestant Religion, the
immortal Gustavus Adolphus ; which, though it happened
nearly four years before, had only now reached the village

of Elsingburgh. Accordingly, the Snow Ball Bombie was set to work in the cooking of a mortal supper; which, agreeably to the taste of West Indian epicures, she seasoned with such enormous quantities of red pepper, that whoever ate was obliged to drink, to keep his mouth from getting on fire, like unto a chimney.

Exactly at ten o'clock, the guests sat down to the table where they ate and drank to the success of the Protestant cause, the glory of the great Gustavus, the downfall of Popery and the Quakers, with equal zeal and patriotism The instant the clock struck twelve, a round was fired from the fort, and a vast and bottomless bowl, supposed to be the identical one in which the famous wise men of Gotham went to sea, was brought in, filled to the utmost brim with smoking punch. The memory of the departed year, and the hopes of the future, were then drank in a special bumper, after which the ladies retired, and noise and fun became the order of the night. The Heer told his great story of having surprised and taken a whole picket-guard, under the great Gustavus; and each of the guests contributed his tale, taking special care, however, not to outdo their host in the marvellous,—a thing which always put the Governor out of humour.

Counsellor Langfanger talked wonderfully about public improvements; Counsellor Varlett sung, or rather roared, a hundred verses of a song in praise of Rhenish wine; and Othman Pfegel smoked and tippled, till he actually came to a determination of bringing matters to a crisis with the fair Christina the very next day. Such are the wonder-working powers of hot punch! As for the Dominie, he departed about the dawn of day, in such a plight, that, if it had not been impossible, we should have suspected him of being, as it were, a little overtaken with the said punch. To one or two persons, who chanced to see him, he actually appeared to stagger a little; but such was the stout faith of the good Dominie's parishioners, that neither of these worthy fellows would believe his own eyes sufficiently to state these particulars.

A couple of hours' sleep sufficed to disperse the vapours of punch and pepper-pot; for heads in those days were much harder than now, and the Heer, as well as his rois-

tering companions, rose betimes to give and receive the
compliments and good wishes of the season. The morning
was still, clear, and frosty. The sun shone with the lustre, though not with the warmth, of summer, and his bright
beams were reflected, with indescribable splendour, from
the glassy, smooth expanse of ice, that spread across, and
up and down the broad river, far as the eye could see.
The smoke of the village chimneys rose straight into the
air, looking like so many inverted pyramids, spreading
gradually broader and broader, until they melted away,
and mixed imperceptibly with ether. Scarce was the sun
above the horizon, when the village was alive with rosy
boys and girls, dressed in their new suits, and going forth
with such warm anticipations of happiness, as time and experience imperceptibly fritter away into languid hopes, or
strengthening apprehensions. "Happy New Year!" came
from every mouth and every heart. Spiced beverages
and lusty cakes were given away with liberal, open hand ;
every body was welcomed to every house ; all seemed to
forget their little heart-burnings and disputes of yore ; all
seemed happy, and all were so ; and the Dominie, who always wore his coat with four great pockets on new-year
day, came home and emptied them seven times of loads
of new-year cookies.

When the gay groups had finished their rounds in the
village, the ice in front was seen all alive with the small
fry of Elsingburgh, gamboling and skating, sliding and
tumbling, helter skelter, and making the frost-bit ears of
winter glad with the sounds of mirth and revelry. In one
place was a group playing at burley, with crooked sticks,
with which they sometimes hit the ball, and sometimes
each other's shins ; in another, a knot of sliders, following
in a row, so that, if the foremost fell, the rest were sure to
tumble over him. A little farther might be seen a few, that
had the good fortune to possess a pair of skates, luxuriat-
ing in that most graceful of all exercises, and emulated by
some half a dozen little urchins, with smooth bones fastened to their feet, in imitation of the others, skating away
with a gravity and perseverance worthy of better implements. All was rout, laughter, revelry and happiness;
and that day the icy mirror of the noble Delaware reflect

ed as light hearts as ever beat together in the new world.
At twelve o'clock, the jolly Heer, according to his imme-
morial custom, went forth from the edge of the river, dis-
tributing apples, and other dainties, together with handsful
of wampum, which, rolling away on the ice in different directions, occasioned innumerable contests and squabbles
among the fry, whose disputes, tumbles, and occasional
buffetings for the prizes, were inimitably ludicrous upon
the slippery element.   Among the most obstreperous and
mischievous of the crowd was that likely fellow Cupid,
who made more noise, and tripped up more heels, that day,
than any half a dozen of his cotemporaries.   His voice
could be heard above all the rest, especially after the arrival of the Heer, before whom he seemed to think it his
duty to exert himself, while his unrestrained, extravagant
laugh, exhibited that singular hilarity of spirit, which dis-
tinguishes the deportment of the African slave from the
invariable gravity of the free red man of the western
world.

All day, and until after the sun had set, and the shadows
of night succeeded, the sports of the ice continued, and the
merry sounds rung far and near, occasionally interrupted
by those loud noises, which sometimes shoot across the ice
like a rushing earthquake, and are occasioned by its crack-
ing, as the water rises or falls.

Conclusion of "Observations on the Boston Port Bill."—
JOSIAH QUINCY, JUN.

THUS, my countrymen, from the days of Gardiner and
Morton, Gorges and Mason, Randolph and Cranfield, down
to the present day, the inhabitants of this northern region
have constantly been in dangers and troubles, from foes
open and secret, abroad and in their bosom.   Our freedom
has been the object of envy, and to make void the charter
of our liberties the work and labour of an undiminished
race of villains.   One cabal having failed of success, new
conspirators have risen, and what the first could not make
"void," the next "humbly desired to revoke."   To this

purpose one falsehood after another hath been fabricated
and spread abroad with equal turpitude and equal effronte-
ry. That minute detail, which would present actors now
on the stage, is the province of History. She, inexorably
severe towards the eminently guilty, will delineate their
characters with the point of a diamond; and, thus blazon-
ed in the face of day, the abhorrence and execrations of
mankind will consign them to an infamous immortality.

So great has been the credulity of the British court from
the beginning, or such hath been the activity of false
brethren, that no tale inimical to the Northern Colonies,
however false or absurd, but what hath found credit with
the administration, and operated to the prejudice of the
country. Thus it was told and believed in England, that
we were not in earnest in the expedition against Canada
at the beginning of this century, and that the country did
every thing in its power to defeat the success of it, and
that the misfortune of that attempt ought to be wholly attributed to the Northern Colonies: while nothing could be
more obvious, than that New England had exhausted her
youngest blood, and all her treasures, in the undertaking;
and that every motive of self-preservation, happiness and
safety must have operated to excite these provinces to the
most spirited and persevering measures against Canada.

The people, who are attacked by bad men, have a testimony of their merit, as the constitution, which is invade
by powerful men, hath an evidence of its value. The
path of our duty needs no minute delineation; it lies level
to the eye. Let us apply, then, like men sensible of its
importance, and determined on its fulfilment. The inroads
on our public liberty call for reparation; the wrongs we
have sustained call for justice. That reparation and that
justice may yet be obtained by union, spirit and firmness.
But to divide and conquer was the maxim of the devil in
the garden of Eden; and to disunite and enslave hath
been the principle of all his votaries from that period to the
present. The crimes of the guilty are to them the cords
of association, and dread of punishment the indissoluble
bond of union. The combinations of public robbers ought,
therefore, to cement patriots and heroes: and, as the former
plot and conspire to undermine and destroy the common

wealth, the latter ought to form a compact for opposition,—
a band of vengeance.

What insidious arts, and what detestable practices, have
been used to deceive, disunite and enslave the good people of this continent! The mystic appellations of *loyalty*
and *allegiance*, the venerable names of *government* and
good order, and the sacred ones of *piety* and *public virtue*,
have been alternately prostituted to that abominable purpose. All the windings and guises, subterfuges and doub-
lings, of which the human soul is susceptible, have been
displayed on the occasion. But secrets, which were thought
impenetrable, are no longer hid; characters deeply disguised are openly revealed; and the discovery of gross
impostors hath generally preceded but a short time their
utter extirpation.

Be not again, my countrymen, " easily captivated with
the appearances only of wisdom and piety,—professions
of a regard to liberty, and of a strong attachment to the
public interest." Your fathers have been explicitly
charged with this folly by one of their posterity. Avoid
this and all similar errors. Be cautious against the deception of appearances. " By their fruits ye shall know
them," was the saying of one, who perfectly knew the
human heart. Judge of affairs which concern social happiness by facts : judge of man by his deeds. For it is very
certain, that pious zeal for days and times, for mint and
cumin, hath often been pretended by those who were infidels at bottom ; and it is as certain, that attachment to the
dignity of government and the king's service, hath often
flowed from the mouths of men, who harboured the darkest machinations against the true end of the former, and
were destitute of every right principle of loyalty to the
latter. Hence, then, care and circumspection are necessary branches of political duty. And, as " it is much easier
to restrain liberty from running into licentiousness, than
power from swelling into tyranny and oppression," so much
more caution and resistance are required against the over-
bearing of rulers, than the extravagance of the people.

To give no more authority to any order of state, and to
place no greater public confidence in any man, than is
necessary for the general welfare, may be considered by

the people as an important point of policy. But though craft and hypocrisy are prevalent, yet piety and virtue have a real existence : duplicity and political imposture abound, yet benevolence and public spirit are not altogether banished the world. As wolves will appear in sheep's clothing, so superlative knaves and parricides will assume the vesture of the man of virtue and patriotism.

These things are permitted by Providence, no doubt, for wise and good reasons. Man was created for a rational, and was designed for an active being. His faculties of intelligence and force were given him for use. When the wolf, therefore, is found devouring the flock, no hierarchy forbids a seizure of the victim for sacrifice ; so, also, when dignified impostors are caught destroying those whom their arts deceive, though their stations destined them to protect,—the sabre of justice flashes righteousness at the stroke of execution.

Yet be not amused, my countrymen ! The extirpation of bondage and the re-establishment of freedom are not of easy acquisition. The worst passions of the human heart and the most subtle projects of the human mind, are leagued against you ; and principalities and powers have acceded to the combination. Trials and conflicts you must, therefore, endure ; hazards and jeopardies of life and fortune will attend the struggle. Such is the fate of all noble exertions for public liberty and social happiness. Enter not the lists without thought and consideration, lest you arm with timidity, and combat with irresolution. Having engaged in the conflict, let nothing discourage your vigour, or repel your perseverance. Remember that submission to the yoke of bondage is the worst that can befall a people, after the most fierce and unsuccessful resistance. What can the misfortunes of vanquishment take away, which despotism and rapine would spare ? " It had been easy," said the great lawgiver Solon to the Athenians, " to repress the advances of tyranny, and prevent its establishment ; but, now it is established and grown to some height, it would be more glorious to demolish it." But nothing glorious is accomplished, nothing great is attained, nothing valuable is secured, without magnanimity of mind, and devotion of heart to the service. Brutus-like, therefore, dedicate yourselves at this day to the service of you country; and henceforth live a life of liberty and glory. " On the ides of March,"—said the great and good man to his friend Cassius, just before the battle of Philippi,—" on the ides of March I devoted my life to my country, and since that time I have lived a life of liberty and glory."

Inspired with public virtue, touched with the wrongs, and indignant at the insults, offered his country, the high-spirited Cassius exhibits an heroic example;—" Resolved as we are,"—replied the hero to his friend,—" resolved as we are, let us march against the enemy; for, though we should not conquer, we have nothing to fear."

Spirits and genii like these rose in Rome, and have since adorned Britain; such also will one day make glorious this more western world. America hath in store her Bruti and Cassii—her Hampdens and Sydneys—patriots and heroes, who will form a band of brothers;—men, who will have memories and feelings, courage and swords,—courage, that shall inflame their ardent bosoms till their hands cleave to their swords, and their swords to their enemies' hearts.

Necessity of Union between the States.—Jay.

It has often given me pleasure to observe that independent America was not composed of detached and distant territories, but that one connected, fertile, wide-spreading country was the portion of our western sons of liberty. Providence has, in a particular manner, blessed it with a variety of soils and productions, and watered it with innumerable streams for the delight and accommodation of its inhabitants. A succession of navigable waters forms a kind of chain round its borders, as if to bind it together; while the most noble rivers in the world, running at convenient distances, present them with highways for the easy communication of friendly aids, and the mutual transportation and exchange of their various commodities.

With equal pleasure I have as often taken notice, that Providence has been pleased to give this one connected country to one united people ; a people descended from the

22

same ancestors, speaking the same language, professing the same religion, attached to the same principles of government, very similar in their manners and customs; and who, by their joint counsels, arms and efforts, fighting side by side, through a long and bloody war, have nobly established their general liberty and independence.

This country and this people seem to have been made for each other; and it appears as if it were the design of Providence, that an inheritance so proper and convenient for a band of brethren united to each other by the strongest ties, should never be split into a number of unsocial, jealous and alien sovereignties.

Similar sentiments have hitherto prevailed among all orders and denominations of men among us. To all general purposes we have uniformly been one people—each individual citizen every where enjoying the same national rights, privileges and protection. As a nation we have made peace and war; as a nation we have vanquished our common enemies; as a nation we have formed alliances, and made treaties, and entered into various compacts and conventions with foreign states.

A strong sense of the value and blessings of union induced the people, at a very early period, to institute a federal government in order to preserve and perpetuate i They formed it almost as soon as they had a political exis ence; nay, at a time when their hal ations were in flames, when many of them were bleeding in the field, and when the progress of hostility and desolation left little room for those calm and mature inquiries and reflections, which must ever precede the formation of a wise and well-balanced government for a free people. It is not to be wondered, that a government instituted in times so inauspicious should, on experiment, be found greatly deficient, and inadequate to the purpose it was intended to answer.

This intelligent people perceived and regretted these defects. Still continuing no less attached to union than enamoured of liberty, they observed the danger, which immediately threatened the former, and more remotely the latter, and, being persuaded that ample security for both could only be found in a national government more wisely framed, they, as with one voice, convened the late conven·

tion at Philadelphia, to take that important subject under consideration.

This convention, composed of men who possessed the confidence of the people, and many of whom had become highly distinguished for their patriotism, virtue and wisdom, in times which tried the souls of men, undertook the arduous task. In the mild season of peace, with minds unoccupied by other subjects, they passed many months in cool, uninterrupted and daily consultations. And finally, without having been awed by power, or influenced by any passion except love for their country, they presented and recommended to the people the plan produced by their joint and very unanimous counsels.

It is not yet forgotten, that well-grounded apprehensions of imminent danger induced the people of America to form the memorable congress of 1774. That body recommended certain measures to their constituents, and the event proved their wisdom; it yet is fresh in our memories how soon the press began to teem with pamphlets and weekly papers against those very measures. Not only many of the officers of government, who obeyed the dictates of personal interest, but others, from a mistaken estimate of consequences, from the undue influence of ancient attachments, or whose ambition aimed at objects which did not correspond with the public good, were indefatigable in their endeavours to persuade the people to reject the advice of that patriotic congress. Many, indeed, were deceived and deluded, but the great majority reasoned and decided judiciously; and happy they are in reflecting that they did so.

But if the people at large had reason to confide in the men of that congress, few of whom had then been fully tried or generally known, still greater reason have they now to respect the judgment and advice of the convention; for it is well known that some of the most distinguished members of that congress, who have been since tried and justly approved for patriotism and abilities, and who have grown old in acquiring political information, were also members of this convention, and carried into it their accumulated knowledge and experience.

It is worthy of remark, that not only the first, but every succeeding congress, as well as the late convention, have joined with the people in thinking that the prosperity of America depended on its union. To preserve and perpetuate it was the great object of the people in forming that convention; and it is also the great object of the plan, which the convention has advised them to accept. With what propriety therefore, or for what good purposes, are attempts at this particular period made by some men to depreciate the importance of the union?—or why is it suggested, that three or four confederacies would be better than one? I am persuaded in my own mind, that the people have always thought right on this subject, and that their universal and uniform attachment to the cause of the union rests on great and weighty reasons.

They who promote the idea of substituting a number of distinct confederacies in the room of the plan of the convention, seem clearly to foresee, that the rejection of it would put the continuance of the union in the utmost jeopardy. That certainly would be the case; and I sincerely wish it may be as clearly foreseen by every good citizen, that, whenever the dissolution of the union arrives, America will have reason to exclaim, in the words of the poet,—"Farewell, a long farewell, to all my greatness!"

Character of Hamilton.—AMES.

MEN of the most elevated minds have not always the readiest discernment of character. Perhaps he was sometimes too sudden and too lavish in bestowing his confidence: his manly spirit, disdaining artifice, suspected none. But, while the power of his friends over him seemed to have no limits, and really had none, in respect to those things which were of a nature to be yielded, no man, not the Roman Cato himself, was more inflexible on every point that touched, or only seemed to touch, his integrity and honour. With him it was not enough to be unsuspected; his bosom would have glowed like a furnace at its own whispers of reproach. Mere purity would have seemed to him below praise ; and such were his habits, and such his nature, that the pecuniary temptations, which many others can only with great exertion and self-denial resist, had no attractions for him. He was very far from obstinate ; yet as his friends assailed his opinions with less profound thought than he had devoted to them, they were seldom shaken by discussion. He defended them, however, with as much mildness as force, and evinced that, if he did not yield, it was not for want of gentleness or modesty.

His early life we pass over ; though his heroic spirit in the army has furnished a theme that is dear to patriotism, and will be sacred to glory.

In all the different stations, in which a life of active usefulness has placed him, we find him not more remarkably distinguished by the extent, than by the variety and versatility, of his talents. In every place, he made it apparent, that no other man could have filled it so well ; and in times of critical importance, in which alone he desired employment, his services were justly deemed absolutely indispensable. As secretary of the treasury, his was the powerful spirit that presided over the chaos.

> " Confusion heard his voice, and wild Uproar
> Stood ruled."————

Indeed, in organizing the federal government in 1789, every man, of either sense or candour, will allow, the difficulties seemed greater than the first-rate abilities could surmount. The event has shown that his abilities were greater than those difficulties. He surmounted them ; and Washington's administration was the most wise and beneficent, the most prosperous, and ought to be the most popular, that ever was intrusted with the affairs of a nation. Great as was Washington's merit, much of it in plan, much in execution, will of course devolve upon his minister.

As a lawyer, his comprehensive genius reached the principles of his profession : he compassed its extent, he fathomed its profound, perhaps, even more familiarly and easily than the rules of its practice. With most men law is a trade ; with him it was a science

22 *

As a statesman, he was not more distinguished for the great exter* of h's views, than by the caution with which he provided against impediments, and the watchfulness of his care over the right and liberty of the subject.   In none of the many revenue bills which he framed, though committees reported them, is there to be found a single clause that savours of despotic power; not one that the sagest champions of law and liberty would, on that ground, hesitate to approve and adopt.

It is rare that a man, who owes so much to nature, descends to seek more from industry; but he seemed to depend on industry as if nature had done nothing for him. His habits of investigation were very remarkable; his mind seemed to cling to his subject till he had exhausted it.   Hence the uncommon superiority of his reasoning powers—a superiority that seemed to be augmented from every source, and to be fortified by every auxiliary—learning, taste, wit, imagination and eloquence.   These were embellished and enforced by his temper and manners, by his fame and his virtues.   It is difficult, in the midst of such various excellence, to say in what particular the effect of his greatness was most manifest.   No man more promptly discerned truth; no man more clearly displayed it: it was not merely made visible,—it seemed to come bright with illumination from his lips.   But, prompt and clear as he was,—fervid as Demosthenes, like Cicero full of resource,—he was not less remarkable for the copiousness and completeness of his argument, that left little for cavil, and nothing for doubt.   Some men take their strongest argument as a weapon, and use no other; but he left nothing to be inquired for—nothing to be answered.   He not only disarmed his adversaries of their pretexts and objections, but he stripped them of all excuse for having urged them; he confounded and subdued as well as convinced.   He indemnified them, however, by making his discussion a complete map of his subject; so that his opponents might, indeed, feel ashamed of their mistakes, but they could not repeat them.   In fact it was no common effort that could preserve a really able antagonist from becoming his convert; for the truth, which his researches so distinctly presented to the understanding of others, was rendered almost irresistibly commanding and impressive by the love and reverence, which, it was ever apparent, he profoundly cherished for it in his own. While patriotism glowed in his heart, wisdom blended in his speech her authority with her charms.

Unparalleled as were his services, they were nevertheless no otherwise requited than by the applause of all good men, and by his own enjoyment of the spectacle of that national prosperity and honour, which was the effect of them. After facing calumny, and triumphantly surmounting an unrelenting persecution, he retired from office with clean though empty hands, as rich as reputation and an unblemished integrity could make him.

The most substantial glory of a country is in its virtuous great men : its prosperity will depend on its docility to learn from their example. That nation is fated to ignominy and servitude, for which such men have lived in vain. Power may be seized by a nation that is yet barbarous ; and wealth may be enjoyed by one that it finds or renders sordid : the one is the gift and the sport of accident, and the other is the sport of power. Both are mutable, and have passed away without leaving behind them any other memorial than ruins that offend taste, and traditions that baffle conjecture. But the glory of Greece is imperishable, or will last as long as learning itself, which is its monument : it strikes an everlasting root, and bears perennial blossoms on its grave. The name of Hamilton would have honoured Greece in the age of Aristides. May Heaven, the guardian of our liberty, grant that our country may be fruitful of Hamiltons, and faithful to their glory !

Morality of Poetry.—GEORGE BANCROFT.

IF poetry is the spirit of God within us, that spirit must be a pure one ; if it is the strongest and most earnest expression of generous enthusiasm, it must be allied with the noblest feelings of human nature. Genius can, it is true, of itself, attract attention ; but it cannot win continued and universal admiration, except in alliance with virtue. Who

can measure the loss, which the world would sustain, if
the sublimest work of Milton were to be struck from the
number of living books? Yet the world would be the
gainer, if Don Juan were as if it had never been written.
The one poet cherishes loftiness of purpose, and tends to
elevate his reader to a kindred magnanimity; while the
other exposes, it may be with inimitable skill and graphic
power, the vices and weaknesses of man, and so tends to
degrade the mind to the level which he establishes for the
race.   But we go to poetry as a relief and a support.   We
need no books to ring changes to us on man's selfishness;
and if at times, in a moment of despondency or disappointment, when the confused judgment cannot rightly estimate
the progress of good amidst the jar of human passions, and
the collision of human interests, we forget the dignity of
our nature, and revile it, the poet should reinstate it in our
favour, and make us forget our disgust with the world.

While on this subject, we cannot forbear to remark on
that tendency to moralize, which many mistake in themselves for wise observation. True, to the eye of a contemplative man, books may be found in the running brooks,
and sermons in stones; but it is the mark of an inferior
mind to be constantly repeating the common-places of morality: one, who does it often, is sure to be esteemed by
his neighbours as a tedious proser; and to have this strain
of puny thinking put into verse, and set before us as sublime, is really intolerable. In that which is to produce a
grand effect, every thing must be proportionably grand.
The historians of nature tell us, that gold is diffused
throughout creation, may be extracted from the stones we
tread upon, and enters into the composition of the plants ou
which we feed. But it is a very slow and troublesome
process to extract it from most stones and plants; and, after
all, it is obtained in so small quantities, that it is not worth
the trouble it costs. And it may be so with the elements
of poetry. They exist every where; the dreams of the
drunkard may sometimes have a gleam of bright fancy; a
mother, setting out in pursuit of an idiot boy, who has run
away on an ass, may have very proper thoughts, and weep
as sincerely as Andromache herself; and the reformation
of a knave like Peter Bell may be psychologically as re-

markable as the downfall of Macbeth, the scepticism of Hamlet, the madness of Lear. But still it is not the thing we want. To the observer of the human mind, the mere collector of facts, one man's experience may ,offer nearly as much as another's; but cannot, in the same degree, promote the purposes of the poet. At a ball in any village in the country, there are probably the self-same passions at work, as were ever called into action on similar occasions. The beauty and pride of a country town, dancing to an imperfect band, may afford illustrations of all the moral phenomena of vanity, admiration and love, the hours whirled away very agreeably in lively dances, and blushes excited by the praise of loveliness. But all this is a common, every day sort of business; and hardly any one would think of weaving it into poetry. But when the imagination is wrought up by the expectation of an ap-proaching battle; when the capital of Belgium has gather-ed its own beauty and the chivalry of England; when the blow, that is to decide the destiny of empires, is suspended for a season, while youth and pleasure revel in careless gayety, till they are recalled from the charm that creeps over the senses by a peal, which is the death-larum of thousands,—we find the scenes of the ball room contribut-ing to heighten the power and the splendour of poetry. If we hear of a blind boy, who goes to sea in a shell, we should think the story would make a very curious and proper paragraph for the miscellaneous department of a newspaper, provided the fact be well authenticated; but what is there of poetry about it ?* If we were to meet a little girl, who had lost her pet lamb, it would be proper to be extremely sorry; and the matter is a fit one for pro-portionate sympathy. But these are trivial things; they hardly claim much attention in life; they are of no gen-eral interest for the exercise of the imagination. The poet must exalt and satisfy the mind; must fill us with glorious aspirations and lofty thoughts; must lead us out

---

* Trifling as this incident might appear, if related in the com mon and desultory manner of a newspaper paragraph, it has yet been wrought, by the genius of Wordsworth, into one of the most beautiful and natural pieces of poetry which it has been our lot to meet with.— Ed.

through the high heaven of invention, and call up before us the master passions of man's mind in all their majesty ;—not show us the inside of a baby-house, nor furnish us with a comment on the catalogue of a toy-shop.

The Consequences of Atheism.—CHANNING.

FEW men suspect, perhaps no man comprehends, the extent of the support given by religion to every virtue No man, perhaps, is aware how much our moral and social sentiments are fed from this fountain; how powerless conscience would become without the belief of a God; how palsied would be human benevolence, were there not the sense of a higher benevolence to quicken and sustain it; now suddenly the whole social fabric would quake, and with what a fearful crash it would sink into hopeless ruins, were the ideas of a Supreme Being, of accountableness, and of a future life, to be utterly erased from every mind. Once let men thoroughly believe, that they are the work and sport of chance; that no Superior Intelligence concerns itself with human affairs; that all their improvements perish forever at death; that the weak have no guardian, and the injured no avenger; that there is no recompense for sacrifices to uprightness and the public good; that an oath is unheard in heaven; that secret crimes have no witness but the perpetrator; that human existence has no purpose, and human virtue no unfailing friend; that this brief life is every thing to us, and death is total, everlasting extinction,—once let men *thoroughly* abandon religion, and who can conceive or describe the extent of the desolation which would follow?

We hope, perhaps, that human laws and natural sympathy would hold society together. As reasonably might we believe, that, were the sun quenched in the heavens, *our* torches could illuminate, and *ur* fires quicken and fertilize the creation. What is there in human nature to awaken respect and tenderness, if man is the unprotected insect of a day? and what is he more, if atheism be true? Erase all thought and fear of God from a community, and selfishness and sensuality would absorb the whole man. Appetite, knowing no restraint, and poverty and suffer- ing, having no solace or hope, would trample in scorn on the restraints of human laws. Virtue, duty, principle, would be mocked and spurned as unmeaning sounds. A sordid self-interest would supplant every other feeling, and man would become in fact, what the theory of atheism declares him to be, a companion for brutes!

The blind Preacher.—WIRT.

IT was one Sunday, as I travelled through the county of Orange, that my eye was caught by a cluster of horses tied near a ruinous, old, wooden house in the forest, not far from the road-side. Having frequently seen such objects before, in travelling through these States, I had no diffi- culty in understanding that this was a place of religious worship.

Devotion alone should have stopped me, to join in the duties of the congregation; but I must confess, that curi- osity to hear the preacher of such a wilderness, was not the least of my motives. On entering, I was struck with his preternatural appearance. He was a tall and very spare old man; his head, which was covered with a white linen cap, his shrivelled hands, and his voice, were all shaking under the influence of a palsy; and a few moments ascertained to me that he was perfectly blind.

The first emotions that touched my breast were those of mingled pity and veneration. But how soon were all my feelings changed! The lips of Plato were never more worthy of a prognostic swarm of bees, than were the lips of this holy man! It was a day of the administration of the sacrament; and his subject was, of course, the passion of our Saviour. I had heard the subject handled a thou- sand times: I had thought it exhausted long ago. Little did I suppose that in the wild woods of America, I was to meet with a man, whose eloquence would give to this topic a new and more sublime pathos, than I had ever be- fore witnessed.

As he descended from the pulpit to distribute the mystic symbols, there was a peculiar, a more than human solemnity in his air and manner, which made my blood run cold, and my whole frame shiver.

He then drew a picture of the sufferings of our Saviour; his trial before Pilate; his ascent up Calvary; his crucifixion; and his death. I knew the whole history; but never until then had I heard the circumstances so selected, so arranged, so coloured! It was all new; and I seemed to have heard it for the first time in my life. His enunciation was so deliberate, that his voice trembled on every syllable; and every heart in the assembly trembled in unison. His peculiar phrases had that force of description, that the original scene appeared to be at that moment acting before our eyes. We saw the very faces of the Jews; the staring, frightful distortions of malice and rage We saw the buffet: my soul kindled with a flame of indignation; and my hands were involuntarily and convulsively clinched.

But when he came to touch on the patience, the forgiving meekness of our Saviour; when he drew, to the life, his blessed eyes streaming in tears to heaven; his voice breathing to God a soft and gentle prayer of pardon on his enemies, "Father, forgive them, for they know not what they do,"—the voice of the preacher, which had all along faltered, grew fainter and fainter, until, his utterance being entirely obstructed by the force of his feelings, he raised his handkerchief to his eyes, and burst into a loud and irrepressible flood of grief. The effect is inconceivable The whole house resounded with the mingled groans, and sobs, and shrieks of the congregation.

It was sometime before the tumult had subsided, so far as to permit him to proceed. Indeed, judging by the usual, but fallacious standard of my own weakness, I began to be very uneasy for the situation of the preacher. For I could not conceive how he would be able to let his audience down from the height to which he had wound them, without impairing the solemnity and dignity of his subject, or perhaps shocking them by the abruptness of the fall But—no: the descent was as beautiful and sublime as the elevation had been rapid and enthusiastic.

The first sentence, with which he broke the awful silence, was a quotation from Rousseau : " Socrates died like a philosopher, but Jesus Christ, like a God !"

I despair of giving you any idea of the effect produced by this short sentence, unless you could perfectly conceive the whole manner of the man, as well as the peculiar crisis in the discourse. Never before did I completely understand what Demosthenes meant by laying such stress on delivery. You are to bring before you the venerable figure of the preacher; his blindness, constantly recalling to your recollection old Homer, Ossian, and Milton, and associating with his performance the melancholy grandeur of their geniuses; you are to imagine that you hear his slow, solemn, well-accented enunciation, and his voice of affecting, trembling melody; you are to remember the pitch of passion and enthusiasm, to which the congregation were raised; and then the few moments of portentous, deathlike silence, which reigned throughout the house : the preacher, removing his white handkerchief from his aged face, (even yet wet from the recent torrent of his tears,) and slowly stretching forth the palsied hand which holds it, begins the sentence, " Socrates died like a philosopher"—then, pausing, raising his other hand, pressing them both, clasped together, with warmth and energy, to his breast, lifting his " sightless balls" to heaven, and pouring his whole soul into his tremulous voice—" but Jesus Christ—like a God !" If he had been indeed and in truth an angel of light, the effect could scarcely have been more divine. Whatever I had been able to conceive of the sublimity of Massillon or the force of Bourdaloue, had fallen far short of the power which I felt from the delivery of this simple sentence.

If this description give you the impression, that this incomparable minister had any thing of shallow, theatrical trick in his manner, it does him great injustice. I have never seen, in any other orator, such a union of simplicity and majesty. He has not a gesture, an attitude, or an accent, to which he does not seem forced by the sentiment he is expressing. His mind is too serious, too earnest, too solicitous, and, at the same time, too dignified, to stoop to artifice. Although as far removed from ostentation as a

23

man can be, yet it is clear, from the train, the style and substance of his thoughts, that he is not only a very polite scholar, but a man of extensive and profound erudition. I was forcibly struck with a short yet beautiful character, which he drew of your learned and amiable countryman, Sir Robert Boyle : he spoke of him, as if " his noble mind had, even before death, divested herself of all influence from his frail tabernacle of flesh ;" and called him, in his peculiarly emphatic and impressive manner, "a pure intelligence : the link between men and angels."

This man has been before my imagination almost ever since. A thousand times, as I rode along, I dropped the reins of my bridle, stretched forth my hand, and tried to imitate his quotation from Rousseau ; a thousand times I abandoned the attempt in despair, and felt persuaded, that his peculiar manner and power arose from an energy of soul, which nature could give, but which no human being could justly copy. As I recall, at this moment, several of his awfully striking attitudes, the chilling tide, with which my blood begins to pour along my arteries, reminds me of the emotions produced by the first sight of Gray's introductory picture of his Bard.

The humble Man and the proud.—THACHER.

COMPARE, then, the proud man with the man of humility, and tell me which is the more dignified being. Pride, like humility, supposes an act of comparison. But the comparison of the proud man is not between himself and the standard of his duty ; between what he is and what he ought to be ; but between himself and his fellow-men. He looks around him, forgets his own defects and weaknesses, infirmities and sins, and because he finds, or imagines he finds, in some respects, a little superiority to his fellow-men—at the greatest it can be *but* a little—because he, one worm of the dust, believes himself to be somewhat more rich, more learned, more successful than another, he thinks this to be a sufficient ground for swelling with self-complacency, and regarding those around him with disdain

and contempt. The humble man, on the contrary, is so
full of the thought of the exceeding breadth of the com
mandments of God, and of that supreme excellence, to
which his religion teaches him to aspire ; and he so constantly recollects the imperfection of his approaches to it,
that every idea of a vain-glorious comparison of himself
with his neighbour dies away within him. He can only
remember that God is every thing, and that in his august
presence all distinctions are lost, and all human beings reduced to the same level. Say, then, my friends; is it not
pride, that is so mean, so poor-spirited and low ? is it not
pride, that is a mark of a little, and narrow, and feeble
mind ? and is not humility alone the truly noble, the truly
generous and sublime quality ?

There is this further proof of the superior elevation of
the humble man. The man of pride, with all his affected
contempt of the world, must evidently estimate it very
highly ; else, whence so much complacency at the idea of
surpassing others? Whence that restless desire of distinction, that passion for theatrical display, which inflames
his heart, and occupies his whole attention ? Why is it
that his strongest motive to good actions is their notoriety,
and that he considers every worthy deed as lost, when it
is not publicly displayed? It is only because the world
and the world's applause are every thing to him ; and that
he cannot live but on the breath of popular favour. But
the humble man, with all his real lowliness, has yet risen
above the world. He looks for that honour, which cometh
down from on high, and the whispers of worldly praise
die away upon his ear. When his thoughts return from
the contemplation of the infinite excellence of God, and
the future glories of virtue, the objects of this life appear
reduced in their importance ; in the same way as the landscape around appears little and low to him, whose eye has
been long directed to the solemn grandeur and wide magnificence of the starry heavens. I appeal to you, my
friends, to decide on the comparative dignity of the characters of the proud and the humble man. I call on you
to say, whether our blessed Master has given to humility
too high a rank in the scale of excellence.

The Son.—From " The Idle Man."—RICHARD DANA

THERE is no virtue without a characteristic beauty to
make it particularly loved of the good, and to make the
bad ashamed of their neglect of it.   To do what is right
argues superior taste as well as morals ; and those, whose
practice is evil, feel an inferiority of intellectual power and
enjoyment, even where they take no concern for a principle.   Doing well has something more in it than the
fulfilling of a duty.   It is a cause of a just sense of elevation of character ; it clears and strengthens the spirits ; it
gives higher reaches of thought ; it widens our benevolence, and makes the current of our peculiar affections
swift and deep.

A sacrifice was never yet offered to a principle, that was
not made up to us by self-approval, and the consideration
of what our degradation would have been had we done
otherwise.   Certainly, it is a pleasant and a wise thing.
then, to follow what is right, when we only go along with
our affections, and take the easy way of the virtuous propensities of our nature.

The world is sensible of these truths, let it act as it may.
It is not because of his integrity alone that, it relies on an
honest man ; but it has more confidence in his judgment and
wise conduct in the long run, than in the schemes of those
of greater intellect, who go at large without any landmarks of principle.   So that virtue seems of a double nature, and to stand oftentimes in the place of what we call
talent.

The reasoning, or rather feeling, of the world is all right,
for the honest man only falls in with the order of nature,
which is grounded in truth, and will endure along with it.
And such a hold has a good man upon the world, that, even
where he has not been called upon to make a sacrifice to a
principle, or to take a stand against wrong, but has merely
avoided running into vices, and suffered himself to be
borne along by the delightful and virtuous affections of pri
vate life, and has found his pleasure in practising the du
ties of home,—he is looked up to with respect, as well as
regarded with kindness.   We attach certain notions of re

finement to his thoughts, and of depth to his sentiment. The impression he makes on us is beautiful and peculiar. Other men in his presence, though we have nothing to object to them, and though they may be very well in their way, affect us as lacking something—we can hardly tell what—a certain sensitive delicacy of character and manner, without which they strike us as more or less vulgar.

No creature in the world has this character so finely marked in him, as a respectful and affectionate son—particularly in his relation to his mother. Every little attention he pays her is not only an expression of filial attachment, and grateful acknowledgment of past cares, but is an evidence of a tenderness of disposition, which moves us the more, because not looked on so much as an essential property in a man's character, as an added grace, which is bestowed only upon a few. His regards do not appear like mere habits of duty, nor does his watchfulness of his mother's wishes seem like taught submission to her will. They are the native courtesies of a feeling mind, showing themselves amidst stern virtues and masculine energies like gleams of light on points of rocks. They are delightful as evidences of power yielding voluntary homage to the delicacy of the soul. The armed knee is bent, and the heart of the mailed man laid bare.

Feelings, that would seem to be at variance with each other, meet together and harmonize in the breast of a son. Every call of the mother which he answers to, and every act of submission which he performs, are not only so many acknowledgments of her authority, but, also, so many instances of kindness, and marks of protecting regard. The servant and defender, the child and guardian, are all mingled in him. The world looks on him in this way; and to draw upon a man the confidence, the respect, and the love of the world, it is enough to say of him, He is an excellent son.

In looking over some papers of a deceased acquaintance, I found the following fragment. He had frequently spoken to me of the person whom it concerned, and who had been his school-fellow. I remember well his one day telling me, that, thinking the character of his friend, and some circumstances in his life, were of such a kind, that an in

23 *

teresting moral little story might be made from them, he
had undertaken it; but considering, as he was going on,
that bringing the private character and feelings of a deceased friend before the world was something like sacrilege,
though done under a fictitious name, he had stopped soon
after beginning the tale; that he had laid it away amongst
his papers, and had never looked at it again.

As the person it concerns has been a long time dead,
and no relation survives, I do not feel that there can be
any impropriety in my now making it public. I give it
as it was written, though evidently not revised by my
friend. Though hastily put together, and beginning as
abruptly as it ends, and with little of story, and no novelty,
in the circumstances, yet there is a mournful tenderness
in it, which, I trust will interest others in some portion
as it did me.

"The sun not set yet, Thomas?" "Not quite, sir. It
blazes through the trees on the hill yonder as if their
branches were all on fire."

Arthur raised himself heavily forward, and, with his ha-
still over his brow, turned his glazed and dim eyes towards
the setting sun. It was only the night before that he had
heard his mother was ill, and could survive but a day or
two. He had lived nearly apart from society, and, being
a lad of a thoughtful, dreamy mind, had made a world to
himself. His thoughts and feelings were so much in it,
that, except in relation to his own home, there were the
same vague and strange notions in his brain, concerning
the state of things surrounding him, as we have of a foreign
land.

The main feeling, which this self-made world excited in
him, was love, and, like most of his age, he had formed to
himself a being suited to his own fancies. This was the
romance of life, and though men, with minds like his, make
imagination to stand oftentimes in the place of real existence, and to take to itself as deep feeling and concern, yet,
in domestic relations, which are so near, and usual, and
private, they feel longer and more deeply than those who
look upon their homes as only a better part of the world

which they belong to. Indeed, in affectionate and good men of a visionary cast, it is in some sort only realizing their hopes and desires, to turn them homeward. Arthur felt that it was so, and he loved his household the more that they gave him an earnest of one day realizing all his hopes and attachments.

Arthur's mother was peculiarly dear to him, in having a character so much like his own. For, though the cares and attachments of life had long ago taken place of a fanciful existence in her, yet her natural turn of mind was strong enough to give to these something of the romance of her disposition. This had led to a more than usual openness and intimacy between Arthur and his mother, and now brought to his remembrance the hours they had sat together by the fire light, when he listened to her mild and melancholy voice, as she spoke of what she had undergone at the loss of her parents and husband. Her gentle rebuke of his faults, her affectionate look of approval when he had done well, her care that he should be a just man, and her motherly anxiety lest the world should go hard with him, all crowded into his mind, and he thought that every worldl; attachment was hereafter to be a vain thing.

He had passed the night between violent, tumultuous grief, and numb insensibility. Stepping into the carriage, with a slow, weak motion, like one who was quitting his sick chamber for the first time, he began his journey homeward. As he lifted his eyes upward, the few stars, that were here and there over the sky, seemed to look down in pity, and shed a religious and healing light upon him. But they soon went out, one after another, and as the last faded from his imploring sight, it was as if every thing good and holy had forsaken him. The faint tint in the east soon became a ruddy glow, and the sun, shooting upward, burst over every living thing in full glory. The sight went to Arthur's sick heart, as if it were in mockery of his misery.

Leaning back in his carriage, with his hand over his eyes, he was carried along, hardly sensible it was day. The old servant, Thomas, who was sitting by his side, went on talking in a low, monotonous tone; but Arthur only heard something sounding in his ears, scarcely heeding

that it was a human voice. He had a sense of wearisome-
ness from the motion of the carriage, but in all things
else the day passed as a melancholy dream.

Almost the first words Arthur spoke were those I have
mentioned. As he looked out upon the setting sun, he
shuddered through his whole frame, and then became sick
and pale. He thought he knew the hill near him ; and, as
they wound round it, some peculiar old trees appeared, and
he was in a few minutes in the midst of the scenery near
his home. The river before him, reflecting the rich evening sky, looked as if poured out from a molten mine. The
birds, gathering in, were shooting across each other, bursting into short, gay notes, or singing their evening songs in
the trees. It was a bitter thing to find all so bright and
cheerful, and so near his own home too. His horses' hoofs
struck upon the old wooden bridge. The sound went to
his heart. It was here his mother took her last leave of
him, and blessed him.

As he passed through the village, there was a feeling of
strangeness, that every thing should be just as it was when
he left it. There was an undefined thought floating in his
mind, that his mother's state should produce a visible change
in all that he had been familiar with. But the boys were at
their noisy games in the street, the labourers returning,
talking together, from their work, and the old men sitting
quietly at their doors. He concealed himself as well as
he could, and bade Thomas hasten on.

As they drew near the house, the night was shutting in
about it, and there was a melancholy gusty sound in the
trees. Arthur felt as if approaching his mother's tomb
He entered the parlour. All was as gloomy and still as a
deserted house. Presently he heard a slow, cautious step,
over head. It was in his mother's chamber. His sister
had seen him from the window. She hurried down, and
threw her arms about her brother's neck, without uttering
a word. As soon as he could speak, he asked, " Is she
alive ?"—he could not say, *my mother*. " She is sleeping," answered his sister, " and must not know to-night
that you are here ; she is too weak to bear it now." " I
will go look at her then, while she sleeps," said he, drawing his handkerchief from his face. His sister's sympathy

had made him shed the first tears which had fallen from
him that day, and he was more composed.

He entered the chamber with a deep and still awe upon
him ; and, as he drew near his mother's bed-side, and looked on her pale, placid, and motionless face, he scarcely
dared breathe, lest he should disturb the secret communion that the soul was holding with the world into which it
was about to enter. The loss that he was about suffering,
and his heavy grief, were all forgotten in the feeling of a
holy inspiration, and he was, as it were, in the midst of invisible spirits, ascending and descending. His mother's
lips moved slightly as she uttered an indistinct sound. He
drew back, and his sister went near to her, and she spoke
It was the same gentle voice which he had known and
felt from his childhood. The exaltation of his soul left
him—he sunk down—and his misery went over him like
a flood.

The next day, as soon as his mother became composed
enough to see him, Arthur went into her chamber. She
stretched out her feeble hand, and turned towards him, with
a look that blessed him. It was the short struggle of a
meek spirit. She covered her eyes with her hand, and the
tears trickled down between her pale, thin fingers. As soon
as she became tranquil, she spoke of the gratitude she felt
at being spared to see him before she died.

" My dear mother," said Arthur—but he could not go
on. His voice was choked, his eyes filled with tears, and
the agony of his soul was visible in his face. " Do not be
so afflicted, Arthur, at the loss of me. We are not to part
for ever. Remember, too, how comfortable and happy you
have made my days   Heaven, I know, will bless so good
a son as you have been to me. You will have that consolation, my son, which visits but a few—you will be able to
look back upon your past conduct to me, not without pain
only, but with a holy joy. And think hereafter of the peace
of mind you give me, now that I am about to die, in the
thought that I am leaving your sister to your love and care.
So long as you live, she will find you a father and brother
to her." She paused for a moment. " I have always felt
that I could meet death with composure ; but I did not
know," she said, with a tremulous voice, her lips quivering

—" I did not know how hard a thing it would be to eave my children, till now that the hour has come."

After a little while, she spoke of his father, and said, she had lived with the belief that he was mindful of her, and with the conviction, which grew stronger as death approached, that she should meet him in another world. She said but little more, as she grew weaker and weaker every hour. Arthur sat by in silence, holding her hand He saw that she was sensible he was watching her countenance, for every now and then she opened her dull eye, and looked towards him, and endeavoured to smile.

The day wore slowly away. The sun went down, and the melancholy and still twilight came on. Nothing was heard but the ticking of the watch, telling him with a resistless power, that the hour was drawing nigh. He gasped, as if under some invisible, gigantic grasp, which it was not for human strength to struggle against.

It was now quite dark, and, by the pale light of the night-lamp in the chimney corner, the furniture in the room threw huge and uncouth figures over the walls. All was unsubstantial and visionary, and the shadowy ministers of death appeared gathering round, waiting the duty of the hour appointed them. Arthur shuddered for a moment with superstitious awe; but the solemn elevation which a good man feels at the sight of the dying, took possession of him, and he became calm again.

The approach of death has so much which is exalting, that our grief is, for the time, forgotten. And could one, who had seen Arthur a few hours before, now have looked upon the grave and grand repose of his countenance, he would hardly have known him.

The livid hue of death was fast spreading over his mother's face. He stooped forward to catch the sound of her breathing. It grew quick and faint.—"My mother!"— She opened her eyes, for the last time, upon him—a faint flush passed over her cheek—there was the serenity of an angel in her look—her hand just pressed his. It was all over.

His spirit had endured to its utmost. It sunk down from its unearthly height; and, with his face upon his mother's pillow, he wept like a child. He arose with a violent effort, and, stepping into the adjoining chamber, spoke to his aunt. "It is past," said he. "Is my sister asleep?—Well, then, let her have rest; she needs it." He then went to his own chamber, and shut himself in.

It is a merciful thing that the intense suffering of sensitive minds makes to itself a relief. Violent grief brings on a torpor, and an indistinctness, and dimness, as from long watching. It is not till the violence of affliction has subsided, and gentle and soothing thoughts can find room to mix with our sorrow, and holy consolations can minister to us, that we are able to know fully our loss, and see clearly what has been torn away from our affections. It was so with Arthur. Unconnected and strange thoughts, with melancholy, but half-formed images, were floating in his mind, and now and then a gleam of light would pass through it, as if he had been in a troubled trance, and all was right again. His worn and tired feelings at last found rest in sleep.

It is an impression, which we cannot rid ourselves of if we would, when sitting by the body of a friend, that he has still a consciousness of our presence , that, though the common concerns of the world have no more to do with him, he has still a love and care of us. The face which we had so long been familiar with, when it was all life and motion, seems only in a state of rest. We know not how to make it real to ourselves, that the body before us is not a living thing.

Arthur was in such a state of mind, as he sat alone in the room by his mother, the day after her death. It was as if her soul had been in paradise, and was now holding communion with pure spirits there, though it still abode in the body that lay before him. He felt as if sanctified by the presence of one to whom the other world had been laid open—as if under the love and protection of one more holy. The religious reflections that his mother had early taught him, gave him strength ; a spiritual composure stole over him, and he found himself prepared to perform the last offices to the dead.

Is 't not enough to see our friends die, and part with them for the remainder of our days ; to reflect that we shall hear their voices no more, and that they will never look on us again ; to see that turning to corruption, which was but just now alive, and eloquent, and beautiful with all the sensations of the soul ? Are our sorrows so sacred and peculiar as to make the world as vanity to us, and the men of it as strangers ? and shall we not be left to our afflictions for a few hours ? Must we be brought out at such a time to the concerned or careless gaze of those we know not, or be made to bear the formal proffers of consolations from acquaintances who will go away and forget it all ? Shall we not be suffered, a little while, a holy and healing communion with the dead ? Must the kindred stillness and gloom of our dwelling be changed for the solemn show of the pall, the talk of the passers-by, and the broad and piercing light of the common sun ? Must the ceremonies of the world wait on us even to the open graves of our friends ?

When the hour came, Arthur rose with a firm step and fixed eye, though his whole face was tremulous with the struggle within him. He went to his sister, and took her arm within his. The bell struck. Its heavy, undulating sound rolled forward like a sea. He felt a violent beating through his whole frame, which shook him that he reeled It was but a momentary weakness. He moved on, passing those who surrounded him, as if they had been shadows While he followed the slow hearse, there was a vacancy in his eye, as it rested on the coffin, which showed him hardly conscious of what was before him. His spirit was with his mother's. As he reached the grave, he shrunk back, and turned deadly pale ; but, sinking his head upon his breast, and drawing his hat over his face, he stood motionless as a statue till the service was over.

He had gone through all that the forms of society required of him. For, as painful as the effort was, and as little suited as such forms were to his own thoughts upon the subject, yet he could not do any thing that might appear to the world like a want of reverence and respect for his mother. The scene was ended, and the inward struggle over ; and now that he was left to himself, the greatness of his loss came up full and distinctly before him.

It was a dreary and chilly evening when he returned home. When he entered the house from which his mother had gone for ever, a sense of dreary emptiness oppressed him, as if his very abode had been deserted by every living thing. He walked into his mother's chamber. The naked bedstead, and the chair in which she used to sit, were all that was left in the room. As he threw himself back into the chair, he groaned in the bitterness of his spirit. A feeling of forlornness came over him, which was not to be relieved by tears. She, whom he had watched over in her dying hour, and whom he had talked to as she lay before him in death, as if she could hear and answer him, had gone from him. Nothing was left for the senses to fasten fondly on, and time had not yet taught him to think of her only as a spirit. But time and holy endeavours brought this consolation; and the little of life that a wasting disease left him, was past by him, when alone, in thoughtful tranquillity; and amongst his friends he appeared with that gentle cheerfulness, which, before his mother's death, had been a part of his nature.

Neglect of foreign Literature in America.—AMERICAN QUARTERLY REVIEW.

THE curiosity of our nation in literature is not sufficiently expansive; our public refuses its attention to works written for another hemisphere, and a different state of society. This is natural, but it is not wise.

The facility of receiving enjoyment from a variety of sources is an advantage of high value. It is well to rejoice in every exhibition of genius. What should we think of the man, who not only clings to the pleasures rendered dear by habit, but denies that there are others to be set in comparison with them? And yet we hear hasty judgments on the merits of whole classes of writers. Every man has, indeed, the right to choose his own guides to the summit of Olympus; but we question the soundness of those who deny that there are more ways than one. Such or

24

opinion could be explained, only as the result of mental imbecility, of a narrowness that submits to the
shackles of prejudice.   Born and bred in a temperate
zone, we all admire the loveliness of our landscape, where
the graceful foliage of our trees is mingled with the rich
verdure of our meadows, and the abundance of our harvests.   But shall we have no eye for other charms?   Shall a
Swiss scene, where the glaciers énter the fertile valley, and
winter and summer are seen side by side, have no power to
please us?   or a scene beneath a southern sky, where the
palm trees lift their heads in slender magnificence, the forests are alive with birds, and glitter with the splendour of
variegated plumage, and earth is gay with all the colours
that gain their deep tints under a tropic sun?   The eye,
that communes with nature, and understands it, discerns
loveliness in all its forms.   And shall we, who are certainly not incurious as to the concerns of this world, be indifferent to foreign letters?   Must we be so engrossed with
the language and concerns of business, that we cannot listen to the language of poetic inspiration?   And must we
forever and unceasingly be deafened by the din of con-
gressional rivalries?   Is there, between the acclamations
and rebukes of partisans, and the hot warfare of canvass
for office, no happy moment of tranquillity, in which Learning may raise her head fearlessly, and be respected, and
the pursuits of contemplative life be cheered by the free
expression of general approbation, and quickened into ex
cellence by the benignity of an attentive nation?   We
cannot as yet be said to have a national literature ; but
we already have the promise of one, and the first fruits
As the literary character of the country is developed, it
should resemble our political institutions in liberality, and
welcome excellence from every quarter of the world.

Death a sublime and universal Moralist.—Sparks.[*]

No object is so insignificant, no event so trivial, as not to carry with it a moral and religious influence. The trees that spring out of the earth are moralists. They are emblems of the life of man. They grow up; they put on the garments of freshness and beauty. Yet these continue but for a time; decay seizes upon the root and the trunk, and they gradually go back to their original elements. The blossoms that open to the rising sun, but are closed at night never to open again, are moralists. The seasons are moralists, teaching the lessons of wisdom, manifesting the wonders of the Creator, and calling on man to reflect on his condition and destiny. History is a perpetual moralist, disclosing the annals of past ages, showing the impotency of pride and greatness, the weakness of human power, the folly of human wisdom. The daily occurrences in society are moralists. The success or failure of enterprise, the prosperity of the bad, the adversity of the good, the disappointed hopes of the sanguine and active, the sufferings of the virtuous, the caprices of fortune in every condition of life, all these are fraught with moral instructions, and, if properly applied, will fix the power of religion in the heart.

But there is a greater moralist still; and that is, Death. Here is a teacher, who speaks in a voice, which none can mistake; who comes with a power, which none can resist. Since we last assembled in this place as the humble and united worshippers of God, this stern messenger, this mysterious agent of Omnipotence, has come among our numbers, and laid his withering hand on one, whom we have been taught to honour and respect, whose fame was a nation's boast, whose genius was a brilliant spark from the ethereal fire, whose attainments were equalled only by the grasp of his intellect, the profoundness of his judgment, the exuberance of his fancy, the magic of his eloquence.

---

* From a Sermon on the death of the Hon. William Pinckney, preached March 3d, 1822, in the hall of the house of representatives in congress.—Ed

It is not my present purpose to ask your attention to any picture drawn in the studied phrase of eulogy. I aim not to describe the commanding powers and the eminent qualities, which conducted the deceased to the superiority he held, and which were at once the admiration and the pride of his countrymen. I shall not attempt to analyze his capacious mind, nor to set forth the richness and variety of its treasures. The trophies of his genius are a sufficient testimony of these, and constitute a monument to his memory, which will stand firm and conspicuous amidst the faded recollections of future ages. The present is not the time to recount the sources or the memorials of his greatness He is gone. The noblest of Heaven's gifts could not shield even him from the arrows of the destroyer. And this behest of the Most High is a warning summons to us all. When Death comes into our doors, we ought to feel that he is near. When his irreversible sentence falls on the great and the renowned, when he severs the strongest bonds, which can bind mortals to earth, we ought to feel that our hold on life is slight, that the thread of existence is slender, that we walk amidst perils, where the next wave in the agitated sea of life may baffle all our struggles, and carry us back into the dark bosom of the deep.

When we look at the monuments of human greatness, and the powers of human intellect, all that genius has invented, or skill executed, or wisdom matured, or industry achieved, or labour accomplished; when we trace these through the successive gradations of human advancement, what are they? On these are founded the pride, glory, dignity of man. And what are they? Compared with the most insignificant work of God, they are nothing, less than nothing. The mightiest works of man are daily and hourly becoming extinct. The boasted theories of religion, morals, government, which took the wisdom, the ingenuity of ages to invent, have been proved to be shadowy theories only. Genius has wasted itself in vain ; the visions it has raised have vanished at the touch of truth. Nothing is left but the melancholy certainty, that all things human are imperfect, and must fail and decay. And man himself, whose works are so fragile, where is he ? The

history of his works is the history of himself. He existed;
he is gone.

The nature of human life cannot be more forcibly described than in the beautiful language of eastern poetry,
which immediately precedes the text: "Man, that is born
of woman, is of few days, and full of trouble. He cometh
forth like a flower, and is cut down; he fleeth as a shadow,
and continueth not. There is hope of a tree, if it be cut
down, that it will sprout again, and that the tender branch
thereof will not cease. Though the root thereof wax old
in the earth, and the stock thereof die in the ground; yet,
through the scent of water, it will bud and bring forth
boughs like a plant. But man wasteth away; yea, man
giveth up the ghost, and where is he?" Such are the striking emblems of human life; such is the end of all that is
mortal in man. And what a question is here for us to
reflect upon! "Man giveth up the ghost, *and where
is he?*"

Yes, when we see the flower of life fade on its stalk,
and all its comeliness depart, and all its freshness wither;
when we see the bright eye grow dim, and the rose on the
cheek lose its hue; when we hear the voice faltering its
last accents, and see the energies of nature paralyzed;
when we perceive the beams of intelligence grow fainter
and fainter on the countenance, and the last gleam of life
extinguished; when we deposit all that is mortal of a fel-
low-being in the dark, cold chamber of the grave, and drop
a pitying tear at a spectacle so humiliating, so mournful;
then let us put the solemn question to our souls, Where is
he? His body is concealed in the earth; but where is
the spirit? Where is the intellect that could look through
the works of God, and catch inspiration from the Divinity
which animates and pervades the whole? Where are the
powers that could command, the attractions that could
charm? where the boast of humanity, wisdom, learning,
wit, eloquence, the pride of skill, the mystery of art, the
creations of fancy, the brilliancy of thought? where the
virtues that could win, and the gentleness that could soothe?
where the mildness of temper, the generous affections, the
benevolent feelings, all that is great and good, all that is
noble, and lovely, and pure, in the human character.—

24 *

where are they? They are gone. We can see nothing the eye of faith only can dimly penetrate the region to which they have fled. Lift the eye of faith; follow the light of the Gospel; and let your delighted vision be lost in the glories of the immortal world. Behold, there, the spirits of the righteous dead rising up into newness of life, gathering brightness and strength, unencumbered by the weight of mortal clay and mortal sorrows, enjoying a happy existence. and performing the holy service of their Maker.

Let our reflections on death have a weighty and immediate influence on our minds and characters. We cannot be too soon nor too entirely prepared to render the account, which we must all render to our Maker and Judge. All things earthly must fail us; the riches, power, possessions and gifts of the world will vanish from our sight; friends and relatives will be left behind; our present support will be taken away; our strength will become weakness; and the earth itself, and all its pomps, and honours, and attractions will disappear. Why have we been spared even till this time? We know not why, nor yet can we say that a moment is our own. The summons for our departure may now be recorded in the book of Heaven. The angel may now be on his way to execute his solemn commission. Death may already have marked us for his victims. But, whether sooner or later, the event will be equally awful, and demand the same preparation.

One, only, will then be our rock and our safety. The kind Parent, who has upheld us all our days, will remain our unfailing support. With him is no change; he is unmoved from age to age; his mercy, as well as his being, endures forever; and, if we rely on him, and live in obedience to his laws, all tears shall be wiped from our eyes, and all sorrow banished from our hearts. If we are rebels to his cause, slaves to vice, and followers of evil, we must expect the displeasure of a holy God, the just punishment of our folly and wickedness; for a righteous retribution will be awarded to the evil as well as to the good.

Let it be the highest, the holiest, the unceasing concern of each one of us, to live the life, that we may be prepared to die the death of the righteous; that, when they

who come after us shall ask, Where is he? uncumbered
voices shall be raised to testify, that, although his mortal
remains are mouldering in the cold earth, his memory is
embalmed in the cherished recollections of many a friend
who knew and loved him ; and all shall say, with tokens
o' joy and confident belief, If God be just, and piety be
rewarded, his pure spirit is now at rest in the regions of
the blessed.

Battle of Bunker Hill.—COOPER.

THE whole scene now lay before them.   Nearly in
their front was the village of Charlestown, with its deserted streets, and silent roofs, looking like a place of the dead ;
or, if the signs of life were visible within its open avenues,
'twas merely some figure moving swiftly in the solitude,
like one who hastened to quit the devoted spot.   On the
opposite point of the south-eastern face of the peninsula,
and at the distance of a thousand yards, the ground was
already covered by masses of human beings, in scarlet,
with their arms glittering in a noon-day sun.   Between the
two, though in the more immediate vicinity of the silent
town, the rounded ridge, already described, rose abruptly
from a flat that was bounded by the water, until, having
attained an elevation of some fifty or sixty feet, it swelled
gradually to the little crest, where was planted the humble object that had occasioned all this commotion.   The
meadows, on the right, were still peaceful and smiling, as
in the most quiet days of the province, though the excited
fancy of Lionel imagined that a sullen stillness lingered
about the neglected kilns in their front, and over the whole
landscape, that was in gloomy consonance with the approaching scene.   Far on the left, across the waters of the
Charles, the American camp had poured forth its thousands
to the hills ; and the whole population of the country, for
many miles inland, had gathered to a point, to witness a
struggle charged with the fate of their nation.   Beacon
Hill rose from out the appalling silence of the town of Boston, like a pyramid of living faces, with every eye fixed

on the fatal point; and men hung along the yards of the
shipping, or were suspended on cornices, cupolas, and steeples, in thoughtless security, while every other sense was
lost in the absorbing interest of the sight.   The vessels of
war had hauled deep into the rivers, or, more properly,
those narrow arms of the sea, which formed the peninsula,
and sent their iron missiles with unwearied industry across
the low passage, which alone opened the means of communication between the self-devoted yeomen on the hill and
their distant countrymen. While battalion landed after
battalion on the point, cannon-balls from the battery of
Copp's, and the vessels of war, were glancing up the natural glacis that surrounded the redoubt, burying themselves
in its earthen parapet, or plunging with violence into the
deserted sides of the loftier height which lay a few hundred yards in its rear ; and the black and smoking bombs
appeared to hover above the spot, as if pausing to select
the places in which to plant their deadly combustibles.

Notwithstanding these appalling preparations, and ceaseless annoyances, throughout that long and anxious morning, the stout husbandmen on the hill had never ceased
their steady efforts to maintain, to the uttermost extremity,
the post they had so daringly assumed. In vain the English exhausted every means to disturb their stubborn foes ;
the pick, the shovel and the spade continued to perform
their offices, and mound rose after mound, amidst the din
and danger of the cannonade, steadily, and as well as if the
fanciful conceits of Job Pray embraced their real objects,
and the labourers were employed in the peaceful pursuits
of their ordinary lives. This firmness, however, was not
like the proud front which high training can impart to the
most common mind ; for, ignorant of the glare of military
show ; in the simple and rude vestments of their calling ;
armed with such weapons as they had seized from the
hooks above their own mantels ; and without even a banner to wave its cheering folds above their heads, they
stood, sustained only by the righteousness of their cause,
and those deep moral principles, which they had received
from their fathers, and which they intended this day should
show were to be transmitted untarnished to their children.
It was afterwards known, that they endured their labours

and their dangers even in want of that sustenance, which is so essential to support animal spirits in moments of calmness and ease; while their enemies, on the point, awaiting the arrival of their latest bands, were securely devouring a meal, which, to hundreds amongst them, proved to be their last. The fatal instant now seemed approaching. A general movement was seen among the battalions of the British, who began to spread along the shore, under cover of the brow of the hill—the lingering boats having arrived with the rear of their detachments—and officers hurried from regiment to regiment with the final mandates of their chief. At this moment a body of Americans appeared on the crown of Bunker Hill, and, descending swiftly by the road, disappeared in the meadows to the 'left of their own redoubt. This band was followed by others, who, like themselves, had broken through the dangers of the narrow pass, by braving the fire of the shipping, and who also hurried to join their comrades on the low land. The British general determined at once to anticipate the arrival of further re-enforcements, and gave forth the long-expected order to prepare for the attack.

The Americans had made a show, in the course of that fearful morning, of returning the fire of their enemies, by throwing a few shot from their light field-pieces, as if in mockery of the tremendous cannonade which they sustained. But as the moment of severest trial approached, the same awful stillness, which had settled upon the deserted streets of Charlestown, hovered around the redoubt. On the meadows, to its left, the recently arrived bands hastily threw the rails of two fences into one, and, covering the whole with the mown grass that surrounded them, they posted themselves along the frail defence, which answered no better purpose than to conceal their weakness from their adversaries. Behind this characteristic rampart, several bodies of husbandmen, from the neighbouring provinces of New Hampshire and Connecticut, lay on their arms, in sullen expectation. Their line extended from the shore to the base of the ridge, where it terminated several hundred feet behind the works; leaving a wide opening, in a diagonal direction, between the fence and an earthen breastwork, which ran a short distance

down the declivity of the hill, from the north-eastern angle
of the redoubt. A few hundred yards in the rear of this
rude disposition, the naked crest of Bunker Hill rose unoccupied and undefended; and the streams of the Charles
and Mystick, sweeping around its base, approached so near
each other as to blend the sounds of their rippling. It was
across this low and narrow isthmus, that the royal frigates
poured a stream of fire, that never ceased, while around
it hovered the numerous parties of the undisciplined Americans, hesitating to attempt the dangerous passage.

In this manner Gage had, in a great degree, surrounded the devoted peninsula with his power; and the bold
men, who had so daringly planted themselves under the
muzzles of his cannon, were left, as already stated, unsupported, without nourishment, and with weapons from their
own gunhooks, singly to maintain the honour of their nation. Including men of all ages and conditions, there
might have been two thousand of them; but, as the day
advanced, small bodies of their countrymen, taking counsel
of their feelings, and animated by the example of the old
partisan of the woods, who crossed and recrossed the neck,
loudly scoffing at the danger, broke through the fire of the
shipping in time to join in the closing and bloody business
of the hour.

On the other hand, Howe led more than an equal number of the chosen troops of his prince; and as boats continued to ply between the two peninsulas throughout the
afternoon, the relative disparity continued undiminished to
the end of the struggle. It was at this point in our narrative that, deeming himself sufficiently strong to force the
defences of his despised foes, the arrangements immediately preparatory to such an undertaking were made in full
view of the excited spectators. Notwithstanding the security with which the English general marshalled his warriors, he felt that the approaching contest would be a battle of no common incidents. The eyes of tens of thousands
were fastened on his movements, and the occasion demanded the richest display of the pageantry of war.

The troops formed with beautiful accuracy, and the columns moved steadily along the shore, and took their assigned stations under cover of the brow of the eminence. Their

force was in some measure divided ; one moiety attempting
the toilsome ascent of the hill, and the other moving along
the beach, or in the orchards of the more level ground, towards the husbandmen on the meadows.   The latter soon
disappeared behind some fruit-trees and the brick-kilns just
mentioned.   The advance of the royal columns up the ascent was slow and measured, giving time to their field-
guns to add their efforts to the uproar of the cannonade,
which broke out with new fury as the battalions prepared
to march.   When each column arrived at the allotted point,
it spread the gallant array of its glittering warriors under
a bright sun.

" It is a glorious spectacle," murmured the graceful
chieftain by the side of Lionel, keenly alive to all the poetry of his alluring profession; " how exceeding soldier-
like ! and with what accuracy his ' first-arm ascends the
hill,' towards his enemy !"

The intensity of his feelings prevented Major Lincoln
from replying, and the other soon forgot that he had spoken,
in the overwhelming anxiety of the moment.   The advance of the British line, so beautiful and slow, resembled
rather the ordered steadiness of a drill, than an approach
to a deadly struggle.   Their standards fluttered proudly
above them ; and there were moments when the wild music of their bands was heard rising on the air, and temper-
ing the ruder sounds of the artillery.   The young and
thoughtless in their ranks turned their faces backward, and
smiled exultingly, as they beheld steeples, roofs, masts, and
heights, teeming with their thousands of eyes, bent on the
show of their bright array.   As the British lines moved
in open view of the little redoubt, and began slowly to
gather around its different faces, gun after gun became silent, and the curious artillerist, or tired seaman, lay extended on his heated piece, gazing in mute wonder at the
spectacle.   There was just then a minute when the roar
of the cannonade seemed passing away like the rumbling
of distant thunder.

" They will not fight, Lincoln," said the animated leader
at the side of Lionel—" the military front of Howe has
chilled the hearts of the knaves, and our victory will be
bloodless !"

" We shall see, sir—we shall see !"

These words were barely uttered, when platoon after platoon, among the British, delivered its fire, the blaze of musketry flashing swiftly around the brow of the hill, and was immediately followed by heavy volleys that ascended from the orchard. Still no answering sound was heard from the Americans, and the royal troops were soon lost to the eye, as they slowly marched into the white cloud which their own fire had alone created.

" They are cowed, by heavens !—the dogs are cowed !" once more cried the gay companion of Lionel, " and Howe is within two hundred feet of them unharmed !"

At that instant a sheet of flame glanced through the smoke, like lightning playing in a cloud, while at one report a thousand muskets were added to the uproar. It was not altogether fancy, which led Lionel to imagine that he saw the smoky canopy of the hill to wave, as if the trained warriors it enveloped faltered before this close and appalling discharge ; but, in another instant, the stimulating war-cry, and the loud shouts of the combatants, were borne across the strait to his ears, even amid the horrid din of the combat. Ten breathless minutes flew by like a moment of time, and the bewildered spectators on Copp's were still gazing intently on the scene, when a voice was raised among them, shouting—

" Hurrah ! let the rake-hellies go up to Breed's ; the people will teach 'em the law !"

" Throw the rebel scoundrel from the hill ! Blow him from the muzzle of a gun !" cried twenty soldiers in a breath.

" Hold !" exclaimed Lionel—" 'tis a simpleton, an idiot, a fool !"

But the angry and savage murmurs as quickly subsided, and were lost in other feelings, as the bright red lines of the royal troops were seen issuing from the smoke, waving and recoiling before the still vivid fire of their enemies.

" Ha !" said Burgoyne—" 'tis some feint to draw the rebels from their hold !"

" 'Tis a palpable and disgraceful retreat !" muttered the stern warrior nigh him, whose truer eye detected at a glance the discomfiture of the assailants.—" 'Tis another bare retreat before the rebels!"

"Hurrah!" shouted the reckless changeling again; "there come the reg'lars out of the orchard too!—see the grannies skulking behind the kilns! Let them go on to Breed's; the people will teach 'em the law!"

No cry of vengeance preceded the act this time, but fifty of the soldiery rushed, as by a common impulse, on their prey. Lionel had not time to utter a word of remonstrance, before Job appeared in the air, borne on the uplifted arms of a dozen men, and at the next instant he was seen rolling down the steep declivity, with a velocity that carried him to the water's edge. Springing to his feet, the undaunted changeling once more waved his hat in triumph, and shouted forth again his offensive challenge. Then turning, he launched his canoe from its hiding place among the adjacent lumber, amid a shower of stones, and glided across the strait; his little bark escaping unnoticed in the crowd of boats that were rowing in all directions. But his progress was watched by the uneasy eye of Lionel, who saw him land and disappear, with hasty steps, in the silent streets of the town.

While this trifling by-play was enacting, the great drama of the day was not at a stand. The smoky veil, which clung around the brow of the eminence, was lifted by the air, and sailed heavily away to the south-west, leaving the scene of the bloody struggle again open to the view. Lionel witnessed the grave and meaning glances which the two lieutenants of the king exchanged as they simultaneously turned their glasses from the fatal spot, and, taking the one proffered by Burgoyne, he read their explanation in the numbers of the dead that lay profusely scattered in front of the redoubt. At this instant, an officer from the field held an earnest communication with the two leaders; when, having delivered his orders, he hastened back to his boat, like one who felt himself employed in matters of life and death.

"It shall be done, sir," repeated Clinton, as the other departed, his own honest brow sternly knit under high martial excitement.—" The artillery have their orders, and the work will be accomplished without delay."

25

" This, Major Lincoln !" cried his more sophisticated
companion, " this is one of the trying duties of the soldier !
To fight, to bleed, or even to die, for his prince, is his happy privilege ; but it is sometimes his unfortunate lot to become the instrument of vengeance."

Lionel waited but a moment for an explanation—the
flaming balls were soon seen taking their wide circuit in
the air, and carrying their desolation among the close and
inflammable roofs of the opposite town. In a very few
minutes, a dense, black smoke arose from the deserted
buildings, and forked flames played actively along the heated shingles, as though rioting in their unmolested possession of the place. He regarded the gathering destruction
in painful silence ; and, on bending his looks towards his
companions, he fancied, notwithstanding the language of
the other, that he read the deepest regret in the averted
eye of him, who had so unhesitatingly uttered the fatal
mandate to destroy.

In scenes like these we are attempting to describe, hours
appear to be minutes, and time flies as imperceptibly as life
slides from beneath the feet of age. The disordered ranks of
the British had been arrested at the base of the hill, and were
again forming under the eyes of their leaders, with admirable discipline, and extraordinary care. Fresh battalions,
from Boston, marched with high military pride into the line,
and every thing betokened that a second assault was at
hand. When the moment of stupid amazement, which
succeeded the retreat of the royal troops, had passed, the
troops and batteries poured out their wrath with tenfold
fury on their enemies. Shot were incessantly glancing
up the gentle acclivity, madly ploughing across its grassy
surface, while black and threatening shells appeared to
hover above the work, like the monsters of the air, about
to stoop upon their prey.

Still all lay quiet and immoveable within the low mounds
of earth, as if none there had a stake in the issue of the
bloody day. For a few moments only, the tall figure of
an aged man was seen slowly moving along the summit of
the ramparts calmly regarding the dispositions of the English general in the more distant part of his line, and, after
exchanging a few words with a gentleman, who joined

him in his dangerous lookout, they disappeared together behind the grassy banks.   Lionel soon detected the name of Prescott of Pepperel, passing through the crowd in low murmurs, and his glass did not deceive him when he thought, in the smaller of the two, he had himself descried the graceful person of the unknown leader of the " caucus."

All eyes were now watching the advance of the battalions, which once more drew nigh the point of contest.   The heads of the columns were already in view of their enemies, when a man was seen swiftly ascending the hill from the burning town : he paused amid the peril, on the natural glacis, and swung his hat triumphantly, and Lionel even fancied he heard the exulting cry, as he recognised the ungainly form of the simpleton, before it plunged into the work.

The right of the British once more disappeared in the orchard, and the columns in front of the redoubt again opened with all the imposing exactness of their high discipline.   Their arms were already glittering in a line with the green faces of the mound, and Lionel heard the experienced warrior at his side murmuring to himself—

" Let him hold his fire, and he will go in at the point of the bayonet !"

But the trial was too great for even the practised courage of the royal troops.   Volley succeeded volley, and in a few moments they had again curtained their ranks behind the misty screen produced by their own fire.   Then came the terrible flash from the redoubt, and the eddying volumes from the adverse hosts rolled into one cloud, enveloping the combatants in its folds, as if to conceal their bloody work from the spectators.   Twenty times, in the short space of as many minutes, Major Lincoln fancied he heard the incessant roll of the American musketry die away before the heavy and regular volleys of the troops; and then he thought the sounds of the latter grew more faint, and were given at longer intervals.

The result, however, was soon known.   The heavy bank of smoke, which now even clung along the ground, was broken in fifty places ; and the disordered masses of the British were seen driven before their deliberate foes in wild confusion.   The flashing swords of the officers in vain attempted to arrest the torrent, nor did the flight cease, with many of the regiments, until they had even reached their boats. At this moment a hum was heard in Boston, like the sudden rush of wind, and men gazed in each other's faces with undisguised amazement. Here and there a low sound of exultation escaped some unguarded lip, and many an eye gleamed with a triumph that could no longer be suppressed. Until this moment the feelings of Lionel had vacillated between the pride of country and his military spirit; but, losing all other feelings in the latter sensation, he now looked fiercely about him, as if he would seek the man who dare exult in the repulse of his comrades. The poetic chieftain was still at his side, biting his nether lip in vexation; but his more tried companion had suddenly disappeared. Another quick glance fell upon his missing form in the act of entering a boat at the foot of the hill. Quicker than thought, Lionel was on the shore, crying, as he flew to the water's edge—

"Hold! for God's sake, hold! remember the 47th is in the field, and that I am its major!"

"Receive him," said Clinton, with that grim satisfaction, with which men acknowledge a valued friend in moments of great trial; "and then row for your lives, or, what is of more value, for the honour of the British name."

The brain of Lionel whirled as the boat shot along its watery bed, but, before it had gained the middle of the stream, he had time to consider the whole of the appalling scene. The fire had spread from house to house, and the whole village of Charlestown, with its four hundred buildings, was just bursting into flames. The air seemed filled with whistling balls, as they hurtled above his head, and the black sides of the vessels of war were vomiting their sheets of flame with unwearied industry. Amid this tumult, the English general and his companions sprung to land. The former rushed into the disordered ranks, and by his presence and voice recalled the men of one regiment to their duty. But long and loud appeals to their spirit and their ancient fame were necessary to restore a moiety of their former confidence to men, who had been thus rudely repulsed, and who now looked along their thinned and exhausted ranks, missing, in many instances, more than half the well-known

countenances of their fellows.   In the midst of the faltering
troops stood their stern and unbending chief; but of all
those gay and gallant youths, who followed in his train as
he had departea from Province-House that morning, not
one remained, but in his blood.   He alone seemed undisturbed in that disordered crowd ; and his mandates went
forth as usual, calm and determined.   At length the panic,
in some degree, subsided, and order was once more restored,
as the high-spirited and mortified gentlemen of the detachment regained their lost authority.

The leaders consulted together, apart, and the dispositions were immediately renewed for the assault. Military
show was no longer affected, but the soldiers laid down all
the useless implements of their trade, and many even cast
aside their outer garments, under the warmth of a broiling
sun, added to the heat of the conflagration, which began to
diffuse itself along the extremity of the peninsula.   Fresh
companies were placed in the columns, and most of the
troops were withdrawn from the meadows, leaving merely
a few skirmishers to amuse the Americans who lay behind
the fence.   When each disposition was completed, the final
signal was given to advance.

Lionel had taken post in his regiment, but, marching on
the skirt of the column, he commanded a view of most of
the scene of battle.   In his front moved a battalion, reduced to a handful of men in the previous assaults.   Behind
these came a party of the marine guards, from the shipping,
led by their own veteran major ; and next followed the dejected Nesbitt and his corps, amongst whom Lionel looked
in vain for the features of the good-natured Polwarth.
Similar columns marched on their right and left, encircling
three sides of the redoubt by their battalions.

A few minutes brought him in full view of that humble
and unfinished mound of earth, for the possession of which
so much blood had that day been spilt in vain.   It lay, as
before, still as if none breathed within its bosom, though
a terrific row of dark tubes were arrayed along its top,
following the movements of the approaching columns, as
the eyes of the imaginary charmers of our own wilderness
are said to watch their victims   As the uproar of the artillery again grew fainter, the crash of falling streets, and
25 *

the appalling sounds of the conflagration, on their left, be
came more audible. Immense volumes of black smoke issued from the smouldering ruins, and, bellying outward,
fold beyond fold, it overhung the work in a hideous cloud,
casting its gloomy shadow across the place of blood.

A strong column was now seen ascending, as if from out
the burning town, and the advance of the whole became quick
and spirited. A low call ran through the platoons, to note
the naked weapons of their adversaries, and it was followed by the cry of " To the bayonet! to the bayonet!"

" Hurrah! for the Royal Irish!" shouted M'Fuse, at the
head of the dark column from the conflagration.

" Hurrah!" echoed a well-known voice from the silent
mound; " let them come on to Breed's; the people will
teach 'em the law!"

Men think at such moments with the rapidity of lightning, and Lionel had even fancied his comrades in possession of the work, when the terrible stream of fire flashed
in the faces of the men in front.

" Push on with the ——th," cried the veteran major
of marines—" push on, or the 18th will get the honour of
the day!"

" We cannot," murmured the soldiers of the ——th;
" their fire is too heavy!"

" Then break, and let the marines pass through you!"

The feeble battalion melted away, and the warriors of
the deep, trained to conflicts of hand to hand, sprang forward, with a loud shout, in their places. The Americans,
exhausted of their ammunition, now sunk sullenly back, a
few hurling stones at their foes, in desperate indignation.
The cannon of the British had been brought to enfilade
their short breast-work, which was no longer tenable; and,
as the columns approached closer to the low rampart, it became a mutual protection to the adverse parties.

" Hurrah! for the Royal Irish!" again shouted M'Fuse,
rushing up the trifling ascent, which was but of little more
than his own height.

" Hurrah!" repeated Pitcairn, waving his sword on
another angle of the work—" the day's our own!"

One more sheet of flame issued out of the bosom of the
work, and all those brave men, who had emulated the ex-

amples of their officers, were swept away, as though a whirlwind had passed along. The grenadier gave his war cry once more, before he pitched headlong among his enemies; while Pitcairn fell back into the arms of his own child. The cry of "Forward, 47th," rung through their ranks, and in their turn this veteran battalion gallantly mou ted the ramparts. In the shallow ditch Lionel passed the expiring marine, and caught the dying and despairing look from his eyes, and in another instant he found himself in the presence of his foes. As company followed company into the defenceless redoubt, the Americans sul lenly retired by its rear, keeping the bayonets of the soldiers at bay with clubbed muskets and sinewy arms. When the whole issued upon the open ground, the husbandmen received a close and fatal fire from the battalions, which were now gathering around them on three sides. A scene of wild and savage confusion then succeeded to the order of the fight, and many fatal blows were given and taken, the mêlée rendering the use of fire-arms nearly impossible for several minutes.

Lionel continued in advance, pressing on the footsteps of the retiring foe, stepping over many a lifeless body in his difficult progress. Notwithstanding the hurry, and vast disorder of the fray, his eye fell on the form of the graceful stranger, stretched lifeless on the parched grass, which had greedily drank his blood. Amid the ferocious cries, and fiercer passions of the moment, the young man paused, and glanced his eyes around him, with an expression that said, he thought the work of death should cease. At this instant the trappings of his attire caught the glaring eye-balls of a dying yeoman, who exerted his wasting strength to sacrifice one more worthy victim to the manes of his countrymen. The whole of the tumultuous scene vanished from the senses of Lionel at the flash of the musket of this man, and he sunk beneath the feet of the combatants, insensible of further triumph, and of every danger.

The fall of a single officer, in such a contest, was a circumstance not to be regarded; and regiments passed over him, without a single man stooping to inquire into his fate. When the Americans had disengaged themselves from the troops, they descended into the little hollow between the two hills, swiftly, and like a disordered crowd, bearing off most of their wounded, and leaving but few prisoners in the hands of their foes. The formation of the ground favoured their retreat, as hundreds of bullets whistled harmlessly above their heads; and, by the time they gained the acclivity of Bunker, distance was added to their security. Finding the field lost, the men at the fence broke away in a body from their position, and abandoned the meadows; the whole moving in confused masses behind the crest of the adjacent height. The shouting soldiery followed in their footsteps, pouring in fruitless and distant volleys; but, on the summit of Bunker, their tired platoons were halted, and they beheld the throng move fearlessly through the tremendous fire that enfiladed the low pass, as little injured as though most of them bore charmed lives.

The day was now drawing to a close. With the disappearance of their enemies, the ships and batteries ceased their cannonade; and, presently, not a musket was heard in that place, where so fierce a contest had so long raged. The troops commenced fortifying the outward eminence, on which they rested, in order o maintain their barren conquest; and nothing further mained for the achievement of the royal lieutenants,   it to go and mourn over their victory.

———

Autumn and Spring.—PAULDING.

THE Summer passed away, and Autumn began to hang out his many-coloured flag upon the trees, that, smitten by the nightly frosts, every morning exhibited less of the green, and more of the gaudy hues, that mark the waning year in our western climate. The farmers of Elsingburgh were out in their fields, bright and early, gathering in the fruits of their spring and summer's labours, or busily employed in making their cider; while the urchins passed their holydays in gathering nuts to crack by the winter's fire. The little quails began to whistle their autumnal notes: the grasshopper, having had his season of idle sport and chirping jollity, began now to pay the penalty of his thoughtless improvidence, and might be seen sunning himself at mid-day, in melancholy silence, as if anticipating the period when his short and merry race would be run. Flocks of robins were passing to the south, to seek a more genial air; the sober cattle began to assume their rough, wintry coat, and to put on that desperate appearance of ennui, with which all nature salutes the approach of winter. The little blue-bird alone, the last to leave us, and the first to return in the spring, sometimes poured out his pensive note, as if bidding farewell to the nest where it had reared its young.

* * * * * * * * * * * * * *

Now the laughing, jolly Spring began sometimes to show her buxom face in the bright morning ; but ever and anon, meeting the angry frown of Winter, loath to resign his rough sway over the wide realm of nature, she would retire again into her southern bower. Yet, though her visits were but short, her very look seemed to exercise a magic influence. The buds began slowly to expand their close winter folds ; the dark and melancholy woods to assume an almost imperceptible purple tint ; and here and there a little chirping blue-bird hopped about the orchards of Elsingburgh. Strips of fresh green appeared along the brooks, now released from their icy fetters ; and nests of little variegated flowers, nameless, yet richly deserving a name, sprung up in the sheltered recesses of the leafless woods. By and by, the shad, the harbinger at once of spring and plenty, came up the river before the mild southern breeze ; the ruddy blossoms of the peach tree exhibited their gorgeous pageantry ; the little lambs appeared frisking and gamboling about the sedate mother ; young, innocent calves began their first bleatings ; the cackling hen announced her daily feat in the barn-yard with clamorous astonishment ; every day added to the appearance of that active vegetable and animal life, which nature presents in the progress of the genial spring ; and, finally, the flowers, the zephyrs, and the warblers, and the maiden's rosy cheeks, announced to the eye, the ear, the senses, the fancy. and the heart, the return and the stay of the vernal year.

The Storm-Ship.—IRVING.

IN the golden age of the province of the New Nether
lands, when it was under the sway of Wouter Van Twiller
otherwise called the Doubter, the people of the Manhat‑
toes were alarmed, one sultry afternoon, just about the time
of the summer solstice, by a tremendous storm of thunder
and lightning.   The rain descended in such torrents as ab‑
solutely to spatter up and smoke along the ground. It seem‑
ed as if the thunder rattled and rolled over the very roofs
of the houses; the lightning was seen to play about the
church of St. Nicholas, and to strive three times, in vain,
to strike its weathercock.   Garret Van Horne's new chim‑
ney was split almost from top to bottom; and Doffue Mil‑
deberger was struck speechless from his bald-faced mare,
just as he was riding into town.   In a word, it was one of
those unparalleled storms, that only happen once within
the memory of that venerable personage known in all towns
by the appellation of " the oldest inhabitant."

Great was the terror of the good old women of the Man‑
hattoes.   They gathered their children together, and took
refuge in the cellars; after having hung a shoe on the iron
point of every bed-post, lest it should attract the lightning.
At length the storm abated; the thunder sunk into a growl,
and the setting sun, breaking from under the fringed bor‑
ders of the clouds, made the broad bosom of the bay to gleam
like a sea of molten gold.

The word was given from the fort that a ship was stand‑
ing up the bay.   It passed from mouth to mouth, and street
to street, and soon put the little capital in a bustle.   The
arrival of a ship, in those early times of the settlement,
was an event of vast importance to the inhabitants.   It
brought them news from the old world, from the land of
their birth, from which 'hey were so completely severed:
to the yearly ship, too, they looked for their supply of lux‑
uries, of finery, of comforts, and almost of necessaries.
The good vrouw could not have her new cap nor new
gown until the arrival of the ship; the artist waited for it
for his tools, the burgomaster for his pipe and his supply
of Hollands, the schoolboy for his top and marbles, and the

ordly landholder for the bricks with which he was to build
his new mansion. Thus every one, rich and poor, great
and small, looked out for the arrival of the ship. It was
the great yearly event of the town of New Amsterdam ;
and, from one end of the year to the other, the ship—the
ship—the ship—was the continual topic of conversation.

The news from the fort, therefore, brought all the populace down to the battery, to behold the wished-for sight.
It was not exactly the time when she had been expected
to arrive, and the circumstance was a matter of some speculation. Many were the groups collected about the battery. Here and there might be seen a burgomaster, of
slow and pompous gravity, giving his opinion with great
confidence to a crowd of old women and idle boys. At
another place was a knot of old, weather-beaten fellows,
who had been seamen or fishermen in their times, and were
great authorities on such occasions ; these gave different
opinions, and caused great disputes among their several
adherents : but the man most looked up to, and followed
and watched by the crowd, was Hans Van Pelt, an old
Dutch sea captain retired from service, the nautical oracle
of the place. He reconnoitred the ship through an ancient
telescope, covered with tarry canvass, hummed a Dutch
tune to himself, and said nothing. A hum, however, from
Hans Van Pelt, had always more weight with the public,
than a speech from another man.

In the mean time the ship became more distinct to the
naked eye : she was a stout, round, Dutch built vessel,
with high bow and poop, and bearing Dutch colours. The
evening sun gilded her bellying canvass, as she came riding
over the long waving billows. The sentinel, who had given
notice of her approach, declared, that he first got sight of
her when she was in the centre of the bay ; and that she
broke suddenly on his sight, just as if she had come out
of the bosom of the black thunder-cloud. The bystanders
looked at Hans Van Pelt, to see what he would say to this
report : Hans Van Pelt screwed his mouth closer together,
and said nothing ; upon which some shook their heads, and
others shrugged their shoulders.

The ship was now repeatedly hailed, but made no reply,
and, passing by the fort, stood on up the Hudson. A gun

was brought to bear on her, and, with some difficulty, loaded and fired by Hans Van Pelt, the garrison not being expert in artillery. The shot seemed absolutely to pass through the ship, and to skip along the water on the other side ; but no notice was taken of it ! What was strange, she had all her sails set, and sailed right against wind and tide, which were both down the river. Upon this Hans Van Pelt, who was likewise harbour-master, ordered his boat, and set off to board her ; but, after rowing two or three hours, he returned without success. Sometimes he would get within one or two hundred yards of her, and then, in a twinkling, she would be half a mile off. Some said it was because his oars-men, who were rather pursy and short-winded, stopped every now and then to take breath, and spit on their hands ; but this, it is probable, was a mere scandal. He got near enough, however, to see the crew ; who were all dressed in the Dutch style, the officers in doublets and high hats and feathers : not a word was spoken by any one on board ; they stood as motionless as so many statues, and the ship seemed as if left to her own government. Thus she kept on, away up the river, lessening and lessening in the evening sunshine, until she faded from sight, like a little white cloud melting away in the summer sky.

The appearance of this ship threw the governor into one of the deepest doubts that ever beset him in the whole course of his administration. Fears were entertained for the security of the infant settlements on the river, lest this might be an enemy's ship in disguise, sent to take possession. The governor called together his council repeatedly, to assist him with their conjectures. He sat in his chair of state, built of timber from the sacred forest of the Hague, and smoking his long jasmin pipe, and listened to all that his counsellors had to say on a subject about which they knew nothing ; but, in spite of all the conjecturing of the sagest and oldest heads, the governor still continued to doubt.

Messengers were despatched to different places on the river ; but they returned without any tidings—the ship had made no port. Day after day, and week after week, elapsed, but she never returned down the Hudson. As, however-

the council seemed solicitous for intelligence, they had it
in abundance. The captains of the sloops seldom arrived
without bringing some report of having seen the strange
ship at different parts of the river; sometimes near the
Palisadoes, sometimes off Croton Point, and sometimes in
the Highlands; but she never was reported as having been
seen above the Highlands. The crews of the sloops, it is
true, generally differed among themselves in their accounts
of these apparitions; but that may have arisen from the
uncertain situations in which they saw her. Sometimes
it was by the flashes of the thunder-storm lighting up a
pitchy night, and giving glimpses of her careering across
Tappaan Zee, or the wide waste of Haverstraw Bay. At
one moment she would appear close upon them, as if likely to run them down, and would throw them into great
bustle and alarm; but the next flash would show her far
off, always sailing against the wind. Sometimes, in quiet
moonlight nights, she would be seen under some high bluff
of the Highlands, all in deep shadow, excepting her top-
sails glittering in the moonbeams; by the time, however,
that the voyagers would reach the place, there would be
no ship to be seen; and, when they had passed on for some
distance, and looked back, behold! there she was again,
with her top-sails in the moonshine! Her appearance was
always just after, or just before, or just in the midst of unruly weather; and she was known by all the skippers
and voyagers of the Hudson by the name of " the storm-
ship."   •

These reports perplexed the governor and his council
more than ever; and it would be endless to repeat the conjectures and opinions that were uttered on the subject.
Some quoted cases in point, of ships seen off the coast of
New England, navigated by witches and goblins. Old
Hans Van Pelt, who had been more than once to the Dutch
colony at the Cape of Good Hope, insisted that this must
be the flying Dutchman, which had so long haunted Table
Bay; but, being unable to make port, had now sought another harbour Others suggested, that, if it really was a supernatural apparition, as there was every natural reason to believe, it might be Hendrick Hudson, and his crew of the
Halfmoon; who, it was well known, had once run aground

26

in the upper part of the river, in seeking a north-west passage to China. This opinion had very little weight with the governor, but it passed current out of doors; for, indeed it had already been reported, that Hendrick Hudson and his crew haunted the Kaatskill Mountain; and it appeared very reasonable to suppose, that his ship might infest the river where the enterprise was baffled, or that it might bear the shadowy crew to their periodical revels in the mountain.

Other events occurred to occupy the thoughts and doubts f the sage Wouter and his council, and the storm-ship ceased to be a subject of deliberation at the board. It continued, however, to be a matter of popular belief and marvellous anecdote through the whole time of the Dutch government, and particularly just before the capture of New Amsterdam, and the subjugation of the province by the English squadron. About that time the storm-ship was repeatedly seen in the Tappaan Zee, and about Weehawk, and even down as far as Hoboken; and her appearance was supposed to be ominous of the approaching squall in public affairs, and the downfall of Dutch domination.

Since that time we have no authentic accounts of her, though it is said she still haunts the Highlands, and cruises about Point-no-point. People, who live along the river, insist that they sometimes see her in summer moonlight; and that, in a deep, still midnight, they have heard the chant of her crew, as if heaving the lead; but sights and sounds are so deceptive along the mountainous shores, and about the wide bays and long reaches of this great river, that I confess I have very strong doubts upon the subject.

It is certain, nevertheless, that strange things have been seen in these Highlands in storms, which are considered as connected with the old story of the ship. The captains of the river craft talk of a little bulbous-bottomed Dutch goblin, in trunk hose and sugar-loafed hat, with a speaking trumpet in his hand, which they say keeps about the Dunderberg.* They declare that they have heard him, in stormy weather, in the midst of the turmoil, giving orders in low Dutch for the piping up of a fresh gust of wind, or

---

* That is, the " Thunder Mountain," so called from its echoes

the rattling off of another thunder-clap; that sometimes he
has been seen surrounded by a crew of little imps in broad
breeches and short doublets; tumbling head over heels in
the rack and mist, and playing a thousand gambols in the
air; or buzzing like a swarm of flies about Antony's
Nose; and that, at such times, the hurry-scurry of the storm
was always greatest. One time a sloop, in passing by the
Dunderberg, was overtaken by a thunder-gust, that came
scouring round the mountain, and seemed to burst just
over the vessel. Though tight and well ballasted, yet she
laboured dreadfully, until the water came over the gun-
wale. All the crew were amazed, when it was discovered
that there was a little white sugar-loaf hat on the mast-
head, which was known at once to be the hat of the Heer
of the Dunderberg. Nobody, however, dared to climb to
the mast-head, and get rid of this terrible hat. The sloop
continued labouring and rocking, as if she would have rolled her mast overboard. She seemed in continual danger,
either of upsetting or of running on shore. In this way
she drove quite through the Highlands, until she had passed Pollopol's Island, where, it is said, the jurisdiction of
the Dunderberg potentate ceases. No sooner had she passed this bourn, than the little hat, all at once, spun up into
the air like a top; whirled up all the clouds into a vortex,
and hurried them back to the summit of the Dunderberg;
while the sloop righted herself, and sailed on as quietly as
if in a mill-pond. Nothing saved her from utter wreck
but the fortunate circumstance of having a horse-shoe nail-
ed against the mast,—a wise precaution against evil spirits,
which has since been adopted by all the Dutch captains
that navigate this haunted river.

There is another story told of this foul-weather urchin,
by Skipper Daniel Ouslesticker, of Fish Hill, who was never known to tell a lie. He declared, that, in a severe
squall, he saw him seated astride of his bowsprit, riding the
sloop ashore, full butt against Antony's Nose, and that he
was exorcised by Dominie Van Gieson, of Esopus, who
happened to be on board, and who sung the hymn of St.
Nicholas; whereupon the goblin threw himself up in the
air like a ball, and went off in a whirlwind, carrying away
with him the night-cap of the Dominie's wife; which was

discovered the next Sunday morning hanging on the weather-cock of Esopus' church steeple, at least forty miles off! After several events of this kind had taken place, the regular skippers of the river, for a long time, did not venture to pass the Dunderberg, without lowering their peaks, out of homage to the Heer of the mountain; and it was observed that all such as paid this tribute of respect were suffered to pass unmolested.*

Anecdote of James Otis.—J. Adams.

Otis belonged to a club who met on evenings; of which club William Molineux† was a member. Molyneux had a petition before the legislature, which did not succeed to his wishes, and he became for several evenings sour, and wearied the company with his complaints of services, losses, sacrifices, &c., and said—"That a man who has behaved as I have should be treated as I am is

---

* Among the superstitions which prevailed in the colonies, during the early times of the settlements, there seems to have been a singular one about phantom ships. The superstitious fancies of men are always apt to turn upon those objects which concern their daily occupations. The solitary ship, which, from year to year, came like a raven in the wilderness, bringing to the inhabitants of a settlement the comforts of life from the world from which they were cut off, was apt to be present to their dreams, whether sleeping or waking. The accidental sight from shore of a sail gliding along the horizon in those, as yet, lonely seas, was apt to be a matter of much talk and speculation. There is mention made in one of the early New England writers, of a ship navigated by witches, with a great horse that stood by the mainmast. I have met with another story, somewhere, of a ship that drove on shore, in fair, sunny, tranquil weather, with sails all set, and a table spread in the cabin, as if to regale a number of guests, yet not a living being on board. These phantom ships always sailed in the eye of the wind, or ploughed their way with great velocity, making the smooth sea foam before their bows, when not a breath of air was stirring.

Moore has finely wrought up one of these legends of the sea into a little tale, which, within a small compass, contains the very essence of this species of supernatural fiction. I allude to his Spectre-Ship bound to Deadman's Isle.

† Mr Molineux was a merchant, but much more of a sportsman and a *bon vivant*, than a man of business. His sentiments were warmly in favour of his country; and, though often a companion of the English officers, he was yet an intimate acquaintance of the leading patriots of the day.—Tudor.

intolerable !" Otis had said nothing; but the company were disgusted and out of patience, when Otis rose from his seat, and said—" Come, come, Will, quit this subject, and let us enjoy ourselves. I also have a list of grievances ; will you hear it ?" The club expected some fun, and all cried out, " Ay ! ay ! let us hear your list."

" Well, then, Will : in the first place, I resigned the office of advocate-general, which I held from the crown, that produced me—how much do you think ?" " A great deal, no doubt," said Molineux. " Shall we say two hundred sterling a year ?" " Ay, more, I believe," said Molineux. " Well, let it be two hundred ; that, for ten years, is two thousand.

" In the next place, I have been obliged to relinquish the greatest part of my business at the bar. Will you set that at two hundred more ?" " Oh ! I believe it much more than that." " Well, let it be two hundred ; this, for ten years, is two thousand more. You allow, then, I have lost four thousand pounds sterling.". " Ay, and much more too," said Molineux.

" In the next place, I have lost an hundred friends ; among whom were the men of the first rank, fortune and power in the province. At what price will you estimate them ?" " At nothing," said Molineux ; " you are better without them, than with them." A loud laugh. " Be it so," said Otis.

" In the next place, I have made a thousand enemies, among whom are the government of the province and the nation. What do you think of this item ?" " That is as it may happen," said Molineux.

" In the next place, you know, I love pleasure ; but I have renounced all amusement for ten years. What is that worth to a man of pleasure ?" " No great matter," said Molineux ; " you have made politics your amusement." A hearty laugh.

" In the next place, I have ruined as fine health, and as good a constitution of body, as nature ever gave to man." " This is melancholy indeed," said Molineux ; " there is nothing to be said on that point."

" Once more," said Otis, holding his head down before Molineux ; " look upon this head !" (where was a scar, in

26 *

which a man might bury his finger ;*) " what do you
think of this? and, what is worse, my friends think I
have a monstrous crack in my skull."

This made all the company very grave, and look very
solemn. But Otis, setting up a laugh, and with a gay
countenance, said to Molineux—" Now, Willy, my advice to you is, to say no more about your grievances ; for
you and I had better put up our accounts of profit and loss
in our pockets, and say no more about them, lest the world
should laugh at us."

This whimsical dialogue put all the company, and Molineux himself, into good humour, and they passed the rest
of the evening in joyous conviviality.

Interesting Passage in the Life of James Otis.— Tudor.

Otis had long been so conspicuous as a leader of the
patriotic party, his power of exciting public feeling was so
irresistible, his opposition to the administration was so bold
and vehement, his detestation against those who were
bringing ruin on the country was so open and mortifying,
that secret representations had long been making to render
him particularly obnoxious to the ministry, and to stimulate
them to arrest and try him for treason. At length, in the
course of this summer, copies of several of the letters of
Governor Bernard, and of the commissioners, filled with
insinuations, and even charges of a treasonable nature,
were procured at the public offices in England, and transmitted to him ; leaving no doubt, that, if these persons had
ventured on such a crimination in official letters, they had
gone much further in their private correspondence.

He was stung to madness by the discovery and proofs
of these malignant calumnies, and this secret treachery.
Agitated as he was by the actual and impending evils, that
threatened the whole country, and that were more espe-

---

* The manner in which he received this wound is related in the fol
lowing extract.—Ed.

cially directed, at this period, against his own province, and his own town ; penetrated with anxious responsibility for the expediency of those measures of opposition, of which he was one of the chief advisers, and had long been the ostensible leader ; these attempts to destroy his character, if not his life, excited the deepest indignation. In defending the cause of the colonies, he had looked forward to the time when justice would be done them, and when he should derive advantage and honour for all his exertions and sacrifices. He was not acting as a demagogue, nor as a revolutionist. He was proud of his rank in society ; and in opposing the ministerial schemes he still felt loyalty towards the sovereign, and affection for England ; and longed for the period, when he might give proofs of both, not in opposing, but in supporting the views of government; while, at this very time, he found that the crown officers had been assiduously labouring to blast his reputation, and endeavouring to have him torn from his home, to undergo imprisonment and persecution in the mother country. With the proofs of their conduct in his possession, he could no longer restrain himself, but hurled his defiance and contempt in the following notice.*

" Advertisement. Whereas I have full evidence, that *Henry Hutton, Charles Paxton, William Burch,* and *John Robinson,*† Esquires, have frequently and lately treated the characters of all true North Americans in a manner that is not to be endured, by *privately* and publicly representing them as *traitors* and *rebels,* and in a general combination to revolt from Great Britain ; and whereas the said *Henry, Charles, William* and *John,* without the least provocation or colour, have represented me by name, as inimical to the rights of the crown, and disaffected to his majesty, to whom I annually swear, and am determined at all events to bear true and faithful allegiance ; for all which general as well as personal abuse and insult, satisfaction has been personally demanded, due warning given, but no sufficient answer obtained ; these are humbly to

---

* Boston Gazette, September 4th, 1769.

† These were the commissioners of the customs.

desire the lords commissioners of his majesty's treasury, his principal secretaries of state, particularly my lord Hillsborough, the board of trade, and all others whom it may concern, or who may condescend to read this, to pay no kind of regard to any of the abusive representations of me or my country, that may be transmitted by the said *Henry*, *Charles*, *William* and *John*, or their confederates; for they are no more worthy of credit, than those of Sir Francis Bernard, of Nettleham, Bart., or any of his cabal; which cabal may be well known, from the papers in the house of commons, and at every great office in England."

JAMES OTIS.

There were some further documents inserted in the same Gazette, such as a correspondence with the collector, and some extracts from the letters of these officers to the treas ury and board of trade in England.

The next evening, about seven o'clock, Mr. Otis went to the British coffee-house, where Mr. Robinson, one of the commissioners, was sitting, as also a number of army, navy, and revenue officers. As soon as he came in, an altercation took place, which soon terminated in Robinson's striking him with a cane, which was returned with a weapon of the same kind. Great confusion then ensued. The lights were extinguished, and Otis, without a friend, was surrounded by the adherents of Robinson. A young man, by the name of Gridley, passing by, very boldly entered the coffee-house to take the part of Otis against so many foes; but he was also assaulted, beaten, and turned out of the house. After some time the combatants were separated, Robinson retreated by a back passage, and Otis was led home wounded and bleeding.

This affair naturally excited much attention. Various and contradictory statements were given in the newspapers respecting it. It was said, that this intentional assault was the result of a meditated plan of assassination. Five or six bludgeons and one scabbard were found on the floor after the struggle. Otis received a deep wound on the head, which the surgeons, Doctors Perkins and Lloyd, testified must have been given by a sharp instrument. The accusation of a preconcerted intention to murder, is doubtless unfounded; but, from all the evidence in the case, it is plain, that it was a brutal and cowardly assault, in which several persons took part, with a disposition, that, in the fury of the moment, sought to disable this great patriot, whom they so rancorously hated. If such was their purpose, it to a considerable degree succeeded.

The natural indignation that was roused against the authors of this ruffian-like attack, the animosity that existed towards the revenue officers, for their insolent and oppressive conduct; the keen feelings natural to a state of violent political excitement; the sympathy and admiration that were cherished for the liberal character, powerful talents and efficient services of the leading patriot of his day,—all conspired to make the public give this transaction the odium of a scheme of assassination. Pity for the sufferer made them also impute the impairment of his reason to this event exclusively. It is not, however, necessary to believe, that an assassination had been planned, in order to cover the perpetrators of this barbarous assault with ignominy. Nor can the mental alienation, which afterwards afflicted him, and deprived the world of his great talents, in the vigour of manhood,—for he was at this time only in his forty-sixth year,—be wholly attributed to the wound he received. His disposition was so ardent, and his mind so excitable, that its natural tendency, under aggravating circumstances, was to insanity. Had he lived in ordinary times, in the usual exercise of professional or political duties, undisturbed by adverse events, he might have escaped the misfortune that befell him. His generous and social humour, his wit and ready talent, would have rendered his career easy and tranquil. But he was called upon to act in public affairs at a most arduous epoch: he had to maintain a continual struggle against insidious placemen and insolent oppressors: he himself was denounced, proscribed, and frequently insulted. The feelings of his own injuries, joined to those for his country, kept his mind in constant action, anxiety and irritation. Having espoused the cause of his fellow-citizens, with all his strength and all his mind, at a time when new wrongs and new difficulties were incessantly recurring, he knew no repose. His faculties were perpetually agitated, and he did not sufficiently master and subdue his indignation against subaltern agents, though prime movers in this ni3 chief, yet who were in reality deserving only of his con tempt. It was an unfortunate yielding to his anger, th● placing himself, as he did in some degree, on a level with the commissioners of the customs, whom he ought merely to have unmasked and left to public scorn, without degrading himself to a personal rencounter. The injuries he sustained in it impaired his power of self-control, and con tributed essentially to his subsequent derangement.

Close of the Lives of Adams and Jefferson.—Webster.

In 1820 Mr. Adams acted as elector of president and vice-president, and in the same year we saw him, then at the age of eighty-five, a member of the convention of this commonwealth, called to revise the constitution. Forty years before, he had been one of those who formed that constitution; and he had now the pleasure of witnessing that there was little which the people desired to change. Possessing all his faculties to the end of his long life, with an unabated love of reading and contemplation, in the centre of interesting circles of friendship and affection, he was blessed in his retirement with whatever of repose and felicity the condition of man allows. He had, also, other enjoyments. He saw around him that prosperity and general happiness, which had been the object of his public cares and labours. No man ever beheld more clearly, and for a longer time, the great and beneficial effects of the services rendered by himself to his country. That liberty, which he so early defended, that independence, of which he was so able an advocate and supporter, he saw, we trust, firmly and securely established. The population of the country thickened around him faster, and extended wider, than his own sanguine predictions had anticipated, and the wealth, respectability and power of the nation sprang up to a magnitude, which it is quite impossible he could have expected to witness in his day. He lived, also, to behold those principles of civil freedom, which had been developed, established, and practically applied, in

America, attract attention, command respect, and awaken imitation, in other regions of the globe; and well might, and well did, he exclaim, " Where will the consequences of the American revolution end !"

If any thing yet remain to fill this cup of happiness, let it be added, that he lived to see a great and intelligent people bestow the highest honour in their gift, where he had bestowed his own kindest parental affections, and lodged his fondest hopes. Thus honoured in life, thus happy at death, he saw the Jubilee, and he died ; and with the last prayers which trembled on his lips, was the fervent supplication for his country, " Independence forever !"

From the time of his final retirement from public life, in 1807, Mr. Jefferson lived as became a wise man. Surrounded by affectionate friends, his ardour in the pursuit of knowledge undiminished, with uncommon health, and unbroken spirits, he was able to enjoy largely the rational pleasures of life, and to partake in that public prosperity, which he had so much contributed to produce. His kindness and hospitality, the charm of his conversation, the ease of his manners, the extent of his acquirements, and especially the full store of revolutionary incidents, which he possessed, and which he knew when and how to dispense, rendered his abode in a high degree attractive to his admiring countrymen, while his high public and scientific character drew towards him every intelligent and educated traveller from abroad. Both Mr. Adams and Mr. Jefferson had the pleasure of knowing, that the respect, which they so largely received, was not paid to their official stations. They were not men made great by office, but great men, on whom the country, for its own benefit, had conferred office. There was that in them, which office did not give, and which the relinquishment of office did not, and could not, take away. In their retirement, in the midst of their fellow-citizens, themselves private citizens, they enjoyed as high regard and esteem, as when filling the most important places of public trust.

There remained to Mr. Jefferson yet one other work of patriotism and beneficence,—the establishment of a university in his native state. To this object he devoted years

of incessant and anxious attention, and, by the enlightened
liberality of the legislature of Virginia, and the co-opera-
tion of other able and zealous friends, he lived to see it accomplished. May all success attend this infant seminary ;
and may those who enjoy its advantages, as often as their
eyes shall rest on the neighbouring height, recollect what
they owe to their disinterested and indefatigable benefactor ; and may letters honour him, who thus laboured in
the cause of letters.

Thus useful, and thus respected, passed the old age of
Thomas Jefferson. But time was on its ever-ceaseless
wing, and was now bringing the last hour of this illustrious man. He saw its approach with undisturbed serenity.
He counted the moments, as they passed, and beheld that
his last sands were falling. That day, too, was at hand,
which he had helped to make immortal. One wish, one
hope,—if it were not presumptuous,—beat in his fainting
breast. Could it be so—might it please God—he would
desire once more to see the sun,—once more to look abroad
on the scene around him,—on the great day of liberty.
Heaven, in its mercy, fulfilled that prayer. He saw that
sun—he enjoyed its sacred light—he thanked God for his
mercy, and bowed his aged head in the grave. " *Felix, non vitæ tantum claritate, sed etiam opportunitate
mortis.*"

Morals of Chess.—FRANKLIN.

PLAYING at chess is the most ancient and universal
game known among men ; for its original is beyond the
memory of history, and it has for numberless ages been
the amusement of all the civilized nations of Asia,—the
Persians, the Indians, and the Chinese. Europe has had
it above a thousand years ; the Spaniards have spread it
over their part of America, and it begins to make its appearance in these States. It is so interesting in itself as
not to need the view of gain to induce engaging in it ; and
thence it is never played for money. Those, therefore
who have leisure for such diversions cannot find one that

is more innocent; and the following piece, written with a
view to correct (among a few young friends) some little
improprieties in the practice of it, shows, at the same time,
that it may, in its effects on the mind, be not merely innocent, but advantageous, to the vanquished as well as the
victor.

The game of chess is not merely an idle amusement.
Several very valuable qualities of the mind, useful in the
course of human life, are to be acquired, or strengthened,
by it, so as to become habits, ready on all occasions. For
life is a kind of chess, in which we have points to gain,
and competitors or adversaries to contend with, and in which
there is a vast variety of good and ill events, that are, in
some degree, the effects of prudence or the want of it. By
playing at chess, then, we learn,

1. *Foresight*, which looks a little into futurity, considers
the consequences that may attend an action; for it is continually occurring to the player, "If I move this piece,
what will be the advantage of my new situation?   What
use can my adversary make of it to annoy me ? What other
moves can I make to support it, and to defend myself from
his attacks ?"

2. *Circumspection*, which surveys the whole chess-
board, or scene of action, the relations of the several pieces
and situations, the dangers they are respectively exposed
to, the several possibilities of their aiding each other, the
probabilities that the adversary may take this or that move,
and attack this or the other piece, and what different means
can be used to avoid his stroke, or turn its consequences
against him.

3. *Caution*, not to make our moves too hastily. This
habit is best acquired by observing strictly the laws of the
game; such as, "If you touch a piece, you must move it
somewhere ; if you set it down, you must let it stand :"
and it is therefore best that these rules should be observed;
as the game thereby becomes more the image of human
life, and particularly of war ; in which, if you have incau-
tiously put yourself into a bad and dangerous position, you
cannot obtain your enemy's leave to withdraw your troops,
and place them more securely, but you must abide all the
consequences of your rashness.

27

And, lastly, we learn by chess the habit of *not being discouraged by present bad appearances in the state of our affairs*, the habit of *hoping for a favourable change*, and that of *persevering in the search of resources*. The game is so full of events, there is such a variety of turns in it, the fortune of it is so subject to sudden vicissitudes, and one so frequently, after long contemplation, discovers the means of extricating one's self from a supposed insur mountable difficulty, that one is encouraged to continue the contest to the last, in hope of victory by our own skill, or at least of giving a stale mate, by the negligence of our adversary. And whoever considers, what in chess he often sees instances of, that particular pieces of success are apt to produce presumption, and its consequent inattention, by which the loss may be recovered, will learn not to be too much discouraged by the present success of his adversary, nor to despair of final good fortune, upon every little check he receives in the pursuit of it.

That we may, therefore, be induced more frequently to choose this beneficial amusement, in preference to others, which are not attended with the same advantages, every circumstance which may increase the pleasure of it should be regarded; and every action or word that is unfair, disrespectful, or that in any way may give uneasiness, should be avoided, as contrary to the immediate intention of both the players, which is, to pass the time agreeably.

Therefore, first, If it is agreed to play according to the strict rules; then those rules are to be exactly observed by both parties, and should not be insisted on for one side, while deviated from by the other—for this is not equitable.

Secondly, If it is agreed not to observe the rules exactly, but one party demands indulgences, he should then be as willing to allow them to the other.

Thirdly, No false move should ever be made to extricate yourself out of a difficulty, or to gain an advantage. There can be no pleasure in playing with a person once detected in such unfair practices.

Fourthly, If your adversary is long in playing, you ought not to hurry him, or to express any uneasiness at his delay You should not sing, nor whistle, nor look at your watch nor take up a book to read, nor make a tapping with your feet on the floor, or with your fingers on the table, nor do any thing that may disturb his attention. For all these things displease ; and they do not show your skill in playing, but your craftiness or your rudeness.

Fifthly, You ought not to endeavour to amuse and deceive your adversary, by pretending to have made bad moves, and saying that you have now lost the game, in order to make him secure and careless, and inattentive to your schemes ; for this is fraud and deceit, not skill in the game.

Sixthly, You must not, when you have gained a victory, use any triumphing or insulting expression, nor show too much pleasure ; but endeavour to console your adversary, and make him less dissatisfied with himself, by every kind of civil expression that may be used with truth ; such as, " You understand the game better than I, but you are a little inattentive ; or, you play too fast ; or, you had the best of the game, but something happened to divert your thoughts, and that turned it in my favour."

Seventhly, If you are a spectator while others play, observe the most perfect silence. For if you give advice, you offend both parties ; him against whom you give it, because it may cause the loss of his game ; and him in whose favour you give it, because, though it be good, and he follows it, he loses the pleasure he might have had, if you had permitted him to think until it had occurred to himself. Even after a move or moves, you must not, by replacing the pieces, show how it might have been placed better ; for that displeases, and may occasion disputes and doubts about their true situation. All talking to the players lessens or diverts their attention, and is therefore unpleasing. Nor should you give the least hint to either party, by any kind of noise or motion. If you do, you are unworthy to be a spectator. If you have a mind to exercise or show your judgment, do it in playing your own game, when you have an opportunity, not in criticising, or meddling with, or counselling the play of others.

Lastly, If the game is not to be played rigorously, according to the rules above-mentioned, then moderate your desire of victory over your adversary, and be pleased with

one over yourself. Snatch not eagerly at every advantage
offered by his unskilfulness or inattention; but point out to
him kindly, that by such a move he places or leaves a piece
in danger and unsupported; that by another he will put his
king in a perilous situation, &c. By this generous civility
(so opposite to the unfairness above forbidden) you may, indeed, happen to lose the game to your opponent; but you
will win what is better,—his esteem, his respect, and his
affection; together with the silent approbation and good
will of impartial spectators.

The Hospital in Philadelphia during the Pestilence.— C. B. BROWN.

I was seized with a violent fever. I knew in what manner
patients were treated at the hospital, and removal thither
was to the last degree abhorred.

The morning arrived, and my situation was discovered.
At the first intimation, Thetford rushed out of the house,
and refused to re-enter it till I was removed. I knew not
my fate, till three ruffians made their appearance at my
bedside, and communicated their commission.

I called on the name of Thetford and his wife. I en-
treated a moment's delay, till I had seen these persons, and
endeavoured to procure a respite from my sentence. They
were deaf to my entreaties, and prepared to execute their
office by force. I was delirious with rage and terror. I
heaped the bitterest execrations on my murderer; and by
turns invoked the compassion of, and poured a torrent of re-
proaches on, the wretches whom he had selected for his
ministers. My struggles and outcries were vain.

I have no perfect recollection of what passed till my arrival at the hospital. My passions combined with my disease
to make me frantic and wild. In a state like mine, the
slightest motion could not be endured without agony. What
then must I have felt, scorched and dazzled by the sun,
sustained by hard boards, and borne for miles over a rugged pavement?

I cannot make you comprehend the anguish of my feelings. To be disjointed and torn piece-meal by the rack, was a torment inexpressibly inferior to this. Nothing excites my wonder, but that I did not expire before the cart had moved three paces.

I knew not how, or by whom, I was moved from this vehicle. Insensibility came at length to my relief. After a time I opened my eyes, and slowly gained some knowledge of my situation. I lay upon a mattress, whose condition proved that a half-decayed corpse had recently been dragged from it. The room was large, but it was covered with beds like my own. Between each, there was scarcely the interval of three feet. Each sustained a wretch, whose groans and distortions bespoke the desperateness of his condition.

The atmosphere was loaded by mortal stenches. A vapour, suffocating and malignant, scarcely allowed me to breathe. No suitable receptacle was provided for the evacuations produced by medicine or disease. My nearest neighbour was struggling with death, and my bed, casually extended, was moist with the detestable matter which had flowed from his stomach.

You will scarcely believe that, in this scene of horrors, the sound of laughter should be overheard. While the upper rooms of this building are filled with the sick and the dying, the lower apartments are the scene of carousals and mirth. The wretches who are hired, at enormous wages, to tend the sick and convey away the dead, neglect their duty, and consume the cordials, which are provided for the patients, in debauchery and riot.

A female visage, bloated with malignity and drunkenness, occasionally looked in. Dying eyes were cast upon her, invoking the boon, perhaps, of a drop of cold water, or her assistance to change a posture which compelled him to behold the ghastly writhings or deathful *smile* of his neighbour.

The visitant had left the banquet for a moment, only to see who was dead. If she entered the room, blinking eyes and reeling steps showed her to be totally unqualified for ministering the aid that was needed. Presently, she dis-
27 *

appeared, and others ascended the staircase : a coffin was deposited at the door : the wretch, whose heart still quivered, was seized by rude hands, and dragged along the floor into the passage.

Oh ! how poor are the conceptions which are formed, by the fortunate few, of the sufferings to which millions of their fellow-beings are condemned ! This misery was more frightful, because it was seen to flow from the depravity of the attendants. My own eyes only would make me credit the existence of wickedness so enormous. No wonder that to die in garrets, and cellars, and stables, unvisited and unknown, had, by so many, been preferred to being brought hither.

A physician cast an eye upon my state. He gave some directions to the person who attended him. I did not comprehend them ; they were never executed by the nurses, and, if the attempt had been made, I should probably have refused to receive what was offered. Recovery was equally beyond my expectations and my wishes. The scene which was hourly displayed before me, the entrance of the sick, most of whom perished in a few hours, and their departure to the graves prepared for them, reminded me of the fate to which I, also, was reserved.

Three days passed away, in which every hour was expected to be the last. That, amidst an atmosphere so contagious and deadly, amidst causes of destruction hourly accumulating, I should yet survive, appears to me nothing less than miraculous. That, of so many conducted to this house, the only one who passed out of it alive should be myself, almost surpasses my belief.

Some inexplicable principle rendered harmless those potent enemies of human life. My fever subsided and vanished. My strength was revived, and the first use that I made of my limbs was, to bear me far from the contemplation and sufferance of these evils.

Shipwreck of the Ariel.—COOPER.

THE Ariel continued to struggle against the winds and ocean for several hours longer, before the day broke on the tempestuous scene, and the anxious mariners were enabled to form a more accurate estimate of their real danger. As the violence of the gale increased, the canvass of the schooner had been gradually reduced, until she was unable to show more than was absolutely necessary to prevent her driving, helplessly, on the land. Barnstable watched the appearance of the weather, as the light slowly opened upon them, with an intensity of anxiety, which denoted, that the presentiments of the cockswain were no longer deemed idle. On looking to windward, he beheld the green masses of water that were rolling in towards the land, with a violence that seemed irresistible, crowned with ridges of foam ; and there were moments when the air appeared filled with sparkling gems, as the rays of the rising sun fell upon the spray that was swept from wave to wave. Towards the land, the view was still more appalling. The cliffs, but a short half league under the lee of the schooner, were, at times, nearly hid from the eye by the pyramids of water, which the furious element, so suddenly restrained in its violence, cast high into the air, as if seeking to overstep the boundaries that nature had affix ed to its dominion. The whole coast, from the distant headland at the south, to the well known shoals that stretched far beyond their course, in the opposite direction, displayed a broad belt of foam, into which it would have been certain destruction, for the proudest ship that swam, to have entered. Still the Ariel floated on the billows, lightly and in safety, though yielding to the impulses of the waters, and, at times, appearing to be ingulfed in the yawning chasms, which, apparently, opened beneath her to receive the little fabric. The low rumour of acknowledged danger, had found its way through the schooner, and the seamen, after fastening their hopeless looks on the small spot of canvass that they were enabled to show to the tempest. would turn to view the dreary line of coast, that seemed to offer so gloomy an alternative. Even Dillon, to whom

the report of their danger had found its way, crept from
his place of concealment in the cabin, and moved about
the decks unheeded, devouring, with greedy ears, such
opinions as fell from the lips of the sullen mariners.

At this moment of appalling apprehension, the cockswain
exhibited the most calm resignation.   He knew that all
had been done, that lay in the power of man, to urge their
little vessel from the land, and it was now too evident to
his experienced eyes, that it had been done in vain ; but,
considering himself as a sort of fixture in the schooner, he
was quite prepared to abide her fate, be it for better or
for worse.   The settled look of gloom, that gathered around
the frank brow of Barnstable, was, in no degree, connected with any considerations of himself, but proceeded from
that sort of parental responsibility, from which the sea-
commander is never exempt.   The discipline of the crew,
however, still continued perfect and unyielding.   There
had, it is true, been a slight movement made by two of the
oldest seamen, which indicated an intention to drown the
apprehensions of death in ebriety ; but Barnstable had
called for his pistols, in a tone that checked the procedure
instantly, and, although the fatal weapons were untouched
by him, but were left to lie exposed on the capstan, where
they had been placed by his servant, not another symptom
of insubordination appeared among the devoted crew.
There was even, what to a landsman might seem, a dreadful affectation of attention to the most trifling duties of the
vessel ; and the men, who, it should seem, ought to be devoting the brief moments of their existence to the mighty
business of the hour, were constantly called to attend to the
most trivial details of their profession.   Ropes were coiled,
and the slightest damages occasioned by the waves, that,
at short intervals, swept across the low decks of the Ariel,
were repaired, with the same precision and order, as if she
yet lay embayed in the haven from which she had just been
driven.   In this manner, the arm of authority was kept
extended over the silent crew, not with the vain desire to
preserve a lingering, though useless exercise of power
but with a view to maintain that unity of action, that now
could alone afford them even a ray of hope.

" She can make no head against this sea, under that rag
of canvass," said Barnstable, gloomily; addressing the
cockswain, who, with folded arms, and an air of cool resignation, was balancing his body on the verge of the quarter-
deck, while the schooner was plunging madly into waves
that nearly buried her in their bosom; " the poor little
thing trembles like a frightened child, as she meets the
water."

Tom sighed heavily, and shook his head, before he answered—

" If we could have kept the head of the main-mast an
hour longer, we might have got an offing, and fetched to
windward of the shoals; but, as it is, sir, mortal man can't
drive a craft to windward—she sets bodily in to land, and
will be in the breakers in less than an hour, unless God
wills that the winds shall cease to blow."

" We have no hope left us, but to anchor; our ground
tackle may yet bring her up."

Tom turned to his commander, and replied, solemnly,
and with that assurance of manner, that long experience
only can give a man in moments of great danger—

" If our sheet-cable was bent to our heaviest anchor,
this sea would bring it home, though nothing but her
launch was riding by it. A north-easter in the German
Ocean must and will blow itself out; nor shall we get the
crown of the gale until the sun falls over the land. Then,
indeed, it may lull; for the winds do often seem to reverence the glory of the heavens too much to blow their might
in its very face !"

" We must do our duty to ourselves and the country,"
returned Barnstable, " go, get the two bowers spliced, and
have a kedge bent to a hawser; we'll back our two anchors together, and veer to the better end of two hundred
and forty fathoms; it may yet bring her up. See all clear
there for anchoring, and cutting away the masts—we'll
leave the wind nothing but a naked hull to whistle over."

" Ay, if there was nothing but the wind, we might yet
live to see the sun sink behind them hills," said the cockswain; " but what hemp can stand the strain of a craft
that is buried, half the time, to her foremast in the
water !"

The order was, however, executed by the crew, with a
sort of desperate submission to the will of their commander ; and, when the preparations were completed, the anchors and kedge were dropped to the bottom, and the instant that the Ariel tended to the wind, the axe was applied to the little that was left of her long raking masts.
The crash of the falling spars, as they came, in succession,
across the decks of the vessel, appeared to produce no sensation amid that scene of complicated danger ; but the seamen proceeded in silence in their hopeless duty of clearing the wrecks. Every eye followed the floating timbers,
as the waves swept them away from the vessel, with a sort
of feverish curiosity, to witness the effect produced by their
collision with those rocks that lay so fearfully near them ;
but, long before the spars entered the wide border of foam,
they were hid from view by the furious element in which
they floated. It was, now, felt by the whole crew of the
Ariel, that their last means of safety had been adopted,
and, at each desperate and headlong plunge the vessel took
into the bosom of the seas that rolled upon her forecastle,
the anxious seamen thought they could perceive the yielding of the iron, that yet clung to the bottom, or could hear
the violent surge of the parting strands of the cable, that
still held them to their anchors. While the minds of the
sailors were agitated with the faint hopes that had been
excited by the movements of their schooner, Dillon had
been permitted to wander about the vessel unnoticed ; his
rolling eyes, hard breathing, and clenched hands, exciting
no observation among the men, whose thoughts were yet
dwelling on the means of safety. But now, when, with
a sort of frenzied desperation, he would follow the retiring
waters along the decks, and venture his person nigh the
group that had collected around and on the gun of the cockswain, glances of fierce or of sullen vengeance were cast
at him, that conveyed threats of a nature that he was too
much agitated to understand.

"If ye are tired of this world, though your time, like
my own, is probably but short in it," said Tom to him, as
he passed the cockswain in one of his turns, "you can go
forward among the men ; but if ye have need of the moments to foot up the reck'ning of your doings among men,

afore ye're brought to face your Maker, and hear the log-book of Heaven, 1 would advise you to keep as nigh as possible to Captain Barnstable or myself."

" Will you promise to save me, if the vessel is wreck-ed?" exclaimed Dillon, catching at the first sounds of friendly interest that had reached his ears, since he had been recaptured; "oh! if you will, I can secure you future ease; yes, wealth, for the remainder of your days!"

" Your promises have been too ill kept, afore this, for the peace of your soul," returned the cockswain, without bit-terness, though sternly; " but it is not in me to strike even a whale, that is already spouting blood."

The intercessions of Dillon were interrupted by a dread-ful cry, that arose among the men forward, and which sounded with increased horror, amid the roaring of the tem-pest. The schooner rose on the breast of a wave at the same instant, and, falling off with her broad side to the sea, she drove in towards the cliffs, like a bubble on the rapids of a cataract.

" Our ground tackle has parted," said Tom, with his re-signed patience of manner undisturbed; " she shall die as easy as man can make her!" While he yet spoke, he seized the tiller, and gave to the vessel such a direction, as would be most likely to cause her to strike the rocks with her bows foremost.

There was, for one moment, an expression of exquisite anguish betrayed in the dark countenance of Barnstable; but, at the next, it passed away, and he spoke cheerfully to his men—

" Be steady, my lads; be calm: there is yet a hope of life for *you*—our light draught will let us run in close to the cliffs, and it is still falling water—see your boats clear, and be steady."

The crew of the whale-boat, aroused, by this speech, from a sort of stupor, sprang into their light vessel, which was quickly lowered into the sea, and kept riding on the foam, free from the sides of the schooner, by the powerful exertions of the men. The cry for the cockswain was earnest and repeated, but Tom shook his head, without re-plying, still grasping the tiller, and keeping his eyes steadily bent on the chaos of waters, into which they were driving. The launch, the largest boat of the two, was cut loose from the " gripes," and the bustle and exertion of the moment rendered the crew insensible to the horror of the scene that surrounded them. But the loud, hoarse call of the cockswain, to " look out—secure yourselves :" suspended even their efforts, and at that instant the Ariel settled on a wave that melted from under her, heavily on the rocks. The shock was so violent as to throw all, wh: disregarded the warning cry, from their feet, and the universal quiver that pervaded the vessel was like the last shudder of animated nature. For a time long enough to breathe, the least experienced among the men supposed the danger to be passed ; but a wave of great height followed the one that had deserted them, and, raising the vessel again, threw her roughly still farther on her bed of rocks, and at the same time its crest broke over her quarter, sweeping the length of her decks, with a fury that was almost resistless. The shuddering seamen beheld their loosened boat driven from their grasp, and dashed against the base of the cliffs, where no fragment of her wreck could be traced, at the receding of the waters. But the passing wave had thrown the vessel into a position which, in some measure, protected her decks from the violence of those that succeeded it.

" Go, my boys, go," said Barnstable, as the moment of dreadful uncertainty passed ; " you have still the whale-boat, and she, at least, will take you nigh the shore ; go into her, my boys ; God bless you, God bless you all ; you have been faithful and honest fellows, and I believe he will not yet desert you ; go, my friends, while there is a lull."

The seamen threw themselves, in a mass of human bodies, into the light vessel, which nearly sunk under the unusual burthen ; but when they looked around them, Barnstable, and Merry, Dillon, and the cockswain, were yet to be seen on the decks of the Ariel. The former was pacing, in deep, and perhaps bitter melancholy, the wet planks of the schooner, while the boy hung, unheeded, on his arm, uttering disregarded petitions to his commander, o desert the wreck. Dillon approached the side where

the boat lay, again and again, but the threatening counte
nances of the seamen as often drove him back in despair.
Tom had seated himself on the heel of the bowsprit, where
he continued, in an attitude of quiet resignation, returning no other answers to the loud and repeated calls of
his shipmates, than by waving his hand toward the shore.

"Now hear me," said the boy, urging his request to
tears; "if not for my sake, or for your own sake, Mr.
Barnstable, or for the hopes of God's mercy, go into the
boat, for the love of my cousin Katherine."

The young lieutenant paused in his troubled walk, and,
for a moment, he cast a glance of hesitation at the cliffs;
but, at the next instant, his eyes fell on the ruin of his vessel, and he answered—

"Never, boy, never; if my hour has come, I will not
shrink from my fate."

"Listen to the men, dear sir; the boat will be swamped
along-side the wreck, and their cry is, that without you
they will not let her go."

Barnstable motioned to the boat, to bid the boy enter it,
and turned away in silence.

"Well," said Merry, with firmness, "if it be right that
a lieutenant shall stay by a wreck, it must also be right for
a midshipman; "shove off; neither Mr. Barnstable nor
myself will quit the vessel."

"Boy, your life has been intrusted to my keeping, and
at my hands will it be required," said his commander, lifting the struggling youth, and tossing him into the arms of
the seamen. "Away with ye, and God be with you;
there is more weight in you, now, than can go safe to
land."

Still, the seamen hesitated, for they perceived the cockswain moving, with a steady tread, along the deck, and
they hoped he had relented, and would yet persuade the
lieutenant to join his crew. But Tom, imitating the example of his commander, seized the latter, suddenly, in
his powerful grasp, and threw him over the bulwarks with
an irresistible force. At the same moment, he cast the
last of the boat from the pin that held it, and, lifting his
broad hands high in to the air, his voice was heard in the
tempest.

28

"God's will be done with me," he cried; "I saw the first timber of the Ariel laid, and shall live just long enough to see it torn out of her bottom; after which I wish to live no longer."

But his shipmates were swept far beyond the sounds of his voice, before half these words were uttered. All command of the boat was rendered impossible, by the numbers it contained, as well as the raging of the surf; and, as it rose on the white crest of a wave, Tom saw his beloved little craft for the last time; it fell into a trough of the sea, and in a few moments more its fragments were ground into splinters on the adjacent rocks. The cockswain still remained where he had cast off the rope, and beheld the numerous heads and arms that appeared rising, at short intervals, on the waves; some making powerful and well-directed efforts to gain the sands, that were becoming visible as the tide fell, and others wildly tossed, in the frantic movements of helpless despair. The honest old seaman gave a cry of joy, as he saw Barnstable issue from the surf, bearing the form of Merry in safety to the sands, where, one by one, several seamen soon appeared also, dripping and exhausted. Many others of the crew were carried, in a similar manner, to places of safety; though, as Tom returned to his seat on the bowsprit, he could not conceal, from his reluctant eyes, the lifeless forms, that were, in other spots, driven against the rocks, with a fury that soon left them but few of the outward vestiges of humanity.

Dillon and the cockswain were now the sole occupants of their dreadful station. The former stood, in a kind of stupid despair, a witness of the scene we have related; but, as his curdled blood began again to flow more warmly through his heart, he crept close to the side of Tom, with that sort of selfish feeling that makes even hopeless misery more tolerable, when endured in participation with another.

"When the tide falls," he said, in a voice that betrayed the agony of fear, though his words expressed the renewal of hope, "we shall be able to walk to land."

"There was One, and only One, to whose feet the waters were the same as a dry deck," returned the cock swain; " and none but such as have his power will ever be able to walk from these rocks to the sands." The old seaman paused, and, turning his eyes, which exhibited a mingled expression of disgust and compassion, on his companion, he added, with reverence—" Had you thought more of him in fair weather, your case would be less to be pitied in this tempest."

" Do you still think there is much danger ?" asked Dillon.

" To them that have reason to fear death : listen! do you hear that hollow noise beneath ye ?"

" 'Tis the wind, driving by the vessel !"

" 'Tis the poor thing herself," said the affected cockswain, " giving her last groans. The water is breaking up her decks, and, in a few minutes more, the handsomest model that ever cut a wave will be like the chips that fell from her timbers in framing !"

" Why, then, did you remain here ?" cried Dillon, wildly.

" To die in my coffin, if it should be the will of God," returned Tom : " these waves to me are what the land is to you ; I was born on them, and I have always meant that they should be my grave."

" But I—I," shrieked Dillon, " I am not ready to die !— I cannot die !—I will not die !"

" Poor wretch !" muttered his companion ; " you must go, like the rest of us ; when the death-watch is called, none can skulk from the muster."

" I can swim," Dillon continued, rushing, with frantic eagerness, to the side of the wreck. " Is there no billet of wood, no rope, that I can take with me ?"

" None ; every thing has been cut away, or carried off by the sea. If ye are about to strive for your life, take with ye a stout heart and a clean conscience, and trust the rest to God !"

" God !" echoed Dillon, in the madness of his frenzy ; " I know no God ! there is no God that knows me !"

" Peace !" said the deep tones of the cockswain, in a voice that seemed to speak in the elements ; " blasphemer, peace !"

The heavy groaning, produced by the water, in the timbers of the Ariel, at that moment, added its impulse to
the raging feelings of Dillon, and he cast himself headlong
into the sea.

The water, thrown by the rolling of the surf on the beach,
was necessarily returned to the ocean, in eddies, in different places, favourable to such an action of the element.
Into the edge of one of these counter-currents, that was
produced by the very rocks on which the schooner lay, and
which the watermen call the " under-tow," Dillon had,
unknowingly, thrown his person, and when the waves had
driven him a short distance from the wreck, he was met
by a stream that his most desperate efforts could not overcome. He was a light and powerful swimmer, and the
struggle was hard and protracted. With the shore immediately before his eyes, and at no great distance, he was
led, as by a false phantom, to continue his efforts, although
they did not advance him a foot. The old seaman, who,
at first, had watched his motions with careless indifference,
understood the danger of his situation at a glance, and, forgetful of his own fate, he shouted aloud, in a voice that
was driven over the struggling victim, to the ears of his
shipmates on the sands—

" Sheer to port, and clear the under-tow ! sheer to the
southward !"

Dillon heard the sounds, but his faculties were too much
obscured by terror to distinguish their object ; he, however, blindly yielded to the call, and gradually changed his
direction, until his face was once more turned towards the
vessel. The current swept him diagonally by the rocks,
and he was forced into an eddy, where he had nothing to
contend against but the waves, whose violence was much
broken by the wreck. In this state he continued still to
struggle, but with a force that was too much weakened to
overcome the resistance he met. Tom looked around him
for a rope, but not one presented itself to his hands ; all
had gone over with the spars, or been swept away by the
waves. At this moment of disappointment, his eyes met
those of the desperate Dillon. Calm, and inured to horrors, as was the veteran seaman, he involuntarily passed
his hand before his brow, as if to exclude the look of despau

he encountered; and when, a moment afterwards, he removed the rigid member, he beheld the sinking form of
the victim, as it gradually settled in the ocean, still struggling, with regular but impotent strokes of the arms and
feet, to gain the wreck, and to preserve an existence that
had been so much abused in its hour of allotted probation.

"He will soon know his God, and learn that his God
knows him!" murmured the cockswain to himself. As he
yet spoke, the wreck of the Ariel yielded to an overwhelming sea, and, after a universal shudder, her timbers and
planks gave way, and were swept towards the cliffs, bearing the body of the simple-hearted cockswain among the
ruins.

Destruction of a Family of the Pilgrims by the Savages.—
MISS SEDGWICK.

———ALL was joy in Mrs. Fletcher's dwelling. "My
dear mother," said Everell, "it is now quite time to look
out for father and Hope Leslie. I have turned the hour-
glass three times since dinner, and counted all the sands, I
think. Let us all go on the front portico, where we can
catch the first glimpse of them, as they come past the elm
trees. Here, Oneco," he continued, as he saw assent in
his mother's smile, "help me out with mother's rocking
chair: rather rough rocking,"—he added, as he adjusted
the rockers lengthwise with the logs that served for the floor-
ing,—"but mother won't mind trifles just now. Ah!
blessed babe, brother," he continued, taking in his arms
the beautiful infant, "you shall come, too, even though
you cheat me out of my birthright, and get the first embrace from father." Thus saying, he placed the laughing
infant in his go-cart, beside his mother. He then aided
his little sisters in their arrangement of the playthings they
had brought forth to welcome and astonish Hope; and
finally he made an elevated position for Faith Leslie, where
she might, he said, as she ought, catch the very first glimpse
at her sister.

23 *

" Thank, thank you, Everell," said the little girl, as she
mounted her pinnacle: "if you knew Hope, you would
want to see her first, too; every body loves Hope. We
shall always have pleasant times when Hope gets here."

It was one of the most beautiful afternoons at the close
of the month of May. The lagging Spring had at last
come forth in all her power; "her work of gladness" was
finished, and forests, fields and meadows were bright with
renovated life. The full Connecticut swept triumphantly
on, as if still exulting in its release from the fetters of winter. Every gushing rill had the spring-note of joy. The
meadows were, for the first time, enriched with patches
of English grain, which the new settlers had sown scantily,
by way of experiment, prudently occupying the greatest
portion of the rich mould with the native Indian corn
This product of our soil is beautiful in all its progress, from
the moment when, as now it studded the meadow with hil-
locks, shooting its bright pointed spear from its mother
earth, to its maturity, when the long golden ear bursts from
the rustling leaf.

The grounds about Mrs. Fletcher's house had been prepared with the neatness of English taste; and a rich bed
of clover, that overspread the lawn immediately before the
portico, already rewarded the industry of the cultivators.
Over this delicate carpet, the domestic fowls, the first civilized inhabitants of the country of their tribe, were now
treading, picking their food here and there like dainty little
epicures.

The scene had also its minstrels; the birds, those ministers and worshippers of nature, were on the wing, filling
the air with melody, while, like diligent little housewives,
they ransacked the forest and field for materials for their
house-keeping.

A mother, encircled by healthful, sporting children, is
always a beautiful spectacle—a spectacle that appeals to
nature in every human breast. Mrs. Fletcher, in obedience to matrimonial duty, or, it may be, from some lingering
of female vanity, had on this occasion attired herself with
extraordinary care. What woman does not wish to look
handsome in the eyes of her husband!

"Mother," said Everell, putting aside the exquisitely fine lace that shaded her cheek, " I do not believe you looked more beautiful than you do to-day, when, as I have heard, they called you ' the rose of the wilderness.' Our little Mary's cheek is as round and as bright as a peach, but it is not so handsome as yours, mother. Your heart has sent this colour here," he continued, kissing her tenderly; " it seems to have come forth to tell us that our father is near."

" It would shame me, Everell," replied his mother, embracing him with a feeling that the proudest drawing-room belle might have envied, " to take such flattery from any lips but thine."—" Oh, do not call it flattery, mother—look, Magawisca—for Heaven's sake cheer up—look, would you know mother's eye ? just turn it, mother, one minute from that road—and her pale cheek too—with this rich colour on it ?"

" Alas ! alas !" replied Magawisca, glancing her eyes at Mrs. Fletcher, and then, as if heart struck, withdrawing them, " how soon the flush of the setting sun fades from the evening cloud !"

" Oh, Magawisca !" said Everell, impatiently, " why are you so dismal ? your voice is too sweet for a bird of ill-omen. I shall begin to think as Jennet says—though Jennet is no text book for me—I shall begin to think old Nelema has really bewitched you."—" You call me a bird of ill-omen," replied Magawisca, half proud, half sorrowful, " and you call the owl a bird of ill-omen, but we hold him sacred ; he is our sentinel, and, when danger is near, he cries, ' Awake ! awake !' "

" Magawisca, you are positively unkind. Jeremiah's lamentations on a holyday would not be more out of time than your croaking is now. The very skies, earth, and air, seem to partake of our joy at father's return, and you only make a discord. Do you think, if your father was near, I would not share your joy ?"

Tears fell fast from Magawisca's eyes, but she made no reply, and Mrs. Fletcher, observing and compassionating her emotion, and thinking it probably arose from comparing her orphan state to that of the merry children about her, called her, and said, " Magawisca, you are neither a stran-

ger nor a servant; will you not share our joy? Io you
not love us?"

"Love you!" she exclaimed, clasping her hands, "love
you! I would give my life for you."

"We do not ask your life, my good girl," replied Mrs.
Fletcher, kindly smiling on her, "but a light heart, and
a cheerful look. A sad countenance doth not become this
joyful hour Go and help Oneco; he is quite out of breath
blowing those soap bubbles for the children." Oneco
smiled, and shook his head, and continued to send off one
after another of the prismatic globes, and, as they rose and
floated on the air, and brightened with the many-coloured ray, the little girls clapped their hands, and the baby
stretched his to grasp the brilliant vapour. "Oh!" said
Magawisca, impetuously covering her eyes, "I do not
like to see any thing so beautiful pass so quickly away."

Scarcely had she uttered these words, when suddenly,
as if the earth had opened on them, three Indian warriors
darted from the forest, and pealed on the air their horrible
yells.

"My father! my father!" burst from the lips of Magawisca and Oneco. Faith Leslie sprang towards the Indian boy, and clung fast to him, and the children clustered
about their mother; she instinctively caught her infant,
and held it close within her arms, as if their ineffectual
shelter were a rampart.

Magawisca uttered a cry of agony, and, springing forward with her arms uplifted, as if deprecating his approach,
she sunk down at her father's feet, and, clasping her hands,
"Save them!—save them!" she cried; "the mother—the
children—oh! they are all good: take vengeance on your
enemies, but spare, spare our friends! our benefactors! I
bleed when they are struck; oh! command them to stop!"
she screamed, looking to the companions of her father, who,
unchecked by her cries, were pressing on to their deadly
work.

Mononotto was silent and motionless: his eye glanced
wildly from Magawisca to Oneco. Magawisca replied to
the glance of fire: "Yes, they have sheltered us—they
have spread the wing of love over us—save them—save
them—oh! it will be too late," she cried, springing from

her father, whose silence and fixedness showed that, if his
better nature rebelled against the work of revenge, there
was no relenting of purpose.   Magawisca darted before the
Indian, who was advancing towards Mrs. Fletcher with an
uplifted hatchet.   " You shall hew me to pieces ere you
touch her," she said, and planted herself as a shield before
her benefactress.   The warrior's obdurate heart, untouched by the sight of the helpless mother and her little ones,
was thrilled by the courage of the heroic girl · he paused,
and grimly smiled on her, when his companion, crying,
" Hasten ! the dogs will be on us !" levelled a deadly blow
at Mrs. Fletcher; but his uplifted arm was penetrated by
a musket shot, and the hatchet fell harmless to the floor.

" Courage, mother !" cried Everell, reloading the piece;
but neither courage nor celerity could avail : the second
Indian sprang upon him, threw him on the floor, wrested
his musket from him, and, brandishing his tomahawk over
his head, he would have aimed the fatal stroke, when a
cry from Mononotto arrested his arm.

Everell extricated himself from his grasp, and, a ray of
hope flashing into his mind, he seized a bugle horn, which
hung beside the door, and winded it.   This was the con-
ventional signal of alarm, and he sent forth a blast long
and loud—a death-cry.   .

Mrs. Grafton and her attendants were just mounting
their horses to return home.   Digby listened for a moment:
then, exclaiming, " It comes from our 1 ·ter's dwelling !
ride for your life, Hutton !" he tossed away a bandbox that
encumbered him, and spurred his horse to its utmost speed.

The alarm was spread through the village, and, in a brief
space, Mr. Pynchon, with six armed men, was 'pressing
towards the fatal scene.   In the mean time the tragedy
was proceeding at Bethel.   Mrs. Fletcher's senses had
been stunned with terror.   She had neither spoken nor
moved after she grasped her infant.   Everell's gallant interposition restored a momentary consciousness; she screamed to him, " Fly, Everell, my son, fly ; for your father's
sake, fly !"

" Never !" he replied, springing to his mother's side.

The savages, always rapid in their movements, were
now aware that their safety depended on despatch.   " Fin

ish your work, warriors!" cried Mononotto. Obedient to
the command, and infuriated by his bleeding wound, the
Indian, who, on receiving the shot, had staggered back,
and leaned against the wall, now sprang forward, and tore
the infant from its mother's breast. She shrieked, and
in that shriek passed the agony of death. She was unconscious that her son, putting forth a strength beyond nature, for a moment kept the Indian at bay; she neither
saw nor felt the knife struck at her own heart. She felt
not the arms of her defenders, Everell and Magawisca, as
they met around her neck. She fainted and fell to the floor,
dragging her impotent protectors with her.

The savage, in his struggle with Everell, had tossed the
infant boy to the ground : he fell, quite unharmed, on the
turf at Mononotto's feet; there, raising his head, and looking up into the chieftain's face, he probably perceived a
gleam of mercy; for, with the quick instinct of infancy,
that with unerring sagacity directs its appeal, he clasped
the naked leg of the savage with one arm, and stretched
the other towards him with a piteous supplication, that no
words could have expressed.

Mononotto's heart melted within him : he stooped to
raise the sweet suppliant, when one of the Mohawks fiercely seized him, tossed him wildly around his head, and dashed him on the door-stone. But the silent prayer, perhaps
the celestial inspiration of the innocent creature, was not
lost. " We have had blood enough," cried Mononotto;
" you have well avenged me, brothers."

Then, looking at Oneco, who had remained in one corner of the portico, clasping Faith Leslie in his arms, he
commanded him to follow him with the child. Everell was
torn from the lifeless bodies of his mother and sisters, and
dragged into the forest. Magawisca uttered one cry of
agony and despair, as she looked for the last time on the
bloody scene, and then followed her father.

As they passed the boundary of the cleared ground,
Mononotto tore from Oneco his English dress, and, casting
it from him, " Thus perish," he said, " every mark of the
captivity of my children. Thou shalt return to our forests,"
he continued, wrapping a skin around him, " with the
badge of thy people." * * * * * * * * * * *

We hope our readers will not think we have wantonly sported with their feelings, by drawing a picture of calamity that only exists in the fictitious tale. No—such events as we have feebly related were common in our early annals, and attended by horrors that it would be impossible for the imagination to exaggerate. Not only families, but villages, were cut off by the most dreaded of all foes—the ruthless, vengeful savage.

In the quiet possession of the blessings transmitted, we are, perhaps, in danger of forgetting or undervaluing the sufferings by which they were obtained. We forget that the noble pilgrims lived and endured for us; that, when they came to the wilderness, they said truly, though, it may be, somewhat quaintly, that they turned their backs on Egypt. They did virtually renounce all dependence on earthly support; they left the land of their birth, of their homes, of their fathers' sepulchres; they sacrificed ease and preferment, and all the delights of sense—and for what?—to open for themselves an earthly paradise?—to dress their bowers of pleasure, and rejoce with their wives and children? No!—they came not for themselves; they lived not to themselves. An exiled and suffering people, they came forth in the dignity of the chosen servants of the Lord, to oper. the forests to the sun-beam, and to the light of the Sun of righteousness; to restore man, man, oppressed and trampled on by his fellow, to religious and civil liberty and equal rights; to replace the creatures of God on their natural level; to bring down the hills, and make smooth the rough places, which the pride and cruelty of man had wrought on the fair creation of the Father of all.

What was their reward? Fortune?—distinctions?—the sweet charities of home? . No—but their feet were planted on the mount of vision, and they saw, with sublime joy, a multitude of people where the solitary savage roamed the forest; the forest vanished, and pleasant villages and busy cities appeared; the tangled foot-path expanded to the thronged highway; the consecrated church was planted on the rock of heathen sacrifice.

And, that we might realize this vision,—enter into this promised land of faith,—they endured hardship, and braved

death, deeming, as said one of their company, that " he is
not worthy to live at all, who, for fear of danger or death,
shunneth his country's service or his own honour—since
death is inevitable, and the fame of virtue immortal "

If these were the fervours of enthusiasm, it was an en
thusiasm kindled and fed by the holy flame that glows cr.
the altar of God ; an enthusiasm that never abates, but
gathers life and strength as the immortal soul expands in
the image of its Creator.

The Emigrant's Abode in Ohio.—FLINT

IN making remoter journeys from the town, beside the
rivulets, and in the little bottoms not yet in cultivation, I
discerned the smoke rising in the woods, and heard the
strokes of the axe, the tinkling of bells, and the baying of
dogs, and saw the newly-arrived emigrant either raising
his log cabin, or just entered into possession. It has afforded me more pleasing reflections, a happier train of associations, to contemplate these beginnings of social toil in the
wide wilderness, than, in our more cultivated regions, to
come in view of the most sumptuous mansion. Nothing
can be more beautiful than these little bottoms, upon which
these emigrants deposit, if I may so say, their household
gods. Springs burst forth in the intervals between the
high and low grounds. The trees and shrubs are of the
most beautiful kind. The brilliant red-bird is seen flitting
among the shrubs, or, perched on a tree, seems welcoming,
in her mellow notes, the emigrant to his abode. Flocks
of paroquets are glittering among the trees, and gray squir-
rels are skipping from branch to branch. In the midst of
these primeval scenes, the patient and laborious father fixes
his family. In a few weeks they have reared a comfortable cabin and other outbuildings. Pass this place in two
years, and you will see extensive fields of corn and wheat,
a young and thrifty orchard, fruit trees of all kinds,—the
guarantee of present abundant subsistence, and of future
luxury. Pass it in ten years, and the log buildings will
have disappeared. The shrubs and forest trees will be

gone. The Arcadian aspect of humble and retired abundance and comfort will have given place to a brick house, with accompaniments like those that attend the same kind of house in the older countries. By this time, the occupant, who came there, perhaps, with a small sum of money, and moderate expectations, from humble life, and with no more than a common school education, has been made, in succession, member of the assembly, justice of the peace, and finally county judge. I admit that the first residence among the trees affords the most agreeable picture to my mind; and that there is an inexpressible charm in the pastoral simplicity of those years, before pride and self-consequence have banished the repose of their Eden, and when you witness the first strugglings of social toil with the barren luxuriance of nature.

Melancholy Decay of the Indians.—CASS.

NEITHER the government nor people of the United States have any wish to conceal from themselves, nor from the world, that there is upon their frontiers a wretched, forlorn people, looking to them for support and protection, and possessing strong claims upon their justice and humanity. Those people received our forefathers in a spirit of friendship, aided them to endure privations and sufferings, and taught them how to provide for many of the wants with which they were surrounded. The Indians were then strong, and we were weak; and, without looking at the change which has occurred in any spirit of morbid affectation, but with the feelings of an age accustomed to observe great mutations in the fortunes of nations and of individuals, we may express our regret that they have lost so much of what we have gained. The prominent points of their history are before the world, and will go down unchanged to posterity. In the revolution of a few ages, this fair portion of the continent, which was theirs, has passed into our possession. The forests, which afforded them food and security, where were their cradles, their homes and their graves

29

have disappeared, or are disappearing, before the progress of civilization.

We have extinguished their council fires, and ploughed up the bones of their fathers. Their population has diminished with lamentable rapidity. Those tribes that remain, like the lone column of a falling temple, exhibit but the sad relics of their former strength ; and many others live only in the names, which have reached through the earlier accounts of travellers and historians. The causes, which have produced this physical desolation, are yet in constant and active operation, and threaten to leave us, at no distant day, without a living proof of Indian sufferings, from the Atlantic to the immense desert, which sweeps along the base of the Rocky Mountains. Nor can we console ourselves with the reflection, that their physical condition has been counterbalanced by any melioration in their moral condition. We have taught them neither how to live, nor how to die. They have been equally stationary in their manners, habits and opinions ; in every thing but their numbers and their happiness ; and, although existing, for more than six generations, in contact with a civilized people, they owe to them no one valuable improvement in the arts, nor a single principle which can restrain their passions, or give hope to despondence, motive to exertion, or confidence to virtue.

Efforts, however, have not been wanting to reclaim the Indians from their forlorn condition ; but with what hopeless results, we have only to cast our eyes upon them to ascertain. Whether the cause of this failure must be sought in the principles of these efforts, or in their application, has not yet been satisfactorily determined ; but the important experiments, which are now making, will probably, ere long, put the question at rest. During more than a century, great zeal was displayed by the French court, and by many of the dignified French ecclesiastics, for the conversion of the American aborigines in Canada ; and learned, and pious, and zealous men devoted themselves, with noble ardour and intrepidity, to this generous work : at what immense personal sacrifices, we can never fully estimate. And it is melancholy to contrast their privations and sufferings, living and dying, with the fleeting memori

als of their labours. A few external ceremonies, affecting
neither the head nor the heart, and which are retained like
idle legends among some of the aged Indians, are all that
remain to preserve the recollection of their spiritual fathers; and I have stood upon the ruins of St. Ignace, on
the shores of Lake Huron, their principal missionary establishment, indulging those melancholy reflections, which
must always press upon the mind, amid the fallen monuments of human piety.

Object and Success of the Missionary Enterprise.—
WAYLAND.

OUR object will not have been accomplished till the
tomahawk shall be buried forever, and the tree of peace
spread its broad branches from the Atlantic to the Pacific;
until a thousand smiling villages shall be reflected from
the waves of the Missouri, and the distant valleys of the
West echo with the song of the reaper; till the wilderness
and the solitary place shall have been glad for us, and the
desert has rejoiced, and blossomed as the rose.

Our labours are not to cease, until the last slave-ship
shall have visited the coast of Africa, and, the nations of
Europe and America having long since redressed her ag-
gravated wrongs, Ethiopia, from the Mediterranean to the
Cape, shall have stretched forth her hand unto God.

How changed will then be the face of Asia! Bramins,
and sooders, and castes, and shasters, will have passed away,
like the mist which rolls up the mountain's side before the
rising glories of a summer's morning, while the land on
which it rested, shining forth in all its loveliness, shall,
from its numberless habitations, send forth the high praises
of God and the Lamb. The Hindoo mother will gaze upon
her infant with the same tenderness, which throbs in the
breast of any one of you who now hears me, and the Hindoo son will pour into the wounded bosom of his widowed
parent the oil of peace and consolation.

In a word, point us to the loveliest village that smiles
upon a Scottish or New England landscape, and compare

it with the filthiness and brutality of a Caffrarian kraal,
and we tell you, that our object is to render that Caffrarian kraal as happy and as gladsome as that Scottish or New
England village.   Point us to the spot on the face of the
earth, where liberty is best understood and most perfectly
enjoyed, where intellect shoots forth in its richest luxuriance, and where all the kindlier feelings of the heart are
constantly seen in their most graceful exercise ; point us
to the loveliest, and happiest neighbourhood in the world,
on which we dwell ; and we tell you, that our object is to
render this whole earth, with all its nations, and kindreds,
and tongues, and people, as happy, nay, happier, than that
neighbourhood.

We do believe, that God so loved the world, that he gave
his only begotten Son, that whosoever believeth in him
should not perish, but have everlasting life.   Our object is
to convey to those who are perishing the news of this salvation.   It is to furnish every family upon the face of the
whole earth with the Word of God written in its own language, and to send to every neighbourhood a preacher of
the cross of Christ.   Our object will not be accomplished
until every idol temple shall have been utterly abolished,
and a temple of Jehovah erected in its room ; until this
earth, instead of being a theatre, on which immortal beings
are preparing by crime for eternal condemnation, shall become one universal temple, in which the children of men
are learning the anthems of the blessed above, and becoming meet to join the general assembly and church of
the first born, whose names are written in heaven.   Our
design will not be completed until

> " One song employs all nations, and all cry,
> ' Worthy the Lamb, for he was slain for us ;'
> The dwellers in the vales and on the rocks
> Shout to each other ; and the mountain tops
> From distant mountains catch the flying joy;
> Till, nation after nation taught the strain,
> Earth rolls the rapturous hosanna round.''

The object of the missionary enterprise embraces every
child of Adam.   It is vast as the race to whom its operations are of necessity limited.   It would confer upon every
individual on earth all that intellectual or moral cultivation
can bestow.   It would rescue a world from the indignation

and wrath, tribulation and anguish, reserved for every son of man that doeth evil, and give it a title to glory, honour, and immortality. You see, then, that our object is, not only to affect every individual of the species, but to affec him in the momentous extremes of infinite happiness and infinite wo. And now, we ask, what object, ever undertaken by man, can compare with this same design of evangelizing the world? Patriotism itself fades away before it, and acknowledges the supremacy of an enterprise, which seizes, with so strong a grasp, upon both the temporal and eternal destinies of the whole family of man.

And now, my hearers, deliberately consider the nature of the missionary enterprise. Reflect upon the dignity of its object; the high moral and intellectual powers which are to be called forth in its execution; the simplicity, benevolence, and efficacy, of the means by which all this is to be achieved; and we ask you, Does not every other enterprise, to which man ever put forth his strength, dwindle into insignificance before that of preaching Christ crucified to a lost and perishing world?

Engaged in such an object, and supported by such an assurance, you may readily suppose, we can very well bear the contempt of those who would point at us the finger of scorn. It is written, "In the last days there shall be scoffers." We regret that it should be so. We regret that men should oppose an enterprise, of which the chief object is, to turn sinners unto holiness. We pity them, and we will pray for them. For we consider their situation far other than enviable. We recollect that it was once said by the Divine Missionary, to the first band which he commissioned, "He that despiseth you despiseth me, and he that despiseth me despiseth him that sent me." So that this very contempt may, at last, involve them in a controversy infinitely more serious than they at present anticipate. The reviler of missions, and the missionary of the cross, must both stand before the judgment seat of him who said, "Go ye into all the world, and preach the Gospel to every creature." It is affecting to think, that, whilst the one, surrounded by the nation who, through his instrumentality, have been rescued from everlasting death, shall receive the plaudit, "Well done, good and faithful servant!"

29 *

the other may be numbered among those despisers, who wonder and perish. "O that they might know, even in this their day, the things which belong to their peace, before they are hidden from their eyes!"

You can also easily perceive how it is that we are not soon disheartened by those who tell us of the difficulties, nay, the hopelessness, of our undertaking. They may point us to countries once the seat of the church, now overspread with Mohammedan delusion; or, bidding us look at nations, who once believed as we do, now contending for what we consider fatal error, they may assure us that our cause is declining. To all this we have two answers. First, the assumption that our cause is declining, is utterly gratuitous. We think it not difficult to prove, that the distinctive principles we so much venerate, never swayed so powerful an influence over the destinies of the human race as at this very moment. Point us to those nations of the earth, to whom moral and intellectual cultivation, inexhaustible resources, progress in arts, and sagacity in council, have assigned the highest rank in political importance, and you point us to nations whose religious opinions are most closely allied to those we cherish. Besides, when was there a period, since the days of the apostles, in which so many converts have been made to these principles, as have been made, both from Christian and Pagan nations, within the last five-and-twenty years? Never did the people of the saints of the Most High look so much like going forth, in serious earnest, to take possession of the kingdom, and dominion, and the greatness of the kingdom, under the whole heaven, as at the present day. We see, then, nothing in the signs of the times, which forebodes a failure, but every thing which promises that our undertaking will prosper. But, secondly, suppose the cause did seem declining; we should see no reason to relax our exertions; for Jesus Christ has said, " Preach the Gospel to every creature." Appearances, whether prosperous or adverse, alter not the obligation to obey a positive command of Almighty God.

Again, suppose all that is affirmed were true. It it must be, let it be. Let the dark cloud of infidelity overspread Europe, cross the ocean, and cover our own beloved land

Let nation after nation swerve from the faith Let iniqui-
ty abound, and the love of many wax cold, even until there
is on the face of the earth but one pure church of our
Lord and Saviour Jesus Christ. All we ask is, that we
may be members of that one church. God grant that we
may throw ourselves into this Thermopylæ of the moral
universe.

But, even then, we should have no fear that the church
of God would be exterminated. We would call to remembrance the years of the right hand of the Most High. We
would recollect there was once a time, when the whole
church of Christ not only could be, but actually was, gathered with one accord in one place. It was then that that
place was shaken as with a rushing, mighty wind, and they
were all filled with the Holy Ghost. That same day, three
thousand were added to the Lord. Soon we hear they
have filled Jerusalem with their doctrine. The church
has commenced her march. Samaria has with one accord
believed the Gospel. Antioch has become obedient to the
faith. The name of Christ has been proclaimed throughout Asia Minor. The temples of the gods, as though
smitten by an invisible hand, are deserted. The citizens
of Ephesus cry out in despair, " Great is Diana of the
Ephesians!" Licentious Corinth is purified by the preaching of Christ crucified. Persecution puts forth her arm to
arrest the spreading "superstition." But the progress of
the faith cannot be stayed. The church of God advances
unhurt, amidst rocks and dungeons, persecutions and death ;
yea, " smiles at the drawn dagger, and defies its point."
She has entered Italy, and appears before the walls of the
Eternal City. Idolatry fails prostrate at her approach.
Her ensigns float in triumph over the capitol. She has
placed upon her brow the diadem of the Cæsars !

Mont Blanc in the Gleam of Sunset.—Griscom.

We arrived, before sundown, at the village of St. Martin, where we were to stay for the night. The evening
being remarkably fine, we crossed the Arve on a beautiful

bridge, and walked over to Salenche, a very considerable village, opposite to St. Martin, and ascended a hill to view the effect of the sun's declining light upon Mont Blanc. The scene was truly grand. The broad range of the mountain was fully before us, of a pure and almost glowing white, apparently to its very base; and which, contrasted with the brown tints of the adjoining mountains, greatly heightened the novelty of the scene. We could scarcely avoid the conclusion, that this vast pile of snow was very near us, and yet its base was not less than fifteen, and its summit, probably, more than twenty miles from the place where we stood. The varying rays of light produced by reflection from the snow, passing, as the sun's rays declined, from a brilliant white through purple and pink, and ending in the gentle light, which the snow gives after the sun has set, afforded an exhibition in optics upon a scale of grandeur, which no other region in the world could probably excel. Never in my life have my feelings been so powerfully affected by merely scenery as they were in this day's excursion. The excitement, though attended by sensations awfully impressive, is nevertheless so finely attempered by the glow of novelty incessantly mingled with astonishment and admiration, as to produce on the whole a feast of delight.

A few years ago, I stood upon Table Rock, and placed my cane in the descending flood of Niagara. Its tremendous roar almost entirely precluded conversation with the friend at my side; while its whirlwind of mist and foam filled the air to a great distance around me. The rainbow sported in its bosom; the gulf below exhibited the wild fury of an immense boiling caldron; while the rapids above, for the space of nearly a mile, appeared like a mountain of billows chafing and dashing against each other with thundering impetuosity, in their eager strife to gain the precipice, and take the awful leap. In contemplating this scene, my imagination and my heart were filled with sublime and tender emotions. The soul seemed to be brought a step nearer to the presence of that incomprehensible Being, whose spirit dwelt in every feature of the cataract, and directed all its amazing energies. Yet in the scenery of this day there was more of a pervading sense of awful and

unlimited grandeur : mountain piled upon mountain in endless continuity throughout the whole extent, and crowned
by the brightest effulgence of an evening sun, upon the
everlasting snows of the highest pinnacle of Europe.

Contrast in the Characters of Cicero and Atticus.—
BUCKMINSTER.

THE history of letters does not, at this moment, suggest
to me a more fortunate parallel between the effects of active
and of inactive learning, than in the well known characters of Cicero and Atticus   Let me hold them up to your
observation, not because Cicero was faultless, or Atticus
always to blame, but because, like you, they were the citizens of a republic.   They lived in an age of learning and
of dangers, and acted upon opposite principles, when Rome
was to be saved, if saved at all, by the virtuous energy of
her most accomplished minds.

If we look now for Atticus, we find him in the quiet of
his library, surrounded by his books; while Cicero was
passing through the regular course of public honours and
services, where all the treasures of his mind were at the
command of his country.   If we follow them, we find Atticus pleasantly wandering among the ruins of Athens,
purchasing up statues and antiques; while Cicero was at
home, blasting the projects of Catiline, and, at the head of
the senate, like the tutelary spirit of his country, as the
storm was gathering, secretly watching the doubtful movements of Cæsar.   If we look to the period of the civil
wars, we find Atticus always reputed, indeed, to belong to
the party of the friends of liberty, yet originally dear to
Sylla, and intimate with Clodius, recommending himself
to Cæsar by his neutrality, courted by Antony, and connected with Octavius, poorly concealing the Epicureanism
of his principles under the ornaments of literature and the
splendour of his benefactions ; till at last this inoffensive
and polished friend of successive usurpers hastens out of
life to escape from the pains of a lingering disease.   Turn

now to Cicero, the only great man at whom Cæsar always
trembled, the only great man, whom falling Rome did *not*
fear. Do you tell me that his hand once offered incense
to the dictator? Remember, it was the gift of gratitude
only, and not of servility; for the same hand launched its
indignation against the infamous Antony, whose power was
more to be dreaded, and whose revenge pursued him till
his father of his country gave his head to the executioner
without a struggle, for he knew that Rome was no longer
to be saved. If, my friends, you would feel what learning, and genius, and virtue, should aspire to in a day of
peril and depravity, when you are tired of the factions of
the city, the battles of Cæsar, the crimes of the triumvi-
rate, and the splendid court of Augustus, do not go and
repose in the easy-chair of Atticus, but refresh your virtues and your spirits with the contemplation of Cicero.

Scenery in the Highlands on the River Hudson.—IRVING.

IN the second day of the voyage they came to the Highlands. It was the latter part of a calm, sultry day, that they
floated gently with the tide between these stern mountains.
There was that perfect quiet, which prevails over nature
in the languor of summer heat; the turning of a plank,
or the accidental falling of an oar on deck, was echoed
from the mountain side, and reverberated along the shores;
and if by chance the captain gave a shout of command,
there were airy tongues that mocked it from every cliff.

Dolph gazed about him in mute delight and wonder at
these scenes of nature's magnificence. To the left the
Dunderberg reared its woody precipices, height over height,
forest over forest, away into the deep summer sky. To
the right strutted forth the bold promontory of Antony's
Nose, with a solitary eagle wheeling about it; while beyond, mountain succeeded to mountain, until they seemed to lock their arms together, and confine this mighty river in their embraces. There was a feeling of quiet luxury
in gazing at the broad, green bosoms here and there scoop-

ed out among the precipices; or at woodlands high in air, nodding over the edge of some beetling bluff, and their foliage all transparent in the yellow sunshine.

In the midst of his admiration, Dolph remarked a pile of bright, snowy clouds peering above the western heights. It was succeeded by another, and another, each seemingly pushing onwards its predecessor, and towering, with dazzling brilliancy, in the deep blue atmosphere: and now muttering peals of thunder were faintly heard rolling behind the mountains. The river, hitherto still and glassy, reflecting pictures of the sky and land, now showed a dark ripple at a distance, as the breeze came creeping up it. The fish hawks wheeled and screamed, and sought their nests on the high dry trees; the crows flew clamorously to the crevices of the rocks, and all nature seemed conscious of the approaching thunder-gust.

The clouds now rolled in volumes over the mountain tops; their summits still bright and snowy, but the lower parts of an inky blackness. The rain began to patter down in broad and scattered drops; the wind freshened, and curled up the waves; at length it seemed as if the bellying clouds were torn open by the mountain tops, and complete torrents of rain came rattling down. The lightning leaped from cloud to cloud, and streamed quivering against the rocks, splitting and rending the stoutest forest trees. The thunder burst in tremendous explosions; the peals were echoed from mountain to mountain; they crashed upon Dunderberg, and then rolled up the long defile of the Highlands, each headland making a new echo, until old Bull Hill seemed to bellow back the storm.

For a time, the scudding rack and mist, and the sheeted rain, almost hid the landscape from the sight. There was a fearful gloom, illumined still more fearfully by the streams of lightning, which glittered among the rain drops. Never had Dolph beheld such an absolute warring of the elements; it seemed as if the storm was tearing and rending its way through this mountain defile, and had brought all the artillery of heaven into action.

The vessel was hurried on by the increasing wind, until she came to where the river makes a sudden bend, the only one in the whole course of its majestic career.* Just as they turned the point, a violent flaw of wind came sweeping down a mountain gully, bending the forest before it, and, in a moment, lashing up the river into white froth and foam. The captain saw the danger, and cried out to lower the sail. Before the order could be obeyed, the flaw struck the sloop, and threw her on her beam-ends. Every thing now was fright and confusion: the flapping of the sails, the whistling and rushing of the wind, the bawling of the captain and crew, the shrieking of the passengers, all mingled with the rolling and bellowing of the thunder. In the midst of the uproar the sloop righted; at the same time the mainsail shifted, the boom came sweeping the quarter deck, and Dolph, who was gazing unguardedly at the clouds, found himself, in a moment, floundering in the river.

For once in his life, one of his idle accomplishments was of use to him. The many truant hours which he had devoted to sporting in the Hudson had made him an expert swimmer; yet, with all his strength and skill, he found great difficulty in reaching the shore. His disappearance from the deck had not been noticed by the crew, who were all occupied with their own danger. The sloop was driven along with inconceivable rapidity. She had hard work to weather a long promontory on the eastern shore, round which the river turned, and which completely shut her from Dolph's view.

It was on a point of the western shore that he landed, and, scrambling up the rocks, he threw himself, faint and exhausted, at the foot of a tree. By degrees the thunder-gust passed over. The clouds rolled away to the east, where they lay piled in feathery masses, tinted with the last rosy rays of the sun. The distant play of the lightning might be still seen about their dark bases, and now and then might be heard the faint muttering of the thunder. Dolph rose, and sought about to see if any path led from the shore, but all was savage and trackless. The rocks were piled upon each other; great trunks of trees lay shattered about, as they had been blown down by the

---

* This must have been the bend at West Point

strong winds which draw through these mountains, or had fallen through age. The rocks, too, were overhung with wild vines and briers, which completely matted themselves together, and opposed a barrier to all ingress ; every movement that he made shook down a shower from the dripping foliage. He attempted to scale one of these almost perpendicular heights ; but, though strong and agile, he found it an Herculean undertaking. Often he was supported merely by crumbling projections of the rock, and sometimes he clung to roots and branches of trees, and hung almost suspended in the air. The wood-pigeon came cleaving his whistling flight by him, and the eagle screamed from the brow of the impending cliff. As he was thus clambering, he was on the point of seizing hold of a shrub to aid his ascent, when something rustled among the leaves, and he saw a snake quivering along like lightning, almost from under his hand. It coiled itself up immediately, in an attitude of defiance, with flattened head, distended jaws, and quickly vibrating tongue, that played like a little flame about its mouth. Dolph's heart turned faint within him, and he had well nigh let go his hold, and tumbled down the precipice. The serpent stood on the defensive but for an instant ; it was an instinctive movement of defence ; and, finding there was no attack, it glided away into a cleft of the rock. Dolph's eye followed it with fearful intensity ; and he saw at a glance that he was in the vicinity of a nest of adders, that lay knotted, and writhing, and hissing in the chasm. He hastened with all speed to escape from so frightful a neighbourhood. His imagination was full of this new horror ; he saw an adder in every curling vine, and heard the tail of a rattle-snake in every dry leaf that rustled.

At length he succeeded in scrambling to the summit of a precipice ; but it was covered by a dense forest. Wherever he could gain a look out between the trees, he saw that the coast rose into heights and cliffs, one rising beyond another, until huge mountains overtopped the whole. There were no signs of cultivation, nor any smoke curling amongst the trees to indicate a human residence. Every thing was wild and solitary. As he was standing on the edge of a precipice that overlooked a deep ravine fringed with trees,

30

his feet detached a great fragment of rock; it fell, crash
ing its way through the tree tops, down into the chasm. A
loud whoop, or rather a yell, issued from the bottom of the
glen; the moment after there was the report of a gun;
and a ball came whistling over his head, cutting the twigs
and leaves, and burying itself deep in the bark of a chest-
nut-tree.

Dolph did not wait for a second shot, but made a precipitate retreat; fearing every moment to hear the enemy
in pursuit. He succeeded, however, in returning unmo
lested to the shore, and determined to penetrate no farther
into a country so beset with savage perils.

He sat himself down, dripping, disconsolately, on a wet
stone. What was to be done? where was he to shelter
himself? The hour of repose was approaching; the birds
were seeking their nests, the bat began to flit about in the
twilight, and the night hawk, soaring high in heaven, seemed to be calling out the stars. Night gradually closed in,
and wrapped every thing in gloom; and though it was the
latter part of summer, yet the breeze, stealing along the
river, and among these dripping forests, was chilly and
penetrating, especially to a half-drowned man.

Eternity of God.—GREENWOOD.

WE receive such repeated intimations of decay in the
world through which we are passing; decline and change
and loss, follow decline and change and loss in such rapid
succession, that we can almost catch the sound of universal wasting, and hear the work of desolation going on busily
around us. "The mountain, falling, cometh to nought,
and the rock is removed out of his place. The waters
wear the stones, the things which grow out of the dust of
the earth are washed away, and the hope of man is destroyed." Conscious of our own instability, we look about
for something to rest on, but we look in vain. The heavens and the earth had a beginning, and they will have an
end. The face of the world is changing daily and hourly.
All animated things grow old and die. The rocks crum-

ble, the trees fall, the leaves fade, and the grass withers. The clouds are flying, and the waters are flowing away from us.

The firmest works of man, too, are gradually giving way ; the ivy clings to the mouldering tower, the brier hangs out from the shattered window, and the wall-flower springs from the disjointed stones. The founders of these perishable works have shared the same fate long ago. If we look back to the days of our ancestors, to the men as well as the dwellings of former times, they become immediately associated in our imaginations, and only make the feeling of instability stronger and deeper than before. In the spacious domes, which once held our fathers, the serpent hisses, and the wild bird screams. The halls, which once were crowded with all that taste, and science, and labour could procure, which resounded with melody, and were lighted up with beauty, are buried by their own ruins, mocked by their own desolation. The voice of merriment, and of wailing, the steps of the busy and the idle, have ceased in the deserted courts, and the weeds choke the entrances, and the long grass waves upon the hearthstone. The works of art, the forming hand, the tombs, the very ashes they contained, are all gone

While we thus walk among the ruins of the past, a sad feeling of insecurity comes over us ; and that feeling is by no means diminished when we arrive at home. If we turn to our friends, we can hardly speak to them before they bid us farewell. We see them for a few moments, and in a few moments more their countenances are changed, and they are sent away. It matters not how near and dear they are. The ties which bind us together are never too close to be parted, or too strong to be broken. Tears were never known to move the king of terrors, neither is it enough that we are compelled to surrender one, or two, or many of those we love ; for, though the price is so great, we buy no favour with it, and our hold on those who remain is as slight as ever. The shadows all elude our grasp, and follow one another down the valley. We gain no confidence, then, no feeling of security, by turning to our contemporaries and kindred. We know that the forms, which are breathing around us, are as short-lived as those

were, which have been dust for centuries. The sensation
of vanity, uncertainty, and ruin, is equally strong, whether we muse on what has long been prostrate, or gaze on
what is falling now, or will fall so soon.

If every thing which comes under our notice has en
dured for so short a time, and in so short a time will be no
more, we cannot say that we receive the least assurance
by thinking on ourselves. When they, on whose fate we
have been meditating, were engaged in the active scenes
of life, as full of health and hope as we are now, what
were we ? We had no knowledge, no consciousness, no
being ; there was not a single thing in the wide universe
which knew us. And after the same interval shall have
elapsed, which now divides their days from ours, what
shall we be ? What they are now. When a few more
friends have left, a few more hopes deceived, and a few
more changes mocked us, " we shall be brought to the
grave, and shall remain in the tomb : the clods of the valley shall be sweet unto us, and every man shall draw after
us, as there are innumerable before us." All power will have
forsaken the strongest, and the loftiest will be laid low, and
every eye will be closed, and every voice hushed, and
every heart will have ceased its beating. And when we
have gone ourselves, even our memories will not stay behind us long. A few of the near and dear will bear our
likeness in their bosoms, till they too have arrived at the
end of their journey, and entered the dark dwelling of un-
consciousness. In the thoughts of others we shall live
only till the last sound of the bell, which informs them of
our departure, has ceased to vibrate in their ears. A stone,
perhaps, may tell some wanderer where we lie, when we
came here, and when we went away ; but even that will
soon refuse to bear us record : " time's effacing fingers"
will be busy on its surface, and at length will wear it
smooth ; and then the stone itself will sink or crumble,
and the wanderer of another age will pass, without a single call upon his sympathy, over our unheeded graves.

Is there nothing to counteract the sinking of the heart,
which must be the effect of observations like these ? Is
there no substance among all these shadows ? If all who
live and breathe around us are the creatures of yesterday

and destined to see destruction to-morrow; if the same condition is our own, and the same sentence is written against us; if the solid forms of inanimate nature and laborious art are fading and falling; if we look in vain for durability to the very roots of mountains, where shall we return, and on what shall we rely? Can no support be offered? can no source of confidence be named? Oh yes! there is one Being, to whom we can look with a perfect conviction of finding that security, which nothing about us can give, and which nothing about us can take away To this Being we can lift up our souls, and on him we may rest them, exclaiming, in the language of the monarch of Israel, " Before the mountains were brought forth, or ever thou hadst formed the earth and the world, even from everlasting to everlasting thou art God. Of old hast thou laid the foundations of the earth, and the heavens are the work of thy hands. They shall perish, but thou shalt endure; yea, all of them shall wax old like a garment, as a vesture shalt thou change them, and they shall be changed , but thou art the same, and thy years shall have no end."

The eternity of God is a subject of contemplation, which, at the same time that it overwhelms us with astonishment and awe, affords us an immoveable ground of confidence in the midst of a changing world. All things which sur· round us, all these dying, mouldering inhabitants of time, must have had a Creator, for the plain reason, that they could not have created themselves. And their Creator must have existed from all eternity, for the plain reason, that the first cause must necessarily be uncaused. As we cannot suppose a beginning without a cause of existence, that which is the cause of all existence must be self-existent, and could have had no beginning. And, as it had no beginning, so also, as it is beyond the reach of all influence and control, as it is independent and almighty, it will have no end.

Here then is a support, which will never fail; here is a foundation, which can never be moved—the everlasting Creator of countless worlds, " the high and lofty One that inhabiteth eternity." What a sublime conception ! *He inhabits eternity,* occupies this inconceivable duration pervades and fills throughout his boundless dwelling

30 *

Ages on ages before even the dust of which we are formed was created, he had existed in infinite majesty, and ages
on ages will roll away, after we have all returned to the
dust whence we were taken, and still he will exist in infinite majesty, living in the eternity of his own nature,
reigning in the plenitude of his own omnipotence, forever
sending forth the word, which forms, supports and governs
all things, commanding new-created light to shine on new-
created worlds, and raising up new-created generations to
inhabit them.

The contemplation of these glorious attributes of God
is fitted to excite in our minds the most animating and con-
soling reflections. Standing, as we are, amid the ruins of
time, and the wrecks of mortality, where every thing about
us is created and dependent, proceeding from nothing, and
hastening to destruction, we rejoice that something is presented to our view, which has stood from everlasting,
and will remain forever. When we have looked on the
pleasures of life, and they have vanished away ; when we
have looked on the works of nature, and perceived that
they were changing ; on the monuments of art, and seen
that they would not stand ; on our friends, and they have
fled, while we were gazing ; on ourselves, and felt that
we were as fleeting as they ; when we have looked on
every object to which we could turn our anxious eyes, and
they have all told us that they could give us no hope nor
support, because they were so feeble themselves,—we can
look to the throne of God : change and decay have never
reached that ; the revolution of ages has never moved it ;
the waves of an eternity have been rushing past it, but it
has remained unshaken ; the waves of another eternity
are rushing toward it, but it is fixed, and can never be disturbed.

And blessed be God, who has assured us, by a revelation
from himself, that the throne of eternity is likewise a throne
of mercy and love ; who has permitted and invited us to
repose ourselves and our hopes on that which al e is everlasting and unchangeab e. We shall soon y finish our
allotted time on earth, even i. it should be constantly prolonged. We shall leave behind us all which is now familiar and beloved, and a world of other days and other

men will be entirely ignorant that once we lived.   But the same unalterable Being will still preside over the universe, through all its changes, and from his remembrance we shall never be blotted.   We can never be where he is not, nor where he sees and loves and upholds us not.   He is our Father and our God forever.   He takes us from earth that he may lead us to heaven, that he may refine our nature from all its principles of corruption, share with us his own immortality, admit us to his everlasting habitation, and crown us with his eternity.

Philosophy and Morality of Tacitus.—FRISBIE.

IT is not for his style, that we principally admire this author: his profound views of the human heart, his just developement of the principles of action, his delicate touches of nature, his love of liberty and independence, and, above all, the moral sensibility, which mingles, and incorporates itself with all his descriptions, are the qualities, which must ever render him a favourite with the friends of philosophy and of man.

Tacitus has been truly called the philosopher of historians; but his philosophy never arrays itself in the robe of the schools, or enters into a formal investigation of causes and motives.   It seems to show itself here and there, in the course of his facts, involuntarily, and from its own fulness, by the manner of narration, by a single word, and sometimes by a general observation.   Events, in his hands, have a soul, which is constantly displaying its secret workings by the attitude, into which it throws the body, by a glance of the eye, or an expression of the face, and now and then a sudden utterance of its emotions.   It is not the prince, the senator, or the plebeian, that he describes; it is always man, and the general principles of human nature; and this in their nicer and more evanescent, as well as their boldest and most definite expressions.   If we were not afraid of giving too violent a shock to classical devotees, we should say, that, in the particulars we have mentioned, Tacitus in history is not unlike Miss Edgeworth in fiction

There are, indeed, many circumstances, unnecessary to be
pointed out, in which they differ ; but there is in both the
same frequent interspersion in the narrative of short remarks, which lay open a principle of human nature, the
same concise developement of character by discrimination
and contrast, and the nice selection of some one trait, or
apparently trifling circumstance, of conduct, as a key to
the whole ; traits and circumstances, which, though none
but a philosopher would have pointed out, find their way
at once to every heart. But the historian has none of the
playfulness, the humour, and the mind at ease, which are
seen in the novelist. He knew himself the register of
facts, and facts, too, in which he took the deepest interest.
He records events, not as one curious in political relations,
or revolutions in empires, but as marking the moral character and condition of the age ; a character and condition,
which he felt were exerting a direct and powerful influence upon himself, upon those whom he loved, and with
whom he lived.

The moral sensibility of Tacitus is, we think, that particular circumstance, by which he so deeply engages his
reader, and is perhaps distinguished from every other writer, in the same department of literature ; and the scenes
he was to describe peculiarly required this quality. His
writings comprise a period the most corrupt within the
annals of man. The reigns of the Neros, and of many
of their successors, seemed to have brought together the
opposite vices of extreme barbarism and excessive luxury ;
the most ferocious cruelty and slavish submission ; voluptuousness the most effeminate, and sensuality worse than
brutal. Not only all the general charities of life, but the
very ties of nature were annihilated by a selfishness, the
most exclusively individual. The minions of power butch-
ered the parent, and the child hurried to thank the emperor for his goodness. The very fountains of abominations
seemed to have been broken up, and to have poured over
the face of society a deluge of pollution and crimes. How
important was it, then, for posterity, that the records of
such an era should be transmitted by one in whose personal character there should be a redeeming virtue, who
would himself feel, and awaken in his readers, that disgust

and abhorrence, which such scenes ought to excite! Such a one was Tacitus. There is in his narrative a seriousness, approaching sometimes almost to melancholy, and sometimes bursting forth in expressions of virtuous indignation. He appears always to be aware of the general complexion of the subjects, of which he is treating; and, even when extraordinary instances of independence and integrity now and then present themselves, you perceive, that his mind is secretly contrasting them with those vices, with which his observation was habitually familiar. Thus, in describing the pure and simple manners of the barbarous tribes of the north, you find him constantly bringing forward and dwelling upon those virtues, which were most strikingly opposed to the enormities of civilized Rome. He could not, like his contemporary Juvenal, treat these enormities with sneering and sarcasm. To be able to laugh at vice, he thought a symptom, that one had been touched at least by its pollution; or, to use his words, and illustrate, at once, both of the remarks we have just made; speaking of the temperance and chastity of the Germans, he says, "Nemo enim illic ridet vitia, nec corrumpere et corrumpi sæculum vocatur." Therefore it is, that, in reading Tacitus, our interest in events is heightened by a general sympathy with the writer; and as, in most instances, it is an excellence, when we lose the author in his story, so, in this, it is no less an excellence, that we have him so frequently in our minds. It is not, that he obtrudes himself upon our notice, but that we involuntarily, though not unconsciously, see with his eyes, and feel with his feelings.

In estimating, however, the moral sentiment of this historian, we are not to judge him by the present standard, elevated and improved as it is by Christianity. Tacitus undoubtedly felt the influence of great and prevalent errors. That war with barbarians was at all times just, and their territory and their persons the lawful prey of whatever nation could seize them, it is well known, had been always the practical maxim of the Greeks, as well as the Romans. Hence we are not to be surprised, that, in various passages of his work, he does not express that abhorrence of many wars, in which his countrymen were engaged, which we might otherwise have expected from him. This apology must especially be borne in mind, as we read the life of Agricola. The invasion of Britain by the Romans was as truly a violation of the rights of justice and humanity, as that of Mexico and Peru by the Spaniards; and their leader little better in principle, than Cortez and Pizarro. Yet, even here, full as was Tacitus of the glory of his father-in-law and of Rome, we have frequent indications of sensibility to the wrongs of the oppressed and plundered islanders. The well known speech of Calgaeus breathes all the author's love of liberty and virtue, and exhibits the simple virtues, the generous self-devotion, of the Caledonians, in their last struggle for independence, in powerful contrast with the vices and ambition of their cruel and rapacious invaders.

We have mentioned what appears to us the most striking characteristics of the author before us. When compared with his great predecessor, he is no less excellent, but essentially different. Livy is only a historian, Tacitus is also a philosopher; the former gives you images, the latter impressions. In the narration of events, Livy produces his effect by completeness and exact particularity, Tacitus by selection and condensation; the one presents to you a panorama—you have the whole scene, with all its complicated movements and various appearances vividly before you; the other shows you the most prominent and remarkable groups, and compensates in depth for what he wants in minuteness. Livy hurries you into the midst of the battle, and leaves you to be borne along by its tide: Tacitus stands with you upon an eminence, where you have more tranquillity for distinct observation; or perhaps, when the armies have retired, walks with you over the field; points out to you the spot of each most interesting particular, and shares with you those solemn and profound emotions, which you have now the composure to feel.

The Village Grave-Yard.—GREENWOOD

"Why is my sleep disquieted?
Who is he that calls the dead?"—BYRON.

IN the beginning of the fine month of October, I was
travelling with a friend in one of our northern states, on a
tour of recreation and pleasure. We were tired of the
city, its noise, its smoke, and its unmeaning dissipation; and,
with the feelings of emancipated prisoners, we had been
breathing, for a few weeks, the perfume of the vales, and
the elastic atmosphere of the uplands. Some minutes before the sunset of a most lovely day, we entered a neat
little village, whose tapering spire we had caught sight of
at intervals an hour before, as our road made an unexpected turn, or led us to the top of a hill. Having no motive
to urge a farther progress, and being unwilling to ride in
an unknown country after night-fall, we stopped at the inn,
and determined to lodge there.

Leaving my companion to arrange our accommodations
with the landlord, I strolled on toward the meeting-house.
Its situation had attracted my notice. There was much
more taste and beauty in it than is common. It did not
stand, as I have seen some meeting-houses stand, in the most
frequented part of the village, blockaded by wagons and
horses, with a court-house before it, an engine-house behind it, a store-house under it, and a tavern on each side;
it stood away from all these things, as it ought, and was
placed on a spot of gently rising ground, a short distance
from the main road, at the end of a green lane; and so
near to a grove of oaks and walnuts, that one of the
foremost and largest trees brushed against the pulpit window. On the left, and lower down, there was a fertile
meadow, through which a clear brook wound its course,
fell over a rock, and then hid itself in the thickest part of
the grove. A little to the right of the meeting-house was
the grave-yard.

I never shun a grave-yard—the thoughtful melancholy
which it inspires is grateful rather than disagreeable to
me—it gives me no pain to tread on the green roof of that
dark mansion, whose chambers I must occupy so soon—

and I often wander from choice to a place, where there is
neither solitude nor society—something human is there—
but the folly, the bustle, the vanities, the pretensions, the
competitions, the pride of humanity, are gone—men are
there, but their passions are hushed, and their spirits are
still—malevolence has lost its power of harming—appetite
is sated, ambition lies low, and lust is cold—anger has done
raving, all disputes are ended, all revelry is over, the fell
est animosity is deeply buried, and the most dangerous sins
are safely confined by the thickly-piled clods of the valley
—vice is dumb and powerless, and virtue is waiting in
silence for the trump of the archangel, and the voice of
God.

I never shun a grave-yard, and I entered this. There
were trees growing in it, here and there, though it was
not regularly planted; and I thought that it looked better
than if it had been. The only paths were those, which
had been worn by the slow feet of sorrow and sympathy,
as they followed love and friendship to the grave; and this
too was well, for I dislike a smoothly rolled gravel-walk in a
place like this. In a corner of the ground rose a gentle
knoll, the top of which was covered by a clump of pines.
Here my walk ended; I threw myself down on the slippery couch of withered pine leaves, which the breath of
many winters had shaken from the boughs above, leaned
my head upon my hand, and gave myself up to the feelings
which the place and the time excited.

The sun's edge had just touched the hazy outlines of
the western hills; it was the signal for the breeze to be
hushed, and it was breathing like an expiring infant, softly
and at distant intervals, before it died away. The trees before me, as the wind passed over them, waved to and fro,
and trailed their long branches across the tomb-stones, with
a low, moaning sound, which fell upon the ear like the voice
of grief, and seemed to utter the conscious tribute of nature's sympathy over the last abode of mortal man. A
low, confused hum came from the village; the brook was
murmuring in the wood behind me; and, lulled by all these
soothing sounds, I fell asleep.

But whether my eyes closed or not, I am unable to say,
for the same scene appeared to be before them, the same

trees were waving, and not a green mound had changed
ts form. I was still contemplating the same trophies of
the unsparing victor, the same mementos of human evan-
escence. Some were standing upright; others were inclined to the ground; some were sunk so deeply in the
earth, that their blue tops were just visible above the long
grass which surrounded them; and others were spotted or
covered with the thin yellow moss of the grave-yard. I
was reading the inscriptions on the stones, which were
nearest to me—they recorded the virtues of those who slept
beneath them, and told the traveller that they hoped for a
happy rising. Ah! said I—or I dreamed that I said so—
this is the testimony of wounded hearts—the fond belief
of that affection, which remembers error and evil no longer; but could the grave give up its dead—could they, who
have been brought to these cold dark houses, go back again
into the land of the living, and once more number the
days which they had spent there, how differently would
they then spend them! and when they came to die, how
much firmer would be their hope! and when they were
again laid in the ground, how much more faithful would
be the tales, which these same stones would tell over them!
the epitaph of praise would be well deserved by their virtues, and the silence of partiality no longer required for
their sins.

I had scarcely spoken, when the ground began to trem
ble beneath me. Its motion, hardly perceptible at first,
increased every moment in violence, and it soon heaved
and struggled fearfully; while in the short quiet between
shock and shock, I heard such unearthly sounds, that the
very blood in my heart felt cold—subterraneous cries and
groans issued from every part of the grave-yard, and these
were mingled with a hollow crashing noise, as if the mouldering bones were bursting from their coffins. Suddenly
all these sounds stopped—the earth on each grave was
thrown up—and human figures of every age, and clad in
the garments of death, rose from the ground, and stood by
the side of their grave-stones. Their arms were crossed
upon their bosoms—their countenances were deadly pale,
and raised to heaven. The looks of the young children
alone were placid and unconscious—but over the features

31

of all the rest a shadow of unutterable meaning passed and
repassed, as their eyes turned with terror from the open
graves, and strained anxiously upward. Some appeared
to be more calm than others, and when they looked above,
it was with an expression of more confidence, though not
less humility ; but a convulsive shuddering was on the
frames of all, and on their faces that same shadow of unutterable meaning. While they stood thus, I perceived that
their bloodless lips began to move, and, though I heard no
voice, I knew, by the motion of their lips, that the word
would have been—Pardon !

But this did not continue long—they gradually became
more fearless—their features acquired the appearance of
security, and at last of indifference—the blood came to
their lips—the shuddering ceased, and the shadow passed
away.

And now the scene before me changed. The tombs and
grave-stones had been turned, I knew not how, into dwellings—and the grave-yard became a village. Every now
and then I caught a view of the same faces and forms,
which I had seen before—but other passions were traced
upon their faces, and their forms were no longer clad in
the garments of death. The silence of their still prayer
was succeeded by the sounds of labour, and society, and
merriment. Sometimes, I could see them meet together
with inflamed features and angry words, and sometimes I
distinguished the outcry of violence, the oath of passion,
and the blasphemy of sin. And yet there were a few
who would often come to the threshold of their dwellings,
and lift their eyes to heaven, and utter the still prayer of
pardon—while others passing by would mock them.

I was astonished and grieved, and was just going to express my feelings, when I perceived by my side a beautiful and majestic form, taller and brighter than the sons of
men, and it thus addressed me—" Mortal ! thou hast now
seen the frailty of thy race, and learned that thy thoughts
were vain. Even if men should be wakened from their
cold sleep, and raised from the grave, the world would still
be full of enticement and trials ; appetite would solicit and
passion would burn, as strongly as before—the imperfec
tions of their nature would accompany their return, and

the commerce of life would soon obliterate the recollection of death. It is only when this scene of things is exchanged for another, that new gifts will bestow new powers, that higher objects will banish low desires, that the mind will be elevated by celestial converse, the soul be endued with immortal vigour, and man be prepared for the course of eternity." The angel then turned from me, and with a voice, which I hear even now, cried, " Back to your graves, ye frail ones, and rise no more, till the elements are melted." Immediately a sound swept by me, like the rushing wind—the dwellings shrunk back into their original forms, and I was left alone in the grave-yard, with nought but the silent stones and the whispering trees around me.

The sun had long been down—a few of the largest stars were timidly beginning to shine, the bats had left their lurking places, my cheek was wet with the dew, and I was chilled by the breath of evening. I arose, and returned to the inn.

Influence of the Habit of Gaming on the Mind and Heart.—NOTT.

IF an occupation were demanded for the express purpose of perverting the human intellect, and humbling, and degrading, and narrowing, I had almost said, annihilating, the soul of man, one more effectual could not be devised, than the one the gamester has already devised and pre-occupied. ¶And the father and mother of a family, who, instead of assembling their children in the reading-room, or conducting them to the altar, seat them, night after night, beside themselves at the gaming-table, do, so far as this part of their domestic economy is concerned, contribute not only to quench their piety, but also to extinguish their intellect, and convert them into automatons, living mummies, the mere mechanical members of a domestic gambling machine, which, though but little soul is necessary, requires a number of human hands to work it.¶And if, under such a blighting culture, they do not degenerate into a state of mechanical existence, and, gradually losing their reason, their taste, their fancy, become incapable of conversation, the fortunate parents may thank the school-house, the church, the library, the society of friends, or some other and less wretched part of their own defective system, for preventing the consummation of so frightful a result.

Such are the morbid and sickly effects of play on the human intellect. But intelligence constitutes no inconsiderable part of the glory of man; a glory which, unless eclipsed by crime, increases, as intelligence increases. Knowledge is desirable with reference to this world, but principally so with reference to the next; not because philosophy, or language, or mathematics, will certainly be pursued in heaven, but because the pursuit of them on earth gradually communicates that quickness of perception, that acumen, which, as it increases, approximates towards the sublime and sudden intuition of celestial intelligences, and which cannot fail to render more splendid the commencement, as well as more splendid the progression, of man's interminable career.

But, while gaming leaves the *mind* to languish, it produces its full effect *on the passions and on the heart.* Here, however, that effect is deleterious. None of the sweet and amiable sympathies are at the card-table called into action. No throb of ingenuous and philanthropic feeling is excited by this detestable expedient for killing time, as it is called; and it is rightly so called; for many a murdered hour will witness, at the day of judgment, against that fashionable idler, who divides her time between her toilet and the card-table, no less than against the profligate, hackneyed in the ways of sin, and steeped in all the filth and debauchery of gambling. But it is only amidst the filth and debauchery of gambling, that the full effects of card-playing on the passions and on the heart of man are seen.

Here that mutual amity that elsewhere subsists, ceases; paternal affection ceases; even that community of feeling that piracy excites, and that binds the very banditti together, has no room to operate; for, at this inhospitable board, every man's interest clashes with every man's interest, and every man's hand is literally against every man.

The love of mastery and the love of money are the purest loves, of which the gamester is susceptible. And even the love of mastery loses all its nobleness, and degenerates into the love of lucre, which ultimately predominates, and becomes the ruling passion.

Avarice is always base; but the gamester's avarice is doubly so. It is avarice unmixed with any ingredient of magnanimity or mercy; avarice, that wears not even the guise of public spirit; that claims not even the meager praise of hoarding up its own hard earnings. On the contrary, it is an avarice, that wholly feeds upon the losses, and only delights itself with the miseries, of others; avarice, that eyes, with covetous desire, whatever is not individually its own; that crouches to throw its fangs over that booty, by which its comrades are enriched; avarice, that stoops to rob a traveller, that sponges a guest, and that would filch the very dust from the pocket of a friend.

But though avarice predominates, other related passions are called into action. The bosom, that was once serene and tranquil, becomes habitually perturbed. Envy rankles; jealousy corrodes; anger rages; and hope and fear alternately convulse the system. The mildest disposition grows morose; the sweetest temper becomes fierce and fiery, and all the once amiable features of the heart assume a malignant aspect! Features of the *heart*, did I say? Pardon my mistake. The finished gambler has none. Though his intellect may not be, though his soul may not be, his heart is quite annihilated.

Thus habitual gambling consummates what habitual play commences. Sometimes its deadening influence prevails, even over female virtue, eclipsing all the loveliness, and benumbing all the sensibility of woman. In every circle, where cards form the bond of union, frivolity and heartlessness become alike characteristic of the mother and the daughter; devotion ceases; domestic care is shaken off, and the dearest friends, even before their burial, are consigned to oblivion.

This is not exaggeration. I appeal to fact. Madame du Deffand was certainly not among the least accomplished females, who received and imparted that exquisite tone of feeling, that pervaded the most fashionable society of modern

31 *

Paris. And yet it is recorded of her, in the correspondence of the Baron De Grimm, whose veracity will not be questioned, that when her old and intimate friend and admirer, M. de Ponte de Vesle, died, this celebrated lady came rather late to a great supper in the neighbourhood; and as it was known that she made it a point of honour to attend him, the catastrophe was generally suspected. She mentioned it, however, herself, immediately on entering; adding, that it was lucky he had gone off so early in the evening, as she might otherwise have been prevented from appearing. She then sat down to table, and made a very hearty and merry meal of it.

Afterwards, when Madame de Chatelet died, Madame du Deffand testified her grief for the most intimate of all her female acquaintance, by circulating over Paris, the very next morning, the most libellous and venomous attack on her person, her understanding, and her morals.

This utter heartlessness, this entire extinction of native feeling, was not peculiar to Madame du Deffand; it pervaded that accomplished and fashionable circle, in which she moved. Hence she herself, in her turn, experienced the same kind of sympathy, and her remembrance was consigned to the same instantaneous oblivion. During her last illness, three of her dearest friends used to come and play cards, every night, by the side of her couch; and, as she chose to die in the middle of a very interesting game, they quietly played it out, and settled their accounts before leaving the apartment.

I do not say that such are the uniform, but I do say, that such are the natural and legitimate, effects of gaming on the female character. The love of play is a demon, which only takes possession as it kills the heart. But if such is the effect of gaming, on the one sex, what must be its effect upon the other? Will nature long survive in bosoms invaded, not by gaming only, but also by debauchery and drunkenness, those sister furies, which hell has let loose, to cut off our young men from without, and our children from the streets? No, it will not. As we have said, the finished gambler has no heart. The club, with which he herds, would meet, though all its members were in mourning. They would meet, though it were in an apartment of

the charnel-house. Not even the death of kindred can
affect the gambler. He would play upon his brother's coffin, he would play upon his father's sepulchre.

The Preservation of the Church.—MASON.

THE long existence of the Christian Church would be
pronounced, upon common principles of reasoning, impossible. She finds in every man a natural and inveterate
enemy. To encounter and overcome the unanimous hostility of the world, she boasts no political stratagem, no disciplined legions, no outward coercion of any kind. Yet
her expectation is that she will live forever. To mock
this hope, and to blot out her memorial from under heaven,
the most furious efforts of fanaticism, the most ingenious
arts of statesmen, the concentrated strength of empires,
have been frequently and perseveringly applied. The blood
of her sons and her daughters has streamed like water;
the smoke of the scaffold and the stake, where they wore
the crown of martyrdom in the cause of Jesus, has ascended in thick volumes to the skies. The tribes of persecution have sported over her woes, and erected monuments,
as they imagined, of her perpetual ruin. But where are
her tyrants, and where their empires? The tyran's have
long since gone to their own place; their names have descended upon the roll of infamy; their empires have passed, like shadows over the rock; they have successively disappeared, and left not a trace behind!

But what became of the Church? She rose from her
ashes fresh in beauty and might; celestial glory beamed
around her; she dashed down the monumental marble of
her foes, and they who hated her fled before her She has
celebrated the funeral of kings and kingdoms that plotted
her destruction; and, with the inscriptions of their pride,
has transmitted to posterity the records of their shame.
How shall this phenomenon be explained? We are, at
the present moment, witnesses of the fact; but who can
unfold the mystery? The book of truth and life has made
our wonder to cease. "THE LORD HER GOD IN THE

MIDST OF HER IS MIGHTY." His presence is a fountain
of health, and his protection a " wall of fire." He has
betrothed her, in eternal covenant, to himself. Her living
Head, in whom she lives, is above, and his quickening
spirit shall never depart from her. Armed with divine virtue, his Gospel, secret, silent, unobserved, enters the hearts
of men, and sets up an everlasting kingdom. It eludes all
the vigilance, and baffles all the power, of the adversary.
Bars, and bolts, and dungeons are no obstacles to its approach : bonds, and tortures, and death cannot extinguish
its influence. Let no man's heart tremble, then, because
of fear. Let no man despair (in these days of rebuke and
blasphemy) of the Christian cause. The ark is launched,
indeed, upon the floods ; the tempest sweeps along the deep ;
the billows break over her on every side. But Jehovah-
Jesus has promised to conduct her in safety to the haven
of *peace.* She *cannot* be lost unless the pilot perish.

Modern Facilities for evangelizing the World.—
BEECHER.

THE means of extending knowledge, and influencing
the human mind by argument and moral power, are multiplied a thousand fold. The Lancasterian mode of instruction renders the instruction of the world cheap and
easy. The improvements of the press have reduced im-
mensely, and will reduce yet more, the price of books,
bringing not only tracts and Bibles, but even libraries,
within the reach of every man and every child. But in
the primitive age, the light of science beamed only on a
small portion of mankind. The mass of mankind were not,
and could not be, instructed to read. Every thing was
transient and fluctuating, because so little was made permanent in books and general knowledge, and so much depended on the character, the life, and energy, of the living
teacher. The press, that lever of Archimedes, which now
moves the world, was unknown.

It was the extinction of science by the invasion of the
northern barbarians, which threw back the world ten cen-

turies; and this it effected through the want of permanent
instruction, and the omnipotent control of opinion which is
exerted by the press. Could Paul have put in requisition
the press, as it is now put in requisition by Christianity, anc
have availed himself of literary societies, and Bible societies,
and Lancasterian schools to teach the entire population to
read, and of Bibles, and libraries, and tracts, Mahomet had
never opened the bottomless pit, and the pope had never
set his foot upon the neck of kings, nor deluged Europe
with the blood of the saints.

Should any be still disposed to insist, that our advan
tages for evangelizing the world are not to be compared with
those of the apostolic age, let them reverse the scene, and
roll back the wheels of time, and obliterate the improvements of science, and commerce, and arts, which now facilitate the spread of the Gospel. Let them throw into darkness all the known portions of the earth, which were then
unknown. Let them throw into distance the propinquity
of nations; and exchange their rapid intercourse for cheerless, insulated existence. Let the magnetic power be forgotten, and the timid navigator creep along the coasts of
the Mediterranean, and tremble and cling to the shore
when he looks out upon the broad waves of the Atlantic.
Inspire idolatry with the vigour of meridian manhood, and
arm in its defence, and against Christianity, all the civilization, and science, and mental power of the world. Give
back to the implacable Jew his inveterate unbelief, and his
vantage-ground, and his disposition to oppose Christianity
in every place of his dispersion, from Jerusalem to every
extremity of the Roman empire. Blot out the means of
extending knowledge and exerting influence upon the human mind. Destroy the Lancasterian system of instruction, and throw back the mass of men into a state of un-
reading, unreflecting ignorance. Blot out libraries and
tracts; abolish Bible, and education, and tract, and missionary societies; and send the nations for knowledge parchment, and the slow and limited productions of the pen. Let
all the improvements in civil government be obliterated,
and the world be driven from the happy arts of self-government to the guardianship of dungeons and chains. Let
liberty of conscience expire, and the Church, now emanci-

pated, and walking forth in her unsullied loveliness, return to the guidance of secular policy, and the perversions and corruptions of an unholy priesthood.   And now reduce the 200,000,000 nominal, and the 10,000,000 of real Christians, spread over the earth, to 500 disciples, and to twelve apostles, assembled, for fear of the Jews, in an upper chamber, to enjoy the blessings of a secret prayer-meeting. And give them the power of miracles, and the gift of tongues, and send them out into all the earth to preach the Gospel to every creature.

Is this the apostolic advantage for propagating Christianity, which throws into discouragement and hopeless imbecility all our present means of enlightening and disenthralling the world ?   They, comparatively, had nothing to begin with, and every thing to oppose them ; and yet, in three hundred years, the whole civilized, and much of the barbarous, world was brought under the dominion of Christianity.   And shall we, with the advantage of their labours, and of our numbers, and a thousand fold increase of opportunity, and moral power, stand halting in unbelief, while the Lord Jesus is still repeating the injunction, Go ye out into all the world, and preach the Gospel to every creature ; and repeating the assurance, Lo I am with you alway, even to the end of the world ? Shame on our sloth ! Shame upon our unbelief !

---

*Speech** of the Chief* SA-GU-YU-WHAT-HAH, *called by the white People* RED JACKET.

FRIEND AND BROTHER—It was the will of the Great Spirit that we should meet together this day. He orders all things, and has given us a fine day for our council. He has taken his garment from before the sun, and caused a

* Delivered in answer to the offer and request of an American missionary, to teach among the Indians the principles of Christianity Some of their speeches have exhibited more of energy and pathos on occasions specially adapted to excite these qualities ; but we have seen none which better illustrates the peculiar sagacity and eloquence of this unfortunate people, than the one before us.—ED

to shine with brightness upon us. Our eyes are opened that we see clearly; our ears are unstopped, that we have been able to hear distinctly the words you have spoken For all these favours we thank the Great Spirit and him only.

Brother—Listen to what we say. There was a time when our forefathers owned this great island. Their seats extended from the rising to the setting sun. The Great Spirit had made it for the use of Indians. He had created the buffalo, deer, and other animals for food. He had made the bear and the beaver. Their skins served us for clothing. He had scattered them over the earth, and taught us how to take them. He had caused the earth to produce corn for bread. All this he had done for his red children, because he loved them. But an evil day came upon us. Your forefathers crossed the great water, and landed on this island. Their numbers were small. They found friends, and not enemies. They told us they had fled from their own country for fear of wicked men, and had come here to enjoy their religion. They asked for a small seat. We took pity on them, and granted their request; and they sat down among us. We gave them corn and meat; they gave us poison in return.

The white people had now found our country. Tidings were carried back, and more came among us. Yet we did not fear them. We took them to be friends. They called us brothers. We believed them, and gave them a larger seat. At length their numbers had greatly increased. They wanted more land. They wanted our country. Our eyes were opened, and our minds became uneasy. Wars took place. Indians were hired to fight against Indians, and many of our people were destroyed. They also brought strong liquor among us. It was strong, and powerful, and has s'ain thousands.

Brother—Our seats were once large, and yours were small. You have now become a great people, and we have scarcely a place left to spread our blankets You have got our country, but are not satisfied; you want to force your religion among us.

Brother—Continue to listen. You say that you are sent to instruct us how to worship the Great Spirit agreeably to his mind, and, if we do not take hold of the religion which you white people teach, we shall be unhappy hereafter You say that you are right, and we are lost. How do we know this to be true? We understand that your religion is written in a book. If it was intended for us as well as you, why has not the Great Spirit given to us, and not only to us, but why did he not give to our forefathers, the knowledge of that book, with the means of understanding it rightly? We only know what you tell us about it. How shall we know when to believe, being so often deceived by the white people?

Brother—You say there is but one way to worship and serve the Great Spirit. If there is but one religion, why do you white people differ so much about it? Why not all agreed, as you can all read the book?

Brother—We do not understand these things. We are told that your religion was given to your forefathers, and has been handed down from father to son. We also have a religion, which was given to our forefathers, and was handed down to their children. We worship in that way. It teaches us to be thankful for all the favours we receive; to love each other, and to be united. We never quarrel about religion.

Brother—The Great Spirit has made us all, but he has made a great difference between his white and red children. He has given us different complexions and different customs. To you he has given the arts. To these he has not opened our eyes. We know these things to be true. Since he has made so great a difference between us in other things, why may we not conclude that he has given us a different religion according to our understanding? The Great Spirit does right: he knows what is best for his children. We are satisfied.

Brother—We do not wish to destroy your religion, or take it from you. We only wish to enjoy our own.

Brother—We are told that you have been preaching to the white people in this place. These people are our neighbours. We are acquainted with them. We will wait a little while, and see what effect your preaching has upon them. If we find it does them good, makes them honest, and less disposed to cheat Indians, we will then consider again of what you have said.

Brother—You have now heard our answer to your talk. This is all we have to say at present. As we are going to part, we will come and take you by the hand, and hope the Great Spirit will protect you on your journey, and return you safe to your friends.

———◆———

Extract from a Speech on the British Treaty.*—
AMES.

THIS, sir, is a cause that would be dishonoured and betrayed, if I contented myself with appealing only to the understanding. It is too cold, and its processes are too slow for the occasion. I desire to thank God, that, since he has given me an intellect so fallible, he has impressed upon me an instinct that is sure. On a question of shame and honour, reasoning is sometimes useless, and worse. I feel the decision in my pulse : if it throws no light upon the brain, it kindles a fire at the heart.

It is not easy to deny, it is impossible to doubt, that a treaty imposes an obligation on the American nation. It would be childish to consider the president and senate obliged, and the nation and house free. What is the obligation ? perfect or imperfect ? If perfect, the debate is brought to a conclusion. If imperfect, how large a part of our faith is pawned ? Is half our honour put at a risk, and is that half too cheap to be redeemed ? How long has this hair-splitting subdivision of good faith been discovered ? and why has it escaped the researches of the writers on the law of nations ? Shall we add a new chapter to that

---

* The celebrated speech, from which this extract is taken, was delivered in the house of representatives, April 28, 1796, in support of the following motion : " Resolved, That it is expedient to pass the laws necessary to carry into effect the treaty lately concluded between the United States and the king of Great Britain."—After the debate, the votes stood, for carrying the treaty into effect, 51 , against carrying it into effect, 48.—ED.

law ? or insert this doctrine as a supplement to, or, more properly, a repeal of the ten commandments ?

On every hypothesis, the conclusion is not to be resisted : we are either to execute this treaty, or break our faith.

To expatiate on the value of public faith, may pass with some men for declamation : to such men I have nothing to say. To others I will urge, can any circumstance mark upon a people more turpitude and debasement ? Can any thing tend more to make men think themselves mean, or degrade to a lower point their estimation of virtue, and their standard of action ? It would not merely demoralize mankind ; it tends to break all the ligaments of society, to dissolve that mysterious charm, which attracts individuals to the nation, and to inspire in its stead a repulsive sense of shame and disgust.

What is patriotism ? Is it a narrow affection for the spot where a man was born ? Are the very clods where we tread entitled to this ardent preference, because they are greener. No, sir : this is not the character of the virtue, and it soars higher for its object. It is an extended self-love, mingling with all the enjoyments of life, and twisting itself with the minutest filaments of the heart. It is thus we obey the laws of society, because they are the laws of virtue. In their authority we see, not the array of force and terror, but the venerable image of our country's honour. Every good citizen makes that honour his own ; and cherishes it not only as precious, but as sacred. He is willing to risk his life in its defence ; and is conscious, that he gains protection while he gives it. For what rights of a citizen will be deemed inviolable, when a state renounces the principles that constitute their security ? Or, if his life should not be invaded, what would its enjoyments be in a country odious in the eyes of strangers, and dishonoured in his own ? Could he look with affection and veneration to such a country as his parent ? The sense of having one would die within him ; he would blush for his patriotism, if he retained any, and justly—for it would be a vice. He would be a banished man in his native land.

I see no exception to the respect that is paid among nations to the law of good faith. If there are cases in this
enlightened period when it is violated, there are none when
it is decried. It is the philosophy of politics, the religion
of governments. It is observed by barbarians : a whiff
of tobacco smoke, or a string of beads, gives not merely
binding force, but sanctity, to treaties. Even in Algiers,
a truce may be bought for money; but, when ratified, even
Algiers is too wise, or too just, to disown and annul its obligation. Thus we see, neither the ignorance of savages,
nor the principles of an association for piracy and rapine,
permit a nation to despise its engagements. If, sir, there
could be a resurrection from the foot of the gallows, if the
victims of justice could live again, collect together and
form a society, they would, however loath, soon find themselves obliged to make justice, that justice under which
they fell, the fundamental law of their state. They would
perceive it was their interest to make others respect, and
they would, therefore, soon pay some respect themselves
to the obligations of good faith.

It is painful, I hope it is superfluous, to make even the
supposition that America should furnish the occasion of this
opprobrium. No : let me not even imagine, that a republican government, sprung, as our own is, from a people
enlightened and uncorrupted, a government whose origin
is right, and whose daily discipline is duty, can, upon solemn debate, make its option to be faithless; can dare to
act what despots dare not avow, what our own example
evinces the states of Barbary are unsuspected of. No :
let me rather make the supposition that Great Britain refuses to execute the treaty, after we have done every thing
to carry it into effect. Is there any language of reproach
pungent enough to express your commentary on the fact ?
What would you say ? or rather what would you not say ?
Would you not tell them, wherever an Englishman might
travel, shame would stick to him ? he would disown his
country. You would exclaim—" England, proud of your
wealth, and arrogant in the possession of power, blush for
these distinctions which become the vehicles of your dishonour !" Such a nation might truly say to corruption,
thou art my father ; and to the worm, thou art my mother

and my sister. We should say of such a race of men, their name is a heavier burden than their debt.

The refusal of the western posts—inevitable if we reject the treaty—is a measure too decisive in its nature to be neutral in its consequences. From great causes we are to look for great effects. Will the tendency to Indian hostilities be contested by any one? Experience gives the answer. The frontiers were scourged with war until the negotiation with Great Britain was far advanced; and then the state of hostility ceased. Perhaps the public agents of both nations are innocent of fomenting the Indian war, and perhaps they are not. We ought not, however, to expect, that neighbouring nations, highly irritated against each other, will neglect the friendship of the savages. The traders will gain an influence, and will abuse it; and who is ignorant that their passions are easily raised, and hardly restrained from violence? Their situation will oblige them to choose between this country and Great Britain in case the treaty should be rejected; they will not be our friends, and at the same time the friends of our enemies.

If any, against all these proofs, should maintain that the peace with the Indians will be stable without the posts, to them I will urge another reply. From arguments calculated to produce conviction, I will appeal directly to the hearts of those who hear me, and ask whether it is not already planted there? I resort especially to the convictions of the western gentlemen, whether, supposing no posts and no treaty, the settlers will remain in security? Can they take it upon them to say, that an Indian peace, under these circumstances, will prove firm? No, sir, it will not be peace, but a sword; it will be no better than a lure to draw victims within reach of the tomahawk. On this theme my emotions are unutterable. If I could find words for them, if my powers bore any proportion to my zeal, I would swell my voice to such a note of remonstrance that it should reach every log-house beyond the mountains. I would say to the inhabitants—Wake from your false security: your cruel dangers, your more cruel apprehensions, are soon to be renewed: the wounds yet unhealed are to be torn open again: in the day time your path through the woods will be ambushed: the darkness of midnight will glitter with the blaze of your dwellings. You are a father—the blood of your sons shall fatten your cornfield : you are a mother—the war-whoop shall wake the sleep of the cradle.

On this subject, you need not suspect any deception on your feelings. It is a spectacle of horror, which cannot be overdrawn. If you have nature in your hearts, they will speak a language, compared with which all I have said, or can say, will be poor and frigid.

Who will accuse me of wandering out of the subject ? Who will say that I exaggerate the tendencies of our measures ? Will any one answer by a sneer, that all this is idle preaching ? Will any one deny that we are bound—and I would hope to good purpose—by the most solemn sanctions of duty for the vote we give ? Are despots alone to be reproached for unfeeling indifference to the tears and blood of their subjects ? Are republicans unresponsible ? Have the principles, on which you ground the reproach upon cabinets and kings, no practical influence, no binding force ? Are they merely themes of idle declamation, introduced to decorate the morality of a newspaper essay, or to furnish pretty topics of harangue from the windows of that statehouse ? I trust it is neither too presumptuous nor too late to ask—Can you put the dearest interest of society at risk without guilt and without remorse ?

By rejecting the posts, we light the savage fires, we bind the victims. This day we undertake to render account to the widows and orphans whom our decision will make, to the wretches that will be roasted at the stake, to our country, and, I do not deem it too serious to say, to conscience and to God. We are answerable ; and if duty be any thing more than a word of imposture, if conscience be not a bugbear, we are preparing to make ourselves as wretched as our country.

There is no mistake in this case, there can be none · experience has already been the prophet of events, and the cries of our future victims have already reached us. The western inhabitants are not a silent and uncomplaining sacrifice. The voice of humanity issues from the shade of the wilderness : it exclaims that, while one hand is held up to reject this treaty, the other grasps a tomahawk. It
32 *

summons our imagination to the scenes that will open. I
is no great effort of the imagination to conceive that events
so near are already begun.   I can fancy that I listen to the
yells of savage vengeance and the shrieks of torture ; already they seem to sigh in the western wind ; already they
mingle with e ery echo from the mountains.

I rose to speak under impressions that I would have resisted if I could.   Those who see me will believe, that
the reduced state of my health has unfitted me, almost
equally, for much exertion of body or mind.   Unprepared
for debate by careful reflection in my retirement, or by
long attention here, I thought the resolution I had taken
to sit silent was imposed by necessity, and would cost me
no effort to maintain.   With a mind thus vacant of ideas,
and sinking, as I really am, under a sense of weakness, I
imagined the very desire of speaking was extinguished by
the persuasion that I had nothing to say.   Yet when I
come to the moment of deciding the vote, I start back with
dread from the edge of the pit into which we are plunging.
In my view, even the minutes I have spent in expostu-
lation have their value, because they protract the crisis,
and the short period in which alone we may resolve to es
cape it.

I have thus been led by my feelings to speak more at
length than I had intended.   Yet I have, perhaps, as little
personal interest in the event as any one here.   There is,
I believe, no member, who will not think his chance to be
a witness of the consequences greater than mine.   If, however, the vote should pass to reject, and a spirit should rise,
as it will with the public disorders, to make "confusion
worse confounded," even I, slender and almost broken as
my hold upon life is, may outlive the government and
constitution of my country.

Appeal in Favour of the Union.—MADISON.

I SUBMIT to you, my fellow-citizens, these considera
tions, in full confidence that the good sense, which has so
often marked your decisions, will allow them their due

weight and effect; and that you will never suffer difficulties, however formidable in appearance, or however fashionable the error on which they may be founded, to drive
you into the gloomy and perilous scenes, into which the
advocates for disunion would conduct you. Hearken not
to the unnatural voice, which tells you that the people of
America, knit together, as they are, by so many cords of
affection, can no longer live together as members of the
same family; can no longer continue the mutual guar-
dians of their mutual happiness; can no longer be fellow-citizens of one great, respectable and flourishing empire. Hearken not to the voice, which petulantly tells
you, that the form of government recommended for your
adoption is a novelty in the political world; that it has
never yet had a place in the theories of the wildest pro-
jectors; that it rashly attempts what it is impossible to accomplish. No, my countrymen; shut your ears against
this unhallowed language. Shut your hearts against the
poison which it conveys; the kindred blood, which flows
in the veins of American citizens, the mingled blood, which
they have shed in defence of their sacred rights, consecrate
their union, and excite horror at the idea of their becoming aliens, rivals, enemies. And if novelties are to be
shunned, believe me, the most alarming of all novelties,
the most wild of all projects, the most rash of all attempts,
is that of rending us in pieces, in order to preserve our liberties and promote our happiness. But why is the experiment of an extended republic to be rejected, merely because it may comprise what is new? Is it not the glory
of the people of America, that, whilst they have paid a decent regard to the opinions of former times and other nations, they have not suffered a blind veneration for antiquity,
for custom, or for names, to overrule the suggestions of
their own good sense, the knowledge of their own situation, and the lessons of their own experience? To this
manly spirit, posterity will be indebted for the possession,
and the world for the example, of the numerous innovations
displayed on the American theatre, in favour of private
rights and public happiness. Had no important step been
taken by the leaders of the revolution, for which a prece
dent could not be discovered: had no government been estab-

lished, of which an exact model did not present itself,—the people of the United States might, at this moment, have been numbered among the melancholy victims of misguided councils; must at best have been labouring under the weight of some of those forms, which have crushed the liberties of the rest of mankind. Happily for America, happily, we trust, for the whole human race, they pursued a new and more noble course. They accomplished a revolution, which has no parallel in the annals of human society. They reared fabrics of government, which have no model on the face of the globe. They formed the design of a great confederacy, which it is incumbent on their successors to improve and perpetuate. If their works betray imperfections, we wonder at the fewness of them. If they erred most in the structure of the union, this was the work most difficult to be executed; this is the work which has been new-modelled by the act of your convention, and it is that act, on which you are now to deliberate and decide.

Grand electrical Experiment of Dr. Franklin.—
STUBER.

IN the year 1749, he first suggested his idea of explaining the phenomena of thunder-gusts, and of the aurora borealis, upon electrical principles. He points out many particulars in which lightning and electricity agree; and he adduces many facts, and reasonings from facts, in support of his positions. In the same year he conceived the astonishingly bold and grand idea of ascertaining the truth of his doctrine, by actually drawing down the lightning, by means of sharp-pointed iron rods raised into the region of the clouds. Even in this uncertain state, his passion to be useful to mankind displays itself in a powerful manner. Admitting the identity of electricity and lightning, and knowing the power of points in repelling bodies charged with electricity, and in conducting their fire silently and imperceptibly, he suggested the idea of securing houses, ships, &c. from being damaged by lightning, by erecting pointed rods, that should rise some feet above the most elevated part, and descend some feet into the ground or the water. The effect of these, he concluded, would be either to prevent a stroke by repelling the cloud beyond the striking distance, or by drawing off the electrical fire which it contained ; or, if they could not effect this, they would at least conduct the electric matter to the earth, without any injury to the building.

It was not until the summer of 1752, that he was enabled to complete his grand and unparalleled discovery by experiment. The plan which he had originally proposed, was, to erect on some high tower, or other elevated place, a sentry box, from which should rise a pointed iron rod, insulated by being fixed in a cake of resin Electrified clouds, passing over this, would, he conceived, impart to it a portion of their electricity, which would be rendered evident to the senses by sparks being emitted, when a key, the knuckle, or other conductor, was presented to it.   Philadelphia, at this time, afforded no opportunity of trying an experiment of this kind. While Franklin was waiting for the erection of a spire, it occurred to him that he might have more ready access to the region of clouds by means of a common kite. He prepared one by fastening two cross sticks to a silk handkerchief, which would not suffer so much from the rain as paper. To the upright stick was affixed an iron point. The string was, as usual, of hemp, except the lower end, which was silk. Where the hempen string terminated, a key was fastened. With tiis apparatus, on the appearance of a thunder-gust approaching, he went out into the commons, accompanied by his son, to whom alone he communicated his intentions, well knowing the ridicule, which, too generally for the interest of science, awaits unsuccessful experiments in philosophy. He placed himself under a shade, to avoid the rain—his kite was raised—a thunder-cloud passed over it—no sign of electricity appeared. He almost despaired of success, when suddenly he observed the loose fibres of his string to move towards an erect position. He now presented his knuckle to the key, and received a strong spark. How exquisite must his sensations have been at this moment! On this experiment depended the fat of his theory. If he succeeded, his name would rank high among those who had improved science ; if he failed, he must inevitably be subjected to the derision of mankind, or, what is worse, their pity, as a well-meaning man, but a weak, silly projector. The anxiety with which he looked for the result of his experiment may be easily conceived. Doubts and despair had begun to prevail, when the fact was ascertained in so clear a manner, that even the most incredulous could no longer withhold their assent. Repeated sparks were drawn from the key, a phial was charged, a shock given, and all the experiments made which are usually performed with electricity.

* * * * * * * * * * * * *

By these experiments Franklin's theory was established in the most convincing manner. When the truth of it could no longer be doubted, envy and vanity endeavoured to detract from its merit. That an American, an inhabitant of the obscure city of Philadelphia, the name of which was hardly known, should be able to make discoveries, and to frame theories, which had escaped the notice of the enlightened philosophers of Europe, was too mortifying to be admitted. He must certainly have taken the idea from some one else. An American, a being of an inferior order, make discoveries !—Impossible. It was said, that the Abbé Nollet, 1748, had suggested the idea of the similarity of lightning and electricity in his *Leçons de Physique.* It is true that the abbé mentions the idea, but he throws it out as a bare conjecture, and proposes no mode of ascertaining the truth of it   He himself acknowledges, that Franklin first entertained the bold thought of bringing lightning from the heavens, by means of pointed rods fixed in the air. The similarity of lightning and electricity is so strong, that we need not be surprised at notice being taken of it, as soon as electrical phenomena became familiar. We find it mentioned by Dr. Wall and Mr. Grey, while the science was in its infancy. But the honour of forming a regular theory of thunder-gusts, of suggesting a mode of determining the truth of it by experiments, and of putting these experiments in practice, and thus establishing the theory upon a firm and solid basis. is incontestably due to Franklin

Extrication of a Frigate from the Shoals.—
COOPER.

THE extraordinary activity of Griffith, which communicated itself with promptitude to the whole crew, was
produced by a sudden alteration in the weather. In place
of the well-defined streak along the horizon, that has been
already described, an immense body of misty light appeared to be moving in, with rapidity, from the ocean, while a
distinct but distant roaring announced the sure approach
of he tempest, that had so long troubled the waters. Even
Griffith, while thundering his orders through the trumpet,
and urging the men, by his cries, to expedition, would
pause, for instants, to cast anxious glances in the direction
of the coming storm, and the faces of the sailors who lay
on the yards were turned, instinctively, towards the same
quarter of the heavens, while they knotted the reef-points,
or passed the gaskets, that were to confine the unruly canvass to the prescribed limits.

The pilot alone, in that confused and busy throng, where
voice rose above voice, and cry echoed cry, in quick succession, appeared as if he held no interest in the important
stake. With his eyes steadily fixed on the approaching
mist, and his arms folded together, in composure, he stood
calmly awaiting the result.

The ship had fallen off, with her broadside to the sea,
and was become unmanageable, and the sails were already
brought into the folds necessary to her security, when the
quick and heavy fluttering of canvass was thrown across
the water, with all the gloomy and chilling sensations that
such sounds produce, where darkness and danger unite to
appal the seaman.

"The schooner has it!" cried Griffith; "Barnstable
has held on, like himself, to the last moment—God send
that the squall leave him cloth enough to keep him from
the shore!"

"His sails are easily handled," the commander observed, "and she must be over the principal danger. We
are falling off before it, Mr. Gray; shall we try a cast of
the lead?"

The pilot turned from his contemplative posture, and moved slowly across the deck, before he returned any reply to this question—like a man who not only felt that every thing depended on himself, but that he was equal to the emergency.

" 'Tis unnecessary," he at length said ; " 'twould be certain destruction to be taken aback, and it is difficult to say, within several points, how the wind may strike us."

" 'Tis difficult no longer," cried Griffith ; " for here it comes, and in right earnest !"

The rushing sounds of the wind were now, indeed, heard at hand, and the words were hardly passed the lips of the young lieutenant, before the vessel bowed down heavy to one side, and then, as she began to move through the water, rose again majestically to her upright position, as if saluting, like a courteous champion, the powerful antagonist with which she was about to contend. Not another minute elapsed, before the ship was throwing the waters aside, with a lively progress, and, obedient to her helm, was brought as near to the desired course, as the direction of the wind would allow. The hurry and bustle on the yards gradually subsided, and the men slowly descended to the deck, all straining their eyes to pierce the gloom in which they were enveloped, and some shaking their heads in melancholy doubt, afraid to express the apprehensions they really entertained. All on board anxiously waited for the fury of the gale ; for there were none so ignorant or inexperienced in that gallant frigate, as not to know, that they, as yet, only felt the infant efforts of the wind. Each moment, however, it increased in power, though so gradual was the alteration, that the relieved mariners began to believe that all their gloomy forebodings were not to be realized. During this short interval of uncertainty, no other sounds were heard than the whistling of the breeze, as it passed quickly through the mass of rigging that belonged to the vessel, and the dashing of the spray, that began to fly from her bows, like the foam of a cataract.

" It blows fresh," cried Griffith, who was the first to speak in that moment of doubt and anxiety ; " but it is no more than a cap-full of wind, after all. Give us elbow-room, and the right canvass, Mr. Pilot, and I'll handle the ship like a gentleman's yacht, in this breeze."

" Will she stay, think ye, under this sail?" said the low voice of the stranger.

" She will do all that man, in reason, can ask of wood and iron," returned the lieutenant; " but the vessel don't float the ocean that will tack under double-reefed topsails alone, against a heavy sea. Help her with the courses, pilot, and you'll see her come round like a dancing-master."

" Let us feel the strength of the gale first," returned the man who was called Mr. Gray, moving from the side of Griffith to the weather gang-way of the vessel, where he stood in silence, looking ahead of the ship, with an air of singular coolness and abstraction.

All the lanterns had been extinguished on the deck of the frigate, when her anchor was secured, and as the first mist of the gale had passed over, it was succeeded by a faint light, that was a good deal aided by the glittering foam of the waters, which now broke in white curls around the vessel, in every direction. The land could be faintly discerned, rising, like a heavy bank of black fog, above the margin of the waters, and was only distinguishable from the heavens, by its deeper gloom and obscurity. The last rope was coiled, and deposited in its proper place, by the seamen, and for several minutes the stillness of death pervaded the crowded decks. It was evident to every one, that their ship was dashing at a prodigious rate through the waves; and, as she was approaching, with such velocity, the quarter of the bay where the shoals and dangers were known to be situated, nothing but the habits of the most exact discipline could suppress the uneasiness of the officers and men within their own bosoms. At length the voice of Captain Munson was heard, calling to the pilot.

" Shall I send a hand into the chains, Mr. Gray," he said, " and try our water?"

* * * * * * * * * * * *

" Tack your ship, sir, tack your ship; I would see how she works, before we reach the point, where she *must* behave well, or we perish."

33

Griffith gazed after him in wonder, wh:le the pilot slowly paced the quarter-deck, and then, rousing from his
trance, gave forth the cheering order that called each man
to his station, to perform the desired evolution. The confident assurances which the young officer had given to the
pilot, respecting the qualities of his vessel, and his own
ability to manage her, were fully realized by the result.
The helm was no sooner put a-lee, than the huge ship bore
up gallantly against the wind, and, dashing directly through
the waves, threw the foam high into the air, as she looked
boldly into the very eye of the wind, and then, yielding
gracefully to its power, she fell off on the other tack, with
her head pointed from those dangerous shoals that she had
so recently approached with such terrifying velocity. The
heavy yards swung round, as if they had been vanes to
indicate the currents of the air, and in a few moments the
frigate again moved, with stately progress, through the
water, leaving the rocks and shoals behind her on one side
of the bay, but advancing towards those that offered equal
danger on the other.

During this time, the sea was becoming more agitated,
and the violence of the wind was gradually increasing.
The latter no longer whistled amid the cordage of the vessel, but it seemed to howl, surlily, as it passed the compli
cated machinery that the frigate obtruded on its path. An
endless succession of white surges rose above the heavy
billows, and the very air was glittering with the light that
was disengaged from the ocean. The ship yielded, each
moment, more and more before the storm, and, in less than
half an hour from the time that she had lifted her anchor,
she was driven along, with tremendous fury, by the full
power of a gale of wind. Still, the hardy and experienced
mariners, who directed her movements, held her to the
course that was necessary to their preservation, and still
Griffith gave forth, when directed by their unknown pilot,
those orders that turned her in the narrow channel where
safety was, alone, to be found.

So far, the performance of his duty appeared easy to the
stranger, and he gave the required directions in those still,
calm tones, that formed so remarkable a contrast to the
responsibility of his situation. But when the land was be-

coming dim, in distance as well as darkness, and the agitated sea was only to be discovered as it swept by them in foam; he broke in upon the monotonous roaring of the tempest, with the sounds of his voice, seeming to shake off his apathy, and rouse himself to the occasion.

"Now is the time to watch her closely, Mr. Griffith," he cried; "here we get the true tide and the real danger. Place the best quarter-master of your ship in those chains, and let an officer stand by him, and see that he gives us the right water."

"I will take that office on myself," said the captain; "pass a light into the weather main-chains."

"Stand by your braces!" exclaimed the pilot, with startling quickness. "Heave away that lead!"

These preparations taught the crew to expect the crisis, and every officer and man stood in fearful silence, at his assigned station, awaiting the issue of the trial. Even the quarter-master at the cun gave out his orders to the men at the wheel in deeper and hoarser tones than usual, as if anxious not to disturb the quiet and order of the vessel.

While this deep expectation pervaded the frigate, the piercing cry of the leadsman, as he called, "By the mark seven!" rose above the tempest, crossed over the decks, an l appeared to pass away to leeward, borne on the blast, like the warnings of some water spirit.

"'Tis well," returned the pilot, calmly; "try it again."

The short pause was succeeded by another cry, "and a half-five!"

"She shoals! she shoals!" exclaimed Griffith; "keep her a good full."

"Ay! you must hold the vessel in command, now," said the pilot, with those cool tones that are most appalling in critical moments, because they seem to denote most preparation and care.

The third call of "By the deep four!" was followed by a prompt direction from the stranger to tack.

Griffith seemed to emulate the coolness of the pilot, in issuing the necessary orders to execute this manœuvre.

The vessel rose slowly from the inclined position into which she had been forced by the tempest, and the sails were shaking violently, as if to release themselves from their confinement, while the ship stemmed the billows, when the well-known voice of the sailing-master was heard shouting from the forecastle—

"Breakers! breakers, dead ahead!"

This appalling sound seemed yet to be lingering about the ship, when a second voice cried—

"Breakers on our lee-bow!"

"We are in a bight of the shoals, Mr. Gray," said the commander. "She loses her way; perhaps an anchor might hold her."

"Clear away that best-bower!" shouted Griffith through his trumpet.

"Hold on!" cried the pilot, in a voice that reached the very hearts of all who heard him; "hold on every thing."

The young man turned fiercely to the daring stranger, who thus defied the discipline of his vessel, and at once demanded—

"Who is it that dares to countermand my orders?—is it not enough that you run the ship into danger, but you must interfere to keep her there! If another word—"

"Peace, Mr. Griffith," interrupted the captain, bending from the rigging, his gray locks blowing about in the wind, and adding a look of wildness to the haggard care that he exhibited by the light of his lantern; "yield the trumpet to Mr. Gray; he alone can save us."

Griffith threw his speaking trumpet on the deck, and, as he walked proudly away, muttered in bitterness of feeling—

"Then all is lost, indeed, and, among the rest, the foolish hopes with which I visited this coast."

There was, however, no time for reply; the ship had been rapidly running into the wind, and, as the efforts of the crew were paralyzed by the contradictory orders they had heard, she gradually lost her way, and, in a few seconds, all her sails were taken aback.

Before the crew understood their situation, the pilot had applied the trumpet to his mouth, and, in a voice that rose above the tempest, he thundered forth his orders. Each command was given distinctly, and with a precision that showed him to be master of his profession.   The helm was kept fast, the head yards swung up heavily against the wind, and the vessel was soon whirling round on her heel, with a retrograde movement.

Griffith was too much of a seaman, not to perceive that the pilot had seized, with a perception almost intuitive, the only method that promised to extricate the vessel from her situation.   He was young, impetuous, and proud; but he was also generous.   Forgetting his resentment and his mortification, he rushed forward among the men, and, by his presence and example, added certainty to the experiment.   The ship fell off slowly before the gale, and bowed her yards nearly to the water, as she felt the blast pouring its fury on her broadside, while the surly waves beat violently against her stern, as if in reproach at departing from her usual manner of moving.

The voice of the pilot, however, was still heard, steady and calm, and yet so clear and high as to reach every ear; and the obedient seamen whirled the yards at his bidding, in despite of the tempest, as if they handled the toys of their childhood.   When the ship had fallen off dead before the wind, her head sails were shaken, her after yards trimmed, and her helm shifted, before she had time to run upon the danger that had threatened, as well to leeward as to windward.   The beautiful fabric, obedient to her government, threw her bows up gracefully towards the wind again, and, as her sails were trimmed, moved out from amongst the dangerous shoals, in which she had been embayed, as steadily and swiftly as she had approached them.

A moment of breathless astonishment succeeded the accomplishment of this nice manœuvre, but there was no time for the usual expressions of surprise.   The stranger still held the trumpet, and continued to lift his voice amid the howlings of the blast, whenever prudence or skill directed any change in the management of the ship.   For an hour longer, there was a fearful struggle for their preservation, the channel becoming, at each step, more complicated, and the shoals thickening around the mariners, on every side.   The lead was cast rapidly, and the quick eye of the pilot seemed to pierce the darkness, with a keenness of vision that exceeded human power.   It was appa-

33 *

rent to all in the vessel, that they were under the guidance
of one who understood the navigation thoroughly, and their
exertions kept pace with their reviving confidence. Again
and again the frigate appeared to be rushing blindly on
shoals, where the sea was covered with foam, and where
destruction would have been as sudden as it was certain,
when the clear voice of the stranger was heard warning
them of the danger, and inciting them to their duty.
The vessel was implicitly yielded to his government, and
during those anxious moments, when she was dashing the
waters aside, throwing the spray over her enormous yards,
each ear would listen eagerly for those sounds that had
obtained a command over the crew, that can only be acquired, under such circumstances, by great steadiness and
consummate skill. The ship was recovering from the in-
action of changing her course, in one of those critical tacks
that she had made so often, when the pilot, for the first
time, addressed the commander of the frigate, who still
continued to superintend the all-important duty of the
leadsman.

"Now is the pinch," he said; "and if the ship behaves
well, we are safe—but if otherwise, all we have yet done
will be useless."

The veteran seaman whom he addressed left the chains
at this portentous notice, and, calling to his first lieutenant, required of the stranger an explanation of his warning.

"See you yon light on the southern headland?" returned the pilot; "you may know it from the star near
it by its sinking, at times, in the ocean. Now observe
the hummoc, a little north of it, looking like a shadow in
the horizon—'tis a hill far inland. If we keep that light
open from the hill, we shall do well—but if not, we surely
go to pieces."

"Let us tack again!" exclaimed the lieutenant.

The pilot shook his head, as he replied—

"There is no more tacking or box-hauling to be done to-
night. We have barely room to pass out of the shoals on
this course, and if we can weather the 'Devil's-Grip,' we
clear their outermost point—but if not, as I said before,
there is but an alternative."

"If we had beaten out the way we entered," exclaimed Griffith, "we should have done well."

"Say, also, if the tide would have let us do so," returned the pilot calmly. "Gentlemen, we must be prompt; we have but a mile to go, and the ship appears to fly. That topsail is not enough to keep her up to the wind; we want both jib and mainsail."

"'Tis a perilous thing to loosen canvass in such a tempest!" observèd the doubtful captain.

"It must be done," returned the collected stranger; "we perish, without it—see! the light already touches the edge of the hummoc; the sea casts us to leeward!"

"It shall be done!" cried Griffith, seizing the trumpet from the hand of the pilot.

The orders of the lieutenant were executed almost as soon as issued, and, every thing being ready, the enormous folds of the mainsail were trusted, loose, to the blast. There was an instant when the result was doubtful; the tremendous threshing of the heavy sails, seeming to bid defiance to all restraint, shaking the ship to her centre; but art and strength prevailed, and gradually the canvass was distended, and, bellying as it filled, was drawn down to its usual place, by the power of a hundred men. The vessel yielded to this immense addition of force, and bowed before it, like a reed bending to a breeze. But the success of the measure was announced by a joyful cry from the stranger, that seemed to burst from his inmost soul.

"She feels it! she springs her luff! observe," he said, "the light opens from the hummoc already; if she will only bear her canvass, we shall go clear!"

A report, like that of a cannon, interrupted his exclamation, and something resembling a white cloud was seen drifting before the wind from the head of the ship, till it was driven into the gloom far to leeward.

"'Tis the jib, blown from the bolt-ropes," said the commander of the frigate. "This is no time to spread light duck—but the mainsail may stand it yet."

"The sail would laugh at a tornado," returned the lieutenant; "but that mast springs like a piece of steel."

"Silence all!" cried the pilot. "Now, gentlemen, we shall soon know our fate. Let her luff—luff you can

This warning effectually closed all discourse, and the hardy mariners, knowing that they had already done all in the power of man to ensure their safety, stood in breathless anxiety, awaiting the result. At a short distance ahead of them, the whole ocean was white with foam, and the waves, instead of rolling on, in regular succession, appeared to be tossing about in mad gambols. A single streak of dark billows, not half a cable's length in width, could be discerned running into this chaos of water; but it was soon lost to the eye, amid the confusion of the disturbed element. Along this narrow path the vessel moved more heavily than before, being brought so near the wind as to keep her sails touching. The pilot silently proceeded to the wheel, and, with his own hands, he undertook the steerage of the ship. No noise proceeded from the frigate to interrupt the horrid tumult of the ocean, and she entered the channel among the breakers, with the silence of a desperate calmness. Twenty times, as the foam rolled away to leeward, the crew were on the eve of uttering their joy, as they supposed the vessel past the danger; but breaker after breaker would still rise before them, following each other into the general mass, to check their exultation. Occasionally, the fluttering of the sails would be heard; and, when the looks of the startled seamen were turned to the wheel, they beheld the stranger grasping its spokes, with his quick eye glancing from the water to the canvass. At length the ship reached a point, where she appeared to be rushing directly into the jaws of destruction, when, suddenly, her course was changed, and her head receded rapidly from the wind. At the same instant, the voice of the pilot was heard, shouting—

" Square away the yards!—in mainsail !"

A general burst from the crew echoed, " Square away the yards !" and, quick as thought, the frigate was seen gliding along the channel, before the wind. The eye had hardly time to dwell on the foam, which seemed like clouds driving in the heavens, and directly the gallant vessel issued from her perils, and rose and fell on the heavy waves of the open sea.

Lafayette's first Visit to America.—TICKNOR

WHEN only between sixteen and seventeen, Lafayette was married to the daughter of the Duke d'Ayen, son of the Duke de Noailles, and grandson to the great and good Chancellor d'Aguesseau; and thus his condition in life seemed to be assured to him among the most splendid and powerful in the empire. His fortune, which had been accumulating during a long minority, was vast; his rank was with the first in Europe; his connexions brought him the support of the chief persons in France; and his individual character—the warm, open and sincere manners, which have distinguished him ever since, and given him such singular control over the minds of men—made him powerful in the confidence of society wherever he went. It seemed, indeed, as if life had nothing further to offer him, than he could surely obtain by walking in the path that was so bright before him.

It was at this period, however, that his thoughts and feelings were first turned towards these thirteen colonies, then in the darkest and most doubtful passage of their struggle for independence. He made himself acquainted with our agents at Paris, and learned from them the state of our affairs. Nothing could be less tempting to him, whether he sought military reputation, or military instruction; for our army, at that moment retreating through New Jersey, and leaving its traces of blood from the naked and torn feet of the soldiery, as it hastened onward, was in a state too humble to offer either. Our credit, too, in Europe was entirely gone, so that the commissioners, (as they were called, without having any commission,) to whom Lafayette still persisted in offering his services, were obliged, at last, to acknowledge, that they could not even give him decent means for his conveyance. "Then," said he, "I shall purchase and fit out a vessel for myself." He did so. The vessel was prepared at Bordeaux, and sent round to one of the nearest ports in Spain, that it might be beyond the reach of the French government. In order more effectually to conceal his purposes, he made, just before his embarkation, a visit of a few weeks in England, (the only

time he was ever there,) and was much sought in English
society. On his return to France, he did not stop at all
in the capital, even to see his own family, but hastened,
with all speed and secrecy, to make good his escape from
the country. It was not until he was thus on his way
to embark, that his romantic undertaking began to be
known.

The effect produced in the capital and at court by its
publication was greater than we should now, perhaps, imagine. Lord Stormont, the English ambassador, required
the French ministry to despatch an order for his arrest, not
only to Bordeaux, but to the French commanders on the
West India station ; a requisition with which the ministry
readily complied, for they were at that time anxious to preserve a good understanding with England, and were seriously angry with a young man who had thus put in jeopardy the relations of the two countries. In fact, at Passage, on the very borders of France and Spain, a *lettre de
cachet* overtook him, and he was arrested and carried back
to Bordeaux. There, of course, his enterprise was near
being finally stopped; but, watching his opportunity, and
assisted by one or two friends, he disguised himself as a
courier, with his face blacked and false hair, and rode on,
ordering post horses for a carriage, which he had caused
to follow him at a suitable distance, for this very purpose,
and thus fairly passed the frontiers of the two kingdoms,
only three or four hours before his pursuers reached them.
He soon arrived at the port where his vessel was waiting
for him. His famil/, however, still followed him with so-
licitations to return, which he never received ; and the society of the court and capital, according to Madame du
Deffand's account of it, was in no common state of excitement on the occasion. Something of the same sort happened in London. " We talk chiefly," says Gibbon, in a
letter dated April 12th, 1777, " of the Marquis de Lafayette, who was here a few weeks ago. He is about twenty,
with a hundred and thirty thousand livres a year ; the
nephew of Noailles, who is ambassador here. He has
bought the Duke of Kingston's yacht. [a mistake,] and is
gone to join the Americans. The court appear to be angry
with him."

Immediately on arriving the secord time at Passage, the wind being fair, he embarked. The usual course, for French vessels attempting to trade with our colonies at that period, was, to sail for the West Indies, and then, coming up along our coast, enter where they could. But this course would have exposed Lafayette to the naval commanders of his own nation, and he had almost as much reason to dread them as to dread British cruisers. When, therefore, they were outside of the Canary Islands, Lafayette required his captain to lay their course directly for the United States. The captain refused, alleging that, if they should be taken by a British force, and carried into Halifax, the French government would never reclaim them, and they could hope for nothing but a slow death in a dungeon or a prison-ship. This was true, but Lafayette knew it before he made the requisition. He therefore insisted, until the captain refused in the most positive manner. Lafayette then told him that the ship was his own private property, that he had made his own arrangements concerning it, and that if he, the captain, would not sail directly for the United States, he should be put in irons, and his command given to the next officer. The captain, of course, submitted, and Lafayette gave him a bond for forty thousand francs, in case of any acciden' They therefore now made sail directly for the southern portion of the United States, and arrived unmolested at Charleston, South Carolina, on the 25th of April, 1777.

The sensation produced by his appearance in this country was, of course, much greater than that produced in Europe by his departure. It still stands forth as one of the most prominent and important circumstances in our revolutionary contest ; and, as has often been said by one who bore no small part in its trials and success, none but those, who were then alive, can believe what an impulse it gave to the hopes of a population almost disheartened by a long series of disasters. And well it might ; for it taught us, that, in the first rank of the first nobility in Europe, men could still be found, who not only took an interest in our struggle, but were willing to share our sufferings ; that our obscure and almost desperate contest for freedom, in a remote quarter of the world, could yet find supporters

among those, who were the most natural and powerful allies of a splendid despotism ; that we were the objects of a
regard and interest throughout the world, which would add
to our own resources sufficient strength to carry us safely
through to final success.

Goffe the Regicide.—Dwight.

In the course of Philip's war, which involved almost all
the Indian tribes in New England, and among others those
in the neighbourhood of Hadley, the inhabitants thought
it proper to observe the first of September, 1675, as a day
of fasting and prayer. While they were in the church,
and employed in their worship, they were surprised by a
band of savages. / The people instantly betook themselves
to their arms,—which, according to the custom of the
times, they had carried with them to the church,—and,
rushing out of the house, attacked their invaders. The
panic, under which they began the conflict, was, however,
so great, and their number was so disproportioned to that
of their enemies, that they fought doubtfully at first, and
in a short time began evidently to give way. At this moment an ancient man, with hoary locks, of a most venera
ble and dignified aspect, and in a dress widely differing
from that of the inhabitants, appeared suddenly at their
head, and with a firm voice and an example of undaunted
resolution, reanimated their spirits, led them again to the
conflict, and totally routed the savages. / When the battle
was ended, the stranger disappeared ; and no person knew
whence he had come, or whither he had gone. The relief
was so timely, so sudden, so unexpected, and so providen-
tial ; the appearance and the retreat of him who furnished
it were so unaccountable ; his person was so dignified and
commanding, his resolution so superior, and his interference
so decisive, that the inhabitants, without any uncommon
exercise of credulity, readily believed him to be an angel,
sent by Heaven for their preservation. Nor was this
opinion seriously controverted, until it was discovered, several years afterward, that Goffe and Whalley had been

lodged in the house of Mr. Russell. Then it was known
that their deliverer was Goffe; Whalley having become
superannuated some time before the event took place.*

General Washington resigning the Command of the Army.—RAMSAY.

THE hour now approached, in which it became necessary for the American chief to take leave of his officers, who
had been endeared to him by a long series of common sufferings and dangers. This was done in a solemn manner.
The officers having previously assembled for the purpose,
General Washington joined them, and, calling for a glass
of wine, thus addressed them:—"With a heart full of
love and gratitude, I now take leave of you. I most devoutly wish that your latter days may be as prosperous and
happy as your former ones have been glorious and honourable." Having drank, he added,—"I cannot come to
each of you to take my leave, but shall be obliged to you
if each of you will come and take me by the hand."
General Knox, being next, turned to him. Incapable of
utterance, Washington grasped his hand, and embraced
him. The officers came up successively, and he took an
affectionate leave of each of them. Not a word was articulated on either side. A majestic silence prevailed.
The tear of sensibility glistened in every eye. The tenderness of the scene exceeded all description. When the
last of the officers had taken his leave, Washington left
the room, and passed through the corps of light infantry to
the place of embarkation. The officers followed in a solemn, mute procession, with dejected countenances. On
his entering the barge to cross the North River, he turned
towards the companions of his glory, and, by waving his
hat, bid them a silent adieu. Some of them answered this
last signal of respect and affection with tears; and all of

---

* The magic pencil of Sir Walter Scott has wrought up this romantic incident into a most eloquent and beautiful description. It is contained in Bridgenorth's relation of his adventures in America to Julian
Peveril, in one of the volumes of " Peveril of the Peak."—ED

them gazed upon the barge, which conveyed him from their sight, till they could no longer distinguish in it the person of their beloved commander-in-chief.

The army being disbanded, Washington proceeded to Annapolis, then the seat of congress, to resign his commission. On his way thither, he, of his own accord, delivered to the comptroller of accounts in Philadelphia an account of the expenditure of all the public money he had ever received. This was in his own hand-writing, and every entry was made in a very particular manner. Vouchers were produced for every item, except for secret intelligence and service, which amounted to no more than 1,982 pounds 10 shillings sterling. The whole, which, in the course of eight years of war, had passed through his hands, amounted only to 14,479 pounds, 18 shillings 9 pence sterling. Nothing was charged or retained for personal services; and actual disbursements had been managed with such economy and fidelity, that they were all covered by the above moderate sum.

After accounting for all his expenditures of public money, (secret service money, for obvious reasons, excepted,) with all the exactness which established forms required from the inferior officers of his army, he hastened to resign into the hands of the fathers of his country the powers with which they had invested him. This was done in a public audience. Congress received him as the founder and guardian of the republic. While he appeared before them, they silently retraced the scenes of danger and distress, through which they had passed together. They recalled to mind the blessings of freedom and peace purchased by his arm. They gazed with wonder on their fellow-citizen, who appeared more great and worthy of esteem in resigning his power, than he had done in gloriously using it. Every heart was big with emotion. Tears of admiration and gratitude burst from every eye. The general sympathy was felt by the resigning hero, and wet his cheek with a manly tear. After a decent pause, he addressed Thomas Mifflin, the president of congress, in the following words:

"The great events on which my resignation depended having at length taken place, I have now the honour of

offering my sincere congratulations to congress, and of pre
senting myself before them, to surrender into their hands
the trust committed to me, and to claim the indulgence of
retiring from the service of my country.

" Happy in the confirmation of our independence and
sovereignty, and pleased with the opportunity afforded the
United States of becoming a respectable nation, I resign
with satisfaction the appointment I accepted with diffidence ;
a diffidence in my abilities to accomplish so arduous a task,
which, however, was superseded by a confidence in the
rectitude of our cause, the support of the supreme power
of the union, and the patronage of Heaven.

" The successful termination of the war has verified the
most sanguine expectations ; and my gratitude for the interposition of Providence, and for the assistance I have received from my countrymen, increases with every review
of the momentous contest.

" While I repeat my obligations to the army in general,
I should do injustice to my own feelings not to acknowledge
in this place the peculiar services and distinguished merits
of the persons, who have been attached to my person during the war. It was impossible that the choice of confidential officers to compose my family should have been
more fortunate. Permit me, sir, to recommend, in particular, those who have continued in the service to the present moment, as worthy of the favourable notice and patronage of congress.

" I consider it as an indispensable duty to close this last
solemn act of my official life, by commending the interests
of our dearest country to the protection of Almighty God,
and those who have the superintendence of them to his
holy keeping.

" Having now finished the work assigned me, I retire
from the great theatre of action ; and, bidding an affectionate farewell to this august body, under whose orders I have
long acted, I here offer my commission, and take my leave
of all the employments of public life."

This address being ended, General Washington advanced
and delivered his commission into the hands of the president
of congress, who replied as follows :

" The United States, in congress assembled, receive, with emotions too affecting for utterance, the solemn resignation of the authorities under which you have led their troops with success through a perilous and doubtful war.

" Called upon by your country to defend its invaded rights, you accepted the sacred charge before it had formed alliances, and whilst it was without friends or a government to support you.

" You have conducted the great military contest with wisdom and fortitude, invariably regarding the rights of the civil power through all disasters and changes. You have, by the love and confidence of your fellow-citizens, enabled them to display their martial genius, and transmit their fame to posterity : you have persevered, till these United States, aided by a magnanimous king and nation, have been enabled, under a just Providence, to close the war in safety, freedom and independence ; on which happy event we sincerely join you in congratulations.

" Having defended the standard of liberty in this new world, having taught a lesson useful to those who inflict, and to those who feel oppression, you retire from the great theatre of action with the blessings of your fellow-citizens ; but the glory of your virtues will not terminate with your military command ; it will continue to animate remotest ages. We feel with you our obligations to the army in general, and will particularly charge ourselves with the interest of those confidential officers, who have attended your person to this affecting moment.

" We join you in commending the interests of our dearest country to the protection of Almighty God, beseeching him to dispose the hearts and minds of its citizens to improve the opportunity afforded them of becoming a happy and respectable nation ; and for you we address to him our earnest prayers, that a life so beloved may be fostered with all his care ; that your days may be happy as they have been illustrious, and that he will finally give you that reward, which this world cannot give."

The military services of General Washington, which ended with this interesting day, were as great as ever were rendered by any man to any nation. They were at the same time disinterested. How dear would not a mercena-

ry man have sold such toils, such dangers, and, above all,
such successes!   What schemes of grandeur and of power
would not an ambitious man have built upon the affections
of the people and of the army!   The gratitude of America was so lively, that any thing asked by her resigning
chief would have been readily granted.   He asked nothing for himself, his family or relations; but indirectly solicited favours for the confidential officers, who were attached to his person.   These were young gentlemen, without fortune, who had served him in the capacity of aids-
de-camp.   To have omitted the opportunity which then
offered of recommending them to their country's notice,
would have argued a degree of insensibility in the breast
of their friend.   The only privilege distinguishing him
from other private citizens, which the retiring Washington
did or would receive from his grateful country, was a
right of sending and receiving letters free of postage.

The American chief, having by his own voluntary act
become one of the people, hastened, with ineffable delight,
to his seat at Mount Vernon, on the banks of the Potomac.
There, in a short time, the most successful general in the
world became the most diligent farmer in Virginia.

To pass suddenly from the toils of the first commission
in the United States to the care of a farm, to exchange
the instruments of war for the implements of husbandry,
and to become at once the patron and example of ingenious
agriculture, would, to most men, have been a difficult task.
To the elevated mind of Washington it was natural and
delightful.

His own sensations, after retiring from public business,
are thus expressed in his letters:—"I am just beginning
to experience the ease and freedom from public cares,
which, however desirable, it takes some time to realize; for,
strange as it may seem, it is nevertheless true, that it was
not until lately I could get the better of my usual custom
of ruminating, as soon as I awoke in the morning, on the
business of the ensuing day; and of my surprise on finding, after revolving many things in my mind, that I was
no longer a public man, or had any thing to do with public
transactions.   I feel as I conceive a wearied traveller must

34

do, who, after treading many a painful step with a heavy
burden on his shoulders, is eased of the latter, having
reached the haven to which all the former were directed
and, from his housetop is looking back, and tracing with
an eager eye the meanders by which he escaped the quick-
sands and mires, which lay in his way, and into which
none but the all-powerful Guide and Dispenser of human
events could have prevented his falling."

"I have become a private citizen on the banks of the
Potomac ; and, under the shadow of my own vine and my
own fig-tree, free from the bustle of a camp, and the busy
scenes of public life, I am solacing myself with those tranquil enjoyments, of which the soldier, who is ever in pursuit of fame,—the statesman, whose watchful days and
sleepless nights are spent in devising schemes to promote
the welfare of his own, perhaps the ruin of other countries,
as if this globe was insufficient for us all,—and the cour-
tier, who is always watching the countenance of his prince,
in the hope of catching a gracious smile,—can have very
little conception.   I have not only retired from all public
employments, but am retiring within myself, and shall be
able to view the solitary walk, and tread the paths of private life, with heartfelt satisfaction.   Envious of none, I
am determined to be pleased with all ; and this, my dear
friend, being the order of my march, I will move gently
down the stream of life, until I sleep with my fathers."

Mr. MARSHALL thus finishes this beautiful picture.—ED.

For several months after reaching Mount Vernon, almost every day brought him the addresses of an affectionate and grateful people.   The glow of expression, in which
the high sense universally entertained of his services was
conveyed, manifested a warmth of feeling seldom equalled in the history of man.   It is worthy of remark, that this
unexampled tribute of applause made no impression on the
unassuming modesty of his character and deportment.   The
same firmness of mind, the same steady and well-tempered
judgment, which had guided him through the most perilous seasons of the war, still regulated his conduct ; and
the enthusiastic applauses of an admiring nation appeared

only to cherish sentiments of gratitude, and to give greater activity to the desire still further to contribute to the prosperity of his country.

Alexander Wilson.—NORTH AMERICAN REVIEW.

HE was a Scotchman by birth. The first years of his residence in this country were devoted to school-keeping in Pennsylvania. An early acquaintance with the venerable Bartram kindled within him a love of science; and after he commenced his ornithological inquiries, he pursued them for the remaining short period of his life with an enthusiasm, perseverance, and self-devotion, which have rarely been equalled. He died in Philadelphia, August 23d, 1813, at the age of forty-seven. His American Ornithology, executed under every possible disadvantage, and with encouragement so slender, as hardly to keep him from the heavy pressure of want, is a monument to his name that will never decay. The old world and the new will regard it with equal admiration. "We may add without hesitation," says Mr. Bonaparte, "that such a work as he has published in a new country, is still a desideratum in Europe." To accomplish such a work, with all the facilities which the arts and knowledge of Europe afford, would confer no common distinction. But when it is considered that Wilson taught himself, almost unassisted, the arts of drawing and engraving; that he made his way in the science with very little aid from books or teachers; that he entered a path in which he could find no companions, none to stimulate his ardour by a similarity of pursuits or communion of feeling, none to remove his doubts, guide his inquiries, or to be deeply interested in his success; when these things are considered, the labours of Wilson must claim a praise, which is due to a few only of the solitary efforts of talent and enterprise.

In the strictest sense of the terms, Wilson was a man of genius; his perceptions were quick, his impressions vivid; a bright glow of feeling breathes through his compositions. In the professed walks of poetry, his attempts

were not often fortunate; but his prose writings partake
of the genuine poetic spirit. A lively fancy, exuberance
of thought, and minute observation of the natural world,
are strongly indicated in whatever has flowed from his pen.
He travelled for the double purpose of procuring subscriptions to his book, and searching the forest for birds; and
some of his graphic descriptions of the scenery of nature,
and the habits of the winged tribes, are inimitable. Sometimes he walked; at others descended rivers in a canoe;
again he was on horseback, in a stage-coach or a farmer's
wagon, as the great ends of his wanderings could be most
easily attained. The cold repulses of the many from
whom he solicited subscriptions he bore with equanimity;
undaunted by disappointment, unsubdued by toil and pri-
vation. The acquisition of a new bird, or of new facts
illustrating the habitudes of those already known, was a
fountain of joy in his gloomiest moments; it poured the waters of oblivion over the past, and gave him new energy
in his onward course. The following are his descriptions
of the mocking bird and bald eagle ·

"This distinguished bird, [the eagle,] as he is the most
beautiful of his tribe in this part of the world, and the
adopted *emblem* of our country, is entitled to particular notice. He has been long known to naturalists, being common to both continents, and occasionally met with from a
very high northern latitude to the borders of the torrid
zone, but chiefly in the vicinity of the sea, and along the
shores and cliffs of our lakes and large rivers. Formed by
nature for braving the severest cold; feeding equally upon
the produce of the sea and of the land; possessing powers
of flight capable of outstripping even the tempests themselves; unawed by any thing but man; and, from the
ethereal heights to which he soars, looking abroad at one
glance on an immeasurable expanse of forests, fields, lakes
and ocean, deep below him; he appears indifferent to the
little localities of change of seasons, as in a few minutes
he can pass from summer to winter, from the lower to the
higher regions of the atmosphere, the abode of eternal cold,
and thence descend at will to the torrid or the arctic regions of the earth. He is therefore found at all seasons
in the countries which he inhabits, but prefers such places

as have been mentioned above, from the great partiality he has for fish.

"In procuring these he displays, in a very singular manner, the genius and energy of his character, which is fierce, contemplative, daring and tyrannical; attributes not exerted but on particular occasions, but, when put forth, overwhelming all opposition. Elevated upon a high, 'ead limb of some gigantic tree, that commands a wide view of the neighbouring shore and ocean, he seems calmly to contemplate the motions of the various feathered tribes that pursue their busy avocations below,—the snow-white gulls, slowly winnowing the air,—the busy tringæ, coursing along the sands,—trains of ducks, streaming over the surface,—silent, and watchful cranes, intent and wading,—clamorous crows, and all the winged multitudes that subsist by the bounty of this vast liquid magazine of nature. High over all these hovers one, whose action instantly arrests his attention. By his wide curvature of wing, and sudden suspension in air, he knows him to be the fish-hawk settling over some devoted victim of the deep. His eye kindles at the sight, and, balancing himself with half-opened wings on the branch, he watches the result. Down, rapid as an arrow from heaven, descends the distant object of his attention, the roar of its wings reaching the ear as it disappears in the deep, making the surges foam around. At this moment the looks of the eagle are all ardour; and, levelling his neck for flight, he sees the fish-hawk emerge, struggling with his prey, and mounting into the air with screams of exultation. These are the signal for our hero, who, launching into the air, instantly gives chase, soon gains on the fish-hawk, each exerts his utmost to mount above the other, displaying in these rencounters the most elegant and sublime aerial evolutions. The unincumbered eagle rapidly advances, and is just on the point of reaching his opponent, when, with a sudden scream, probably of despair and honest execration, the latter drops his fish; the eagle, poising himself for a moment, as if to take a more certain aim, descends like a whirlwind, snatches it in his grasp ere it reaches the water, and bears his ill-gotten booty silently away to the woods."

" The plumage of the mocking-bird, though none of the
homeliest, has nothing gaudy or brilliant in it; and, had
he nothing else to recommend him, would scarcely entitle
him to notice; but his figure is well proportioned, and even
handsome. The ease, elegance and rapidity of his movements, the animation of his eye, and the intelligence he
displays in listening, and laying up lessons from almost
every species of the feathered creation within his hearing,
are really surprising, and mark the peculiarity of his genius.
To these qualities we may add that of a voice full, strong
and musical, and capable of almost every modulation, from
the clear, mellow tones of the wood-thrush, to the savage
screams of the bald eagle. In measure and accent, he
faithfully follows his originals. In force and sweetness of
expression, he greatly improves upon them. In his native
groves, mounted upon the top of a tall bush, or half-grown
tree, in the dawn of dewy morning, while the woods are
already vocal with a multitude of warblers, his admirable
song rises pre-eminent over every competitor. The ear
can listen to *his* music alone, to which that of all the others
seems a mere accompaniment. Neither is this strain altogether imitative. His own native notes, which are easily
distinguishable by such as are acquainted with those of our
various song birds, are bold and full, and varied seemingly
beyond all limits. They consist of short expressions of two,
three, or, at the most, five or six syllables, generally interspersed with imitations, and all of them uttered with
great emphasis and rapidity, and continued with undiminished ardour for half an hour or an hour at a time; his
expanded wings and tail, glistening with white, and the
buoyant gayety of his action, arresting the eye as his song
most irresistibly does the ear. He sweeps round with
enthusiastic ecstasy. He mounts and descends as his song
swells or dies away; and, as my friend Mr. Bartram has
beautifully expressed it, ' he bounds aloft with the celerity
of an arrow, as if to recover or recall his very soul, which
expired in the last elevated strain.' While thus exerting
himself, a bystander, destitute of sight, would suppose that
the whole feathered tribes had assembled together on a
trial of skill, each striving to produce his utmost effect;—
so perfect are his imitations. He many times deceives the

sportsman, and sends him in search of birds that perhaps are not within miles of him, but whose notes he exactly imitates. Even birds themselves are frequently imposed on by this admirable mimic, and are decoyed by the fancied calls of their mates ; or dive with precipitati n into the depths of thickets, at the scream of what they suppose to be the sparrow-hawk."

Female Education and Learning.—STORY.

IF Christianity may be said to have given a permanent elevation to woman, as an intellectual and moral being, it is as true that the present age, above all others, has given play to her genius, and taught us to reverence its influence. It was the fashion of other times to treat the literary acquirements of the sex as starched pedantry, or vain pretension ; to stigmatize them as inconsistent with those domestic affections and virtues, which constitute the charm of society. We had abundant homilies read upon their amiable weaknesses and sentimental delicacy, upon their timid gentleness and submissive dependence ; as if to taste the fruit of knowledge were a deadly sin, and ignorance were the sole guardian of innocence. Their whole lives were " sicklied o'er with the pale cast of thought," and concealment of intellectual power was often resorted to, to escape the dangerous imputation of masculine strength. In the higher walks of life, the satirist was not without colour for the suggestion, that it was

" A youth of folly, an old age of cards ;"

and that, elsewhere, " most women had no character at all," beyond that of purity and devotion to their families. Admirable as are these qualities, it seemed an abuse of the gifts of Providence to deny to mothers the power of instructing their children, to wives the privilege of sharing the intellectual pursuits of their husbands, to sisters and daughters the delight of ministering knowledge in the fireside circle, to youth and beauty the charm of refined sense, to age and infirmity the consolation of studies, which

elevate the soul, and gladden the listless hours of despondency.

These things have, in a great measure, passed away.
The prejudices, which dishonoured the sex, have yielded
to the influence of truth. By slow but sure advances,
education has extended itself through all ranks of female
society. There is no longer any dread, lest the culture
of science should foster that masculine boldness or restless
independence, which alarms by its sallies, or wounds by its
inconsistencies. We have seen that here, as every where
else, knowledge is favourable to human virtue and human
happiness ; that the refinement of literature adds lustre to
the devotion of piety ; that true learning, like true taste,
is modest and unostentatious ; that grace of manners receives a higher polish from the discipline of the schools ;
that cultivated genius sheds a cheering light over domestic
duties, and its very sparkles, like those of the diamond,
attest at once its power and its purity. There is not a rank
of female society, however high, which does not now pay
homage to literature, or that would not blush even at the
suspicion of that ignorance, which, a half century ago,
was neither uncommon nor discreditable. There is not a
parent, whose pride may not glow at the thought, that his
daughter's happiness is in a great measure within her own
command, whether she keeps the cool, sequestered vale of
life, or visits the busy walks of fashion.

A new path is thus opened for female exertion, to alleviate the pressure of misfortune, without any supposed
sacrifice of dignity or modesty. Man no longer aspires to
an exclusive dominion in authorship. He has rivals or allies in almost every department of knowledge ; and they
are to be found among those, whose elegance of manners
and blamelessness of life command his respect, as much as
their talents excite his admiration. Who is there that does
not contemplate with enthusiasm the precious fragments of
Elizabeth Smith, the venerable learning of Elizabeth Car-
ter, the elevated piety of Hannah More, the persuasive
sense of Mrs. Barbauld, the elegant memoirs of her accomplished niece, the bewitching fiction of Madame D'Ar-
blay, the vivid, picturesque and terrific imagery of Mrs
Radcliffe, the glowing poetry of Mrs. Hemans, the match

less wit, the inexhaustible conversations, the fine character painting, the practical instructions of Miss Edgeworth,
the great Known, standing in her own department by the
side of the great Unknown!

———◆———

Poetical Character of Gray.—BUCKMINSTER.

IT has been the fortune of Gray, as well as of other poets of the first order, to suffer by the ignorance and the
envy of contemporaries, and at last to obtain from posterity, amid the clamours of discordant criticism, only a divided
suffrage.   The coldness of his first reception by the public
has, however, been more than compensated by the warmth
of his real admirers ; for he is one of those few poets, who
at every new reading recompenses you double for every
encomium, by disclosing some new charm of sentiment or
of diction.   The many, who have ignorantly or reluctantly
praised, may learn, as they study him, that they have nothing to retract ; and those, who have delighted to depreciate
his excellence, will understand, if they ever learn to admire him, that their former insensibility was pardonable,
though they may be tempted to wish, that it had never
been known.   Gray was not destitute of those anticipations
of future fame, which God has sometimes granted to
neglected genius, as he gives the testimony of conscience
to suffering virtue.   His letters to Mason and Hurd show
how pleasantly he could talk of those, who could neither
admire nor understand his odes.   He knew, that it was
not of much consequence to be neglected by that public,
which suffered Thomson's Winter to remain for years unnoticed, and which had to be told by Addison, at the expi-
ration of half a century, of the merit of the Paradise Lost
Still less could his fame be endangered by Colman's exquisitely humorous parody of his odes, especially since it
is now known, that Colman has confessed to Warton, that
he repented of the attempt ; and, at the present day, I
know not whether it would add any thing to the final reputation of a lyric poet, to have been praised by that great
man, who could pronounce Dryden's ode on Mrs. Killigrew
35

the finest in our language, and who could find nothing in
Collins' but " clusters of consonants."

* * * * * * * * * * * * *

If Gray has any claim to the character of a poet, he
must hold an elevated rank or none.   If he is not excellent,
he is supremely ridiculous; if he has not the living spirit
of verse, he is only besotted and bewildered with the fumes
of a vulgar and stupifying draught, which he found in
some stagnant pool at the foot of Parnassus, and which he
mistook for the Castalian spring.   But if Pindar and Horace were poets, so too was Gray.   The finest notes of their
lyre were elicited by the breath of inspiration breathing
on the strings; and he, who cannot enter into the spirit
which animates the first Pythian of Pindar, or the " Quem
virum aut heroa" of Horace, must be content to be *shown*
beauties in Gray, which it is not yet granted him to feel,
or spontaneously to discern.   I am willing to rest the merit
of Gray on Horace's definition of a poet,—

> " Ingenium cui sit, cui mens divinior, atque os,
> Magna sonaturum, sed nominis hujus honorem."

* * * * * *   *   * * * * * *

We shall be more ready to admit, that the sole perfection of poetry consists not merely in faithful description,
fine sense, or pointed sentiment in polished verse, if we
attend to some curious remarks of Burke, in the last part
of his Essay on the Sublime and Beautiful.   He has there
sufficiently shown that many fine passages, which produce
the most powerful effect on a sensible mind, present no
ideas to the fancy, which can be strictly marked or imbodied.   The most thrilling touches of sublimity and beauty are consistent with great indistinctness of images and
conceptions.   Indeed, it is hardly to be believed, before
making the experiment, that we should be so much affected as we are, by passages which convey no definite picture
to the mind.   To those who are insensible to Gray's curious junction of phrases and hardy personifications, we recommend the study of this chapter of Burke.   There they
will see, that the effect of poetical expression depends more
upon particular and indefinable associations, than upon the

precise images which the words convey. Thus, of Gray's
poetry, the effect, like that of Milton's finest passages in
the Allegro and Penseroso, is to raise a glow, which it is
not easy to describe ; but the beauty of a passage, when
we attempt to analyze it, seems to consist in a certain exquisite felicity of terms, fraught with pictures which it is
impossible to transfer with perfect exactness to the canvass.

* * * * * * * * * * * *

If the perfection of poetry consists in imparting every
impression to the mind in the most exquisite degree, and
the ode has, by the consent of critics in all ages, been indulged in irregularities which are not pardonable in other
kinds of verse, because it is supposed to follow the rapid
and unrestrained passage of images through the mind, it is
surely enough to satisfy even Aristotle himself, that in
Gray's odes the subject is never entirely deserted, and that
a continued succession of sublime or beautiful impressions
is conveyed to the mind, in language the most grateful to
the ear which our English tongue can furnish. For my
own part, I take as much delight in contemplating the rich
hues that succeed one another without order in a deep cloud
in the west, which has no prescribed shape, as in viewing the seven colours of the rainbow disposed in a form
exactly semicircular. The truth is, that, after having read
any poem once, we recur to it afterwards not as a whole,
but for the beauty of particular passages.

It would be easy to reply in order to the invidious and
contemptible criticisms of Johnson on particular passages
in these odes, and to show their captious futility. This,
however, has been frequently and successfully attempted.
Those faults, which must at last be admitted in Gray's
poetry, detract little from his merit. That only two
flat lines should be found in a whole volume of poems, is
an honour which even Virgil might be permitted to envy.
He who can endure to dwell upon these petty blemishes
in the full stream of Gray's enthusiasm, must be as insensible to the pomp and grandeur of poetic phrase, as that
traveller would be to the sentiment of the sublime in nature, who could sit coolly by the cataract of Niagara, spec-

ulating upon the chips and straws that were carried over
the fal'.

That his digressions are sometimes abrupt, is a character
which he shares with his Grecian master; and that an
obscurity sometimes broods over his sublimest images, is not
to be denied. But violence of transition, if it is a fault in
this kind of poetry, must be excused by those laws of lyrical
composition, which we have hitherto been content to receive, like the laws of the drama and the epic, implicitly
from the ancients; and the obscurity of Gray is never invincible. It is not the fog of dulness; but, like the darkness which the eye at first perceives in excessive brightness, it vanishes the longer it is contemplated, and when
the eye is accommodated to the flood of light.

* * * * * * * * * * * * * *

The distinguishing excellence of Gray's poetry is, I
think, to be found in the astonishing force and beauty of
his epithets. In other poets, if you are endeavouring to
recollect a passage, and find that a single word still eludes
you, it is not impossible to supply it occasionally with
something equivalent or superior. But let any man attempt this in Gray's poetry, and he will find that he does
not even approach the beauty of the original. Like the
single window in Aladdin's palace, which the grand vizier
undertook to finish with diamonds equal to the rest, but
found, after a long trial, that he was not rich enough to
furnish the jewels, nor ingenious enough to dispose them,
so there are lines in Gray, which critics and poets might
labour forever to supply, and without success. This wonderful richness of expression has perhaps injured his fame.
For sometimes a single word, by giving rise to a succession of images, which preoccupy the mind, obscures
the lustre of the succeeding epithets. The mind is fatigued and retarded by the crowd of beauties, soliciting
the attention at the same moment to different graces of
thought and expression. Overpowered by the blaze of
embellishment, we cry out with Horace, " Parce, Liber!
parce! gravi metuende thyrso." Hence Gray, more than
any other lyric poet, will endure to be read in detached
portions, and again and again.

Another characteristic of Gray, which, while it detracts something from his originality, increases the charm of his verse, is the classical raciness of his diction. . Milton is the only English poet who rivals him in the remote learning of his allusions, and this has greatly restrained the number of their admirers. * * * * The meaning of the word *rage*, in this line of the Elegy, a poem which all profess to relish and admire,

> " Chill penury repressed their noble rage,"

cannot be understood without reverting to a common use of the word ορχη among the Greeks, to which Gray refers, signifying a strong bent of genius. The Progress of Poesy is peculiarly full of allusions to the Heathen Mythology The sublime imitation of Pindar, in the description of the bird of Jupiter, in the second stanza, is almost worth the learning of Greek to understand.

The last perfection of verse, in which Gray is unrivalled, is the power of his numbers. These have an irresistible charm even with those, who understand not his meaning and without this musical enchantment, it is doubtful whether he would have surmounted the ignorance and insensibility, with which he was at first received. His rhythm and cadences afford a perpetual pleasure, which, 'n the full contemplation of his other charms, we sometimes forget to acknowledge. There is nothing, surely, in the whole compass of English versification, to be compared in musical structure with the third stanza of his ode on the Progress of Poesy. The change of movement, in the six last lines, is inexpressibly fine. The effect of these varied cadences and measures is, to my ear at least, full as great as that of an adagio in music immediately following a rondo; and I admire in silent rapture the genius of that man, who could so mould our untractable language as to produce all the effect of the great masters of musical composition. If the ancient lyrics contained many specimens of numerous verse equal to this, we need no longer wonder that they were always accompanied with music. Poetry never approached nearer to painting, than verse does in this stanza to the most ravishing melody.

35 *

Republics of Greece and Italy.—HAMILTON.

IT is impossible to read the history of the petty republics
of Greece and Italy, without feeling sensations of horror
and disgust at the distractions with which they were continually agitated, and at the rapid succession of revolutions,
by which they were kept perpetually vibrating between
the extremes of tyranny and anarchy. If they exhibit occasional calms, these only serve as short-lived contrasts to
the furious storms that are to succeed. If now and then intervals of felicity open themselves to view, we behold them
with a mixture of regret, arising from the reflection, that
the pleasing scenes before us are soon to be overwhelmed
by the tempestuous waves of sedition and party rage. If
momentary rays of glory break forth from the gloom, while
they dazzle as with a transient and fleeting brilliancy, they
at the same time admonish us to lament that the vices of
government should pervert the direction and tarnish the
lustre of those bright talents and exalted endowments, for
which the favoured soils that produced them have been so
justly celebrated.

From the disorders that disfigure the annals of those
republics, the advocates of despotism have drawn arguments, not only against the forms of republican government,
but against the very principles of civil liberty. They have
decried all free governments as inconsistent with the order
of society, and have indulged themselves in malicious exultation over its friends and partisans. Happily for mankind, stupendous fabrics, reared on the basis of liberty,
which have flourished for ages, have, in a few instances,
refuted their gloomy sophisms. And I trust America will
be the broad and solid foundation of other edifices not less
magnificent, which will be equally permanent monuments
of their error.

But it is not to be denied, that the portraits they have
sketched of republican government were but too just copies
of the originals from which they were taken. If it had
been found impracticable to have devised models of a more
perfect structure, the enlightened friends of liberty would
have been obliged to abandon the cause of that species of

government as indefensible. The science of politics, how·
ever, like most other sciences, has received great improve·
ment. The efficacy of various principles is now well understood, which were either not known at all, or imperfectly known to the ancients. The regular distribution of
power into distinct departments—the introduction of legislative balances and checks—the institution of courts composed of judges holding their offices during good behaviour
—the representation of the people in the legislature, by
deputies of their own election—these are either wholly
new discoveries, or have made their principal progress
towards perfection in modern times. They are means, and
powerful means, by which the excellences of republican
government may be retained, and its imperfections lessened
or avoided.

Professional Character of William Pinkney.— HENRY WHEATON.

IN tracing the principal outlines of his public character,
his professional talents and attainments must necessarily
occupy the most prominent place. To extraordinary nat·
ural endowments, Mr. Pinkney added deep and various
knowledge in his profession. A long course of study and
practice had familiarized his mind with the science of ju-
risprudence. His intellectual powers were most conspicuous
in the investigations connected with that science. He had
felt himself originally attracted to it by invincible inclination ; it was his principal pursuit in life ; and he never entirely lost sight of it in his occasional deviations into other
pursuits and employments. The lures of political ambition
and the blandishments of polished society, or perhaps a
vague desire of universal accomplishment and general
applause, might sometimes tempt him to stray, for a season, from the path which the original bent of his genius
had assigned him. But he always returned with fresh
ardour and new delight to his appropriate vocation. He
was devoted to the law with a true enthusiasm ; and his
other studies and pursuits, so far as they had a serious ai

ject, were valued chiefly as they might minister to this
idol of his affections.

It was in his profession that he found himself at home;
in this consisted his pride and his pleasure; for, as he said,
" the bar is not the place to acquire or preserve a false and
fraudulent reputation for talents." And on that theatre
he felt conscious of possessing those powers which would
command success.

This entire devotion to his professional pursuits was continued with unremitting perseverance to the end of his
career. If the celebrated Denys Talon could say of the
still more celebrated D'Aguesseau, on hearing his first
speech at the bar, " *that he would willingly* END *as that
young man* COMMENCED," every youthful aspirant to
forensic fame among us might wish to begin his professional exertions with the same love of labour, and the same ardent desire of distinction, which marked the efforts of
William Pinkney throughout his life.

What might not be expected from professional emulation,
directed by such an ardent spirit and such singleness of
purpose, even if sustained by far inferior abilities! But
no abilities, however splendid, can command success at the
bar, without intense labour and persevering application.
It was this which secured to Mr. Pinkney the most extensive and lucrative practice ever acquired by any American lawyer, and which raised him to such an enviable
height of professional eminence. For many years he was
the acknowledged leader of the bar in his native state;
and, during the last ten years of his life, the principal period of his attendance in the supreme court of the nation,
he enjoyed the reputation of having been rarely equalled,
and perhaps never excelled, in the power of reasoning upon
legal subjects. This was the faculty which most remarkably distinguished him. His mind was acute and subtile,
and, at the same time, comprehensive in its grasp, rapid
and clear in its conceptions, and singularly felicitous in
the exposition of the truths it was employed in investigating.

Of the extent and solidity of his legal attainments it would
be difficult to speak in adequate terms, without the appearance of exaggeration. He was profoundly versed in the

ancient learning of the common law; its technical peculiarities and feudal origin. Its subtile distinctions and artificial logic were familiar to his early studies, and enabled him to expound, with admirable force and perspicuity, the rules of real property. He was familiar with every branch of commercial law; and superadded, at a later period of his life, to his other legal attainments, an extensive acquaintance with the principles of international law, and the practice of the prize courts. In his legal studies he preferred the original text-writers and reporters, (è *fontibus hauríri*,) to all those abridgments, digests, and elementary treatises, which lend so many convenient helps and facilities to the modern lawyer, but which he considered as adapted to form sciolists, and to encourage indolence and superficial habits of investigation. His favourite law book was the Coke Littleton, which he had read many times. Its principal texts he had treasured up in his memory, and his arguments at the bar abounded with perpetual recurrences to the principles and analogies drawn from this rich mine of common law learning.

External Appearance of England.—A. H. EVERETT

WHATEVER may be the extent of the distress in England, or the difficulty of finding any remedies for it, which shall be at once practicable and sufficient, it is certain that the symptoms of decline have not yet displayed themselves on the surface; and no country in Europe, at the present day, probably none that ever flourished at any preceding period of ancient o of modern times, ever exhibited so strongly the outward marks of general industry, wealth and prosperity. The misery that exists, whatever it may be, retires from public view; and the traveller sees no 'traces of it except in the beggars,—which are not more numerous than they are on the continent,—in the courts of justice, and in the newspapers. On the contrary, the impressions he receives from the objects that meet his view are almost uniformly agreeable. He is pleased with the great attention paid to his personal accommodation as a traveller, with the excellent roads, and the conveniences of the public carriages and inns. The country every where exhibits the appearance of high cultivation, or else of wild and picturesque beauty; and even the unimproved lands are disposed with taste and skill, so as to embellish the landscape very highly, if they do not contribute, as they might, to the substantial comfort of the people. From every eminence extensive parks and grounds, spreading far and wide over hill and vale, interspersed with dark woods, and variegated with bright waters, unroll themselves before the eye, like enchanted gardens. And while the elegant constructions of the modern proprietors fill the mind with images of ease and luxury, the mouldering ruins that remain of former ages, of the castles and churches of their feudal ancestors, increase the interest of the picture by contrast, and associate with it poetical and affecting recollections of other times and manners. Every village seems to be the chosen residence of Industry, and her handmaids, Neatness and Comfort; and, in the various parts of the island, her operations present themselves under the most amusing and agreeable variety of forms. Sometimes her votaries are mounting to the skies in manufactories of innumerable stories in height, and sometimes diving in mines into the bowels of the earth, or dragging up drowned treasures from the bottom of the sea. At one time the ornamented grounds of a wealthy proprietor seem to realize the fabled Elysium; and again, as you pass in the evening through some village engaged in the iron manufacture, where a thousand forges are feeding at once their dark-red fires, and clouding the air with their volumes of smoke, you might think yourself, for a moment, a little too near some drearier residence.

The aspect of the cities is as various as that of the country. Oxford, in the silent, solemn grandeur of its numerous collegiate palaces, with their massy stone walls, and vast interior quadrangles, seems like the deserted capital of some departed race of giants. This is the splendid sepulchre, where Science, like the Roman Tarpeia, lies buried under the weight of gold that rewarded her ancient services, and where copious libations of the richest Port and Madeira are daily poured out to her memory. At Liver-

COMMON-PLACE BOOK OF PROSE.

pool, on the contrary, all is bustle, brick and business. Every
thing breathes of modern times, every body is occupied
with the concerns of the present moment, excepting one
elegant scholar, who unites a singular resemblance to the
Roman face and dignified person of our Washington, with
the magnificent spirit and intellectual accomplishments of
his own Italian hero.

At every change in the landscape, you fall upon monuments of some new race of men, among the number that
have in their turn inhabited these islands. The mysterious
monument of Stonehenge, standing remote and alone upon a
bare and boundless heath, as much unconnected with the
events of past ages as it is with the uses of the present, carries you back, beyond all historical records, into the obscurity
of a wholly unknown period. Perhaps the Druids raised it;
but by what machinery could these half barbarians have
wrought and moved such immense masses of rock? By
what fatality is it, that, in every part of the globe, the most
durable impressions that have been made upon its surface
were the work of races now entirely extinct? Who were
the builders of the pyramids, and the massy monuments
of Egypt and India? Who constructed the Cyclopean
walls of Italy and Greece, or elevated the innumerable
and inexplicable mounds, which are seen in every part of
Europe, Asia, and America; or the ancient forts upon the
Ohio, on whose ruins the third growth of trees is now more
than four hundred years old? All these constructions have
existed through the whole period within the memory of
man, and will continue, when all the architecture of the
present generation, with its high civilization and improved
machinery, shall have crumbled into dust. Stonehenge
will remain unchanged, when the banks of the Thames
shall be as bare as Salisbury heath. But the Romans had
something of the spirit of these primitive builders, and
they left every where distinct traces of their passage.
Half the castles in Great Britain were founded, according
to tradition, by Julius Cæsar; and abundant vestiges remain, throughout the island, of their walls, and forts, and
military roads. Most of their castles have, however, been
built upon and augmented at a later period, and belong,
with more propriety, to the brilliant period of Gothic archi-

tecture. Thus the keep of Warwick dates from the time of Cæsar, while the castle itself, with its lofty battlements, extensive walls, and large enclosures, bears witness to the age, when every Norman chief was a military despot within his own barony. To this period appertains the principal part of the magnificent Gothic monuments, castles, cathedrals, abbeys, priories and churches, in various stages of preservation and of ruin; some, like Warwick and Alnwick castles, like Salisbury cathedral and Westminster abbey, in all their original perfection; others, like Kenilworth and Canterbury, little more than a rude mass of earth and rubbish; and others again in the intermediate stages of decay, borrowing a sort of charm from their very ruin, and putting on their dark-green robes of ivy to conceal the ravages of time, as if the luxuriant bounty of nature were purposely throwing a veil over the frailty and feebleness of art. What a beautiful and brilliant vision was this Gothic architecture, shining out as it did from the deepest darkness of feudal barbarism! And here again, by what fatality has it happened that the moderns, with all their civilization and improved taste, have been as utterly unsuccessful in rivalling the divine simplicity of the Greeks, as the rude grandeur of the Cyclopeans and ancient Egyptians? Since the revival of art in Europe, the builders have confined themselves wholly to a graceless and unsuccessful imitation of ancient models. Strange, that the only new architectural conception of any value, subsequent to the time of Phidias, should have been struck out at the worst period of society that has since occurred! Sometimes the moderns, in their laborious poverty of invention, heap up small materials in large masses, and think that St. Peter's or St. Paul's will be as much more sublime than the Parthenon, as they are larger; at others, they condescend to a servile imitation of the wild and native graces of the Gothic; as the Chinese, in their stupid ignorance of perspective, can still copy, line by line, and point by point, an European picture. But the Norman castles and churches, with all their richness and sublimity, fell with the power of their owners at the rise of the commonwealth. The Independents were levellers of substance as well as form: and the material traces they left of their existence are the ruins of what their predecessors had built. They, too, had an architecture, but it was not in wood nor stone. It was enough for them to lay the foundation of the nobler fabric of civil liberty. The effects of the only change in society that has since occurred, are seen in the cultivated fields, the populous and thriving cities, the busy ports, and the general prosperous appearance of the country.

All the various aspects, that I have mentioned, present themselves in turns; and, having gradually succeeded to each other, their contrasts are never too rude, and they harmonize together so as to make up a most agreeable picture. Sometimes, as at Edinburgh, the creations of ancient and of modern days, the old and new towns, have placed themselves very amicably side by side, like Fitz James and Rhoderic Dhu reposing on the same plaid; while at London, the general emporium and central point of the whole system, every variety of origin and social existence is defaced, and all are coagulate ¹ in one uniform though heterogeneous mass.

Features of American Scenery.—Tudor.

THE numerous waterfalls, the enchanting beauty of Lake George and its pellucid flood, of Lake Champlain and the lesser lakes, afford many objects of the most picturesque character; while the inland seas, from Superior to Ontario, and that astounding cataract, whose roar would hardly be increased by the united murmurs of all the cascades of Europe, are calculated to inspire vast and sublime conceptions. The effects, too, of our climate, composed of a Siberian winter and an Italian summer, furnish new and peculiar objects for description. The circumstances of remote regions are here blended, and strikingly opposite appearances witnessed in the same spot at different seasons of the year. In our winters, we have the sun at the same altitude as in Italy, shining on an unlimited surface of snow, which can only be found in the higher latitudes of Europe, where the sun in the winter rises little above the horizon. The dazzling brilliance of a winter's day and a moonlight

night, in an atmosphere astonishingly clear and frosty, when
the utmost splendour of the sky is reflected from a surface
of spotless white, attended with the most excessive cold, is
peculiar to the northern part of the United States. What,
too, can surpass the celestial purity and transparency of the
atmosphere in a fine autumnal day, when our vision and
our thought seem carried to the third heaven; the gorgeous
magnificence of the close, when the sun sinks from our
view, surrounded with various masses of clouds fringed
with gold and purple, and reflecting, in evanescent tints,
all the hues of the rainbow!

<hr>

Literary Character of Jefferson and Adams — WEBSTER.

THE last public labour of Mr. Jefferson naturally suggests the expression of the high praise which is due, both
to him and to Mr. Adams, for their uniform and zealous
attachment to learning, and to the cause of general know'-
edge. Of the advantages of learning, indeed, and of li-
erary accomplishments, their own characters were striking
recommendations and illustrations. They were scholars,
ripe and good scholars; widely acquainted with ancient as
well as modern literature, and not altogether uninstructed
in the deeper sciences. Their acquirements doubtless were
different, and so were the particular objects of their literary pursuits; as their tastes and characters in these respects differed like those of other men. Being also men
of busy lives, with great objects requiring action constantly before them, their attainments in letters did not become
showy or obtrusive. Yet I would hazard the opinion,
that, if we could now ascertain all the causes which gave
them eminence and distinction in the midst of the great
men with whom they acted, we should find not among the
least their early acquisition in literature, the resources
which it furnished, the promptitude and facility which it
communicated, and the w de field it opened for analogy and
illustration; giving them thus, on every subject, a larger

view and a broader range, as well for discussion as for the government of their own conduct.

Literature sometimes, and pretensions to it much oftener, disgusts, by appearing to hang loosely on the character, like something foreign or extraneous; not a part, but an ill-adjusted appendage; or by seeming to overload and weigh it down by its unsightly bulk, like the productions of bad taste in architecture, when there is massy and cumbrous ornament, without strength or solidity of column. This has exposed learning, and especially classical learning, to reproach. Men have seen that it might exist without mental superiority, without vigour, without good taste, and without utility. But, in such cases, classical learning has only not inspired natural talent; or, at most, it has but made original feebleness of intellect and natural bluntness of perception somewhat more conspicuous. The question, after all, if it be a question, is, whether literature, ancient as well as modern, does not assist a good understanding, improve natural good taste, add polished armour to native strength, and render its possessor not only more capable of deriving private happiness from contemplation and reflection, but more accomplished also for action in the affairs of life, and especially for public action. Those, whose memories we now honour, were learned men; but their learning was kept in its proper place, and made subservient to the uses and objects of life. They were scholars, not common nor superficial; but their scholarship was so in keeping with their character, so blended and inwrought, that careless observers or bad judges, not seeing an ostentatious display of it, might infer that it did not exist; forgetting, or not knowing, that classical learning, in men who act in conspicuous public stations, perform duties which exercise the faculty of writing, or address popular, judicial, or deliberative bodies, is often felt where it is little seen, and sometimes felt more effectually because it is not seen at all.

Eloquence and Humour of Patrick Henry.—WIRT.

HOOK was a Scotchman, a man of wealth, and suspected of being unfriendly to the American cause. During the distresses of the American army, consequent on the joint invasion of Cornwallis and Phillips in 1731, a Mr. Venable, an army commissary, had taken two of Hook's steers for the use of the troops. The act had not been strictly legal; and, on the establishment of peace, Hook, on the advice of Mr. Cowan, a gentleman of some distinction in the law, thought proper to bring an action of trespass against Mr. Venable, in the district court of New London. Mr. Henry appeared for the defendant, and is said to have disported himself in this cause to the infinite enjoyment of his hearers, the unfortunate Hook always excepted. After Mr. Henry became animated in the cause, says a correspondent, he appeared to have complete control over the passions of his audience: at one time he excited their indignation against Hook: vengeance was visible in every countenance: again, when he chose to relax, and ridicule him, the whole audience was in a roar of laughter. He painted the distresses of the American army, exposed, almost naked, to the rigours of a winter's sky, and marking the frozen ground over which they trod with the blood of their unshod feet. Where was the man, he said, who had an American heart in his bosom, who would not have thrown open his fields, his barns, his cellars, the doors of his house, the portals of his breast, to have received with open arms the meanest soldier in that little band of famished patriots? Where is the man? *There* he stands—but whether the heart of an American beats in his bosom, you, gentlemen, are to judge. He then carried the jury by the powers of his imagination to the plains around York, the surrender of which had followed shortly after the act complained of: he depicted the surrender in the most glowing and noble colours of his eloquence—the audience saw before their eyes the humiliation and dejection of the British as they marched out of their trenches—they saw the triumph which lighted up every patriot face, and heard the shouts of victory, and the cry of ' Washington and liberty,' as it rung and echoed through the American ranks, and was reverberated from the hills and shores of the neighbouring river—"but, hark! what notes of discord are these, which disturb the general joy, and silence the acclamation of victory—they are the notes of John Hook, hoarsely bawling through the American camp, '*Beef! beef! beef!*' "

The whole audience were convulsed: a particular incident will give a better idea of the effect than any general description. The clerk of the court, unable to command himself, and unwilling to commit any breach of decorum in his place, rushed out of the court-house, and threw himself on the grass, in the most violent paroxysm of laughter, where he was rolling, when Hook, with very different feelings, came out for relief into the yard also. "Jemmy Steptoe," said he to the clerk, "what the devil ails ye, mon?" Mr. Steptoe was only able to say that *he could not help it.* "Never mind ye," said Hook; "wait till Billy Cowan gets up; he'll show him the la'!" Mr. Cowan, however, was so completely overwhelmed by the torrent which bore upon his client, that, when he rose to reply to Mr. Henry, he was scarcely able to make an intelligible or audible remark. The cause was decided almost by acclamation. The jury retired for form's sake, and instantly returned with a verdict for the defendant. Nor did the effect of Mr. Henry's speech stop here. The people were so highly excited by the tory audacity of such a suit, that Hook began to hear around him a cry more terrible than that of *beef*, it was the cry of *tar and feathers;* from the application of which it is said, that nothing saved him but a precipitate flight and the speed of his horse.

Valley of the Commanches.—FRANCIS BERRIAN.

I AROSE early in the morning to make the circuit of this lovely vale. At the extremity of the village, the torrent whose sources were in the mountains, poured down, from a prodigious elevation, a white and perpendicular cascade, which seemed a sheet suspended in the air. It falls into a circular basin, paved with blue limestone, of some rods circuit. The dash near at hand has a startling effect upon the ear. But at a little distance, it is just the murmur to inspire repose, and it spreads a delicious coolness all around the place. From the basin the stream seems to partake of the repose of the valley ; for it broadens into a transparent and quiet water, whose banks are fringed with pawpaws, persimon, laurel, and catalpa shrubs and trees, interlaced with vines, under which the green carpet is rendered gay with flowers of every scent and hue. The soil is black, tender, and exuberantly fertile. The coolness of the vale and the shade, together with the irrigation of the stream, cover the whole valley with a vivid verdure. The beauti- ful red-bird, with its crimson-tufted crest, and the nightin- gale sparrow, pouring from a body scarcely larger than an acorn a continued stream of sound, a prolonged, plaintive and sweetly-modulated harmony, that might be heard at the distance of half a mile, had commenced their morning voluntary. The mocking bird, the buffoon of songsters, was parodying the songs of all the rest. Its short and jerking notes at times imitated bursts of laughter. Sometimes, laying aside its habitual levity, it shows that it knows the notes of seriousness, and trills a sweetly-melancholy strain Above the summits of these frowning mountains, that mor- tal foot had never yet trodden, soared the mountain eagle, drinking the sunbeam in the pride of his native indepen- dence. Other birds of prey, apparently poised on their wings, swam slowly round in easy curves, and seemed to look with delight upon the green spot embosomed in the mountains. They sallied back and forwards, as though they could not tire of the view. The sun, which had burnished all the tops of the mountains with gold, and here and there glistened on banks of snow, would not shine into the val- ley, until he had almost gained his meridian height. The natives, fleet as the deer when on expeditions abroad, and at home lazy and yawning, were just issuing from their cabins, and stretching their limbs supinely in the cool of the morn- ing. The smoke of their cabin fires had begun to undulate and whiten in horizontal pillars athwart the valley it was a charming assemblage of strong contrasts, rocky and inaccessible mountains, the deep and incessant roar of the stream, a valley that seemed to sleep between these impregnable ramparts of nature, a little region of landscape surrounded by black and ragged cliffs, on every side dotted thick with brilliant and beautiful vegetation, and fragrant with hundreds of acacias, and catalpas in full flower, a spot sequestered like a lonely isle in the midst of the ocean; in the midst of it a simple, busy, and undescribed people, whose forefathers had been born and had died here for uncounted generations; a people who could record wars, loves, and all the changes of fortune, if they had had their historian. Such was the valley of the Commanches.

There are places where I am at once at home with Nature, and where she seems to take me to her bosom with all the fondness of a mother. I forget at once that I am a stranger in a strange land; and this was one of those places. I cannot describe the soothing sensations I felt. I listened to the mingled sounds of a hundred birds, the barking of the dogs on the acclivities of the hills, the cheerful sounds of the domestic animals, and the busy hum of the savages. The morning was fresh and balmy. The sublime nature above me, and the quiet and happy animated nature on my own level, seemed to be occupied in morning orisons to the Creator. I, too, felt the glad thrill of devotion come over my mind. "These are thy works, Parent of good." Here, thought I, in this delightful vale, with a few friends, is the place where one would choose to dream away his short day and night, forgetting and forgotten.

> " Here would I live, unnoticed and unknown,
> Here, unlamented, would I die;
> Steal from the world, and not a stone
> Tell where I lie."

Pleasures of the Man of a refined Imagination.— IDLE MAN.

WHEN such a one turns away from men, and is left alone in silent communion with nature and his own thoughts, and there are no bounds to the movements of the feelings, and nothing on which he would shut his eyes, but God's

own land has made all before him as it is, he feels his
spirit opening upon a new existence—becoming as broad
as the sun and the air—as various as the earth over which
it spreads itself, and touched with that love which God has
imaged in all he has formed. His senses take a quicker
life,—his whole frame becomes one refined and exquisite
emotion, and the etherealized body is made, as it were, a
spirit in bliss. His soul grows stronger and more active
within him as he sees life intense and working throughout
nature ; and that which passes away links itself with the
eternal, when he finds new life beginning even with decay,
and hastening to put forth in some other form of beauty,
and become a sharer in some new delight. His spirit
is ever awake with happy sensations, and cheerful, and innocent, and easy thoughts. Soul and body are blending
into one—the senses and thoughts mix in one delight—he
sees a universe of order, and beauty, and joy, and life, of
which he becomes a part, and he finds himself carried
along in the eternal going on of nature. Sudden and short-
lived passions of men take no hold upon him, for he has
sat in holy thought by the roar and hurry of the stream,
which has rushed on from the beginning of things ; and
he is quiet in the tumult of the multitude, for he has watched the tracery of leaves playing over the foam.

The innocent face of nature gives him an open and
fair mind. Pain and death seem passing away, for all
about him is cheerful and in its spring. His virtues are
not taught him as lessons, but are shed upon him, and enter
into him, like the light and warmth of the sun. Amidst all
the variety of earth, he sees a fitness which frees him
from the formalities of rule, and lets him abroad to find a
pleasure in all things, and order becomes a simple feeling
of the soul.   .

Religion to such a one has thoughts, and visions, and
sensations, tinged as it were with a holier and brighter
light than falls on other men. The love and reverence of
the Creator make their abode in his imagination, and he
gathers about them the earth, and air, and ideal worlds
His heart is made glad with the perfectness in the works
of God, when he considers that even of the multitude of
things that are growing up and decaying, and of those

which have come and gone, on which the eye of man has never rested, each was as fair and complete as if made to live forever for our instruction and delight.

Freedom, and order, and beauty, and grandeur, are it accordance with his mind, and give largeness and height to his thoughts,—he moves amongst the bright clouds, he wanders away into the measureless depth of the stars, and is touched by the fire with which God has lighted them—all that is made partakes of the eternal, and religion becomes a perpetual pleasure.

Scene at Niag ra.—MISS SEDGWICK.

THE vehement dashing of the rapids ; the sublime falls the various hues of the mass of waters ; the snowy whiteness and the deep bright green ; the billowy spray that veils in deep obscurity the depths below ; the verdant island that interposes between the two falls half veiled in a misty mantle, and placed there, it would seem, that the eye and the spirit may repose on it ; the little island on the brink of the American fall, that looks, amidst the commotion of the waters, like the sylvan vessel of a woodland nymph gayly sailing onward,—or as if the wish of the Persian girl were realized, and the " little isle *had* wings,"—a thing of life and motion that the spirit of the waters had inspired.

The profound caverns, with their overarching rocks ; the quiet habitations along the margin of the river,—peaceful amid all the uproar,—as if the voice of the Creator had been heard, saying, " It is I ; be not afraid ;" the green hill, with its graceful projections, that skirts and overlooks Table Rock ; the deep and bright verdure of the foliage—every spear of grass that penetrates the crevices of the rocks, gemmed by the humid atmosphere, and sparkling in the sunbeams ; the rainbow that rests on the mighty torrent—a symbol of the smile of God upon his wondrous work.

" What is it, mother ?" asked Edward, as he stood with his friends on Table Rock, where they had remained gazing on the magnificent scene for fifteen minutes without uttering a syllable, "what is it, mother, that makes us all so silent?"

"It is the spirit of God moving on the face of the waters; it is this new revelation to our senses of his power and majesty, which ushers us, as it were, into his visible presence, and exalts our affections above language. What, my dear children, should we be, without the religious sentiment that is to us as a second sight, by which we see, in all this beauty, the hand of the Creator; by which we are permitted to join in the hymn of nature; by which, I may say, we are permitted to enter into the joy of our Lord? Without it, we should be like those sheep, who are at this moment grazing on the verge of this sublime precipice, alike unconscious of all these wonders, and of their Divine Original. This religious sentiment is, in truth, Edward, that Promethean fire, that kindles nature with a living spirit, infuses life and expression into inert matter, and invests the mortal with immortality." Mrs. Sackville's eye was upraised, and her countenance illumined with a glow of devotion that harmonized with the scene. "It is, my dear children," she continued, "this religious sentiment, enlightened and directed by reason, that allies you to external nature, that should govern your affections, direct your pursuits, exalt and purify your pleasures, and make you feel, by its celestial influence, that the kingdom is within you: but," she added, smiling, after a momentary pause, "this temple does not need a preacher."

Procession of Nuns in a Catholic Hospital.—
MISS FRANCIS.

IT was autumn,—and the earth, as if weary of the vanities of her children, was rapidly changing her varied and gorgeous drapery for robes as sad and unadorned as those of the cloister. The tall and almost leafless trees stood amid black and mouldering stumps, like giants among the tombstones : the faint murmuring voice of the St. Lawrence was heard in the distance, and the winds rustled among the leaves, as if imitating the sound of its waters.

The melancholy that we feel when gazing on natural scenes in the vigour of young existence, is but pleasure in a softened form. It has none of the bitterness, none of that soul-sickening sense of desolation, which visits us in our riper years, when we have had sad experience of the jarring interests, the selfish coldness, and the heartless caprice of the world. A rich imagination, like the transparent mantle of light, which the Flemish artists delight to throw around their pictures, gives its own glowing hues to the dreariness of winter and the sobriety of autumn, as well as to the freshness of spring and the verdure of summer; and, if the affections are calm and pure, forests and streams, sky and ocean, sunrise and twilight, will always bring deep, serene, and holy associations. Under the influence of such feelings, our young traveller entered Quebec, just as the rays of the declining sun tinged the windows and spires with a fiery beam, and fell obliquely on the distant hills in tranquil radiance. At the sign of St. George and the Dragon, the horse made a motion to pause; and, thus reminded of the faithful creature's extreme fatigue, he threw the bridle over his neck, and gave him into the care of a ragged hostler, who in bad French demanded his pleasure. In the same language his hostess gave her brief salutation, " A clever night to ride, please your honour."

Percival civilly replied to her courtesy, and gave orders for supper. The inn was unusually crowded and noisy; and, willing to escape awhile from the bustling scene, he walked out into the city. The loud ringing of the cathedral bells, summoning the inhabitants to evening prayer, and the rolling of drums from the neighbouring garrison, were at variance with the quietude of his spirit. He turned from the main street, and rambled along until he reached the banks of the little river St. Charles, about a mile westward from the town. He paused before the extensive and venerable-looking hospital, founded by M. de St. Valliere, the second bishop of Quebec. The high, steep roof, and the wide portals, beneath which various images of the saints were safely ensconced in their respective niches, were indistinctly seen in the dimness of twilight; but a rich gush of sound from the interior of the building poured on the ear, mingling the deep tones of the organ with woman's sweetest melody.

All that painting and music, pomp and pageantry, can do to dazzle the imagination and captivate the heart, has ever been employed by that tremendous hierarchy, "whose roots were in another world, and whose far-stretching shadow awed our own." At this time, the effect was increased by that sense of mystery so delightful to the human soul. "Ora, ora pro nobis," was uttered by beings seclueed from the world, taking no part in the busy game of life, and separated from all that awakens the tumult of passion and the eagerness of pursuit. How, then, could fancy paint them otherwise than lovely, placid and spotless? Had Percival been behind the curtain during these sanctified dramas,—had he ever searched out the indolence, the filth and the profligacy, secreted in such retreats, the spell that bound him would have been broken; but it had been riveted by early association, and now rendered peculiarly delightful by the excited state of his feelings. Resigning himself entirely to its dominion, he inquired of one who stood within the door, whether it was possible for him to gain admittance.

The man held out his hand for money, and, having received a livre, answered, "Certainly, sir. You must be a stranger in Quebec, or you would know that there is to be a procession of white nuns to-night, in honour of M. de St. Valliere." So saying, he led the way into the building.

An old priest, exceedingly lazy in his manner, and monotonous in his tone, was reading mass, to which most of the audience zealously vociferated a response.

An arch, ornamented with basso relievo figures of the saints on one side of the chancel, surmounted a door which apparently led to an interior chapel; and beneath a similar one, on the opposite side, was a grated window shaded by a large, flowing curtain of black silk.

Behind this provoking screen were the daughters of earth, whom our traveller supposed to be as beautiful as angels, and as pure.

For some time a faint response, a slight cough, or a deep drawn sigh, alone indicated the vicinity of the seraphic beings.

At length, however, the mass, with all its thousand ceremonies, was concluded. There was silence for a moment, and then there was heard one of the low, thrilling chants of the church of Rome.

There was the noise of light, sandalled feet. The music died away to a delicious warbling, faint, yet earnest;—then gradually rising to a bold, majestic burst of sound, the door on the opposite side opened, and the sisterhood entered amid a glare of light.

That most of them were old and ugly passed unnoticed; for whatever visions an enthusiastical imagination might have conjured up, were certainly realized by the figure that preceded the procession.

Her forehead was pale and lofty,—her expression proud, but highly intellectual. A white veil, carelessly pinned about her brow, fell over her shoulders in graceful drapery; and, as she glided along, the loose, white robe, that constituted the uniform of her order, displayed to the utmost advantage that undulating outline of beauty, for which the statues of Psyche are so remarkable.

A silver crucifix was clasped in her hands, and her eyes were steadily raised towards heaven; yet there was something in her general aspect, from which one would have concluded that the fair devotee had never known the world, rather than that she had left it in weariness or disgust. Her eye happened to glance on our young friend as she passed near him; and he fancied it rested a moment with delighted attention.

The procession moved slowly on in pairs, the apostles bearing waxen lights on either side, until the last white robe was concealed behind an arch at the other end of the extensive apartment.

The receding sounds of " O sanctissima, O purissima," floated on the air mingled with clouds of frankincense; and the young man pressed his hand to his forehead with a bewildered sensation, as if the airy phantoms of the magic lantern had just been flitting before him. A notice from

37

the porter, that the nuns were now at the altar performing
silent mass, and that the doors were shortly to be closed, re
ca'led his recollection.

Grandeur of astronomical Discoveries.—WIRT.

IT was a pleasant evening in the month of May; and
my sweet child, my Rosalie, and I had sauntered up to the
castle's top to enjoy the breeze that played around it, and
to admire the unclouded firmament, that glowed and sparkled with unusual lustre from pole to pole. The atmosphere was in its purest and finest state for vision; the
milky way was distinctly developed throughout its whole
extent; every planet and every star above the horizon,
however near and brilliant or distant and faint, lent its lam-
bent light or twinkling ray to give variety and beauty to
the hemisphere; while the round, bright moon (so distinctly defined were the lines of her figure, and so clearly visible even the rotundity of her form) seemed to hang off
from the azure vault, suspended in midway air; or stooping forward from the firmament her fair and radiant face,
as if to court and return our gaze.

We amused ourselves for some time, in observing through
a telescope the planet Jupiter, sailing in silent majesty with
his squadron of satellites along the vast ocean of space between us and the fixed stars; and admired the felicity of
that design, by which those distant bodies had been par-
celled out and arranged into constellations; so as to have
served not only for beacons to the ancient navigator, but,
as it were, for landmarks to astronomers at this day; ena-
bling them, though in different countries, to indicate to
each other with ease the place and motion of those planets,
comets and magnificent meteors, which inhabit, revolve,
and play in the intermediate space.

We recalled and dwelt with delight on the rise and progress of the science of astronomy; on that series of astonishing discoveries through successive ages, which display
in so strong a light, the force and reach of the human
mind and on those bold conjectures and sublime reveries,

which seem to tower even to the confines of divinity, and
denote the high destiny to which mortals tend:—that
thought, for instance, which is said to have been first started by Pythagoras, and which modern astronomers approve;
that the stars which we call fixed, although they appear to
us to be nothing more than large spangles of various sizes
glittering on the same concave surface, are, nevertheless,
bodies as large as our sun, shining, like him, with original
and not reflected light, placed at incalculable distances
asunder, and each star the solar centre of a system of planets, which revolve around it as the planets belonging to our
system do around the sun; that this is not only the case
with all the stars which our eyes discern in the firmament,
which the telescope has brought within the sphere of
our vision, but, according to the modern improvements of
this thought, that there are probably other stars, whose
light has not yet reached us, although light moves with a
velocity a million times greater than that of a cannon ball;
that those luminous appearances, which we observe in the
firmament, like flakes of thin, white cloud, are windows, as
it were, which open to other firmaments, far, far beyond the
ken of human eye, or the power of optical instruments, lighted
up, like ours, with hosts of stars or suns; that this scheme
goes on through infinite space, which is filled with thousands upon thousands of those suns, attended by ten thousand times ten thousand worlds, all in rapid motion, yet
calm, regular and harmonious, invariably keeping the paths
prescribed to them; and these worlds peopled with myriads of intelligent beings.

One would think that this conception, thus extended,
would be bold enough to satisfy the whole enterprise of
the human imagination. But what an accession of glory
and magnificence does Dr. Herschell superadd to it, when,
instead of supposing all those suns fixed, and the motion
confined to their respective planets, he loosens those multi-
tudinous suns themselves from their stations, sets them all
into motion with their splendid retinue of planets and satellites, and imagines them, thus attended, to perform a stupendous revolution, system above system, around some
grander, unknown centre, somewhere in the boundless abyss
of space!—and when, carrying on the process, you sup

pose even that centre itself not stationary, but also coun-
terpoised by other masses in the immensity of spaces, with
which, attended by their accumulated trains of

" Planets, suns, and adamantine spheres
Wheeling unshaken through the void immense,"

it maintains harmonious concert, surrounding, in its vast
career, some other centre still more remote and stupendous,
which in its turn——" You overwhelm me," cried Rosalie, as I was labouring to pursue the immense concatena-
tion ;—" my mind is bewildered and lost in the effort to
follow you, and finds no point on which to rest its weary
wing."—" Yet there *is* a point, my dear Rosalie—the throne
of the Most High.   Imagine *that* the ultimate centre, to
which this vast and inconceivably magnificent and august
apparatus is attached, and around ,which it is continually
revolving.   Oh ! what a spectacle for the cherubim and ser-
aphim, and the spirits of the just made perfect, who dwell
on the right hand of that throne, if, as may be, and probably is, the case, their eyes are permitted to pierce through
the whole, and take in, at one glance, all its order, beauty, sublimity and glory, and their ears to distinguish that
celestial harmony, unheard by us, in which those vast globes,
as they roll on in their respective orbits, continual', hymn
their great Creator's praise !"

Scenes on the Prairies.—ANONYMOUS.

ON these level plains some of my dreams of the pleasures of wandering were realized.   We were all in the
morning of life, full of health and spirits, on horseback
and breathing a most salubrious air, with a boundless hori
zon open before us, and, shaping our future fortune and
success in the elastic mould of youthful hope and imagination we could hardly be other than happy.   Sometimes
we saw, scouring away from our path, horses, asses, mules,
buffaloes and wolves, in countless multitudes, and we took,
almost with too much ease to give pleasure in the chase,
whatever we needed for luxurious subsistence.   The pas-

sage of creeks and brooks across the prairies is marked, to the utmost extent of vision, by a fringe of woods and countless flowering shrubs. Sometimes we ascended an elevation of some height, swelling gently from the plain. Here the eye traces, as on an immense map, the formation and gradual enlargement of these rivulets, and sees them curving their meandering lines to a point of union with another of the same kind. The broadened fringe of wood indicates the enlargement of the stream, and the eye takes in at one glance the gradual formation of rivers. The night brought us up on the edge of one of these streams. Our beasts are turned loose to stretch themselves on the short and tender grass to feed and repose. The riders collect round a fire in the centre. Supper is prepared with bread, coffee, and the tenderest parts of the buffalo, venison and other game. The appetite, sharpened by exercise on horseback and by the salubrious air, is devouring. The story circulates. Past adventures are recounted, and if they receive something of the colouring of romance, it may be traced to feelings that grow out of the occasion. The projects and the mode of journeying on the morrow are discussed and settled. The fire flickers in the midst. The wild horses neigh, and the prairie wolves howl in the distance Except the weather threatens storm, the tents are not pitched The temperature of the night air is both salutary and delightful. The blankets are spread upon the tender grass, and under a canopy of the softest blue, decked with all the visible lights of the sky. The party sink to a repose, which the exercise of the preceding day renders as unbroken and dreamless as that of the grave. I awoke more than once unconscious that a moment had elapsed between the time of my lying down and my rising.

The day before we came in view of the Rocky Mountains, I saw, in the greatest perfection, that impressive, and to me almost sublime spectacle, an immense drove of wild horses, for a long time hovering round our path across the prairies. I had often seen great numbers of them before, mixed with other animals, apparently quiet, and grazing like the rest. Here there were thousands, unmixed, unemployed; their motions, if such a comparison might be allowed, as darting and as wild as those of humming-birds

37 *

on the flowers. The tremendous snorts, with which the
front columns of the phalanx made known their approach
to us, seemed to be their wild and energetic way of expressing their pity and disdain for the servile lot of our
horses, of which they appeared to be taking a survey. They
were of all colours, mixed, spotted and diversified with
every hue, from the brightest white to clear and shining
black; and of every form and structure, from the long and
slender racer to those of firmer limbs and heavier mould,
and of all ages, from the curvetting colt to the range of
patriarchal steeds, drawn up in a line, and holding their
high heads for a survey of us in the rear. Sometimes they
curved their necks, and made no more progress than just
enough to keep pace with our advance. There was a kind
of slow and walking minuet, in which they performed various evolutions with the precision of the figures of a country dance. Then a rapid movement shifted the front to
the rear. But still, in all their evolutions and movements,
like the flight of sea-fowl, their lines were regular, and free
from all indications of confusion. At times a spontaneous
and sudden movement towards us almost inspired the apprehension of a united attack upon us. After a moment's
advance, a snort and a rapid retrograde movement seemed
to testify their proud estimate of their wild independence.
The infinite variety of their rapid movements, their tam-
perings and manœuvres, were of such a wild and almost
terrific character, that it required but a moderate stretch
of fancy to suppose them the genii of these grassy plains.
At one period they were formed to an immense depth in
front of us. A wheel, executed almost with the rapidity
of thought, presented them hovering on our flanks. Then
again, the cloud of dust that enveloped their movements
cleared away, and presented them in our rear. They evidently operated as a great annoyance to the horses and
mules of our cavalcade. The frighted movements, the increased indications of fatigue, with their frequent neighings
sufficiently evidenced what unpleasant neighbours they
considered their wild compatriots to be. So much did our
horses appear to suffer from fatigue and terror in consequence of their vicinity, that we were thinking of some
way in which to drive them off; when, on a sudden, a pa-

tient and laborious donkey of the establishment, who appeared to have regarded all their movements with philosophic indifference, pricked up his long ears, and gave a loud and most sonorous bray from his vocal shells. Instantly this prodigious multitude—and there were thousands of them—took what the Spanish call the "stompado." With a trampling like the noise of thunder, or still more like that of an earthquake,—a noise that was absolutely appalling,—they took to their heels, and were all in a few moments invisible in the verdant depths of the plains, and we saw them no more.

Eulogy on William Penn.—Du Ponceau.

WILLIAM PENN stands the first among the lawgivers, whose names and deeds are recorded in history. Shall we compare him with Lycurgus, Solon, Romulus, those founders of military commonwealths, who organized their citizen in dreadful array against the rest of their species, taught them to consider their fellow-men as barbarians, and themselves as alone worthy to rule over the earth ? What benefit did mankind derive from their boasted institutions ? Interrogate the shades of those who fell in the mighty contests between Athens and Lacedæmon, between Carthage and Rome, and between Rome and the rest of the universe. But see William Penn, with weaponless hand, sitting down peaceably with his followers in the midst of savage nations, whose only occupation was shedding the blood of their fellow-men, disarming them by his justice, and teaching them, for the first time, to view a stranger without distrust. See them bury their tomahawks, in his presence, so deep that man shall never be able to find them again. See them, under the shade of the thick groves of Coaquannock, extend the bright chain of friendship, and solemnly promise to preserve it as long as the sun and moon shall endure. See him then, with his companions, establishing his commonwealth on the sole basis of religion, morality and universal ive, and adopting, as the fundamental maxim of his government, the rule handed down to us from heaven, *Glor*

*to God on high, and on earth peace and good will to
men.* Here was a spectacle for the potentates of the earth
to look upon,—an example for them to imitate. But the po
tentates of the earth did not see, or, if they saw, they turn
ed away their eyes from the sight; they did not hear, or,
if they heard, they shut their ears against the voice which
called out to them from the wilderness,

"Discite justitiam moniti, et non temnere Divos."

The character of William Penn alone sheds a never-fad
ing lustre on our history.

Morbid Effects of Envy, Malice, and Hatred.— RUSH.

ENVY is commonly the parent of malice and hatred. Of
this vice it may be truly asserted, that it is deep-seated,
and always painful; hence it has been said by an inspired
writer to resemble "rottenness in the bones;" and by Lord
Bacon "to know no holydays." It is likewise a monopo-
lizing vice. Alexander envied his successful generals,
and Garrick was hostile to all the popular players of his
day. It is moreover a parricide vice, for it not only emits
its poison against its friends, but against the persons, who,
by the favours it has conferred upon those who cherish it,
have become in one respect the authors of their being; and,
lastly, it possesses a polypus life. No kindness, gentleness
or generosity can destroy it. On the contrary, it derives
fresh strength from every act which it experiences of any
of them. It likewise survives and often forgives the resentment it sometimes occasions, but without ceasing to
hate the talents, virtues or personal endowments by which
it was originally excited. Nor is it satiated by the apparent extinction of them in death. This is obvious from its
so frequently opening the sanctuary of the grave, and rob-
bing the possessors of those qualities of the slender remains it had left them of posthumous fame.

However devoid this vice and its offspring may be of remissions, they now and then appear in the form of parox

ysms, which discover themselves in tremors, paleness and a suffusion of the face with red blood. The face in this case performs the vicarious office, which has lately been ascribed to the spleen. But their effects appear more frequently in slow fevers, and in a long train of nervous diseases. Persons affected with them seldom acknowledge their true cause. A single instance, only, of this candour, is mentioned by Dr. Tissot He tells us he was once consulted by a gentleman, who told him that all his complaints were brought on by his intense and habitual hatred of an enemy. Many of the chronic diseases of high life and of professional men, I have no doubt, are induced by the same cause.

I once thought that medicine had not a single remedy ʌ all its stores, that could subdue, or even palliate, the diseases induced by the baneful passions which have been described, and that an antidote to them was to be found only in religion; but I have since recollected one, and heard of another physical remedy, that will at least palliate them. The first is, frequent convivial society between persons who are hostile to each other. It never fails to soften resentments, and sometimes produces reconciliation and friendship. The reader will be surprised when I add that the second physical remedy was suggested to me by a madman in the Pennsylvania hospital. In conversing with him, he produced a large collection of papers, which he said contained his journal. " Here," said he, " I write down every thing that passes in my mind, and particularly malice and revenge. In recording the latter, I feel my mind emptied of something disagreeable to it, just as an emetic relieves the stomach of bile. When I look at what I have written a day or two afterwards, I feel ashamed and disgusted with it, and wish to throw it into the fire." I have no doubt of the utility of this remedy for envy, malice and hatred, from its salutary effects in a similar case. A gentleman in this city informed me, that, after writing an attack for the press upon a person who had offended him, he was so struck with its malignity upon reading it, that he instantly destroyed it. The French nobility sometimes cover the walls and ceiling of a room in their houses with looking glasses The room thus furnished is called a *boudoir*. Did ill-natured people imitate the practice of the madman and gentleman I have mentioned, by putting their envious, malicious and revengeful thoughts upon paper, it would form a mirror that would serve the same purpose of pointing out and remedying the evil dispositions of the mind, that the boudoir in France serves, in discovering and remedying the defects in the attitudes and dress of the body.

To persons who are not ashamed and disgusted with the first sight of their malevolent effusions upon paper, the same advice may be given that Dr. Franklin gave to a gentleman, who read part of a humorous satire which he had written upon the person and character of a respectable cit izen of Philadelphia. After he had finished reading it, he asked the doctor what he thought of his publishing it. " Keep it by you," said the doctor, " for one year, and then ask me that question." The gentleman felt the force of this answer, went immediately to the printer who had composed the first page of it, took it from him, and consigned the whole manuscript to oblivion.

Appearance of the first Settlements of the Pilgrims.— Miss SEDGWICK.

THE first settlers followed the course of the Indians, and planted themselves on the borders of rivers,—the natural gardens of the earth. where the soil is mellowed and enriched by the annual overflowing of the streams, and prepared by the unassisted processes of nature to yield to the indolent Indian his scanty supply of maize and other esculents. The wigwams which constituted the village, or, to use the graphic aboriginal designation, the " smoke,' of the natives, gave place to the clumsy, but more convenient dwellings of the pilgrims.

Where there are now contiguous rows of shops, filled with the merchandise of the East, the manufactures of Europe, the rival fabrics of our own country, and the fruits of the tropics ; where now stand the stately hall of justice, the academy, the bank, church es, orthodox and heretic, and all the symbols of a rich and populous community,—were, at the early period of our history, a few log-houses planted around a fort, defended by a slight embankment and palisade.

The mansions of the proprietors were rather more spacious and artificial than those of their more humble associates, and were built on the well known model of the modest dwelling-house illustrated by the birth of Milton—a form still abounding in the eastern parts of Massachusetts, and presenting to the eye of a New Englander the familiar aspect of an awkward, friendly country cousin.

The first clearing was limited to the plain. The beautiful hill, that is now the residence of the gentry, (for there yet lives such a class in the heart of our democratic community,) and is embellished with stately edifices and expensive pleasure-grounds, was then the border of a dense forest, and so richly fringed with the original growth of trees, that scarce a sunbeam had penetrated to the parent earth

Mr Fletcher was at first welcomed as an important acquisition to the infant establishment, but he soon proved that he purposed to take no part in its concerns, and, in spite of the remonstrances of the proprietors, he fixed his residence a mile from the village, deeming exposure to the incursions of the savages very slight, and the surveillance of an inquiring neighbourhood a certain evil. His domain extended from a gentle eminence, that commanded an extensive view of the bountiful Connecticut to the shore, where the river indented the meadow by one of those sweeping, graceful curves, by which it seems to delight to beautify the land it nourishes.

The border of the river was fringed with all the water-loving trees; but the broad meadows were quite cleared, excepting that a few elms and sycamores had been spared by the Indians, and consecrated by tradition, as the scene of revels or councils. The house of our pilgrim was a low-roofed, modest structure, containing ample accommodation for a patriarchal family ; where children, dependents and servants were all to be sheltered under one roofee. On one side, as we have described, lay an open and extensive plain ; within view was the curling smoke from the little cluster of houses about the fort—the habita's of civilized man; but all else was a savage, howling wilderness.

Never was a name more befitting the condition of a people, than "pilgrim" that of our forefathers. It should be redeemed from the Puritanical and ludicrous associations which have degraded it in most men's minds, and be hallowed by the sacrifices made by these voluntary exiles. They were pilgrims, for they had resigned forever what the good hold most dear—their homes. Home can never be transferred; never repeated in the experience of an individual. The place consecrated by parental love, by the innocence and sports of childhood, by the first acquaintance with nature, by the linking of the heart to the visible creation, is the only home. There, there is a living and a breathing spirit infused into nature: every familiar object has a history—the trees have tongues, and the very air is vocal. There the vesture of decay doth not close in and control the noble functions of the soul. It sees, and hears, and enjoys, without the ministry of gross, material substance

---

Description of a Herd of Bisons.—COOPER.

"THERE come the buffaloes themselves, and a noble herd it is. I warrant me that Pawnee has a troop of his people in some of the ho' jws nigh by; and, as he has gone scampering after them, you are about to see a glorious chase. It will serve to keep the squatter and his brood under cover, and for ourselves there is little reason to fear. A Pawnee is not apt to be a malicious savage."

Every eye was now drawn to the striking spectacle that succeeded. Even the timid Inez hastened to the side of Middleton to gaze at the sight, and Paul summoned Ellen from her culinary labours, to become a witness of the lively scene.

Throughout the whole of these moving events which it has been our duty to record, the prairies had lain in all the majesty of perfect solitude. The heavens had been blackened with the passage of the migratory birds, it is true, but the dogs of the party and the ass of the docter were the only quadrupeds that had enlivened the broad surface of the waste beneath. There was now a sudden exhibition of animal life, which changed the scene, as it were by magic, to the very opposite extreme.

A few enormous bison bulls were first observed scouring along the most distant roll of the prairie, and then succeeded long files of single beasts, which, in their turns, were followed by a dark mass of bodies, until the dun-coloured herbage of the plain was entirely lost in the deeper hue of their shaggy coats. The herd, as the column spread and thickened, was like the endless flocks of the smaller birds, whose extended flanks are so often seen to heave up out of the abyss of the heavens, until they appear as countless as the leaves in those forests, over which they wing their endless flight. Clouds of dust shot up in little columns from the centre of the mass, as some animal more furious than the rest ploughed the plain with his horns, and, from time to time, a deep, hollow bellowing was borne along on the wind, as though a thousand throats vented their plaints in a discordant murmuring.

A long and musing silence reigned in the party, as they gazed on this spectacle of wild and peculiar grandeur. It was at length broken by he trapper, who, having been long accustomed to similar sights, felt less of its influence, or rather felt it in a less thrilling and absorbing manner, than those to whom the scene was more novel.

"There go ten thousand oxen in one drove, without keeper or master, except Him who made them, and gave them these open plains for their pasture! Ay, it is here that man may see the proofs of his wantonness and folly! Can the proudest governor in all the States go into his fields, and slaughter a nobler bullock than is here offered to the meanest hands? and, when he has gotten his sirloin or his steak, can he eat it with as good a relish as he who nas sweetened his food with wholesome toil, and earned it according to the law of natur', by honestly mastering that which the Lord hath put before him?"

"If the prairie platter is smoking with a buffaloe's hump, answer, no," interrupted the luxurious bee-hunter.

"Ay, boy, you have tasted, and you feel the genuine reasoning of the thing. But the herd is heading a little this-a-way, and it behooves us to make ready for their visit. If we hide ourselves, altogether, the horned brutes will break through the place, and trample us beneath their feet, like so many creeping worms; so we will just put the weak ones apart, and take post, as becomes men and hunters, in the van."

As there was but little time to make the necessary arrangements, the whole party set about them in good earnest. Inez and Ellen were placed in the edge of the thicket on the side farthest from the approaching herd. Asinus was posted in the centre, in consideration of his nerves, and then the old man, with his three male companions, divided themselves in such a manner as they thought would enable them to turn the head of the rushing column, should it chance to approach too nigh their position. By the vacillating movements of some fifty or a hundred bulls, that led the advance, it remained questionable, for many moments, what course they intended to pursue. But a tremendous and painful roar, which came from behind the cloud of dust that rose in the centre of the herd, and which was horridly answered by the screams of the carrion birds, that were greedily sailing directly above the flying drove, appeared to give a new impulse to their flight, and at once to remove every symptom of indecision. As if glad to seek the smallest signs of the forest, the whole of the affrighted herd became steady in its direction, rushing in a straight line toward the little cover of bushes, which has already been so often named.

The appearance of danger was now, in reality, of a character to try the stoutest nerves. The flanks of the dark, moving mass, were advanced in such a manner as to make a concave line of the front, and every fierce eye, that was glaring from the shaggy wilderness of hair, in which the entire heads of the males were enveloped, was riveted with mad anxiety on the thicket. It seemed as if each beast strove to outstrip his neighbour in gaining this desired cover, and as thousands in the rear pressed blindly on those in front, there was the appearance of an imminent risk that the leaders of the herd would be precipitated on the concealed party, in which case the destruction of every one of them was certain. Each of our adventurers felt the danger of his situation in a manner peculiar to his individual character and circumstances.

* * * * * * * * * * * * ,

The old man, who had stood all this while leaning on his rifle, and regarding the movements of the herd with a steady eye, now deemed it time to strike his blow. Levelling his piece at the foremost bull, with an agility that would have done credit to his youth, he fired. The animal received the bullet on the matted hair between his horns, and fell to his knees ; but, shaking his head, he instantly arose, the very shock seeming to increase his exertions. There was now no longer time to hesitate. Throwing down his rifle, the trapper stretched forth his arms, and advanced from the cover with naked hands, directly towards he rushing column of the beasts.

The figure of a man, when sustained by the firmness and steadiness that intellect can only impart, rarely fails of commanding respect from all the inferior animals of the creation. The leading bulls recoiled, and, for a single instant, there was a sudden stop to their speed, a dense mass of bodies rolling up in front, until hundreds were seen floundering and tumbling on the plain. Then came another of those hollow bellowings from the rear, and set the herd again in motion. The head of the column, however, divided ; the immoveable form of the trapper cutting it, as it were, into two gliding streams of life. Middleton and Paul instantly profited by his example, and extended the feeble barrier by a similar exhibition of their own persons.

For a few moments, the new impulse given to the animals in front served to protect the thicket. But, as the body of the herd pressed more and more upon the open line of its defenders, and the dust thickened so as to obscure their persons, there was, at each instant, a renewed danger of the beasts breaking through. It became necessary for the trapper and his companions to become still more and more alert ; and they were gradually yielding before the headlong multitude, when a furious bull darted by Mid

dleton, so near as to brush his person, and, at the next
instant, swept through the thicket with the velocity of the
wind.

" Close, and die for the ground," shouted the old man,
' or a thousand of the devils will be at his heels !"

All their efforts would have proved fruitless, however,
against the living torrent, had not Asinus, whose domains
had just been so rudely entered, lifted his voice in the midst
of the uproar. The most sturdy and furious of the bulls
trembled at the alarming and unknown cry, and then each
individual brute was seen madly pressing from that very
thicket, which, the moment before, he had endeavoured to
reach with the same sort of eagerness as that with which
the murderer seeks the sanctuary.

As the stream divided, the place became clear ; the two
dark columns moving obliquely from the copse to unite
again at the distance of a mile on its opposite side. The
instant the old man saw the sudden effect which the voice
of Asinus had produced, he coolly commenced reloading
his rifle, indulging, at the same time, in a most heartfelt fit
of his silent and peculiar merriment.

* * * * * * * * * * * * *

The uproar, which attended the passage of the herd, was
now gone, or rather it was heard rolling along the prairie,
at the distance of a mile. The clouds of dust were already
blown away by the wind, and a clear range was left to the
eye, in that place where, ten minutes before, there existed
such a strange scene of wildness and confusion.

The Character of Jesus.—REV. S. C. THACHER.

WE find in the life of Jesus a union of qualities, which
had never before met in any being on this earth. We find
imbodied in his example the highest virtues both of active
and of contemplative life. We see united in him a devotion to God the most intense, abstracted, unearthly, with
a benevolence to man the most active, affectionate and universal. We see qualities meet and harmonize in his char-

racter, which are usually thought the most uncongenial
We see a force of character, which difficulties cannot conquer, an energy which calamity cannot relax, a fortitude
and constancy which sufferings can neither subdue nor
bend from their purpose; connected with the most melting
tenderness and sensibility of spirit, the most exquisite susceptibility to every soft and gentle impression. We see in
him the rare union of zeal and moderation, of courage and
prudence, of compassion and firmness; we see superiority
to the world without gloom or severity, or indifference or
distaste to its pursuits and enjoyments. In short, there is
something in the whole conception and tenor of our Saviour's character so entirely peculiar, something which so
realizes the ideal model of the most consummate moral
beauty; something so lovely, so gracious, so venerable and
commanding, that the boldest infidels have shrunk from it
overawed, and, though their cause is otherwise desperate,
have yet feared to profane its perfect purity. One of the
most eloquent tributes to its sublimity, that was ever uttered, was extorted from the lips of an infidel. "Is there
any thing in it," he exclaims, " of the tone of an enthusi-
ast, or of an ambitious sectary? What sweetness, what
purity in his manners; what touching grace in his instructions; what elevation in his maxims; what profound wisdom in his discourses; what presence of mind, what skill
and propriety in his answers; what empire over his passions! Where is the man, where is the sage, who knows
how to act, to suffer and to die, without weakness and without ostentation? When Plato paints his imaginary just
man covered with all the ignominy of crime, and yet wor
thy of all the honours of virtue, he paints in every featur
the character of Christ. What prejudice, what blindness
must possess us to compare the son of Soproniscus to the
son of Mary! How vast the distance between them.
Socrates, dying without pain and without ignominy, easily
sustains his character to the last; and, if this gentle death
had not honoured his life, we might have doubted whether
Socrates, with all his genius, was any thing more than a
sophist. The death of Socrates, philosophizing tranquilly
with his friends, is the most easy that one could desire;
but of Jesus, expiring in torture, insulted, mocked, exe-
33 *

crated by a whole people, is the most horrible that one can
ear. Socrates, when he takes the poisoned cup, blesses
him who weeps as he presents it; Jesus, in the midst of
the most dreadful tortures, prays for his infuriated executioners.—Yes! if the life and death of Socrates are those
of a sage, the life and death of Jesus are wholly divine "

Recollections of Josiah Quincy, Jun —J. QUINCY.

By the lapse of half a century, the actors in the scenes
immediately preceding the American revolution begin to
be placed in a light, and at a distance, favourable at once
to right feelings and just criticism. In the possession of
freedom, happiness, and prosperity, seldom if ever before
equalled in the history of nations, the hearts of the American people naturally turn towards the memories of those,
who, under Providence, were the instruments of obtaining
these blessings. Curiosity awakens concerning their characters and motives. The desire grows daily more universal to repay, with a late and distant gratitude, their long
neglected and often forgotten sacrifices and sufferings.

Among the men, whose character and political conduct
had an acknowledged influence on the events of that period, was Josiah Quincy, Jun. The unanimous consent of
his contemporaries has associated his name in an imperishable union with that of Otis, Adams, Hancock, Warren,
and other distinguished men, whose talents and intrepidity
influenced the events which led to the declaration of independence. This honour has been granted to him, notwithstanding his political path was, in every period of its short
extent, interrupted by intense professional labours, and
was terminated by death at the early age of thirty-one
years.

The particular features of a life and character, capable,
under such circumstances, of attaining so great a distinction,
are objects of curiosity and interest. Those, who recollect
aim, speak of his eloquence, his genius, and his capacity
'or ntellectual labour ; of the inextinguishable zeal and
bsorbing ardour of his exertions, whether directed to po-

litical or professional objects; of the entireness with which
he threw his soul into every cause in which he engaged;
of the intrepidity of his spirit, and of his indignant sense
of the wrongs of his country.

It is certain that he made a deep impression on his contemporaries. Those who remember the political debates
in Faneuil Hall consequent on the stamp act, the Boston
massacre, and the Boston port bill, have yet a vivid recol-
ection of the pathos of his eloquence, the boldness of his
invectives, and the impressive vehemence with which he
arraigned the measures of the British ministry, inflaming
he zeal and animating the resentment of an oppressed
people.

The true Pride of Ancestry.—WEBSTER.

IT is a noble faculty of our nature, which enables us to
connect our thoughts, our sympathies, and our happiness,
with what is distant in place or time; and, looking before
and after, to hold communion at once with our ancestors and
our posterity. Human and mortal although we are, we are,
nevertheless, not mere insulated beings, without relation to
the past or the future. Neither the point of time nor the spot
of earth, in which we physically live, bounds our rational
and intellectual enjoyments. We live in the past by a
knowledge of its history, and in the future by hope and
anticipation. By ascending to an association with our ancestors; by contemplating their example and studying their
character; by partaking their sentiments, and imbibing their
spirit; by accompanying them in their toils; by sympathiz-
ing in their sufferings, and rejoicing in their successes and
their triumphs,—we mingle our own existence with theirs,
and seem to belong to their age. We become their contemporaries, live the lives which they lived, endure what
they endured, and partake in the rewards which they enjoyed. And in like manner, by running along the line of
future time; by contemplating the probable fortunes of
hose who are coming after us; by attempting something
which may promote their happiness, and leave some not

dishonourable memorial of ourselves for their regard when
we shall sleep with the fathers,—we protract our own earthly being, and seem to crowd whatever is future, as well as
all that is past, into the narrow compass of our earthly existence.   As it is not a vain and false, but an exalted and
religious imagination, which leads us to raise our thoughts
from the orb which, amidst this universe of worlds, the
Creator has given us to inhabit, and to send them with
something of the feeling which nature prompts, and teaches to be proper among children of the same Eternal Parent,
to the contemplation of the myriads of fellow-beings, with
which his goodness has peopled the infinite of space ; so
neither is it false or vain to consider ourselves as interested
or connected with our whole race through all time ; allied
to our ancestors ; allied to our posterity ; closely compacted
on all sides with others ; ourselves being but links in the
great chain of being, which begins with the origin of our
race, runs onward through its successive generations, binding together the past, the present, and the future, and terminating, at last, with the consummation of all things
earthly, at the throne of God.

     There may be, and there often is, indeed, a regard for
ancestry, which nourishes only a weak pride ; as there is
also a care for posterity, which only disguises an habitual
avarice, or hides the workings of a low and grovelling vanity.   But there is, also, a moral and philosophical respect
for our ancestors, which elevates the character and improves the heart.   Next to the sense of religious duty
and moral feeling, I hardly know what should bear with
stronger obligation on a liberal and enlightened mind, than
a consciousness of alliance with excellence which is departed ; and a consciousness, too, that, in its acts and conduct,
and even in its sentiments, it may be actively operating on
the happiness of those who come after it.   Poetry is found
to have few stronger conceptions, by which it would affect
or overwhelm the mind, than those in which it presents
the moving and speaking image of the departed dead to the
senses of the living.   This belongs to poetry only because
it is congenial to our nature.   Poetry is, in this respect,
but the handmaid of true philosophy and morality.   It deals
with us as human beings, naturally reverencing those

whose visible connexion with this state of being is seve. ed and who may yet exercise, we know not what sympathy with ourselves;—and when it carries us forward, also, and shows us the long-continued result of all the good we do, in the prosperity of those who follow us, till it bears us from our se'ves, and absorbs us in an intense interest for what shall happen to the generations after us, it speaks only in the language of our nature, and affects us with sentiments which belong to us as human beings.

A Slide in the White Mountains.—Mrs. Hale.

Robert looked upward. Awful precipices, to the height of more than two thousand feet, rose above him. Near the highest pinnacle, and the very one over which Abarrocho had been seated, the earth had been loosened by the violent rains. Some slight cause, perhaps the sudder. bursting forth of a mountain spring, had given motion to the mass; and it was now moving forward, gathering fresh streng' from its progress, uprooting the old trees, unbedding the ancient rocks, and all rolling onwards with a force and velocity no human barrier could oppose, no created power resist. One glance told Robert that Mary must perish; that he could not save her. "But I will die with her!" he exclaimed; and, shaking off the grasp of Mendowit as he would a feather, "Mary, oh, Mary!" he continued, rushing towards her. She uncovered her head, made an effort to rise, and articulated, "Robert!" as he caught and clasped her to his bosom. "Oh, Mary, must we die?" he exclaimed "We must, we must," she cried, as she gazed on the rolling mountain in agonizing horror; "why, why did you come?" He replied not; but, leaning against the rock, pressed her closer to his heart; while she, clinging around his neck, burst into a passion of tears, and, laying her head or his bosom, sobbed like an infant. He bowed his face upon her cold, wet cheek, and breathed one cry for mercy; yet, even then, there was in the hearts of both lovers a feeling of wild joy in the thought that they should not be separated.

The mass came down, tearing, and crumbling, and sweeping all before it! The whole mountain trembled, and the ground shook like an earthquake. The air was darkened by the shower of water, stones, and branches of trees, crushed and shivered to atoms, while the blast swept by like a whirlwind, and the crash and roar of the convulsion were far more appalling than the loudest thunder.

It might have been one minute, or twenty,—for neither of the lovers took note of time,—when, in the hush as of deathlike stillness that succeeded the uproar, Robert looked around, and saw the consuming storm had passed by. It had passed, covering the valley, farther than the eye could reach, with ruin. Masses of granite, and shivered trees, and mountain earth, were heaped high around, filling the bed of the Saco, and exhibiting an awful picture of the desolating track of the avalanche. Only one little spot had escaped its wrath, and there, safe, as if sheltered in the hollow of His hand, who notices the fall of a sparrow, and locked in each other's arms, were Robert and Mary! Beside them stood Mendowit; his gun firmly clenched, and his quick eye rolling around him like a maniac. He had followed Robert, though he did not intend it; probably impelled by that feeling which makes us loath to face danger alone; and thus had escaped.

The Twins.—TOKEN.

DURING the period of the war of the revolution, there resided, in the western part of Massachusetts, a farmer by the name of Stedman. He was a man of substance, descended from a very respectable English family, well educated, distinguished for great firmness of character in general, and alike remarkable for inflexible integrity and steadfast loyalty to his king. Such was the reputation he sustained, that, even when the most violent antipathies against royalism swayed the community, it was still admitted on all hands, that farmer Stedman, though a tory, was honest in his opinions, and firmly believed them to be right.

The period came when Burgoyne was advancing from the north. It was a time of great anxiety with both the friends and foes of the revolution, and one which called forth their highest exertions. The patriotic militia flocked to the standard of Gates and Stark, while many of the tories resorted to the quarters of Burgoyne and Baum. Among the latter was Stedman. He had no sooner decided it to be his duty, than he took a kind farewell of his wife, a woman of uncommon beauty, gave his children, a twin boy and girl, a long embrace, then mounted his horse and departed. He joined himself to the unfortunate expedition of Baum, and was taken, with other prisoners of war, by the victorious Stark.

He made no attempt to conceal his name or character, which were both soon discovered, and he was accordingly committed to prison as a traitor. The gaol, in which he was confined, was in the western part of Massachusetts, and nearly in a ruinous condition. The farmer was one night waked from his sleep by several persons in his room "Come," said they, "you can now regain your liberty; we have made a breach in the prison, through which you can escape." To their astonishment, Stedman utterly refused to leave his prison. In vain they expostulated with him; in vain they represented to him that life was at stake. His reply was, that he was a true man, and a servant of king George, and he would not creep out of a hole at night, and sneak away from the rebels, to save his neck from the gallows. Finding it altogether fruitless to attempt to move him, his friends left him, with some expressions of spleen.

The time at length arrived for the trial of the prisoner. The distance to the place where the court was sitting was about sixty miles. Stedman remarked to the sheriff, when he came to attend him, that it would save some expense and inconvenience, if he could be permitted to go alone, and on foot. "And suppose," said the sheriff, "that you should prefer your safety to your honour, and leave me to seek you in the British camp?" "I had thought," said the farmer, reddening with indignation, "that I was speaking to one who knew me." "I do know you, indeed," said the sheriff; "I spoke but in jest; you shall have your way. Go, and on the third day I shall expect to see you at S——." * * * * The farmer departed, and at the appointed time he placed himself in the hands of the sheriff.

I was now engaged as his counsel. Stedman insisted, before the court, upon telling his whole story; and, when I would have taken advantage of some technical points, he sharply rebuked me, and told me that he had not employed me to prevaricate, but only to assist him in telling the truth. I had never seen such a display of simple integrity. It was affecting to witness his love of holy, unvarnished truth, elevating him above every other consideration, and presiding in his breast as a sentiment even superior to the love of life. I saw the tears more than once springing to the eyes of his judges; never before, or since, have I felt such an interest in a client   I plead for him as I would have plead for my own life. I drew tears, but I could not sway the judgment of stern men, controlled rather by a sense of duty than the compassionate promptings of humanity. Stedman was condemned. I told him there was a chance of pardon, if he would ask for it. I drew up a petition, and requested him to sign it; but he refused. "I have done," said he, "what I thought my duty. I can ask pardon of my God, and my king; but it would be hypocrisy to ask forgiveness of these men, for an action which I should repeat, were I placed again in similar circumstances. No! ask me not to sign that petition. If what you call the cause of American freedom requires the blood of an honest man for a conscientious discharge of what he deemed his duty, let me be its victim. Go to my judges, and tell them that I place not my fears nor my hopes in them." It was in vain that I pressed the subject; and I went away in despair.

In returning to my house, I accidentally called on an acquaintance, a young man of brilliant genius, the subject of a passionate predilection for painting. This led him frequently to take excursions into the country, for the purpose of sketching such objects and scenes as were interesting to him. From one of these rambles he had just returned. I found him sitting at his easel, giving the last touches to the picture which attracted your attention. He asked my opinion of it. "It is a fine picture," said I; "is it a fancy

piece, or are they portraits?" "They are portraits," said
he; "and, save perhaps a little embellishment, they are, I
think, striking portraits of the wife and children of your
unfortunate client, Stedman. In the course of my rambles,
I chanced to call at his house in H——. I never saw a
more beautiful group. The mother is one of a thousand
and the twins are a pair of cherubs." "Tell me," said I
laying my hand on the picture, "tell me, are they true and
faithful portraits of the wife and children of Stedman?"
My earnestness made my friend stare. He assured me that,
so far as he could be permitted to judge of his own productions, they were striking representations. I asked no further
questions; I seized the picture, and hurried with it to the
prison where my client was confined. I found him sitting,
his face covered with his hands, and apparently wrung by
keen emotion. I placed the picture in such a situation tha
he could not fail to see it. I laid the petition on the little
table by his side, and left the room.

In half an hour I returned. The farmer grasped my hand,
while tears stole down his cheeks; his eye glanced first upon
the picture, and then to the petition. He said nothing, bu
handed the latter to me. I took it, and left the apartment
He had put his name to it. The petition was granted, and
Stedman was set at liberty.

———◆———

The lone Indian.—MISS FRANCIS.

FOR many a returning autumn, a lone Indian was seen
standing at the consecrated spot we have mentioned; but
just thirty years after the death of Soonseetah, he was
noticed for the last time. His step was then firm, and his
figure erect, though he seemed old and way-worn. Age
had not dimmed the fire of his eye, but an expression of
deep melancholy had settled on his wrinkled brow. It was
Powontonamo—he who had once been the Eagle of the
Mohawks! He came to lie down and die beneath the broad
oak, which shadowed the grave of Sunny-eye. Alas, the
white man's axe had been there! The tree he had planted
was dead; and the vine, which had leaped so vigorously
89

from branch to branch, now, yellow and withering, was
falling to the ground. A deep groan burst from the soul of
the savage. For thirty wearisome years, he had watched
that oak, with its twining tendrils. They were the only
things left in the wide world for him to love, and they were
gone! He looked abroad. The hunting land of his tribe
was changed, like its chieftain. No light canoe now shot
down the river, like a bird upon the wing. The laden boat
of the white man alone broke its smooth surface. The
Englishman's road wound like a serpent around the banks
of the Mohawk; and iron hoofs had so beaten down the
war path, that a hawk's eye could not discover an Indian
track. The last wigwam was destroyed; and the sun
looked boldly down upon spots he had visited only by
stealth, during thousands and thousands of moons. The
few remaining trees, clothed in the fantastic mourning of
autumn; the long line of heavy clouds, melting away before
the coming sun; and the distant mountain, seen through the
blue mist of departing twilight, alone remained as he had
seen them in his boyhood. All things spoke a sad language
to the heart of the desolate Indian. "Yes," said he, "the
young oak and the vine are like the Eagle and the Sunny-
eye. They are cut down, torn, and trampled on. The
leaves are falling, and the clouds are scattering, like my
people. I wish I could once more see the trees standing
thick, as they did when my mother held me to her bosom,
and sung the warlike deeds of the Mohawks."

A mingled expression of grief and anger passed over his
face, as he watched a loaded boat in its passage across the
stream. "The white man carries food to his wife and children, and he finds them in his home," said he. "Where is
the squaw and the pappoose of the red man? They are
here!" As he spoke, he fixed his eye thoughtfully upon
the grave. After a gloomy silence, he again looked round
upon the fair scene, with a wandering and troubled gaze.
"The pale face may like it," murmured he; "but an Indian cannot die here in peace." So saying, he broke his
bow-string, snapped his arrows, threw them on the burial-
place of his fathers, and departed for ever.

A Scene in the Catskill Mountains.—G. MELLEN.

WE first came to the verge of the precipice, from which the water takes its leap upon a platform that projects with the rock many feet over the chasm. Here we gazed into the cell and the basin into which the stream pours itself from the beetling cliff. But the prospect from this point is far less thrilling than from below; and we accordingly began our descent. Winding round the crags, and following a foot-path between the overhanging trees, we gradually, and with some difficulty, descended so far as to have a fine view of the station which we had just left. The scene here is magnificent beyond description. Far under the blackened canopy of everlasting rock, that shoots above to an alarming extent over the abyss, the eye glances round a vast and regular amphitheatre, which seems to be the wild assembling-place of all the spirits of the storms,—so rugged, so deep, so secluded, and yet so threatening does it appear! Down from the midst of the cliff that overarches this wonderful excavation, and dividing in the midst the gloom that seems to settle within it, comes the foaming torrent, splendidly relieved upon the black surface of the enduring walls, and throwing its wreaths of mist along the frowning ceiling. Following the guide that had brought us thus far down the chasm, we passed into the amphitheatre, and, moving under the terrific projection, stood in the centre of this sublime and stupendous work;—the black, ironbound rocks behind us, and the snowy cataract springing between us and the boiling basin, which still lay under our feet. Here the scene was unparalleled. Here seemed to be the theatre for a people to stand in, and behold the prodigies and fearful wonders of the Almighty, and feel their own insignificance. Here admiration and astonishment come unbidden over the soul, and the most obdurate heart feels that there is something to be grateful for. Indeed, the scene from this spot is so sublime and so well calculated to impress the feelings with a sense of the power and grandeur of nature, that, apart from all other considerations, it is worthy of long journeying and extreme toil to behold it. Having taken refreshment, very adroitly managed to be conveyed to us from above by John,—whom, by the way, I would name as an excellent guide as well as a reputable boy,—we descended to the extreme depth of the ravine, and, with certain heroic ladies, who somehow dared the perils of the path, we gazed from this place upon the sheet of water, falling from a height of more than two hundred and fifty feet. This is a matter of which Niagara would not speak lightly; and there is wanting only a heavy fall of water to make this spot not only magnificent,—for that it is now,—but terribly sublime. Mountains ascend and overshadow it; crags and precipices project themselves in menacing assemblage all about, as though frowning over a ruin which they are only waiting some fiat to make yet more appalling. Nature has hewed out a resting place for man, where he may linger, and gaze, and admire! Below him she awakens her thunder, and darts her lightning; above him she lifts still loftier summits, and round him she flings her spray and her rainbows!

The St. Lawrence.—N. P. WILLIS.

IT was a beautiful night. The light lay sleeping on the St. Lawrence like a white mist. The boat, on whose deck our acquaintances were promenading, was threading the serpentine channel of the "Thousand Isles," more like winding through a wilderness than following the passage of a great river. The many thousand islands clustered in this part of the St. Lawrence seem to realize the mad girl's dream when she visited the stars, and found them

"Only green islands, sown thick in the sky."

Nothing can be more like fairy land than sailing among them on a summer's evening. They vary in size, from a quarter of a mile in circumference, to a spot just large enough for one solitary tree, and are at different distances, from a bowshot to a gallant leap, from each other. The universal formation is a rock, of horizontal stratum; and the river, though spread into a lake by innumerable divisions, is almost embowered by the luxuriant vegetation

which covers them.   There is every where sufficient depth
for the boat to run directly alongside; and with the rapidity and quietness of her motion, and the near neighbourhood of the trees which may almost be touched, the illusion
of aerial carriage over land is, at first, almost perfect.   The
passage through the more intricate parts of the channel
is, if possible, still more beautiful.   You shoot into narrow
passes, where you could spring on shore on either side,
catching, as you advance, hasty views to the right and left,
through long vistas of islands, or, running round a project-
ing point of rock or woodland, open into an apparent lake,
and, darting rapidly across, seem running right on shore as
you enter a narrow strait in pursuit of the channel.

It is the finest ground in the world for the "magic of
moonlight."   The water is clear, and, on the night we
speak of, was a perfect mirror.   Every star was repeated.
The foliage of the islands was softened into indistinctness,
and they lay in the water, with their well defined shadows
hanging darkly beneath them, as distinctly as clouds in the
sky, and apparently as moveable.   In more terrestrial company than the lady Viola's, our hero might have fancied himself in the regions of upper air ; but, as he leaned
over the taffrail, and listened to the sweetest voice that ever
melted into moonlight, and watched the shadows of the
dipping trees as the approach of the boat broke them, one
by one, he would have thought twice before he had said
that he was sailing on a fresh water river in the good steam
boat "Queenston."

"*I have seen an End of all Perfection.*"—
MRS. SIGOURNEY.

I HAVE seen a man in the glory of his days and the
pride of his strength.   He was built like the tall cedar that
lifts its head above the forest trees ; like the strong oak that
strikes its root deeply into the earth.   He feared no danger; he felt no sickness; he wondered that any should
groan or sigh at pain.   His mind was vigorous, like his
body : he was perplexed at no intricacy ; he was daunted at
39 *

no difficulty; into hidden things he searched, and wha was crooked he made plain. He went forth fearlessly upon the face of the mighty deep; he surveyed the nations of the earth; he measured the distances of the stars, and called them by their names; he gloried in the extent of his knowledge, in the vigour of his understanding, and strove to search even into what the Almighty had concealed. And when I looked on him I said, " What a piece of work is man! how noble in reason! how infinite in faculties! in form and moving how express and admirable ' in action how like an angel! in apprehension how like a God!"

I returned—his look was no more lofty, nor his step proud; his broken frame was like some ruined tower; his hairs were white and scattered; and his eye gazed vacantly upon what was passing around him. The vigour of his intellect was wasted, and of all that he had gained by study, nothing remained. He feared when there was no danger, and when there was no sorrow he wept. His memory was decayed and treacherous, and showed him only broken images of the glory that was departed. His house was to him like a strange land, and his friends were counted as his enemies; and he thought himself strong and healthful while his foot tottered on the verge of the grave. He said of his son—"He is my brother;" of his daughter, "I know her not;" and he inquired what was his own name. And one who supported his last steps, and ministered to his many wants, said to me, as I looked on the melancholy scene, " Let thine heart receive instruction, for thou hast seen an end of all earthly perfection."

I have seen a beautiful female treading the first stages of youth, and entering joyfully into the pleasures of life. The glance of her eye was variable and sweet, and on her cheek trembled something like the first blush of the morning; her lips moved, and there was harmony; and when she floated in the dance, her light form, like the aspen, seemed to move with every breeze. I returned,—but she was not in the dance; I sought her in the gay circle of her companions, but I found her not. Her eye sparkled not there—the music of her voice was silent—she rejoiced on earth no more. I saw a train, sable and slow-paced, who bore sadly to a opened grave what once was animated and beautiful. They paused as they approached, and a voice broke the awful silence: " Mingle ashes with ashes, and dust with its original dust. To the earth, whence it was taken, consign we the body of our sister." They covered her with the damp soil and the cold clods of the valley; and the worms crowded into her-silent abode. Yet one sad mourner lingered, to cast himself upon the grave; and as he wept he said, " There is no beauty, or grace, or loveliness, that continueth in man; for this is the end of all his glory and perfection."

I have seen an infant with a fair brow, and a frame like polished ivory. Its limbs were pliant in its sports; it rejoiced, and again it wept; but whether its glowing cheek dimpled with smiles, or its blue eye was brilliant with tears, still I said to my heart, " It is beautiful." It was like the first pure blossom, which some cherished plant has shot forth, whose cup is filled with a dew-drop, and whose head reclines upon its parent stem.

I again saw this child when the lamp of reason first dawned in its mind. Its soul was gentle and peaceful; its eye sparkled with joy, as it looked round on this good and pleasant world. It ran swiftly in the ways of knowledge; it bowed its ear to instruction; it stood like a lamb before its teachers. It was not proud, or envious, or stubborn; and it had never heard of the vices and vanities of the world. And when I looked upon it, I remembered that our Saviour had said, " Except ye become as little children, ye cannot enter into the kingdom of heaven."

But the scene was changed, and I saw a man whom the world called honourable, and many waited for his smile. They pointed out the fields that were his, and talked of the silver and gold that he had gathered; they admired the stateliness of his domes, and extolled the honour of his family. And his heart answered secretly, " By my wisdom have I gotten all this;" so he returned no thanks to God, neither did he fear or serve him. And as I passed along, I heard the complaints of the labourers who had reaped down his fields, and the cries of the poor, whose covering he had taken away; but the sound of feasting and revelry was in his apartments, and the unfed beggar came tottering from his door. But he considered not that the cries

of the oppressed were continually entering into the ears
of the Most High. And when I knew that this man was
once the teachable child that I had loved, the beautiful
infant that I had gazed upon with delight, I said in my
bitterness, "I have seen an end of all perfection;" and I
laid my mouth in the dust.

Neatness.—DENNIE.

"Let thy garments be always white, and let thy head lack no
ornament."

THOUGH much occupied in preaching, and noted, as
some of my friends say, for a certain poetical heedlessness
of character, yet, at least every Sunday, if not oftener, I
copy the common custom, and invest my little person in
clean array. As, from a variety of motives, and none of
them, I hope, bad ones, I go with some degree of constancy to church, I choose to appear there decently and
in order. However inattentive through the week, on that
solemn day I brush with more than ordinary pains my best
coat, am watchful of the purity of my linen, and adjust
my cravat with an old bachelor's nicety.

While I was lately busied at my toilet in the work of
personal decoration, it popped into my head that a sermon in
praise of neatness would do good service, if not to the world
at large, at least to many of my reading, writing and thinking brethren, who make their assiduous homage to mind a
pretext for negligence of person.

Among the minor virtues, cleanliness ought to be conspicuously ranked; and in the common topics of praise we
generally arrange some commendation of neatness. It
involves much. It supposes a love of order, and attention
to the laws of custom, and a decent pride. My lord Bacon
says, that a good person is a perpetual letter of recommendation. This idea may be extended. Of a well dressed man
it may be affirmed, that he has a sure passport through the
realms of civility. In first interviews we can judge of no
one except from appearances. He, therefore, whose exterior is agreeable, begins well in any society. Men and

women are disposed to augur favourably rather than other-wise of him who manifests, by the purity and propriety of his garb, a disposition to comply and to please. As in rhetoric a judicious exordium is of admirable use to ren-der an audience docile, attentive and benevolent, so, at our introduction into good company, clean and modish apparel is at least a serviceable herald of our exertions, though an humble one.

As these are very obvious truths, and as literary men are generally vain, and sometimes proud, it is singular that one of the easiest modes of gratifying self-compla-cency should by *them* be, for the most part, neglected ; and that this sort of carelessness is so adhesive to one tribe of writers, that the words *poet* and *sloven* are regarded as synonymous in the world's vocabulary.

This negligence in men of letters sometimes arises from their inordinate application to books and papers, and may be palliated, by a good-natured man, as the natural pro-duct of a mind too intensely engaged in sublime specula-tions, to attend to the blackness of a shoe or the whiteness of a ruffle. Mr. Locke and Sir Isaac Newton might be forgiven by their candid contemporaries, though the first had composed his Essay with unwashen hands, and the second had investigated the laws of nature when he was clad in a soiled night-gown. But slovenliness is often affected by authors, or rather pretenders to authorship, and must then be considered as highly culpable ; as an outrage of decorum ; as a defiance to the world ; as a pitiful scheme to attract notice, by means which are equal-ly in the power of the drayman and the chimney sweeper. I know a poet of this description, who anticipates renown no less from a dirty shirt than from an elegant couplet, and imagines that, when his appearance is the most sordid, the world must conclude, of course, that his mind is splendid and fair. In his opinion " marvellous foul linen" is a token of wit, and inky fingers indicate humour ; he avers that a slouched hat is demonstrative of a well stored brain, and that genius always trudges about in unbuckled shoes He looks for invention in rumpled ruffles, and finds high sounding poetry among the folds of a loose stocking.

Slovenliness, so far from being commendable in an author, is more inexcusable in men of letters than in many others, the nature of whose employment compels them to be conversant with objects sordid and impure. A smith from his forge, or a husbandman from his field, is obliged sometimes to appear stained with the smut of the one or the dust of the other. A writer, on the contrary, sitting in an easy chair at a polished desk, and leaning on white paper, or examining the pages of a book, is by no means obliged to be soiled by his labours. I see no reason why an author should not be a gentleman; or at least as clean and neat as a Quaker. Far from thinking that filthy dress marks a liberal mind, I should suspect the good sense and talents of him, who affected to wear a tattered coat as the badge of his profession. Should I see a reputed genius totally regardless of his person, I should immediately doubt the delicacy of his taste and the accuracy of his judgment. I should conclude there was some obliquity in his mind—a dull sense of decorum, and a disregard of order. I should fancy that he consorted with low society; and, instead of claiming the privilege of genius to knock and be admitted at palaces, that he chose to sneak in at the back door of hovels, and wallow brutishly in the sty of the vulgar.

The orientals are careful of their persons with much care. Their frequent ablutions and change of garments are noticed in every page of their history. My text is not the only precept of neatness, that can be quoted from the Bible. The wise men of the east supposed there was some analogy between the purity of the body and that of the mind; nor is this a vain imagination.

I cannot conclude this sermon better than by an extract from the works of Count Rumford, who, in few and strong words, has fortified my doctrine:

"With what care and attention do the feathered race wash themselves, and put their plumage in order! and how perfectly neat, clean, and elegant, do they ever appear! Among the beasts of the field, we find that those which are the most cleanly are generally the most gay and cheerful, or are distinguished by a certain air of tranquillity and contentment; and singing birds are always remarkable for the neatness of their plumage. So grea. is the effect of cleanliness upon man, that it extends even to his moral character. Virtue never dwelt long with dirt; nor do I believe there ever was a person scrupulously attentive to cleanliness, who was a consummate villain."

Description of King's College Chapel.—SILLIMAN.

THE chapel of King's College is allowed to be the most perfect and magnificent monument of Gothic architectuie in the world. Its dimensions are—length, three hundred and sixteen feet; breadth, eighty-four feet; height of the top of the battlements, ninety feet; to the top of the pinnacles, one hundred and one feet; to the top of the corner towers, one hundred forty-six and a half feet. The inside dimensions are—length, two hundred and ninety-one feet; breadth, forty-five and a half feet; height, seventy-eight. It is all in one room, and the roof is arched with massy stone; the key stones of the arch weigh each a ton, and there is neither brace, beam, nor prop of any kind, to support the roof, all the stones of which are of enormous magnitude. Modern architects, and Sir Christopher Wren among the number, have beheld this roof with astonishment, and have despaired of imitating it. It is reported of Sir Christopher, that he used to say, he would engage to build such an arch, if any one would but show him where to place the first stone.

When you realize the magnitude of this room, the roof of which is sustained entirely by the walls, buttresses and towers, you will say that it is a wonderful monument of human skill and power. The interior is finished in the very finest style of Gothic architecture. The roof is fretted with many curious devices raised on the stones, and the walls are adorned with massy sculpture, where the figures appear as if growing to the solid structure of the building; for, while they project into the room on one side, they remain on the other joined by their natural connexion with the stones from which they were originally carved. The windows are superbly painted, and the sub ects are principally from Scripture history. The panes of glass are separated only by very narrow frames, and the figures painted upon them often extend over a great many panes, without any regard to the divisions: it often happens, therefore, that the figures are as large as the life, and they are always so large as to be distinct at a considerable distance. The windows in Gothic structures are commonly covered, in a great measure, with fine paintings, the colours of which are extremely vivid and beautiful. You can easily conceive, therefore, that, on entering a Gothic church, the eye must be immediately arrested and engrossed by these splendid images: they are rendered very conspicuous by the partial transmission of the light, which they soften and diversify, without impairing it so much as to produce obscurity, while, at the same time, they give the interior of the building an unrivalled air of solemnity and grandeur.

When the spectator retires to one end of the chapel of which I am speaking, and casts his eyes along its beautiful pavements, tesselated with black and white marble, along its roof, impending with a mountain's weight, and along the stupendous columns which support the arch, surveying at the same time the gorgeous transparencies which veil the glass, he is involuntarily filled with awe and astonishment.